BLOOD NUMBERS

The Aleph Null Chronicles: Book Two

A Dark Fantasy Novel

I0629308

DEAN FRANK LAPPI

"Power released from chaos, bound by blood and filled with emptiness."

– *from* **The Black Numbers** *manuscript*

FIRST EDITION

Original artwork by Tea, royalty free and licensed from Dreamstime.com.

ISBN-13: **978-0-9891726-3-9**

Published by DEAN FRANK LAPPI

Cover Design by Dean Frank Lappi

Dedication

To Erica Anderson – You are an amazing editor and the quality of this book reflects your dedication to the art of editing.

To Wayne – Thank you for performing a beta read of the early draft of *Blood Numbers*. Your review comments were immensely helpful.

To Pam – Thank you for your ideas regarding my cover work.

To Lisa Danforth – Your ability to find continuity issues that no one else can find is amazing.

To Paula – You have been so supportive!

To all of my good friends at Myrrdin Publishing Group – Thank you for your support, in-depth conversations about everything relating to books, and your friendships over the years.

To my fans – Thank you for reading my books and providing great support and feedback.

And finally to my mom and dad – You always believed in me.

Other books by DEAN FRANK LAPPI

BLACK NUMBERS

The Aleph Null Chronicles: Book One (Now Available)

BROKEN NUMBERS

The Aleph Null Chronicles: Book Three (Coming 2014)

BEYOND NUMBERS

The Aleph Null Chronicles: Book Four (Coming 2015)

Visit **http://www.deanlappi.com** for the latest news and updates on books and news by Dean Frank Lappi

A Note From the Author

The mathematics in this series were intentionally described without going into any mathematical depth because I wanted the math to be conceptual as a way to explain magic, for it to be more visually spectacular than mathematically precise. I did this because I felt the story transcended the math, and also because I imagine most readers are not mathematicians. My apologies to any true mathematicians who may read this and be disappointed. But I also hope that the story itself pulls you in and that the visual way that I describe the math is just as rewarding and enjoyable.

Audience

While Blood Numbers is a traditional fantasy novel in most ways, it has adult-oriented themes not suitable for children under the age of 17, including sexuality and a few scenes of sexual-based violence. Parental review is recommended before letting your teenager read it.

CONTENTS

Prologue

T he Korpor prowled the dark alleyways of Undaluag. Even in complete darkness it didn't hesitate, for it could see everything in a blue light almost as clearly as if it were the middle of the day. It put a long-clawed paw to the rough stone wall of a building where the alleyway came to a narrow side street and peered around the corner.

An old man shuffled along the side of the building on the opposite side, poking into piles of trash with a stick. He stopped at one particular pile of garbage that looked no different than any other and rummaged about before pulling out a dead dog, its fur matted and caked with blood. He held it up to the meager moonlight, examining it closely before putting the carcass into the sack he carried, talking to himself the whole time. He continued on, poking his stick as he went.

The Korpor stepped onto the street and moved toward the old man, wincing slightly as it did, irritated by the lingering pain in its leg from where the Tulgin had bitten it in the cavern. That had been two days ago, but the pain the Korpor now felt was really more from anger. It still couldn't believe the Aleph Null had gotten away, and all because that Tulgin had attacked it. While the Tulgin could not have seriously harmed the Korpor, the creature's attack, as pathetic as it was, had caused it to drop the Aleph Null and lose its psychic hold just long enough for the boy to imprison it in a mathematical array and escape with the other humans.

The Korpor had been frightened when the Black Robe had arrived in the cavern to set it free from the array. The power that the Black Robe held was dark and violent and the man liked to inflict pain in all forms, something the Korpor did so very well itself with just a gaze. But while the pain that the Korpor inflicted was in its nature, a part of it no different from breathing, the Black Robe's power was malignant, filled with mental sickness and hate. The Korpor shivered. In the thousands of seasons it had lived, it had never before feared any living thing.

The old man sensed the Korpor's presence and jerked his head around in terror as the Korpor glided past him. The Korpor did not care about the human but as it passed, the rotten smell of sickness and filth filled its nose and it stopped. When it turned back to the old man, he shrank back in horror, his eyes wide, before he screamed in pain and fell to his knees, holding his head with dirty hands. The Korpor casually stepped forward and backhanded the man, the blow so powerful that the body cart wheeled backward against the wall and crumbled to the ground unmoving, thick blood dripping down the bricks. The Korpor turned and continued on its way, anxious to get out of the city and hunt for food.

The last of the buildings finally gave way to a pasture of tall grass with short, stunted trees far across the field. The Korpor paused and sniffed, then turned its head to the left and slowly blinked its right eye, followed by its left eye. It sensed two deer hunkered down in the tall grass, trembling in fear. The Korpor smiled, then leapt forward and sprinted across the field, moving like a shadowed blur in the darkness. The deer, sensing its approach, jumped up and bounded away in terror. The Korpor turned toward the large buck and cut across the field at an angle to intercept it, its speed far outpacing that of the animal. The deer changed directions constantly as it ran, but the Korpor was able to turn even quicker and in a final burst of speed, it collided with the deer mid-leap. As it did, it plunged its claws through the animal's chest and ripped the heart from its body before they tumbled to the ground together.

The Korpor stood up slowly, holding the warm, wet heart in one paw and looked down at the dead deer. It crushed the heart and then ripped into the animal and began to feed.

The bloodlust within it subsided after a short while, and it felt the rich meat filling its belly, giving it energy. Finally, the Korpor stood up, the smooth, grey skin of its hideous face covered in blood. It stretched its heavily-muscled arms up and cracked its back, then loped back toward the city.

Back to its master.

The Black Robe.

Chapter 1

The early evening light was fading quickly and the mosquitoes were starting to come out as Mrs. Wessmank sat against a Wilden tree and glanced toward Sidoro. She watched him fondly as he finished packing up the food after a light supper, still amazed that he was safe and they were together again.

The calm voice of Maelon filled her mind, *"He is very powerful, but he has a dark road ahead of him."*

She nodded, answering without speaking out loud, *"Yes, but at least we are here to help him."* She glanced down at the three-legged Tulgin and absently stroked the fur between his eyes. While he looked similar to a dog, the Tulgin was much more. He had three legs, which he used to walk in a strange gait, seeming to glide across the ground rather than walk. He was as smart as a human and could speak telepathically with Mrs. Wessmank. He had suffered abuse and beatings from Father Mansico for years, but had volunteered to do it so he could be her eyes and ears around the evil man, providing her with a constant stream of information about his plans for Sidoro. She had never truly forgiven herself for letting Maelon suffer so much at the hands of that monster.

"Please, mother, do not think such things. I willingly did what had to be done and would do it all over again. What is most important is Sidoro and what will come next."

A tear fell down her cheek as she looked fondly down at Maelon. *"Just the same, we will never be apart again."*

Maelon lay his head on her stomach. *"I promise you that, mother."*

She smiled, content for the first time in a long time. She heard a deep laugh and looked up. Crowdal and Writhgarth had bumped into each other by accident and the little Vringe had fallen backward to the ground. Crowdal had reached down to help him up, apologizing, but the little man had laughed it off as he accepted Crowdal's hand back to his feet.

Everyone had fallen into their own roles since they had escaped through the tunnel system under Yisk two days earlier.

Writhgarth prepared most of the meals and Mrs. Wessmank was surprised that he was quite a good cook in spite of how he looked. The scars on his face and corded muscles in his neck and arms showed a man who knew violence and hard work. She had met a few Vringe in her past and all of them had been gentle intellectuals. Being so short, they were normally not adept at physical labor, but Writhgarth had chosen to live by the sword, to uphold the law and stand against men who used violence and strength to take what they wanted from innocent people. The fact that he also liked to cook showed the multiple layers that made him such an interesting person.

Melinda checked on each member of their small group, cleaning small cuts here and there, and ensuring all were well. Her abilities as a healer were greatly appreciated by all. Mrs. Wessmank was still not sure about Melinda, though. There was something the woman kept hidden, some darkness that simmered just under the surface that showed in the cold and guarded way she kept her distance from everyone, even though she and Crowdal were obviously attracted to each other.

Sid had hunted for small game each of the past two evenings. He had grown up hunting rabbits, pheasant, and deer, so he came back each time with fresh meat for them to eat. He also washed what cookware they had after their meals and put the food away. He was the youngest member of their little group, but everyone treated him with a sense of awe, and perhaps a little fear.

Mrs. Wessmank had been amazed when she found out that Crowdal didn't eat meat. The Trith were legendary in the land and greatly feared by all. They believed in honorable violence, of facing an opponent or opponents in a fight to the death. They usually traveled alone or in pairs, always searching for that single sword event that might challenge them. For over the millennia, the Trith had perfected their mastery of the blade and that life-long ambition had caused an unintended result: they had become bored, for there was never any doubt in the outcome of a fight.

Mrs. Wessmank had read in the archives of the Anderom that young Trith warriors often traveled the land hunting for the mysterious Haissen, hoping to face another warrior that was rumored to be even better with the blade then they were, but not one Trith had ever returned to tell of an encounter with a Haissan. These were only stories she had read though, so she didn't know if they were true. What she did know was that, on average, the Trith stood four to six hand spans taller than a human and although she had only come into contact with three Trith in her long life, Crowdal was the tallest she had ever met, lanky whereas the other Trith had been muscular and bulky. But he was also different in another way, for he was kind, thoughtful, and always ready with an easy laugh, where the other Trith she had met had been quiet, intense, and insular. There was definitely more to Crowdal than met the eye. He also seemed to have a strong bond with Sidoro, and she felt a sense of relief knowing that Sidoro had such a good and powerful friend by his side.

As for her role in the group, she made tea for everyone in the evenings, but that was about all she could do to contribute. She was really feeling her hundred-plus years since she had left Orm-Mina. Her old body was no longer cut out for the physical hardships she now faced.

It was almost completely dark and the early spring air was turning cold. Mrs. Wessmank grunted and wisps of white vapor escaped from her mouth as she adjusted herself to get more comfortable on the hard ground.

She closed her eyes in exhaustion and thought of everything that had happened recently. It seemed like living through a nightmare, one that she often wished she would wake from at any moment and find herself back in her little tobacco store, but she shook her head at such foolish thoughts. Her life in Orm-Mina, where she had lived for so many years, was a place she would never visit again.

She smiled to herself as she remembered a young Sidoro sitting at her table, so small that she had had to put a chunk of firewood on the chair for him to sit on so he could see over the table. He had always loved her cookies and tea, and in the early years his smile would light up a room with its warmth. That was, until his mother, Lorielle, had died when he had been six years old. The light had seemed to go out of him on that day and he had become a quiet boy who rarely showed emotion, and only flashes of the innocent Sidoro would show through his stony features.

A soft sob escaped her at the memory of her daughter Lorielle. When she had died, Mrs. Wessmank couldn't imagine a life without her. But her daughter had been Sidoro's whole world. Mrs. Wessmank had tried her best to be there for Sidoro, but his father Danicu had made that difficult, keeping Sidoro away from her as much as he could. As Sidoro grew up, he had become angry and even more withdrawn, and she had worried about him, wanting nothing more than to take him from Danicu. But she hadn't wanted to call attention to herself as the leader of the Anderom, the secret group of people who opposed the Oblate.

The Oblate was a mysterious and powerful organization that controlled the power centers of commerce and more, all from behind the veneers of the royal houses. Very few in the general population had ever heard of the Oblate or the Anderom, and if they had heard of them, it was just as myth. Of those that had heard of the Oblate, no one knew their secret goal was to find and control the Aleph Null, the one person prophesied to control Black Numbers, a power so great that with it, they could enslave all in the land.

Mrs. Wessmank had a vision when she was young that the Aleph Null would be born in a small village called Orm-Mina. Now, 70 years later, here she was with her grandson Sidoro, the Aleph Null.

She had personally witnessed his awesome power two days earlier and still couldn't believe what she had seen. They had been captured by Father Mansico of the House of Healing, who was secretly the highest-level agent of the Oblate. They had, separately, escaped from him into the tunnels underneath the city and met up by chance in a giant cavern. But as quickly as they had been reunited, they were captured again by

Father Mansico and his Murder of Haissen, thirteen deadly masters of the sword. With all hope for escape lost and the Haissen about to execute them, she had watched in horror as Sidoro had unleashed his power of numbers, burning every Haissan to ash in a matter of moments. The power had almost consumed Sidoro and she had barely been able to bring him back before he had been lost.

She had succeeded, but not before Father Mansico had pulled Sidoro from her embrace. A strange thing happened then. Before Father Mansico could escape with Sidoro, the Korpor had dropped down from a ledge and killed the Father with a single blow to his head. She still couldn't get rid of the image of his face being torn from his head, of him sticking a finger into his own brain, almost in confusion, before he had fallen to the ground dead.

The Korpor had lulled Sidoro to sleep and picked him up. It was at that moment that all hope had fled from her, for no one could get Sidoro away from the Korpor, the mythical creature whose muscled body and powerful claws could kill a man with a single blow, but a strength that paled in comparison to the power of its gaze that dropped even the strongest man to his knees in excruciating pain.

Then Maelon, her three-legged and telepathic Tulgin who had been like her own son, had leapt at the Korpor and bit it in the leg, causing it to drop Sidoro to the ground, releasing him from the creature's trance.

Sidoro, with his last bit of energy, had imprisoned the Korpor in a mathematical array, allowing them to escape through the tunnels.

She let the memories fade away, coming back to the present fully when she heard Crowdal laugh at something Writhgarth had said, and she opened her eyes. Crowdal was building a temporary cover made out of branches over their communal area in case it rained during the night, while Writhgarth unrolled his blanket, looking up at Crowdal and gesturing as he spoke. Crowdal laughed again and Melinda even smiled from where she was sitting.

Mrs. Wessmank was so grateful Sidoro had found such amazing people to help protect him. As if knowing that she was thinking of him, Sidoro strolled over and sat down beside her. She put a hand on his leg and they sat together, neither one speaking.

A cool breeze blew through the trees above them, the swishing of leaves very loud. It was fully dark now and the crickets began their nightly chirping. Mrs. Wessmank leaned her head back against the cold bark of the tree and closed her eyes.

Miraculously, she had a second chance to keep Sidoro safe, to see him through to his destiny. But there were dark forces following them, preparing for them, powers of such evil that she shuddered in fear, knowing Sidoro could be taken from her again and destroyed for the power of numbers inside of him. Images flowed through her mind, images of pain and blood, of death and struggle. She cursed her sight, for it rarely let her see positive events in advance.

She shuddered, the fear of the future almost making her physically ill. She leaned forward from the tree and turned her face to Sidoro, studying the few strands of sandy brown hair that fluttered over his eyes in the light breeze as he sat with his eyes closed. She wanted nothing more than to hug him forever, to keep him from ever having to face the evil that hunted him. But she let that go as the foolish thought it was. It was up to her and his friends to help him as best they could against what was to come.

Sidoro opened his eyes and started when he saw her staring at him. She gazed into his eyes, eyes that seemed to simultaneously swirl with anger and fear, and hatred and love.

She thought back to what Father Mansico had said, that Sidoro had been *Ringed* by the Korpor. A deep shiver ran through her. It was the one thing she had been deathly afraid of happening, the worst-case scenario.

And it had happened.

A wave of sympathy washed over her at what Sidoro had endured. The physical act of *Ringing* was beyond horrible. She knew what had happened. The Korpor had used its powers to sexually excite Sidoro to the point of orgasm, then had used a sharp claw to slice around the base of his penis and slide the skin off the shaft. Then, the Korpor proceeded to have sexual intercourse with the bloody member until Sidoro had a violent and painful orgasm, mixing blood and semen together between them.

The mixture of blood, semen, and the fluids of the Korpor brought about a change in Sidoro, opened up pathways in his brain that had been shut away to protect him. But now, the powers of Black Numbers had not only been awakened, the pathway was expanded exponentially, meaning Sidoro had access to the unlimited depths of Black Numbers. The power had no end.

The amount of power coursing through his head right now was more than enough for anyone to handle, but the exponentially available powers could burn Sidoro's brain beyond repair. His fight to control it would either kill him or drive him mad.

Mrs. Wessmank shivered. She wasn't even sure if the Anderom could help him. It was ultimately up to Sidoro and whether he was strong enough to control the powers that were inside of him, ready to burst at any moment.

If only they had the Black Numbers manuscript, then they would have a chance at understanding the powers of Black Numbers and be able to control them.

Mrs. Wessmank stared at Sid so intently that he lowered his eyes.

"What's wrong? Why are you looking at me that way?"

Mrs. Wessmank gave a start, unaware that she had been staring at him. "I'm sorry, Sidoro. I'm an old woman caught up in her own thoughts."

Shifting to his left and reaching down to pull a small rock from under him, Sidoro sat back with a small sigh. "What were you thinking about?"

"Of you, and everything that has led us to this moment." She was silent for a moment, then made a decision to tell him. "Sidoro, did you know I have the gift of sight?"

Sid nodded. "I always suspected." He grinned. "I always wondered how you always had a boiling pot of water and two cups of tea waiting when I entered your shop. Can you really see the future?"

"In a way, yes, although I rarely see events clearly, or when they will happened exactly. But right now, I can see a malevolent force surrounding your aura, searching for you. It is nothing I have ever felt before and I don't understand what or who it is. But it is dangerous beyond anything I've ever known existed. And it wants you, Sidoro."

He visibly swallowed but didn't look away. A cold breeze ruffled his hair and Mrs. Wessmank shivered, although not just from the cold. Sid got up and walked across camp to pick up a blanket. Melinda noticed him and asked if everything was all right. He nodded and returned to the tree, covering Mrs. Wessmank's legs.

Maelon shifted a little and she covered him up with a corner of the blanket before smiling up at Sidoro. "You always were a considerate young man. Thank you."

Sitting back down, Sidoro pulled his knees up to his chest and wrapped his arms around them. "So what do I do now, then?"

"The only thing we can do is to travel to the Anderom in Undaluag. They can help you to understand the power of numbers coursing through your head. It is too bad we don't have the Black Numbers manuscript. But we will do everything within our power to help you, Sidoro. The Anderom has been gathering knowledge for a thousand years, anything and everything to do with you and the power of numbers."

Sidoro looked up at her and grinned.

"Why are you smiling?"

Sidoro merely stood up and made his way across the camp to Crowdal. She heard Sidoro ask him something, but the breeze carried the actual words away. Crowdal nodded and motioned to the pack leaning against the tree behind him.

Sidoro walked over and tried to lift the pack, but it was so large he couldn't do it, so he dragged it across the camp. It was almost as large as he was himself and he looked comical as he dragged it.

He came to a stop in front of Mrs. Wessmank, breathing hard, and she looked up at him quizzically.

"I assume you have gone through all that work for a reason?"

Sidoro nodded as he opened the large flap of the pack. "Could you reach inside that pocket for me?"

A little irritated at having to stand up, she did so anyway, reaching into the waterproof pocket and removing a thick book. As she raised it to the light of the fire, she gasped loudly, for in her hand she held a manuscript that was so black it didn't reflect any light. The leather was thick and inscribed on the cover was the title "BLACK NUMBERS". She felt a thrill of joy go through her. It was beautiful, and even she felt something of the power that it contained.

She looked over to Sidoro, about to ask him how he got the manuscript, but noticed he was breathing heavy and sweating.

"What's wrong Sidoro?"

He wiped sweat from his forehead. "It's nothing... just the power, now that it is out of the pack, it is... intoxicating."

Mrs. Wessmank frowned and put it away immediately.

Sidoro sighed and sat against the tree again.

She closed the pack back up and sat down next to him. She reached out and put her hand on his shoulder. "For how long have you had that in your possession?"

Taking a deep breath, he glanced up at her through the long hair that covered his eyes. "We found it in Father Mansico's chamber. I felt the power and knew it was important, so I took it."

"I can't believe it. This is wonderful news! I knew it was in Father Mansico's desk, but I couldn't get the drawer open."

"You were in his chambers, too?"

"I was brought there so he and my sister could gloat over their apparent capture of you."

Sidoro raised his eyebrows. "Your sister? I saw a dead woman in the room and for some reason I remember thinking of you. That was your sister?"

Mrs. Wessmank lowered her eyes. "Yes, my twin sister, Ailinora. She was the Black Robe of the Oblate."

Sidoro's eyes grew large. "The Black Robe? Your sister?"

She nodded sadly. "It is a long story. Suffice it to say we parted ways seventy years ago because of a difference of opinion on what should be done with you."

"With me? Seventy years ago? But I'm only sixteen."

"Well not you specifically at the time, but we knew the Aleph Null would be born soon, or at least we hoped. I wanted to protect you, while Ailinora wanted power above all else and wanted to use you for her own ends. The Oblate's ends."

Sidoro looked to be having a difficult time digesting all of this information. "You know, to be honest, all these years I always thought of you as 'Mrs. Wessmank,' just the owner of the tobacco and tea store in town. Your cookies and tea were the highlight of my visits with you. I can't believe your sister was the Black Robe of the Oblate." His eyes widened. "The bite marks on your sister's neck... Maelon killed her, didn't he?"

A tear ran down her cheek and she absently stroked Maelon's head. "I regret asking him to do that, but it had to be done."

Sidoro got a chagrined look on his face. "Here I am, feeling sorry for myself. Yet all my friends have suffered worse than me." He glanced around the camp and continued in a soft tone, "Melinda and Writhgarth were beaten and tortured." He looked over to his tall friend. "And Crowdal was cast out by his own people and is hated by everyone just because he is a Trith." He turned back to her. "And you, most of all, I can't believe how much you have given up. You had to have your twin sister killed." He leaned against her. "I'm sorry about everything you and the others have had to go through for me."

Wiping the tear from her cheek, Mrs. Wessmank scowled. "You are a kind and honest young man, Sidoro, and I wouldn't want anyone else to have become the Aleph Null. But we must be strong, all of us. What has happened is in the past. The future, on the other hand, is much darker. We have to be ready for it, no matter what comes."

Sidoro straightened up and nodded to her. "I know, I just wish it were up to someone else to deal with."

She nodded. "As do I. But we do not choose our futures or who we are."

"So what now?"

Mrs. Wessmank patted his knee. "Now, it is time for bed. I'm an old woman, I need my rest."

He leaned over and hugged her, then stood up. "See you in the morning."

She slid forward a bit as she made room to lay down on her blanket, making soft pained sounds as she did, a habit she'd had for so long that she didn't realize she even made the sounds.

She didn't know what the future held, but she was glad to have Sidoro back with her, to be around him and know he was safe. For a while, she had almost given up hope, but miraculously things had worked out in their favor.

A mosquito buzzed her ear so she pulled the blanket over her head and closed her eyes.

She didn't dream.

Chapter 2

The Black Robe sat behind the beautifully-worked Miq desk, high upon the black dais of the Oblate chamber and lazily glanced down at his fourteen Blue Robes, the most powerful members of the inner circle of the Oblate. They all sat in a semi-circle in comfortable chairs with deep hoods covering their faces. The room was silent as he let his gaze settle on each figure individually before moving on to the next. Finally, he focused on the empty chair on the Red Robe dais to his lower left.

Today was the Fractional Ascension, where he would pick a new Red Robe to take the place of his briefly-held previous position. He thought back to the past few days, of how Ailinora, the previous Black Robe as well as his great-grandmother, had been murdered by her twin sister Elenora, who he had known as Mrs. Wessmank when he had grown up in the village of Orm-Mina.

Everything had happened as he had foreseen.

Well, almost everything.

After the previous Black Robe's death, he had taken the position for himself and assumed control of the Oblate. But what he had not expected was for Sid to escape with the *Black Numbers* manuscript, along with Mrs. Wessmank, the Trith, the Vringe, and the healer, Melinda. That had been troubling at first, but he was not concerned anymore, for he would now initiate the plan he had always wanted to put into place but couldn't before he had become the Black Robe.

Now he was and he no longer needed to work behind everyone's back, for as the new Black Robe, he had the full powers of the position at his disposal. This included having full control of the myriad agents in the field, as well as all of the Haissen.

While his old friend Sid may be the Aleph Null, the one prophesied to manipulate Black Numbers, the fact was that his old friend couldn't control them yet. Even though Sid was powerful, he used his power of numbers like a farmer using a fine sword to chop firewood.

Tris shook his head slightly and smiled inside of his black hood. He didn't foresee much difficulty in imprisoning Sid in the mathematical array he had constructed, which would nullify Sid's control of his own numbers. He still had some work to do on the array, but it was almost complete.

The slightly annoying part was that he would have to imprison Sid next to the Obsidian obelisk in the Srithian Wood. He had found a scroll in the vast Oblate collection that referenced the Srithian Wood as the true power source of Black Numbers. It was a risk because it could affect Sid's control of the numbers, but honestly, he didn't think Sid was smart enough to take advantage of the powers inside of the obelisk.

The other annoying thing was that the Srithian Wood was incredibly far away to the north. He could only create a mathematical portal that would let him instantly jump to places he had either already been to, or where the Korpor was located at any given time. He would have liked to have avoided the long trip by horse and transported there as soon as he took possession of the final piece of the plan, which he was leaving for shortly to acquire. But that wasn't the case. So he would have to do everything the hard way and hope everyone would do their jobs.

This was the part of his plan that worried him slightly, because he hated relying on others without being present to ensure their competency. For Sid would have to be guided to the Srithian Wood by a variety of forces, some of whom would be... difficult to manipulate.

Fortunately, he would have the Korpor as his eyes and ears along the way. The creature had the unique ability to follow the trail of the Aleph Null through the psycho-sexual connection of the *Ringing*. Tris would have to wait until the Korpor reached the Srithian Wood itself, and then he would use his equation to transport there using his own connection to the Korpor.

And once he got Sid to the obelisk, then the fun would begin.

He shivered in anticipation of going inside Sid's brain and ripping out the entirety of his Black Numbers. Sid would die from the ordeal, but Tris didn't care. The only thing that was important was for him to take the numbers and use the power inside the obelisk to help solve the mysterious Black Numbers formula that gave Sid his exceptional and unwarranted abilities.

He heard a small cough come from one of the Blue Robes and he snapped back to attention. He glanced around the room, looking for the one who had coughed, and immediately focused on the offending Blue Robe sitting third from the left.

"Do you have something to say?"

The Blue Robe looked left, then right, and slowly stood up. Silence filled the chamber for a few moments until the Blue robe said, "What happened to the Black Robe? We've not seen her and suddenly you show up wearing her robe. By what right do you sit upon the Black Dais?"

A small murmur rose from the group of Blue Robes as they shifted their feet and rustled their robes in anticipation of conflict.

Tris studied the hooded figure, surprised to hear a woman's voice. He put his head back and looked at the beautiful marble ceiling with its intricately-painted scenes of battles and death. He had expected some dissension, some kind of questioning of his authority. The fact that only one Blue Robe, and a woman at that, had the courage to stand up and voice it made him sad. This group of Blue Robes was useless. Well, except possibly for her.

He brought his hood-covered head back down and stared at her, trying to intimidate her. From her voice, she sounded young. He hated the whole robe thing, hiding the identities of the members of the Oblate. It seemed childish and he would soon change things, but first he had to gain complete control of the Oblate, establish his authority. Too much change too soon would cause troubles that he didn't need, troubles that could have a ripple effect through the royal houses where his agents exerted the most influence.

Tris wished he could see what this woman looked like, for she had a husky voice that was sexy and intoxicating. She stood defiantly tall and still, staring unflinchingly back at him. His pulse raced and he grinned, although no one could see it.

He casually waved his hand as he spoke "The Black Robe was brutally murdered by outside forces. But just as she died, she sent her death equation to me, her *'Quistiim Diest'*, to make me the new Black Robe. I gravely accepted the responsibility and ascended."

There was silence in the chamber for a few heartbeats as everyone digested what he had just said. The *Quistiim Diest* had never been used in the long history of the Oblate, but Tris knew that by invoking the mysterious and frightening act, it would ensure that no Blue Robe would dare question the legitimacy of his position. The fact that he was lying was of no significance.

Then the Blue Robe that had stood up surprised him.

She pointed at him and yelled out in a clear voice, "You lie! We have no proof of that and I don't accept it."

Some of the Blue Robes began whispering, but she turned to them. "Oh shut up!"

The whispering stopped, although Tris could almost feel their hateful glares at the woman.

Tris smiled again inside of his hood. Being brought into the inner circle of the Oblate only recently, he had not had the opportunity to speak with many of the Blue Robes. Things had happened too quickly over the past month; from the old Black Robe being killed by his great-grandmother during the formal challenge for the Black Robe position, to her being killed so soon after by her own sister. The brief amount of time that Tris had spent with the Blue Robes had left him thinking they were all useless.

But he had not yet met this one who spoke now. She was obviously intelligent and aggressive and he needed that for what was to come.

She turned her head back up to him. "I demand a formal challenge for the Black Robe."

The group of Blue Robes held their breaths as one. Two challenges of ascension in one week was beyond their comprehension. Until last week there had not been a formal challenge in seventy years. Now a second one had been issued. No one knew how to react, so they stayed quiet.

The Blue Robe took a step forward and crossed her arms.

Tris felt a thrill of excitement run through him. He stood up and spread his hands wide. "Your formal challenge has been accepted. Let all here witness, the Black Robe position is in flux. In the case of my death, the challenger will become the new Black Robe.

He motioned down at the Blue Robe and spoke casually, "Begin at your leisure."

* * *

Agnes gathered her numbers. They floated in front of her with ease, for she had practiced with them for years, honing her skills. For practically her whole life, she had studied mathematics and the physical manipulation of numbers. It was all she had ever thought about. It was all she knew.

Her mother had been murdered when she had been young and she had been abducted by the very man who had murdered her mother. He had held her captive and trained her relentlessly in mathematics. When Agnes was seventeen years old, she had been brought to the Oblate even after failing the Proofing because she was a powerful mathematician, one that the Oblate had been grooming for many years.

She had become the youngest to ever ascend to the Blue Robe position in the history of the Oblate. That is, until this upstart had come into the Oblate the previous month and had somehow been given the Red Robe position. It had grated on her nerves, for at nineteen years of age, with a control of numbers beyond any of the other Blue Robes, she should have been chosen.

Then, just a few days ago, the Red Robe had the gall to call them all back for an emergency meeting. She had traveled as quickly as she could back to Undaluag, only to see him walk out now onto the Black Robe dais wearing the black robe, telling them all that he had been personally chosen to ascend to the highest position, with no proof. It was more than she could take. No one was going to steal it from her without a fight.

She concentrated hard and created an equation only she knew about. It was based on a theorem she had developed and solved, one that proved the absence of matter. By creating the equation with physical numbers, she theorized that she could create a vacuum to destroy matter. In theory, that is, for she had never tried to actually activate the equation before.

As she nudged the last variable into the equation, it snapped into place.

And disappeared!

In the space where the equation had been, there was now a blackness that seemed to pulse with power. The extraneous numbers that were left over were pulled toward the void, and as they touched it, spiraled inward and popped out of existence.

She had done it! She felt a flush of power fill her.

After all these years of forced study, of late nights alone in her small chamber curled up with manuscripts on advanced mathematics, she now knew it had all been worth it.

She thought briefly back to the day she had faced the Korpor, of the intense pain she had felt at the creature's stare and the great shame that burned inside her at not passing the Proofing. Now, two years later, here she was in the Oblate chamber, facing a pretender for the Black Robe position!

Agnes pushed these thoughts away. She couldn't afford to waste valuable energy on anything but the challenge. She concentrated on the void of energy in front of her and found that she could lift it and move it as if it were solid. She readied herself, about to throw it at the Black Robe pretender.

But she held back because she felt nothing from him, no numbers, no defense, not even acknowledgment that he was about to face a challenge. And that worried her.

The chamber was silent and the torches flickered in their sconces along the walls of the chamber, casting shadows that stretched upward almost to the ceiling.

Then she took a deep breath and threw the equation at him.

* * *

Tris watched the woman create her equation. He didn't understand it at first, it was not something he had ever seen before. He studied it curiously, not even bothering to build his own defenses. There was nothing this woman could do to him, for he was absolutely confident in his own strength and control of numbers.

But she intrigued and excited him. She was not frightened easily like the rest of the Blue Robes.

He mentally reached out and was about to disassemble the base variables of her equation when all of a sudden he felt her gather her energies and throw the mathematical construct at him. He smiled and put up a simple wall of numbers to block it. He would examine the complex structure when it bounced off and possibly throw it back at her.

He watched her equation streak toward him and smiled. He loved coming across something new.

But his smile faltered as the equation made contact with his wall of numbers. Instead of bouncing off the wall and dissipating into its base variables, the equation stuck to the wall and began to devour it. The simple numbers he had put up now melted into her equation, first slowly, then faster and faster as they stretched and finally popped out of existence. The void of her equation grew as it devoured his wall.

Tris arched his eyebrows and his breathing came quickly as he watched the spectacle in front of him, studying it from every angle in pure joy. He was looking at a beauty he had never seen before, of numbers being used by an agile and unique mind.

He studied the singularly complex structure of the equation floating in front of him, watching how it moved as if alive, pulsing as if it had a heartbeat. He may just have found someone actually worth keeping around. As he followed the thread of the equation back to the challenger, he sensed that she was a young woman with a life-force that pulsed in time with the equation.

Tris felt the equation drifting toward his body and knew that it would consume his flesh as easily as it had his numbers, so he casually reached out with his mind and disassembled the base structure of the floating variables. It was a simple matter, but to add theatrics to the situation, for the benefit of the challenger and the surrounding Blue Robes, he casually waved his hand and made the equation burst apart spectacularly, releasing all of the numbers it had devoured.

He sat back in his chair and smiled, for he had found his new Red Robe.

***

Agnes was trembling with power as she watched her equation near the Black Robe pretender. She knew she would defeat him and she flushed with excitement. He had put up a pathetic wall of numbers and she was disappointed, expecting something a little more original from him.

But as her equation-based void approached him, he simply waved his hand and her equation burst apart in all directions.

Stunned, she stumbled backward and sat heavily in her chair.

How did he do that? And with such indifference!

She heard quiet laughter from the Blue Robes around her and her face flushed red with embarrassment. She felt power suddenly emanate from the Black Robe and a force pushed her against her chair, completely immobilizing her. Agnes realized that the man she had challenged was not only a true master of mathematics, he controlled powers beyond anything she could have imagined.

Resigned to her fate, she collapsed all of her defenses and bowed her head. She had lived a good, if short, life and she was not afraid to die.

* * *

Tris sensed the challenger's surrender, her resignation to fate. While he didn't want to harm her, he had to put on a show for both her and the rest of the Blue Robes to ensure he would not be challenged again. Lifting a hand, he called forth a simple equation of pain and light. It swirled and pulsed as he projected it into the physical world. He heard a gasp from the remaining thirteen Blue Robes and felt a sense of anticipation from them. They wanted to see the challenger killed, maimed, tortured. Their bloodlust was palpable, and he felt nothing but disgust for them and their small minds that were so easily occupied with such simple needs.

He pushed the equation so it floated above them, its light reflecting off upraised hoods, except for the woman who had challenged him, whose head remained bowed. Nudging the numbers, he made them descend until they hovered directly over her bowed head. Tris let the suspense build. He knew that every eye was on him and the twisting light that he had created.

"The formal Challenge of Ascension has failed!" He lowered the spinning ball of numbers until it touched and then consumed the challenger. Her blue robe glowed white and she fell to her knees screaming. He knew the pain was exquisite, touching the pain sensors of every nerve in her body at once. It was more pain than any human could normally feel, but he made sure it was not fatal.

Raising his voice, he said, "I am the unchallengeable Black Robe! From this time forward, I rule the Oblate and my word is law!" His voice echoed off of the chamber walls, deep and menacing. He felt the minds of the thirteen Blue Robes shrink back in fear, but even as the challenger writhed in intense pain, she remained fearless.

He let the pain continue, but changed the equation, adding another to it and creating a bridge between the two. The glow around her robe changed to red and pulsed in time with her screams. He made the equation intertwine with every fiber of her robe, and where it did, the robe permanently changed from blue to red.

"And now, I have made my decision. Instead of killing this challenger, I am going to let her ascend. As of this moment, she is now the Red Robe."

He made the equation pulse faster and the woman's screams increased in volume with the tempo. "In case any of you think I am being generous in letting the challenger live, I want you to remember her screams."

He paused, then instantly duplicated the equation thirteen times and let it lightly touch each of the Blue Robes. It was just a slight touch, but the psychosomatic combination of what they were witnessing from the writhing figure on the floor, along with their own fears, caused them all to scream out in pain as one.

He raised his voice and it echoed off the walls. "This is just a touch of the pain that she is experiencing right now, just a hint of what is coursing through every nerve ending of her body. If anyone dares challenge me again, you will feel pain a thousand-times worse than this. Now fall to your knees right now and bow down to me!"

All of the Blue Robes instantly fell to their knees and lowered their heads to the floor, quaking and crying, young and old alike. Nothing like this had ever happened before, for while the Black Robe had always ruled over the Oblate, it had been done fairly and often by consensus. What was happening now was entirely new, and the fear and pain that ran through each one of them was something that they would do anything to avoid in the future.

Except for the new Red Robe.

* * *

Even though she couldn't stop herself from screaming at the intense pain, Agnes had accepted her fate and still felt no fear. She merely waited for her final breath to come. But suddenly the pain evaporated and lifted away from her. She lay on the floor, gasping for air, wondering if she had actually died. Then, as if through a dense fog, she heard the voice of the Black Robe for the first time since the pain had begun.

"Rise now, Red Robe, for you have ascended."

Agnes lifted her head and through tears, saw that all thirteen Blue Robes were prostrate on the floor around her. She glanced up and slowly focused on the Black Robe standing above her on his dais, still as a statue. Expecting the pain to reappear at any moment, she simply lay there enjoying the lack of pain.

The Black Robe seemed to sense her confusion and calmly pointed directly at her. "Stand up and take your place below me."

Agnes looked around and then realized that he was speaking to her. Confused, she pushed herself to her knees, and then to her feet, swaying slightly as she gained her balance. She rubbed her eyes and when she did, she saw the sleeve of her robe was now a deep crimson color. She looked down at herself and couldn't comprehend what she was seeing. She was wearing a red robe.

The Red Robe.

Suddenly she understood, and a thrill of elation coursed through her. But just as quickly, the elation turned to distrust and anger. She wasn't sure that she wanted to be part of this new Oblate. Looking up at the Black Robe standing far above her, she shivered, remembering the intense pain he had inflicted upon her with such ease.

But she pushed all of that aside. If she didn't accept the Red Robe offer, she knew that she would be instantly killed. So she confidently strode across the chamber and ascended to the Red Robe Dais, standing proudly and calmly.

She looked up as the Black Robe spoke from the dais. "From this day forward, there will be thirteen Blue Robes only. And in just a matter of weeks, there will be a new Oblate, one that will rise up into the light for all in the land to see. We will take our places as the true leaders of this land, combining the powers of the royal houses under one rule... *our* rule!" His voice echoed off of the chamber walls, filled with power and strength.

Soft, but excited, whispers rose from the Blue Robes in the silence, but they immediately quieted when the Black Robe continued.

"Everyone will know who we are and will bow down to us, even kings and queens." He stared around the room and then said in a low voice, "For I will control the Black Numbers and no one will dare stand against us!"

No one made a sound.

"Now, you are all dismissed. Return to your posts and await my orders."

The thirteen Blue Robes immediately filed out of the chamber. When the Red Robe also began to descend the steps, the Black Robe spoke softly so only she could hear, "Stay where you are. We have some things to discuss."

Agnes halted and looked up. "Yes, of course."

The Black Robe waited until the last Blue Robe left the chamber and closed the door. Then he stood up and removed his hood.

Agnes gasped and turned away. The core rule of the Oblate was that no one would reveal themselves to any other members. It was a death sentence to do so. It ensured that no single Robe could betray any of the other members of the Oblate.

"Look at me!"

Agnes felt the power of his voice and couldn't help herself from turning back to him. She gazed upon his features in surprise, for he was beautiful.

Without waiting for him to ask it, she reached up and slid her own hood from her head.

Her shoulder-length, black hair framed a beautiful face shaped by a sharp nose, full lips, and dark green eyes.

She looked fearlessly up at the Black Robe. "I take it the old rules truly are no more!"

The Black Robe smiled at her. "That... is an understatement."

Chapter 3

A touch on his shoulder woke Sid from a dream of Mistress Riana. They were in her tavern back in Oiro and she was holding his head against her breasts after a night of lovemaking. He was so tired and her caress felt so nice, that when the touch to his shoulder brought him back to reality, he opened his eyes with a glint of anger until he noticed it was Mrs. Wessmank leaning over him, her face hidden mostly in shadow. He managed a small smile at her as he moved to sit up.

Mrs. Wessmank sat back on her heels, looking stunned as she stared into his eyes. He touched her knee. "Are you all right?"

She quickly nodded and looked down, and he thought he caught just a whisper of the words, "so blue," but she quickly smiled at him. "It is time to get up, Sidoro. We will be leaving soon."

He rolled up his blanket in the fading darkness of dawn. He looked sideways at Mrs. Wessmank as she brushed leaves and dirt from her knees. "How did you sleep?"

She smiled tiredly and shook her head. "My old, aching bones don't enjoy lying on this hard ground." She put up a hand to stop him from speaking. "Don't worry, I'll be fine, Sicoro. This travel will do me good, toughen me up again. I've gotten too soft living the easy life in Orm-Mina." She touched his cheek, then turned and slowly walked away.

Sid followed her with his eyes until she faded from view in the darkness of the trees. He reached inside his pack, looking for his water skin, when he heard Writhgarth shout from some distance away. He snapped his head to his right, but couldn't see anything in the pre-dawn gloom. He heard a whistling sound go by his ear and something smacked against the tree behind him. He turned, almost as if in slow motion, and saw a three-foot-long, black arrow stuck in the tree just above his head, the feathered end still vibrating from the impact. Sid dove to the ground as another arrow buzzed over his head. He turned his head frantically left and right, searching for the enemy, but all he could see were the shadows of trees.

He awkwardly pulled out the sword he had taken from the dead Haissan, struggling because he was lying down. It was heavy and he let it rest against the ground as he continued searching the dark areas between the trees. He had to get to Crowdal to see what was going on, so he pushed himself up to his elbows. He smelled the wet earth and old decaying leaves of last winter as he half-slid, half-crawled to Crowdal's empty bedroll, awkwardly holding the sword in one hand. But Crowdal wasn't there so he stood up and ran toward Mrs. Wessmank when he heard the loud crashing of steel on steel to both his right and left. Mrs. Wessmank was lying down, hands over her head as he slid to a stop next to her.

He was about to bend down and see if she was all right when a blur of motion flew out of the darkness and hit him full-force, knocking him five paces backward. The sword flew from his hands and he landed on his back with a rush of air, looking up into a nightmare face rising above him: a tattered helmet in the shape of a beast, eye slots narrow and cut unevenly out of the metal. The man raised an arm and Sid saw a long knife with rough serrated edges catch the first hints of light from the horizon. It flashed down and Sid reacted, sending a single number smashing through the man's visor and twisting his own head to the side as far as he could at the same time. The knife slammed into the ground and Sid felt pain sear through his ear, then the full weight of the man fell on top of him, unmoving.

Sid tried pushing the body off of him but it was too large and heavy. Sid couldn't breathe from the weight and he panicked. He began to shudder from lack of air and just when he felt he was going to lose consciousness, the body was lifted from him and dropped a few paces away.

Crowdal stood looking down at him with worry on his face and then knelt down. "Are you all right?"

Sid nodded and struggled to sit up. Crowdal reached down and helped him to a sitting position. "Yeah, I'm fine. I think he nicked my ear, but that's all."

Crowdal turned Sid's head. "Your ear lobe has an ugly slice through it, but you'll be all right."

Sid touched his ear and yelped, quickly pulling his hand away, looking at all of the blood. His vision swam as he heard Crowdal calmly call to Melinda. She immediately came over, carrying a small pack that contained her medical supplies. She gently moved Sid's head to the side and pushed a clean piece of cloth against his ear to stop the bleeding and asked him to hold it in place. She removed a small bottle of liquid from her pack and poured some onto the cloth against Sid's ear, causing him to groan from a new burst of pain.

She nodded, "I know it hurts, but the alcohol will help it heal better. This next part you will like even less though." She dug into her pack and removed some string and a sewing needle.

She was right, Sid hated getting stitches. He had once sliced his arm badly on a sharp branch in the woods when he was young and his father had roughly sewn the two bleeding pieces of flesh together. The pain had been terrible and he still had the scar.

Sid closed his eyes and squeezed his hands into fists, preparing himself for the pain. But she expertly sewed the two pieces of his ear lobe together and was done so quickly that he was astonished when he opened his eyes and saw her pour some of the alcohol over the bloody needle and set it back into her pack.

She spoke calmly as she wiped her hands with a cloth. "You'll be all right. I just need to wrap your ear and you'll be good to go."

The pain had lessened now and he marveled at how quickly her hands moved as she placed a new, clean piece of cloth against his ear, then wrapped a long strip of cloth tightly around his head and tied it securely to hold the bandage in place. Satisfied, she spoke as she put the rest of her medical supplies away, "You came very close to losing your ear, but I sewed it back together. You'll have a scar, but it should heal well if you take care of it."

Sid nodded, thankful that it was only his ear that had been cut.

Melinda closed her pack and turned back to Sid. She lifted his eyelids one at a time and peered quickly into them before standing up and brushing leaves from her legs. "You were very lucky that he missed your head like he did."

Crowdal, who was kneeling down next to the man who had attacked Sid, looked up at Melinda and shook his head. "I don't think it was luck." He slid the helmet from the man's head and there was a hole the size of copper coin right between the man's eyes. Crowdal turned the head and Sid saw that the entire back of the man's skull had been blown out. Crowdal turned the helmet upside down and blood, skull matter, and brains oozed out of it and slopped onto the ground. Crowdal looked at Sid with an arched brow. "I guess he upset you when he tried to stab you."

Sid sat up, staring at the blood and brains on the ground. He couldn't believe he had done that by just throwing a single number at the man. He quickly turned away from the grisly scene.

Melinda stared at the remains of the man and then back at Sid. "Well, he's one less man I have to try and fix up, at least."

Sid's hands started to shake, the shock from the recent events setting in, when he remembered Mrs. Wessmank and wildly looked over at her. He was relieved to see her shuffling toward him. "Oh, thank the gods, I thought they had killed you."

She smiled tiredly at him and shook her head. "I don't think they were looking for me. They wanted you, Sidoro."

Writhgarth appeared out of the trees and nodded in agreement. "She is right, the attack was aimed at Sid. There are no arrows anywhere else but where Sid was sleeping, although it seems as if it wasn't coordinated very well."

Crowdal nodded to the little man who barely came up to his waist in height, and their eyes met. "Any of them escape?"

Writhgarth nodded. "Five of them did. I followed their trail quite a ways back, then made a circuit around the camp. It was just the one group and we got three of them." He looked down at the bloody mess of the dead attacker at Crowdal's feet. "You certainly had fun with that one."

Crowdal looked down, then tilted his head toward Sid. "Sid took care of this one himself, although not before he got his ear almost sliced off."

Writhgarth raised an eyebrow but didn't make any comment.

Melinda finally asked the question they were all thinking. "Who are these men, and why did they try to kill Sid? They don't look like Father... I mean Mansico's Haissen."

Crowdal shrugged his shoulders. "They are definitely not Haissen, these are mercenaries. Who sent them, I don't know, but the fact that they found us so quickly worries me." He looked at Writhgarth and said, "We need to break camp immediately and get moving again."

Writhgarth nodded. "I agree, and I think we should avoid the road from this point on. We don't know how many others are hunting us."

Sid shivered as Writhgarth said this and thought of the darkness that he felt around them, all because of him. He climbed to his feet, feeling the pounding of blood in his ear. He saw the sword lying on the ground and picked it up. The sword was worthless to him. He had a constant bruise on his leg where the scabbard, heavy with the sword, constantly bounced against him as he walked. He slid the sword into the scabbard, taking three tries before he was able to find the slot. It slid home with a hiss and Sid immediately unbuckled the scabbard and held it out to Crowdal.

The huge man looked down at Sid and raised an eyebrow in question.

"I don't want this anymore. I'll never learn how to use it, and I hate the way it bounces against me when I walk."

Crowdal took the sword without saying a word.

Sid turned, went back to his bedroll, and started rolling it up.

***

Crowdal watched Sid for a few moments, then put the Haissan sword and scabbard into his pack. He was glad that Sid had given up the sword. It wasn't something that an unskilled person should handle, and he felt better knowing that Sid wouldn't hurt himself or someone else with it.

Then he snorted quietly.

As if Sid needed a sword to hurt someone.

Chapter 4

Tris sat at his desk in his bed chamber reading a particularly old manuscript, being careful to not bend the parchment or put any stress on the binding. His hair stuck up at the back of his head from constantly leaning back against his chair to think before leaning forward again to study a portion of the manuscript. The surface of his desk was covered with a dozen other manuscripts.

He came to a specific section on the second-to-last page and his eyes widened. He bent closer to it, studying the exact mathematical formula that was written. It was very complex, so he took out a blank piece of parchment, a quill, and an ink bottle and wrote the equation on the parchment, then began crossing out symbols and adding new ones. He crossed out the formula entirely after a long time and started over.

He worked through the night, not stopping even for sustenance or water. Then, suddenly, he put down the quill and sat back, exhausted but elated. He believed he had finally solved the second formula for the mathematical array that he would use to trap Sid. If he had it correct, he would combine it with his first formula and generate a new mathematical array that would not only hold the Aleph Null's powers in check, but release the hidden equations in Sid's mind that allowed him his special ability to potentially unlock the secret of Black Numbers.

Tris reached over, picked up a mug of water, and drained it. The water was tepid, but still refreshed him, bringing some of his strength back. Now all he had to do was rebuild both formulas in his mind and bridge them together to unleash the array. He closed his eyes and recreated them one number and symbol at a time, the relationship between pure and theoretical mathematics so complexly entangled that even he wondered if he got it right. He finished, then re-checked every aspect of the formulas, and certain they were correct, he took a deep breath and delicately edged them together until the open symbols at the ends touched and merged.

A crack of energy shook the room and Tris momentarily lost his concentration. The energy blew out in a single direction, disappearing through the rock wall and knocking him to the floor in the process. He hit the stone hard but ignored the pain as he concentrated on the two formulas, trying to see what had happened.

Something was definitely wrong with them, they pulsed with power but they didn't create a mathematical array like he had planned. He studied the formulas intently, dissecting each variable and after some time, he stood up with a sigh.

Somehow, he had inverted a single binomial coefficient and

instead of creating an array, it had done the opposite and released the energy of an existing array from somewhere else. Which array it was, he wasn't sure, nor where it was located, but one thing he was certain of, whatever array he had released, it had been incredibly complex.

He fixed the error in his formula, but the damage had been done. He had likely unleashed something powerful upon the world, something that had been locked in an array for a reason. What it was, he had no idea. He ran shaking hands through his hair and took two deep breaths to calm himself down.

What was done was done. He couldn't worry about it now. He concentrated on his new formula for the rest of the morning, studying and verifying every variable, and finally certain that it was correct this time, he reconnected it to the original formula. When they touched, he felt a swelling of power inside of him and within his mind he saw the mathematical array appear with a soft '*whump*' of energy. He stared at his creation in awe. It floated and pulsed as if alive, a thing of complex beauty that he would use to trap Sid and take his powers.

Tris watched his array for a few moments longer, reveling in his success, until he realized he was exhausted. He set the array in a part of his mind for quick access, then opened his eyes. He reached over his desk and slowly closed the cover of the manuscript, the soft creak of leather making him come fully out of his thoughts.

A soft knock sounded on the thick Miq door. He turned his head. "Yes?"

A Haissan opened the door. "The Red Robe is here to see you."

"Let her in."

A red-robed figure glided into the room and the Haissan shut the door.

Tris stared into the darkness of the red hood for a few moments before forming a matter equation and waving his hand as he threw it. The hood flew back and Agnes stood there, a little shocked.

"You could have just asked me to remove my hood." She patted her hair back into place, looking irritated more than anything.

"Yes, I could have I suppose." He turned back to his desk and slid the manuscripts and his own parchments into a drawer, locked it with the leaf key he had made by a master metal worker whom he had immediately killed, and then leaned back in his chair and closed his eyes with a sigh.

He let the silence extend, testing her patience. When she didn't make a sound for some time, he finally spoke, although he didn't open his eyes, "Come here."

Agnes didn't hesitate. She walked quickly over to him and stood to his left.

Sitting up straight, Tris spun his chair and faced her in one quick movement. "Take off your robe."

Agnes sighed, obviously irritated and she turned to walk away.

Tris became even more excited when he saw her turn. Such a mind in that woman! But he had to make her understand that she couldn't disobey him. So he formed a simple wall of numbers in front of her. When she bumped into it, she would turn and he would see the resignation in her eyes. But when she got to the wall of numbers, she dismantled it without slowing down and reached for the door.

"Agnes."

He had surprised himself by saying her name.

She stopped, her back straight, as if waiting to hear what he was going to say.

He formed another equation of air, they came so easily to him, and with a tug of his mind, opened the door. A Haissan stood on the other side but didn't turn to look into the room.

"You may leave, but I'd prefer you stay."

* * *

Agnes stood for a moment, surprised that he had opened the door, but more surprised by the tone of his voice when he said her name. It almost sounded... human. She looked at the back of the Haissan guarding the door and shuddered.

Unlike those things.

She turned around and faced the Black Robe and was again amazed by his beauty and youth. His black eyes and blond hair made her breath catch in her throat, and she quickly looked down. She would not let herself become his toy. But when he spoke again, asking her to stay, she realized that she wanted to stay. She looked up and the magnetic power of his eyes made the decision for her. She walked back and sat down on a hard wooden chair directly across from his desk.

She spoke gruffly. "Black Robe, I will not be your sex slave. I will be your partner or nothing."

He studied her, and then nodded. "In private, please call me Tris. Now, we have business to attend to. Prepare for a long day, because what I have to tell you will change everything in your life."

Agnes raised an eyebrow and waited. She wouldn't be surprised by anything that he said to her.

He turned toward the still open door, the back of the Haissan blocking most of it. "Bring us some tea and a light meal." The Haissan nodded to its right but didn't move. Footsteps echoed away as some unseen servant rushed to the kitchen.

Agnes waited but Tris did not begin speaking. He just sat quietly, studying her. The silence extended but she would not show her impatience. Then, a harried-looking man hurried into the room and quickly set a tray down on the desk. He bowed awkwardly and left quickly. Agnes looked down at the tray and saw a pitcher of steaming water, two cups, a small container of fragrant tea leaves, two empty round metal balls filled with small holes, and a plate of meats, cheeses, and bread.

She raised her eyes to Tris. "So, even you just eat bread, cheese, and meat?"

He smiled. "Despite what you may think of the Black Robe position, I don't eat small children."

Reaching out to take a piece of bread, Agnes grunted. "That remains to be seen, I think." She took a bite of the coarse black bread and chewed the hard crustiness, relishing it. She so loved good bread.

Tris pulled each of the metal balls open and put two pinches of tea leaves into each, then closed and dropped them into the cups and poured the steaming water in, letting it steep. The sweet flower-smell of jasmine filled the room. He breathed deeply and then placed a piece of bread, some beef, and cheese on his plate. Using his knife and fork, he delicately cut a piece of meat and slowly put it into his mouth.

Agnes watched him eat properly, but she didn't care. She grabbed a hunk of cheese and bit into it, wiping a crumb from her mouth with a finger.

Through a mouthful of food, Tris spoke casually, "As you know, we have found the Aleph Null and we must bring him here for the safety of the entire land."

Agnes rolled her eyes. "Oh, please. You want him for his power, you don't care about the land. I'm neither a peasant, nor a king, I don't need to hear your crap." She took a sip of the hot tea to help wash down the bread and cheese, marveling at the wonderful scent as it filled her nose. She was used to the bitter root tea that most people could afford. This was exquisite. "What kind of tea is this?"

"It's jasmine. And yes, I want the Aleph Null for his power. And no, I don't care about the land." He smiled.

Amazed that he had just admitted that to her, she swallowed hard. The goodness of the Oblate had always been her cornerstone of belief. But with this new Black Robe, she no longer felt comfortable with the direction the organization was going. She tried to sound casual so as not to alert him to her doubts. "So how do you propose to capture him if he is truly the Aleph Null?"

He arched an eyebrow, then casually pushed the plate of food away and sat back. He lifted his right arm behind his head, grabbed it and pulled with his left, stretching. "I haven't decided yet if I will actively catch him, as you say, or make him ask me to take his power from him. I'm not sure which way is more satisfying." He put both arms down and rotated his neck in circles. "But either way, I will have the Aleph Null within two fortnights." He looked directly into her eyes. "We will both travel soon, but in different directions. Would you like me to have the Korpor travel with you to keep you company?"

Agnes' face blanched and she set down her half-eaten piece of cheese, her appetite gone at the mention of the Korpor. "No, that won't be... necessary."

Tris nodded, a glint in his eyes. "If you are sure."

She nodded quickly. There was no way she ever wanted to see the Korpor again. The pain the creature had inflicted upon her during the failed Proofing was still fresh in her mind, the way the agony had seemed to enter her very bones and burn her from the inside out, similar to the pain the Black Robe had inflicted on her the previous day. She shivered.

Tris leaned forward and looked briefly down at her breasts, mostly hidden behind her robe, before looking directly at her. "Now, before I leave, some instructions."

Agnes nodded. This is what she had been waiting for. A chance to be a leader. A chance for her to be *almost* the Black Robe.

"You will travel to Karillon and will order the Masteen Vorn Maghuur to lend us one of his death squads to ensure the Aleph Null and his group make their way to the Srithian Wood on the other side of the Kulkraken mountains."

A chill went down her spine at the mention of the Masteen Vorn Maghuur. 'Masteen' was an old title from far in the past that was similar to 'King', but meaning something more like 'Ruler Of The Dead'. Twenty years earlier, Vorn Maghuur, a man who towered over even the largest of men, attacked Karillon with two thousand of his men and destroyed the King's standing army in a single day.

Vorn Maghuur found King Jangg hiding in a secret room of the castle with his family and had them all dragged into the courtyard by their hair. Vorn Maghuur had his men erect sharpened posts throughout the courtyard, then he picked up the deposed king and slowly impaled the man through the rectum. King Jangg's screams of pain changed to an anguished wail when Vorn Maghuur impaled the King's wife and children, one-by-one, in front of him. The courtyard ran red with blood and it was rumored that King Jangg survived for three days on the post, watching his wife and children die in horrible agony.

Vorn Maghuur proclaimed himself the 'Masteen', and since then, few people willingly entered Karillon, and fewer people returned.

Agnes cocked her head slightly, trying to act casual so the Black Robe wouldn't see her fear. "I'll travel to Karillon and meet with the Masteen, but I've never heard of the Kulkraken Mountains, or the

Srithian Wood. Why there?"

"Because there is an ancient power in the Srithian Wood that is the source of the power of Black Numbers. The rest of my plans I will keep to myself."

"Then what about the Karillon death squad? It will consist of fifty men, if my memory serves me correctly, all of which are hardened killers who will want to be paid in gold?"

Tris smiled, although it was more like the smile of a corpse. "They are inconsequential after they serve their purpose. I will kill them and burn their bodies to ash. No one will know or even care what happened to them."

Agnes swallowed slightly. If anyone else had so casually said something like this, she would have laughed, but she believed him without a doubt. This man was not only powerful beyond measure, she realized that he was psychotic as well. Unfortunately, she was in too deep now, and there was no path for her other than with him. Except for death that is, and she wasn't ready for that yet. Ashamed of her cowardice, she simply nodded slightly.

Unaware of her inner turmoil, Tris continued, "So, it will be your job to go to the Masteen Vorn Maghuur, in person, and obtain the services of one of his death squads. You will join with the death squad to ensure all goes accordingly." He paused briefly as if contemplating something he didn't like. Finally he continued, "The Masteen is a strong-willed man, quite temperamental in nature. There is a chance he will insist on leading the death squad. If that happens, let me know, and if the time comes and he chooses to make direct contact with the Aleph Null, then I want you to go along with it." He stared directly at her, his eyes hard. "If you meet the Aleph Null, I want you to become friendly with him, make him trust you. Do whatever you need to do to make this happen. Do you understand?"

Agnes nodded, although she knew there was a lot going on here that he wasn't telling her.

Tris nodded. "Good. I will stay in contact with you to tell you exactly where to go."

"How do I convince the Masteen to give us so much? I can't reveal myself."

Shaking his head, he waved the question away. "As the Red Robe, I had assumed you were intelligent. He already knows about the Oblate."

Cheeks burning red, Agnes glared at him. But she lowered her eyes after a few moments. "Yes, of course. I will take care of it."

Tris nodded, already forgetting the matter.

Agnes had one more question. "How will I stay in contact with you for instructions?"

"*This way, of course.*"

Agnes jumped in her chair. His voice had appeared in her head, as loud as if he had spoken directly to her. She looked at the young man in front of her with awe. She had never heard of anyone being able to do what she had just witnessed. How did he do that, and could he read her thoughts too? When he didn't answer in her head, she relaxed a little.

She spoke out loud, "So how do I communicate back to you, then?"

Tris tapped his temple. "You can't, yet. You will have to let me into your mind, where I will plant an equation that will open up two-way communication."

Agnes swallowed again, and forced herself to relax. She doubted she could keep him out of her mind anyway. With trembling hands, she nodded. "Go ahead."

He closed his eyes.

Agnes felt nothing at first. She waited for a few moments and was about to say something when she suddenly felt a slight pressure in her head, almost like someone was gently squeezing it with two hands. Then, just as quickly, the pressure was gone. She looked quizzically at him. "Is that it?"

Tris opened his eyes and nodded toward the air in front of her, where an equation appeared. "To activate communication, form the following equation, then just speak to me in your head. When you are done, put this alpha symbol in front of it to close it."

Agnes saw an alpha symbol appear in front of the equation and turn light gray in front of her. She memorized the equation and formed it in her mind with the alpha symbol in front of the first number. She then removed it and the equation turned white. She whispered in her mind, *"Can you hear me?"*

His voice immediately appeared in her mind, contempt dripping from it, *"Of course. It isn't a complicated thing, Agnes."*

"Well excuse me for not being perfect like you!" She said out loud as she added the alpha symbol back to the equation, closing it down.

Tris smiled, and she was surprised that it was genuine. He chuckled. "Oh, don't be such a baby."

She relaxed, a little irritated with herself for letting him get her angry. She marveled at his smile, at his beautiful teeth, and at his perfect face. When he smiled like this, she couldn't imagine any darkness being inside of him. She relaxed a little more. She wiped a lock of hair from her eyes. At least she tried to, but her arm wouldn't move. She looked down at it in confusion. It felt like it was tied down. She looked back up at Tris. His smile was still there, beautiful as ever.

"What is happening?" Her voice had an edge of anger to it, but also fear.

"Now that we are done with business, I am going to fuck you." He raised his hand and her robe literally started falling apart, bits of it floating away, other pieces falling to the floor in tatters, until she was completely naked.

Complete fear filled Agnes and she tried to find her own numbers to protect herself, to somehow keep him away. She formed equations to block his numbers, but the equations broke apart as quickly as she formed them. It was like building a sand castle while someone poured water over it. Finally, Agnes became still and stopped fighting.

"Is that all you have?" He smiled beautifully at her, but now it sent chills up her back.

She kept silent, but her eyes smoldered.

Tris stood up, came around his desk, and stared down at her, then leaned down and cupped her right breast, his fingers playing with her nipple, making it harden. Then he did the same to the left breast, looking into her eyes the whole time.

Agnes shivered and closed her eyes. Suddenly she felt herself being picked up and carried to the large bed and set down. Her legs were forced to straighten out, and she was pushed down until she was lying flat on the bed. She still couldn't move.

Tris looked down at her. She saw the look of lust in his eyes and knew that he was studying every part of her body. She glanced down at her long and muscular legs, her flat stomach, her breasts the size of apples with large nipples. She had once had a suitor who told her that her face was beautiful, especially her green eyes, but she didn't think much about beauty. She kept her hair shoulder-length but didn't take good care of it, washing it only a couple of times a week. She just didn't think of herself that much. She was more interested in mathematics, in mastering the power of numbers. She looked back up at Tris and could tell he was going to hurt her. He dropped his robe and stood staring down at her, his eyes cold and emotionless.

Agnes looked down involuntarily at the hardness sticking up from him and started in surprise. His member was smaller than she had expected, looking like a half-sausage sticking up through the course hair of his groin, and before she could stop herself, she giggled.

Tris backed up and his face turned red. He then lunged forward and punched down into her stomach. She gasped in pain as he leaned over her, his eyes smoldering with anger. "If you laugh again, I will cut your tongue out. Do you understand me?"

Agnes merely nodded, unable to breathe after the punch to her stomach.

Tris glared at her for a moment longer, then stood tall and proud, his penis now soft and almost invisible in the hair of his groin.

Agnes gulped in air and realized that she could move again, so she hesitantly sat up in the bed and swung her legs over the edge.

Tris turned and walked back to his desk. He sat down and opened a manuscript and began writing notes on a piece of parchment, completely ignoring her.

Agnes wasn't sure whether he was going to do anything else to her, so she hesitantly started walking toward the door, still naked because her robe had been destroyed. As she reached for the handle, it swung open. A Haissan stepped back to let her by. She was about to step through when she felt a stab of pain that dropped her to her knees. Through the pain she heard his voice drip like oil over her consciousness.

"You are lucky I don't kill you Agnes, and if you ever think that you can laugh at me again, I want you to remember this pain."

Agnes screamed as the pain became even more severe, something that she hadn't thought possible, even worse than during her challenge for the Black Robe. It felt like someone had flayed the flesh from her entire body and was scraping all of her bones at once with a rusty knife. She screamed until her voice became hoarse.

Then the pain was gone and she found herself lying on the stone floor, gasping and sobbing.

Tris chuckled and said in a mild voice, "That was very enjoyable. Now, go. And Agnes, don't fail me."

Agnes struggled to her feet and knew she was lucky to be alive, so she nodded without turning and stumbled out of the room.

As soon as she was out of sight, she stopped and put a hand to the wall to steady herself. She let out a small moan and began to tremble. After a few moments, she took a deep breath, stood up straight, and made her way to her chamber. Her Haissan walked behind her, always there as protector, although she realized that the creature protected her in only a literal sense, and not from the Black Robe, who was its true master.

She reached her door, opened it with a trembling hand, and entered her opulent room, closing the door with relief, leaving the Haissan outside in the corridor. She suddenly wanted nothing more than a hot bath. Not only would it likely be the last bath she would have for the next two fortnights or so, she wanted to soak her muscles, which were still twitching slightly from the ordeal that she had just endured.

She pulled a cord and a small bell rang in the room adjacent to hers. Within only a few moments, her servant knocked lightly on her door. She opened it and ordered the young woman to bring hot water for a bath. The young woman curtsied and scurried down the hall without a word. All servants at the Oblate had their tongues cut out as the condition of employment. Because they were all from poor homes and the Oblate had offered them a living wage well beyond anything they would ever be able to make elsewhere, they had accepted the condition. Their families were well taken care of, and they could never speak of their employment or what went on at the Oblate. They were also made well aware that if they managed to tell anyone of their employment through writing, then not only they, but every single member of their families, would be killed.

Within moments, the woman returned with five men who each carried a large wooden bucket of steaming water. They crossed the bed chamber and poured the water into a large copper tub in the corner. They left quickly and Agnes locked the door behind them. She immediately crossed the room and gingerly stepped over the lip of the tub, gasping from the hot water. Taking a breath to steel herself, she slowly settled into the steaming hot water with a sigh.

She just lay there for a few moments, eyes closed, as the hot water fully relaxed her and the last of the pain subsided. After a short while, she took a bar of soap, washed and rinsed her hair, then scrubbed herself clean. When she finished, she just lay in the soapy water until it began to cool. She rose, toweled herself dry, and put on some undergarments. With a sad sigh, she slipped on a stiff, woolen travel robe, hating the abrasive material. Wringing her hair, she crossed to her bed and just sat there for some time, staring at the floor.

What Tris had done to her and kept doing to her, his absolute power over her and the casual way he inflicted such pain on her made her feel humiliated. The anger built from deep inside the pit of her stomach. Her temples throbbed and she clenched her fists so hard that she felt her knuckles crack. She then let out a scream, grabbed a crystal candle holder, and threw it as hard as she could against the stone wall across the room, where it shattered into a hundred pieces. Her Haissan immediately opened the door and looked inside. She glared at the creature and it immediately closed the door.

She slowly got her breathing under control, her chest heaving, and then she scowled. She would not be weak now.

She picked up a smaller towel and dried her hair as much as she could, then put a few personal items into a small pack and stood, looking around her chamber. She straightened her shoulders, crossed the room, and opened the door. Her Haissan half-bowed and led her to the stables where two stable boys held the reins of two strong horses. Her horse was laden with two packs, probably holding food and other travel items.

She slid into the saddle and squeezed her legs against the sides of the horse, causing it to instantly start trotting forward. Her Haissen rode by her side on a horse with no saddle, moving easily with the gait of the horse as if it were one with the creature. They traveled through the busy streets, and people jumped out of the way as they passed, some cursing them angrily.

The day was warm and the sun was bright, but inside, Agnes' thoughts were black and dangerous.

She never looked back as they galloped out of Undaluag by the north road.

* * *

Tris sensed that Agnes and her Haissan had left the Oblate. He sat back and smiled, glad she was doing his bidding without question.

He knew the Masteen would insist on accompanying the death squad, in fact, he was counting on it, for the Masteen Vorn Maghuur had a strange ability to nullify the power of numbers. That information had been given to the Oblate a couple of years earlier by one of their agents and he had just recently uncovered it in the archives.

He wasn't sure how the Masteen might affect Sid, but Tris knew he needed every weapon he could gather to ensure that Sid did not fully fight back.

He sat forward again and put some papers into his desk, except for one yellowed piece of parchment. It was dated from ten years ago and filled with a flourishing script, detailing a complex contract. He folded it and placed it into a leather binder. He was ready to go and take possession of perhaps his most potent weapon against Sid.

Chapter 5

Deep within a forest, behind the granite wall of a cliff that rose hundreds of feet into the air, a deep cavern extended back into darkness. It was quiet, as it had been for thousands of seasons, except for the hollow echo of dripping water and the faint squeaking of partially slumbering bats.

One bat, hanging by its feet from a narrow crevice in the damp ceiling, twitched its ears at a peculiar sound. It was a sound that the small creature had never before heard inside this cavern. It turned its head and squeaked questioningly, listening to the return echo off the walls. To its left, something was different, causing the echo to bounce at a strange angle. It let go of its feet and dropped down, spreading its wings. It fluttered into the darkness toward the anomaly, squeaking as it went.

Toward the back of the cavern, something moved. It was a minute movement, but the echo registered something foreign and larger than anything the little bat had ever before come across. It flew closer, twitching its nose at the new smell, but as it angled even closer, it was struck out of the air, the impact shattering every bone in its body, and it fell like a stone, dead before it hit the cavern floor.

Silence filled the cavern for a few brief moments, then the ground shook from a deep and powerful impact, causing stalactites to crack and break loose from the limestone ceiling and crash upon the rocky ground.

All of the bats awoke in fear and panic and flew out through a small crack in the wall, squeaking as they went, into the light of the cool morning. They swerved chaotically, turning and weaving in confusion, unsure of where to go. But the one thing they did as one was to fly as far and as fast from their underground home as they could.

Deep within the cavern all was quiet again, except for the ever-present soft drip of water somewhere in a corner. Then, in the blackest darkness, a scream rose in volume, rising until the very walls shook. It went on, inhumanly long, then slowly died away in a gurgling sigh, the sound bouncing around the cavern until all was quiet again.

In the silence, a wet sniffling started, moving left and right, tasting the air. Then a heavy step crashed to the ground, shaking the cavern again, causing more stalactites to fall to the ground. Another step followed, the wet sniffling interspersed with creaking joints. The heavy steps moved through the blackness until they came to a stop at the far wall. The cavern was quiet again for a few moments, except for a slow inhalation and exhalation of breath. Then the wall shuddered from a mighty impact, followed immediately by another, and another. A scream shrieked out again, this time even longer, and the granite wall started to crack under the blows.

Outside, a deer stood not far from the stone cliff, peeling the soft bark from a young sapling and chewing contentedly, when suddenly a muffled scream echoed as if from far away. The ground trembled and the cliff shook. The deer's eyes dilated and it flicked its ears briefly before standing perfectly still, confused by the strange sounds coming from the cliff.

The rock of the cliff face started to crack and small stones fell to the ground. The deer's eyes widened and it turned and leapt away, but as it did, a hole blew out of the cliff face sending rocks flying. A large gray fist stuck out into the air and one of the rocks hit the deer in the side of the head mid-leap and the animal tumbled to the ground, unconscious.

The hand retreated, then more blows hammered from inside until a portion of the cliff crumbled outward and fell to the ground in a shower of rock and dust.

When the dust settled, a colossal form stepped over the rubble and into the light of day for the first time in many millennia. It stood on two heavily-muscled legs and its ribs showed through gray, hanging skin. The creature's head was large, with a face that drooped down in every direction. It stood almost as tall as the young trees growing next to the cliff. Yellow pus ran from open sores on its gray skin, and from between its legs, two enormous, hairless testicles hung low, framing a deformed and thick member, knobby and covered with more yellow pus. It screamed at the sky, its mouth filled with glistening yellow teeth.

The creature strode forward and picked up the deer, ripping it apart with giant three-fingered hands. It opened its mouth and shrieked at the sky again, its long, black tongue fluttering with spittle as it did so. It then dropped the hind quarters of the deer, reached inside the chest of animal, and ripped out its small heart. It held it up, then dropped the small morsel into its mouth, squishing blood as it did so. It had been so long since it had tasted warm, wet flesh. It swallowed, screamed again briefly, then devoured the entire deer. The fresh blood and meat filled it with a small burst of energy, although an aching hunger still gnawed deeply within the creature.

It turned its head back and forth, then started forward, pushing heavily through the trees, smashing them aside like kindling as it searched for more food. It had to fill its stomach, which had been empty for so very long.

It stopped suddenly, one foot frozen in the air. It breathed in deeply as it caught the scent of something it had not sensed since time began. Its mouth salivated, the viscous liquid dripping in strands to the ground below.

The energy of Numbers tickled its consciousness, just a hint, but enough for its eyes to dilate. A deep rage surged inside and it let out another scream, this one filled with longing and hatred as it raised its head to the sky. The creature turned course without hesitating, heading north, toward the source of the Numbers. As it pushed its way through the woods, the creature's thoughts became more clear, as if a dense fog were lifting inside of its mind.

Images from long ago rose to the surface, of pain and ecstasy, of death and destruction, of fields running with blood as it crushed humans covered in black metal who attacked it with violence and fear. Memories flooded back but then faded away, as if they were floating on the surging ocean surf as it rose up a beach and then retreated as quickly.

The creature screamed in frustration as it entered a dense copse of black trees, which it angrily swatted aside.

Then, a single memory rose to the front of its consciousness and stayed there, pulsing with energy. Darkness retreated like black clouds in a storm, and in its mind, the creature saw a single figure coalesce into clarity, its human face hidden except for eyes bright with intelligence. The figure spoke within the creature's mind, words remembered from thousands of seasons ago as clearly as if they were spoken now.

"These numbers I have, black and powerful, I use to create you in all your magnificence. You are the spear point of my army; you will destroy all that stands before me. Nothing can harm you, for I have created you with the essence of Black Numbers. Go my pet, go forth and destroy all that stands before you, and when you are done, come back to me."

The memory hurt the creature and it raised its head high to scream at the sky again, letting the pain flow through it. The creature came upon a badger and picked it up by the tail, the small animal squirming to get loose. The creature dropped the badger in its mouth and bit down hard, crushing the animal's skull and all bodily organs at once, the burst of blood warm and wonderful in its mouth.

It continued on, not stopping or slowing down, relishing the feeling of being free from its prison after so long, and as it walked, another memory crystallized in its mind, clear and just as painful as the first. The creature faintly remembered having this sense of freedom long ago, and of its choice to destroy the numbers man who threatened to take that free will away. The endless destruction that it had wrought upon the landscape of that long ago time and the vast number of humans it had killed and devoured had strengthened it, made it angry that such a puny being dared to control it. It remembered returning to its maker, but with nothing but violence and destruction on its mind, and as it struck down upon its creator, it found itself immobilized.

The man had spoken with a power that had frightened the creature.

"You defy me, and for that you will suffer... forever. From this moment

forward, you are the Unnamed One, for no one will remember you again."

And without any delay, the man had closed his eyes.

The creature remembered struggling against the bonds that held it, of knowing that it would break through whatever was holding it captive. But before it could free itself, it had felt intense pain fill its body, flowing into its mind, as if it were being stretched in many directions at once, the pain growing until the creature had been slammed hard against a stone wall in a space so dark that it could not see a single thing around it. When it tried to move, it found the bonds that held it were fixed firmly, the power so overwhelming that the creature knew it would never break free. It could not move a muscle, and even flexing was not possible. It tried to scream but couldn't open its mouth.

A final thought had entered its mind, filled with sad anger, *"You will remain in this prison forever, but I leave you a gift, something to remind you of my love for you. I give you this pain to be your companion through the millennia. Enjoy it, revel in it, and may you never fully rest... my pet."* And with that, its maker left its mind, to never return again. But he had left behind a deep and burning pain, an agony that filled every joint of the creature, every muscle, never wavering and never leaving, making time seem to both stand still and stretch on forever.

Time had passed.

Slowly.

Inexorably.

The creature's mind had begun to shut down. Memories faded, until just the pain had remained.

Millennia passed, until suddenly, in the darkness, the bonds that held it had collapsed in a burst of power, snapping as if they were made of dried flesh.

Pushing aside a tree now, the creature slowly came out of its thoughts. It put the memories of the man who had imprisoned it for so long into the back of its mind and concentrated on sating its never-ending hunger.

It traveled through the forest, killing whatever animals it came across, devouring them quickly, always looking for more.

It moved constantly for three days, sleeping only briefly, always making its way toward the tantalizing scent of the Black Numbers.

The Unnamed One burst through a stand of tall, but thin trees and startled two massive grizzly bears. The giant animals, the largest creatures in the forest and fearful of nothing, spun around and bared long fangs, roaring in anger at the intruder, but then their eyes grew huge and they turned and bolted away in fear.

The Unnamed One felt bloodlust fill it for a battle with something more than the small pathetic animals it had come across so far. It felt the ever-existing hunger rear up inside, and it screamed to the sky before giving chase.

Chapter 6

The Korpor knelt down and ran a long claw along the edges of the day-old footprint half-obscured by leaves, then lifted its head and sniffed. It could still smell the boy, although his scent was fading into the natural smells of the forest.

The Korpor stood up and was about to start forward when it hesitated and sniffed again, this time inhaling until its lungs completely filled with air. It caught a new scent. Earthy, yet human. It cocked its head slightly, then slowly blinked its left eye, followed by its right eye.

In its long life, the Korpor had only run across this smell one other time, and it felt a small shiver of fear run through its body. It scanned the forest carefully, letting its eyes wander without focusing on any one tree. The scent was weak, but the fact that it was there at all was enough for the Korpor to turn in a full circle. The forest hummed with life. Birds twittered as they hopped from branch to branch in the brush, and far above, in the top of a tree to its right, the Korpor heard the soft scratching of a sloth as it slowly moved across a branch, its long claws gripping the bark.

The Korpor closed its eyes and inhaled deeply again, confirming that whomever made the scent traveled with the Aleph Null.

The Korpor turned to follow the Aleph Null's trail. The boy was surrounded by powerful forces, and the Korpor felt unsure about its mission for the first time.

For if there was one force that it had feared in all its life, it was the Zranh.

Chapter 7

The forest floor, covered in wet decaying leaves, muffled the group's footsteps as they made their way through thick brush and around trees, some of them tall and strong with dark, rough bark, others smooth and thin with new leaves budding on branches stretching toward the sun. Unseen birds twittered and sang in high branches, and squirrels chased each other through the brush and up and down trees. The sun was high over head, but the trees grew so thickly together that the warm rays had a difficult time reaching them on the ground.

Sid pushed a large branch out of his way and held it for Melinda so she wouldn't get slapped in the face with it. She half-smiled and nodded thanks to him. They had been walking steadily since they had left camp after the attack by the mercenaries, and Sid was starting to run out of energy. He could see in Melinda's eyes that she was also getting tired, so he tapped Writhgarth on the shoulder as the little man was sliding over an old and rotting tree that had fallen long ago.

The little man turned his head as he straddled the tree, neither foot touching the ground, and whispered, "Is something wrong?"

None of them had spoken in anything but a whisper all morning. If they were being searched for by other mercenaries, they didn't want to give their position away by their voices.

Sid put his hand on the rough and slimy bark of the fallen tree, breathing a little hard. "Do you think we can take a break?"

Not looking tired himself, Writhgarth looked at Sid and then at Melinda, a little flushed in the face herself behind Sid, and nodded. He whistled softly. Crowdal, who was about ten paces ahead of the group, immediately stopped and turned his head questioningly. Writhgarth motioned him with his thickly fingered hand, and the large Trith immediately came back, not making a sound even though he was at least three times as tall as the Vringe.

When Crowdal stopped on the other side of the tree, Writhgarth whispered, "Let's stop here for a bit and rest."

Crowdal nodded without arguing. "Sure, sounds good." He looked around and pointed toward a small clearing not far away. "How about over there?"

Writhgarth nodded and slid to the other side of the fallen tree.

They all followed Crowdal to the small area free from brush and trees.

Sid put down a blanket for Mrs. Wessmank and Melinda and they both settled down to the ground, with Mrs. Wessmank making soft pained noises as she got settled. Maelon lay down by her thigh, resting his head on her leg. Sid half-smiled. It was one of the things he remembered, even as a boy, when he would visit her in her tobacco and tea shop in Orm-Mina. She never just sat down, she always made a production of it, making pained noises as she got comfortable. He touched her shoulder lightly. "I'll bring you all some food."

The old woman smiled up at him, resting one hand on Maelon's head, softly caressing one of his ears. "Thank you, Sidoro." She always called him Sidoro. Never Sid.

Melinda nodded and thanked him also.

Sid removed his pack, took out enough food for the group, and set it down on the ground, including dried deer meat, some onions, and bread. He handed some to Melinda and Mrs. Wessmank. He looked down at Maelon, unsure what he ate. So he cut the string to one of the dead rabbits that he had hanging from his pack, which he had just killed that morning, and set the animal down on the ground in front of Maelon.

Maelon merely looked at it, and Mrs. Wessmank chuckled. "Maelon would like you to know that he is not an animal, and he eats his meat cooked medium to well-done."

Sid felt his cheeks blush. "I'm sorry Mrs. Wessmank, please tell him that I didn't know."

The old woman motioned down toward Maelon with her head. "You can tell him yourself, you know. He understands you fully."

Sid glanced down at Maelon and saw the creature staring up at him with intelligent eyes. Then Maelon did something that startled Sid. He winked one eye and seemed to grin. Sid laughed, and immediately shut his mouth to stop when he heard Writhgarth hiss for him to be quiet. Sid picked up the dead rabbit. "My apologies, Maelon. Would you like some dried meat instead?"

Maelon nodded and Mrs. Wessmank didn't bother speaking for him, the gesture clear enough.

Sid rummaged in his pack, took out a large piece of dried deer meat, and set it down by Maelon. "Would you like me to cut it up for you?"

Maelon narrowed his eyes and growled softly before putting one of his paws on the meat and biting off a chunk.

Sid backed away, and Mrs. Wessmank chuckled again. "Maelon wants to know if you'd like to chew his food for him too."

Sid felt his cheeks blush again, aware that he had insulted Maelon. "I'm sorry, Maelon."

Mrs. Wessmank smiled. "He's just having fun with you, Sidoro. He thanks you for the food."

Sid nodded, and still uncomfortable, turned away. He whispered loud enough for Writhgarth and Crowdal to hear him, "Help yourselves to some food." They nodded thanks and Crowdal walked quickly over and picked up a hunk of bread and bit into it. He never was one to pass up food.

Sid sat down against a particularly large tree with black bark. He rested his head back and closed his eyes, wondering if he would ever have time again to just sit and do nothing for a day. Since he had left his home he had been pursued and attacked at every turn, and even with the death of Father Mansico and the imprisonment of the Korpor, he found himself still on the run.

He was so tired.

But as he sat against the tree, sleep would not come to him. He kept thinking of the *Black Numbers* manuscript and what was inside. He needed to find out but hadn't had a chance to look. Well, he had the chance a few times, but he admitted to himself that he hadn't been ready.

Until now, he realized.

He opened his eyes and warily got to his feet. Crowdal was talking to Writhgarth not far away, so he made his way to them and tapped Crowdal on the back.

Crowdal turned to him. "Sid, you should be resting."

"I know, but I can't stop thinking about the manuscript."

"You'll have plenty of time to work through it Sid, you need your energy."

Sid frowned. "But what if I never get another chance to examine it? We are constantly on the move, and I have this feeling that things are going to get worse for us."

Crowdal furrowed his brow. "What do you mean? Have you had a vision or something?"

"No, nothing like that. But the Korpor won't be contained by my array for long." He looked down and kicked at the ground for a few moments.

"What is it, Sid?"

He looked back up at his tall friend and pushed thick hair from his face. "I don't know. I can't say why, but I have a feeling that someone new is searching for me... for us, and it is someone who scares me."

Crowdal put a hand on Sid's shoulder. "You are tired, Sid. You've been through so much, it is understandable that you worry. We will be all right."

Sid wished that his friend was right, but deep down, he knew things were going to get bad for them all. Which is why he needed to look through the manuscript now when he could. "Crowdal, I need to spend some time with the manuscript."

"Are you sure that is a good idea?"

"Probably not, but I need to do it. Will you take it out and help me turn the pages?"

Worry showed on Crowdal's face and he studied Sid for a few

moments, looking like he was prepared to say no. But he finally nodded and walked over to his pack. He removed the manuscript and followed Sid to the tree.

Sid sat down and dug his travel blanket from his pack and laid it on the ground. "Please, put it here."

Crowdal set it carefully down on the blanket, then sat down himself. "What do you need me to do?"

Sid pointed to the manuscript. "Please open it to the first page."

Crowdal grabbed the edge of the black leather cover and it creaked as he opened it.

Sid felt a surge of energy fill him as he bent forward to read.

Black Numbers
Power Exponential Black Mathematics

Sid asked Crowdal to turn the page. His friend slowly lifted the parchment to the next page. Sid saw a poem and read it slowly.

> *Beyond sight, below sound, inside taction*
> *Doors into light, windows into darkness*
> *Numbers float randomly, lifeless, sterile*
> *Until a variable unknown*
> *makes black from white*
> *A true Power Rule*

It didn't make much sense to him. He reread it slowly, then asked Crowdal to turn to the next page, not wanting to waste much time on each one.

Crowdal slowly turned the page, the creak of old parchment comforting. He realized that this third page was the same page Writhgarth had quoted from memory, the one his father had read to him when he had found the manuscript.

What is not visible in this world rules supreme. Chaos and absolute power collide with the awakening of the Aleph Null, true wielder of Black Numbers, bringing that which doesn't exist into existence, or erasing existence for all.

A union of the Aleph Null and the beast, of claws and youth, binding a ring of bloody flesh to burst forth the seed of life. A birth, spawning numbers unknown, here yet there, a worm alive at both ends twisting the world upon itself until only power expands, bringing darkness upon the world. The Aleph Null, falls to infinity holding the Black Numbers in a mind's eye, twisting on an axis.

Sid shuddered again at the last sentence. It scared him and made him want to shut the book and read no more. But he needed to continue, so he motioned for Crowdal to turn the page.

When he saw the next page, all he saw were numbers at first. Then the page grew blurry and shimmered slightly. He closed his eyes and rubbed them. When he opened them, the page was filled with text.

Crowdal touched Sid's back. "Are you all right, Sid?"

"Yes, I... am fine."

Crowdal spoke in a comforting voice, "I'm sorry, the manuscript is just gibberish on this page. I know you were hoping for more."

Sid looked up at Crowdal in confusion. "What do you mean?"

Crowdal nodded down to the page. "It is just a series of numbers."

Sid looked back down at the page. "No it isn't. It is pure text."

Crowdal looked back down at the page and then back to Sid. "All I see are numbers. It makes no sense to me."

Unsure what was causing him to read it differently from Crowdal, Sid sat back against the tree again. Maybe he was able to read it because of his power of numbers. A thrill coursed through him, and hope filled him that this manuscript was meant for him, that it could really, honestly, help him understand the strange powers inside of him.

Sid read the text and as he did, the words seemed to lift off the cracked and yellow page and turn back to numbers and mathematical symbols and letters, some that he had never seen before. The more he read, the more the numbers and symbols seemed to come alive and move to certain spots in front of him. He studied them and then gasped when he realized they were forming a single long mathematical formula, the numbers and symbols and letters popping into place at different points of the formula. Sid bent forward to the page and kept reading until he finished the page. He looked up at Crowdal, feeling feverish. "Please turn the page."

Crowdal did as he was told, and as the next page shimmered and the numbers turned to text. Sid immediately began reading it. And as before, as he read each word, the letters lifted from the page and turned to different mathematical pieces of the formula growing in the air in front of him. He remembered the words as he read them, but they seemed to be an abstract layer of meaning that supported the actual mathematical formula that stretched in front of him.

He read the last word of the paragraph that ended about half-way down the fourth page, and as he did so, the letters turned to numbers, lifted off the page, and snicked into place within the formula in front of him. As it did, the formula glowed white and then faded to black. He could still see the equation, but it was like trying to read the equation based on the absence of it within an existing space. He leaned forward further to study it, furrowing his brow as he concentrated. Starting from the left, Sid scanned to the right and to his surprise, he understood the formula, as if he had created it himself. Where at first it looked like an impossible collection of mathematical equations, now it was as simple to him as $2 + 2 = 4$.

He gasped as the formula twisted around and began flowing toward him. His first instinct was to get away from it, but he held his ground as the formula wrapped around his head. It was warm where it touched him and it felt exquisite. Pleasure flowed into him and each nerve of his body tingled as the equation grew brighter and then it was gone from sight. He could feel it moving inside of his mind. It filled him and he cried out in joy as he mentally caressed the equation. Warmth filled him and he realized he had a throbbing erection that pulsed in time with the equation.

And he knew! He understood what Black Numbers were and why he had been unable to manipulate them in the cavern. They were the absence of his numbers, the space between the space where he normally manipulated his numbers. It wasn't something he could just reach out and grasp, or move with his mind alone. With the formula now wrapped around the inside of his mind, he could unlock the base structure of Black Numbers. But it was not enough to manipulate them, he knew. This formula was the tool to understand their nature, like a basic building block of regular mathematics. He had to master it before he could move on to more complex mathematics. One didn't just jump from addition and subtraction to calculus. It was the same thing for him now. He had the basic understanding of Black Numbers. The rest of the manuscript would teach him how to use them.

Sid let his eyes focus on his surroundings again and he leaned backward against the tree, exhausted. He felt Crowdal touch him on the shoulder again. "Sid, what happened?"

Sid smiled weakly up at Crowdal. "Something amazing. But I need to rest now. Can you put the manuscript away? I believe I am finally ready to take that nap."

Crowdal shut the manuscript and squeezed Sid's shoulder before standing up and walking back to put the black leather book into his pack.

Sid closed his eyes and was instantly asleep.

But after what only seemed like a few moments, he felt a hand gently shake his shoulder. "Sid, it is time to get going again."

He opened his eyes and saw Crowdal kneeling next to him. Sid nodded and blinked his eyes a few times to get the sleep out of them, then stood up. He was surprised to find that he actually felt rested.

"How long was I asleep?"

Crowdal looked at the position of the sun in the sky. "You only slept for a short time, it is still early afternoon. But we need to keep moving, we don't know how many other mercenaries are following us."

Sid nodded as he put his pack on his back and tightened the straps. "Let's get going then."

As Sid walked through the woods, he let his mind study the formula that still existed, fully-formed, in his mind. It was an amazing creation and he marveled at its simplicity now. He reached out to his Numbers and the frequency that they existed on was immediately evident to him now.

He remembered how he had tried to change the frequency in the cavern, to force them to change to Black Numbers, and how he couldn't move them once they turned. It had been futile, he realized, like someone trying to move the molecules inside a large boulder. The hard shell of the rock made them solid and immovable. But with the formula he now possessed, Sid now understood the theory of Black Numbers. With this knowledge, he knew the rest of the Black Numbers manuscript would teach him what he needed in order to master the Black Numbers. He couldn't wait until they stopped again so he could read more of the manuscript.

Sid turned his head to his left, and as he did he caught movement in the woods. He stopped and stared at the spot where he had seen it, but now there was nothing there. He slowly moved his eyes, not concentrating on any particular branch or tree. He knew that when in the woods, it was sometimes very difficult to focus on one particular thing, like a deer. But if he let his eyes move naturally over the trees and brush, not concentrating on any particular tree, that he could pick out what he was looking for. He did that now, moving his eyes as far as he could to the right. He started moving them back to the left when he saw it. There was a bit of brown that was slightly different from the color of the surrounding forest. He focused on it and at first wasn't sure it was anything. Then he saw the shape take form.

Sid gasped and Crowdal turned to him. He immediately saw that Sid was tense and staring into the trees. He quickly turned, pulling out his sword at the same time, and scanned the trees.

Without taking his eyes from the figure in the woods, Sid slowly pointed. Crowdal bent down very low in order to follow Sid's arm, then stiffened slightly, seeing the man standing about forty paces away, half-hidden by brush and trees. Sid saw movement to his right and quickly looked, seeing two more people moving from tree to tree. He was quickly pulled back behind Crowdal, who whispered a warning to Writhgarth.

"Aye, I see them too. They are all around us," Writhgarth whispered back. "From my count, I believe there are more than thirty of them out there. Maybe more. I've been seeing twigs bound together into strange shapes and tied to trees, but I've never seen their like before."

When neither Crowdal or Sid showed any understanding, Writhgarth whispered urgently, "Just be very still and do not attack them or we may all very well be killed. If we are lucky, they may just leave us alone."

Sid turned in a full circle and could now see blurred forms moving from tree to tree all around them. He whispered to Writhgarth, "Who are they?"

Before Writhgarth could respond, Melinda pushed past them and made her way into the trees.

***

Crowdal started after Melinda, but he only got ten paces before he was blocked by twenty dark-eyed and deadly-looking men and women. He yelled her name urgently and saw her turn her head once before she disappeared into the brush. Crowdal was about to attack the people who surrounded him when he saw that they all held long, curved knives, each blackened and very sharp. Weapons like that were used for penetrating flesh, which was the one method that could easily kill him. He hesitated only a few moments before deciding that he would rather die than to let Melinda be killed by these... people.

Suddenly the group that blocked him faded into the trees and disappeared. He couldn't even hear them moving away. He looked wildly around and yelled, "Melinda! Melinda, where are you?" Just as he was about to charge into the thickness of brush and trees, he felt a tug on his trousers. He whirled around, eyes wide with rage, only to see a girl of three or four years of age with large brown eyes staring up at him.

She held out her hand for him, her face innocent and beautiful.

Crowdal stared down at the little girl who barely came up to his knees. He could have lifted his foot and crushed her, but instead he surprised himself and reached down and took her small hand in his.

She smiled up at him and tugged at his hand to follow her into the woods. Crowdal looked back and saw that Writhgarth, Melinda, and Mrs. Wessmank with Maelon by her side were surrounded by fifteen or twenty of the people, full adults. He didn't know what was going on, but they weren't dead yet, which meant that these people were not here to harm them. He looked down at the little girl, who smiled beautifully up at him, still gently tugging at his hand. Crowdal made a decision and put his sword back in his scabbard and allowed himself to be led into the woods in the direction where Melinda had disappeared.

The small child pulled him along, smiling up at him every few steps, until they came to another clearing, this one surrounded by posts stuck in the ground. Tied to the top of each post was the figure of a child made of sticks. And standing next to each post was a man or woman. Crowdal only glanced at the stick figures and people next to them, because in the middle of the circle knelt Melinda, and in front of her was an old woman seated on a tree stump. And although the old woman was dressed plainly in a brown, somewhat tattered robe, and her long white hair was unruly, her face radiated intelligence and power.

Melinda turned her face back to Crowdal and he saw sadness and pain in her eyes. The little girl tugged at his hand and Crowdal stepped into the circle.

"I've brought the big man, like you asked." She smiled again up at Crowdal, then let go of his hand and glided into the woods, leaving him standing only a few paces from Melinda and the old woman.

Melinda turned toward Crowdal, a tear running down her cheek.

"Crowdal, I would like you to meet my great-grandmother, Prennia, matriarch of the Zranh."

Chapter 8

Prennia smiled. "Welcome, Crowdal. Please, sit down, my eyes aren't what they used to be and you are like looking up at a tall tree." The old woman motioned to a spot next to Melinda.

Crowdal looked quickly around him and noticed that all of the people who had previously surrounded them were now gone. He sat down and stretched his legs out in front of him. He was amazed these people would trust him not to hurt the old woman who was surely their leader. He said this out loud.

Melinda turned her head again toward him. "It isn't that they trust you, Crowdal. They just don't fear you. If you chose to attack her, my great-grandmother would kill you as easily as one would swat a mosquito."

Crowdal raised an eyebrow and smiled at her joke. Then he glanced to the old woman and noticed that she wasn't sitting in front of him anymore. He began to turn his head when he felt the cold steel point of a knife against the back of his neck; then he felt the person behind him shift and whisper into his left ear, her breath soft against him, "I've killed a score of Trith in my lifetime, although it was purely business. I took no pleasure in the acts." Then, as if he dreamed it, the knife point was gone from his neck and the old woman hobbled past him and sat down slowly on the old tree stump again.

He had just witnessed what he would have thought impossible. How had the old woman moved so quickly and without him even seeing her move? He glanced back at Melinda, but she was just staring down at the ground. Crowdal didn't know how the old woman did what she had done, but he was a pragmatist, and he accepted that she could have easily killed him. He nodded respectfully to her and grinned. "I think I will compliment your cooking, great-grandmother Prennia, even if it tastes terrible."

She laughed, loudly and genuinely, and then tilted her head in his direction while looking at Melinda. "I never thought I would see the day where I met a Trith with a sense of humor. I think he can teach you a few things about living, Melinda, dear."

Melinda scowled at her.

The smile faded from Prennia's face. She shifted on the stump to get more comfortable. "How is your mother?"

"She is unhappy. But you know that already."

The old woman grimaced. "Your mother would have been killed for leaving the clan had I not forced certain... members to let her go. It is far better for her to be unhappy now than to have been killed in the past."

Melinda scowled again at her great-grandmother. "You are so kind." She motioned around her. "My mother has suffered every day, worried that someone from the Zranh would come for us in the night and slit our throats. She has aged beyond her years because she stays up every night and never sleeps for more than a few hours during the day." She spat on the ground and hissed, "And it is all because of her fear of you!"

Prennia sighed. "I am truly sorry, child. I wished that she would accept that we would never harm her." She stared into Melinda's eyes for a few moments and then said, "All I can say is, thank the gods that you live, for you may just be the one who will save us all."

"No!" Melinda screamed, jumping to her feet.

Crowdal jumped up also, pulling his sword from his scabbard in the same movement.

The old woman never moved. She just sat calmly, looking sadly at Melinda.

"I will not be a part of your world. I have my own life now. I'm a healer!" Melinda spat at the ground and snarled, "I'm not a murderer. I am not a Zranh!"

"It is in you, you cannot rid yourself of the Zranh blood that flows through your veins."

Melinda glared at the old woman, the silence between them crackling with energy. Neither broke the stare, and the silence extended. A cool breeze swirled the air in the small clearing, the soft rustling of new leaves in the high tree branches the only sound.

Crowdal didn't move. A battle of wills was taking place between these two strong women and he instinctively knew that whatever the outcome, Melinda's life would be different from this moment forward. She would no longer be the Melinda he had gotten to know over the past few days. As he looked at each of the women, at the old and wrinkled face of Prennia, then at the smooth and beautiful face of Melinda, he couldn't help but see the resemblance between them. It wasn't so much physical as a sense of power inside of them. Their eyes were the exact same shade of brown and radiated the same intelligence and power.

"You are not here against your will, Melinda. You will not be forced into the Zranh life. But I want you to look inside of yourself, think about the anger that has always been inside of you, and ask yourself why. What is missing in your life? There you will find the answer to what you must do at this moment. It isn't by accident that you are here now."

Melinda put her head down. She stood like this for so long that Crowdal was about to ask her if she were all right, when she twirled quickly and walked into the woods, melting into them and disappearing without a sound.

Crowdal stood up quickly, staring into the woods where she had disappeared. Finally he turned back to Prennia.

The old woman sighed and folded her hands in her lap, then looked up at Crowdal. "Please, sit again. It may be a long wait."

Chapter 9

The brush seemed to melt away from Melinda as she walked through the woods, but she didn't even notice the way she instinctively avoided the snagging branches and prickly brush. She just twisted slightly here and there, ducking and weaving, always searching for the easiest path. Most people would have had to hack their way through, or push branches out of their way, getting scratched and beaten up in the process. But Melinda emerged into a small clearing as if she had just walked the marbled halls of the House of Healing.

The clearing was small, maybe ten paces squared, but it was a perfect place to sit and think. She stepped over to a large boulder that sat off-center of the clearing, shaped low on the bottom and rising up at the back, almost in the shape of a chair, or like a throne in a kingly chamber. She sighed as she sat down and put her head back against the cold, rough stone and closed her eyes. Thoughts swirled in her mind, chaotic and random.

She saw images of her mother, graying at the temples despite her relatively young age. Images of the House of Healing flashed by, of helping burn victims from a tavern fire, a score of them blackened so badly she had wondered how they still breathed as she gave them a mixture of Divvene and Rapter weed to deaden the pain so she could put salve on their charred skin and wrap their bodies in clean bandages. The images faded and she saw the door to the room in the tavern where she had been sent to help a traveler, irritated that she had to do it, and of how she had almost gasped out loud when a Trith had filled the doorway. She had never treated a Trith before and had almost turned away. She almost wished that she had, for she would not be here now.

A light, warm breeze touched her face and she tilted her head up and felt the sun filter through the leaves onto her skin, warming it slightly. A small smile touched her lips as she thought of Crowdal. He was a Trith, a race who excelled at fighting and killing, the complete opposite from her profession as a healer. But Crowdal was different from other Trith, for he had the biggest heart she had ever seen in a person and his love of life was greater than anyone she had ever met. He was gentle and loving, which is why the Trith had sent him away, knowing he would quickly realize he couldn't be a part of the outside world, that he belonged in the Trith nation.

It was the opposite for her. Melinda had trained to be a healer, had tried to be a gentle and caring person, but inside she had often felt anger and contempt for people, even as she healed them. She hated that so many people didn't take care of themselves, that they took stupid risks and she was the person who had to try and make them better, only to have them go back to their same lives and make the same mistakes.

Melinda opened her eyes and gazed at the sun-kissed, deep green leaves whispering to each other as they moved in the breeze. She realized just how different she and Crowdal were. Where he was gentle, she was rough. His love of life made her contempt for everything seem shallow. He was trained to kill from birth and had rejected it. Melinda's mother had given up everything to give her a chance at a normal life, yet deep down Melinda wanted to embrace her heritage. Being a healer was really just a cover for who she really was.

A killer.

A Zranh.

Sighing and tilting her head back down, she stared at the brown and rotting leaf-covered ground. Tears came to her eyes as she realized it was a metaphor for who she was; she was rotting on the inside because she had never accepted her past, in fact, she had run from it. But no matter what she had done in her past, she realized she could never get away from who she really was.

She sensed someone moving toward her through the brush but she ignored it and put her head down. It had to be Crowdal, as no Zranh would come to her. This was a private time for her and they knew she had to make up her own mind. She felt Crowdal come to a stop just outside of the clearing and she raised her head tiredly. "I would rather be alone right now, Crowdal."

There was no answer, so she turned her head to her right. A male Zranh stood just outside of the clearing, glaring at her. He was older, perhaps her mother's age, of medium height and build, but with eyes that burned with hatred. She immediately stood up and faced him.

The man stepped into the clearing, only a few paces from her, and pulled out a blackened dagger. He whispered in barely controlled anger, "So it is true."

A vein pulsed near his right eye as he took a step closer.

Melinda scrunched her eyebrows in confusion, about to speak, but he held up his hand.

"Do not say anything or I will ram this blade down your throat, you little bitch."

Melinda flushed with anger but held her tongue.

The man sneered. "That's my good little girl."

Melinda felt a coldness run through her at his statement.

This was her father!

He raised an eyebrow. "So your mother never told you who your father was. Just like her, to lie like that. Your mother should have been killed for leaving... me. And you should have been killed while you were still inside of her."

"You are my father? All these years, I wondered who you were, what you looked like, how your voice would sound."

She spat on the ground. "Now I don't know why I wasted my time."

Her father snarled, clearly close to losing control.

Melinda smiled cruelly, wanting the violence he promised. "Go ahead, try and kill me now, you coward."

The man nodded slowly. "Oh I will, and then I will hunt down your mother, the whore that she is, and jam this Krypen blade into her mouth." His face turned blotchy in his fury and he hissed, "You are both an... abomination and I will finish what I should have done before you were born, before your mother escaped." He advanced on her, holding the black dagger in front of him.

Melinda went still as he advanced on her with the light of death in his eyes, and a rage greater than any she had ever before experienced filled her. Time slowed down and a warmth grew in her hands, arms, legs... spreading until her whole body started to radiate heat. She felt lighter and noticed the leaves had stopped moving. No, they still moved, but it was as if they were undulating slowly under water.

She looked again to her father and saw his foot hovering in mid-air, then slowly coming down, and as she glanced up to his face she saw a frown slowly forming on his mouth as he sluggishly raised his blade toward her.

She felt a chill run through her. She had just slowed down time. The old stories her mother had told her of the Zranh were true! Though how she had done it, she didn't know. She lifted her hands and they moved like normal, although against the almost still backdrop around her, the movements were confusing to her eyes.

Sadness filled her, for she knew she had just become a true Zranh, the very thing her mother had always seemed to hate.

Her mother had educated her on the secret history of the Zranh when she had been old enough to understand it, in case they came for her. The Zranh were an ancient race of assassins who, over thousands of years, had developed the ability to slow down time. It was how they were able to move and kill without being seen. She had often fantasized what this feeling would be like, but had never dreamed that some day she would be able to do what the Zranh did.

She looked back up to her father and wondered if she should run away. But just as she thought this, the man sped up his movements, although everything around her continued at the same slow pace. She realized he had also slowed down time, matching her shift.

He nodded in something close to respect. "So, your mother taught you the time shift. It was a mistake for you to do that, for I doubt she told you what happens when you die while in a shift."

Melinda didn't answer, and he gloated, "You see, when you die in a time shift, the heat your body generates during the transformation rushes out of your body in real time. This difference in time rates causes your body to burn from the inside out and you will feel a pain unlike any you have ever felt before." He smiled viciously. "This is going to be exquisite."

Melinda panicked. She didn't have a weapon and there was no way she could fight a seasoned Zranh. She stepped back, which was a mistake, for like a predator, the retreat only made her father spring at her with a yell, bringing the knife across her face in a death blow.

A flush of heat exploded in her that filled every part of her body. The feeling wasn't painful or unpleasant; in fact, she felt whole for the first time in her life. To her surprise, her father froze in mid air, the knife touching her cheek. She stepped back in shock, unsure what she had done. She put a finger to her cheek and saw a small amount of blood when she pulled it away.

She took deep breaths to get her breathing under control as she studied her father. He wasn't actually frozen in mid-air, she realized. But he was moving so slowly that it took five of her breaths for him to close his eyes in a blink. It never occurred to her that she shouldn't have been able to do this.

Melinda stepped toward her father and pulled his fingers up from the hilt of his dagger, then grasped the point and slid it from his hand. She saw his eyes slowly begin to widen in shock, but he was unable to move fast enough to keep up with her. She studied the knife, for it was unlike any blade she had ever held. It was heavy and very warm to her touch.

Looking back into her father's eyes, she saw nothing but hatred emanating from him. Without hesitating, she flipped the knife into the air, and catching it by the hilt, plunged it into his mouth, just the way he had promised to do to her mother. The blade crushed his upper teeth, sliced through his tongue and throat, and punched through the back of his skull, shattering it. Blood and bone burst out of the back of his head from the blow but just hung in the air in a spray pattern. The shock in his eyes never left him as he fell backward from the blow and landed on the ground.

But her father's death didn't happen immediately, due to the slowed time shift. She watched his eyes carefully, how they became glassy with tears of pain. Beads of sweat appeared on his face, which evaporated quickly from the heat of his shift releasing. The moments stretched on, his face showing the agony coursing through him. Melinda took a couple steps back and sat on the rock again. Her father's eyes began to boil and then seep thickly down his cheeks and she realized she couldn't let him suffer like this. No matter how much she hated her father, no person deserved a fate such as this. She was a healer, not a killer.

Not a Zranh.

She concentrated and time sped up to the time shift rate she had first entered. Her father instantly began screaming and thrashing on the ground, blood pumping out of his mouth in thick eruptions. Almost as quickly as he thrashed, he arched his back and then lay still, staring up at the sky.

Melinda slipped from the large rock and walked over to her father's corpse. She bent down and yanked the blade from his mouth, staring at the blood on it, bright red and thick. It dripped very slowly, one drop taking many moments to hang down until it broke the liquid bond. The circular drop of blood slowly floated to the ground, and as it impacted, the red edges rose up and around the flat middle of the drop with amazing beauty.

Melinda looked down at her dead father and while she didn't feel sadness at his death, she did feel sick to her stomach that she had so brutally killed him.

She turned and left the clearing, absently holding the knife, and made her way back to Prennia and Crowdal, the time shift silence of the forest strange yet intoxicating. As she entered the larger clearing, she saw the old woman and Crowdal sitting facing each other, almost completely still. Then to her surprise, Prennia turned her head toward her and watched her walk up with sad eyes.

Crowdal never moved.

Prennia nodded slightly to Melinda. "Rollien has joined the earth, and by your hand as I had foreseen."

Melinda started to speak but the old woman raised a hand to stop her. "It is as it was meant to be. You had to do what you did."

Shaking her head angrily, Melinda quietly hissed, "I had to murder my own father? What am I?"

The old woman looked even older, her skin seemed to hang more loosely, her face became more slack, but her eyes were as piercing as ever with light dancing in her pupils. "I don't know what you are, to be honest. You are Zranh, you can enter the Raith world where time moves slower, but you have the pure blood inside of you that allows you to slow time to almost a stop. Your mother had it to some degree, although she couldn't control how she did it, which is why she left us. Few of the Zranh knew that she was pregnant with you, she kept that secret because she knew some of the Zranh were frightened of her and wanted her dead."

Melinda spoke through clenched teeth, "Then how did my father know who I was?"

"Zranh can feel the energy of their children, parent and child are connected by a special bond. He knew your mother was pregnant almost upon conception. But we forbade him to leave, to hunt you and your mother down after she left us. When you entered these woods, he immediately felt your presence, which shocked him and drove him into the final pit of madness."

Melinda angrily broke a twig into smaller and smaller parts as she listened. "Well that was his problem, now, wasn't it? It's not my fault and I don't want any further part of what is happening. I am a healer and that is all I am." Even as she said it though, she knew, deep down, that there was no going back, that she didn't want to go back to who she had been. Her eyes must have shown this because the old woman lowered her eyes to the ground.

Silence stretched between them until Melinda spoke, so quietly that her voice came out more as a whisper, "So what is my future?"

"That, my dear, is for you to find out." When Melinda's eyes blazed angrily, Prennia put up her hand in a conciliatory gesture. "Your mother had to make her own life. In rare, uncontrolled moments, she was able to make time move slower than any Zranh could do, she could walk around us as if we were trying to walk under water. And some of us even thought she could make time stop entirely, but we were never able to prove it. Because of her difference, she was shunned by most of the Zranh, except for me and Rollien. He loved her, in his own, sick way. But he was cruel and beat her. When she chose to leave him while carrying his child, he couldn't bear to think that your mother would reject him, and he would have killed her had I let him. Her betrayal destroyed him. He was forever ruined after she left, but that is in the past. Your future is an emptiness in my vision, which means it is up to you to make your own life. But we would like to have you stay with us. We... need you."

Melinda rubbed her eyes tiredly. This was all too much for her and she needed to leave this place. She lowered her eyes to Crowdal, who had turned toward her and was now halfway to his feet, a surprised expression on his face. He knew she was there, but time was moving so slowly that everything that had just taken place between her and Prennia had only been a moment to Crowdal.

She sighed and turned her eyes back to the old woman and her expression softened. In a tired voice she said, "Thank you for the information. I will be who I will be, whomever that is, but I will not be a Zranh, I will not live like you."

The old woman nodded sadly. "Please don't think of us as monsters, Melinda. We do not kill without reason; when we do, it is always merciful. We respect life more than anyone else outside of our clan because we know how easy it is to take it from someone."

"Whatever... I don't care about you. You are not my people. I am a healer, that is all I am."

Prennia shook her head, "No, whatever you are, you are far from just a healer. You can save us."

Melinda started to protest but Prennia held her hand up. "Please, let me finish. I must give you all the facts so that you know the whole truth. We are dying, Melinda. It is that simple. We need you to save our bloodline, for you carry the pure blood of the ancients within you. You can restore our race to what we once were. You are the key to our survival."

Melinda stood up and screamed at the woman, spittle flying from her mouth, "How dare you put this on me? I owe you nothing!" Her chest heaved and she pushed hair from her sweaty face. "My mother left you for a reason and my place is with my friends. We are going to leave here and you will not stop us."

The old woman visibly sagged. "As you wish. We will not stop you."

Melinda, expecting an argument, didn't know how to answer at first. Finally she lifted her head. "Thank you."

"Before you go, you must do something first."

Melinda's eyes flashed angrily and the old woman held up her hand to stop another outburst. "Please, let me finish. You must take that blade with you."

Melinda glanced down at the bloody blade in her hand; at the blackened steel as sharp as any blade ever made; at the tightly wrapped, black-skinned handle that she instinctively knew was made from the skin of a human. The quillon that kept her hand from sliding from the handle was sharpened to a point so it could also be used as a weapon. It was a beautiful blade, and she hated and loved it at the same time. It called to her, but she angrily dropped it to the ground at the old woman's feet.

"I don't want it!"

But as she said this, a sense of loss immediately filled her, a feeling like a part of her had just died.

Prennia didn't look down, instead she locked her gaze on Melinda. "Pick up the Krypen blade Melinda, it is yours now."

When Melinda merely stood there, the old woman lowered her voice to a grim whisper, "Pick up that blade right now!"

Melinda found herself picking it up before she even realized what she was doing, the power of the woman's voice was so great.

Prennia nodded. "That Krypen blade has the blood of your father in it, and is now a part of you and will be forever. It is a living thing."

At those words, Melinda felt a burning in her hand and looked down at the blade. She instinctively wanted to drop it to the ground again, but she couldn't open her fingers enough to make it happen. The burning intensified and when it got to the point where she didn't think she could take the pain any longer, it stopped. In awe, Melinda turned the blade over and watched in fascination as the blood seemed to sink into the steel. In a few moments the blackened blade was a deep crimson color. She reached out a finger and touched it and warmth infused her, a sense of hatred and love at the same time. She pulled her finger away from the steel and looked at it. The blood was now a part of the blade.

She looked up wonderingly at Prennia, who said, "Your father will forever be a part of that blade now. A part of you. If you lose it, or let it be taken from you, a part of you will die and an emptiness will exist within you."

A male Zranh appeared from the woods and walked over to the old woman, handing a simple black sheath to her, then left as quietly.

Prennia held it toward Melinda. "This was your father's and now it is yours."

Almost in a daze, Melinda stepped forward and took the sheath. She slid the Krypen blade into it, the feeling almost like she were sliding it into flesh. The warmth dissipated, and when she looked up to the old woman, she felt the anger bubble up within her again and she grimaced as she turned away. "Goodbye, grandmother, I hope I never see you again."

Pain briefly flickered in the old woman's eyes, then they cleared. "One last thing before you go. Do not let the Raith world consume you. If you spend too much time in it, you will find it harder and harder to spend time in the real world." She closed her eyes briefly, then whispered. "It will kill you, if you let it. For every heartbeat that you spend in it, you lose a thousand heartbeats of your life."

When Melinda didn't seem to hear her, Prennia spoke sharply, her voice like the crack of a whip, "Do not ignore this warning!"

Melinda jumped.

Prennia continued in a harsh voice, "We only slow down time for those short moments before we kill. If you spent one full day in the Raith world, you would lose almost three years of your life, but that loss would occur all at once and could kill you from the shock to your system, as if you had never slept in all that time." She stopped briefly, as if thinking, then continued, "To be honest, we have no idea how it will affect you with your abilities. It could be ten times worse for you. Your life force could burn away and if you didn't die from it, you could become just a shell of yourself. Even this small portion of time you just now spent in the Raith world will make you feel as if you have not slept for many days. You will be exhausted. Do not enter the Raith world again for at least another fortnight."

She paused, then whispered, "Please don't let your hatred of us consume you."

The old woman seemed to sag and Melinda realized that her grandmother had probably never spent so long a time in the Raith world before.

As much as she wanted to like the old woman, she just couldn't find it within herself to be civil to her. Instead, she nodded stiffly and strapped the sheath to her belt, then bent down to her pack and put it on her back. She looked at Crowdal, whose head was almost completely turned toward her. She closed her eyes and felt the heat flow through her body, and without knowing how she did it, she let it dissipate.

The whispering of the leaves in the trees assaulted her, incredibly loud after the silent world she had just inhabited.

Crowdal's face completed the turn toward her in a smooth motion and his eyes raised in surprise. To Melinda's sadness, she saw a glint of distrust in them. She grunted toward him as she turned, "Come on, we're leaving."

Crowdal looked back toward her great-grandmother but Melinda knew the old woman had stayed in the Raith world long enough to fade into the woods. The clearing was just a place in the woods with no signs anyone had ever been there.

Crowdal quickly got to his feet. "Melinda, what happened?"

Without turning to look at him, she marched into the woods. "Not now, Crowdal."

Chapter 10

Agnes glanced up at the sun. There was maybe a quarter of a day left of light and she and her Haissan had yet to reach the village of Vorllindo, where they would rest for the night. They had been riding at a comfortable pace since leaving the Oblate in Undaluag that morning. The horse that she rode was gentle, yet strong, and the day was comfortably warm.

Since leaving the outskirts of Undaluag, they had traveled through small village after small village, but for the past half-day, they had not come across one. The road had at first led them through what seemed like unending fields of wheat, but for some time now it ran along the western edge of a swamp, with a dark forest of gnarled Cypress trees to her left.

A mosquito bit her neck. She slapped it without thinking and looked at her hand. The insect was just a smudge of blood on her palm, so she wiped it on her horse with a small curse. The black flies were worse than the mosquitoes, though, as they constantly flew around her and her horse, burrowing into her hair and biting her head. It hadn't taken her long to tie a scarf around her head as she rode.

The Haissan, riding to her right, didn't seem to be bothered by the biting insects, which irritated her. Not for the first time, and with a little shiver, she wondered just what kind of creatures the Haissen were. She had studied what little was written about them in the old histories, but every word she had read raised even more questions. That they were brutal killers was obvious; but there was something else underneath their emotionless countenance that intrigued her. Whether it had to do with the calm efficiency with which they did everything, or the fact that they didn't appear to have any faults, she wasn't sure. Maybe it was that they didn't seem to have any agenda. They never played politics; in fact, they never even seemed to care about anything going on around them, yet appeared to be aware of everything. It was a contradiction that frightened and intrigued her.

Her horse snorted softly and Agnes got a whiff of air that made her nose crinkle. She turned in her saddle and saw that her stallion had his tail raised and was dumping an incredible amount of shit onto the road as it walked. How any animal could produce so much feces was amazing to her. She saw flies immediately swarm around the warm piles and she quickly faced forward. She hadn't been raised around farm animals of any kind and still found it difficult to get used to riding a horse. Her back and butt were already getting sore, as were her thighs and legs as they chaffed against the saddle and sides of the horse.

The road was wide and well-cared-for, dry and smooth. The

motion of the walking horse lulled her senses and she found it difficult to keep her eyes open. The sounds of birds twittering in the trees to her left was like music, and the swamp to her right had its own beauty with its stunted and blackened Cypress trees and mossy mounds of earth that seemed to be floating in brackish water. The warm, early-summer air was the perfect temperature. They had not met another rider all afternoon, which was strange for this time of year on a main road. But she didn't worry about it as her chin dropped to her chest and bobbed in time with the constant rocking motion of her horse.

An image of her mother appeared in her head, standing by an open door with a large wooden bowl held in the crook of her arm. She used her other hand to knead the contents and was calling to Agnes, who was playing with her puppy out in the tidy yard.

Agnes stumbled as her puppy ran and jumped at her legs, playfully biting at her fingers. They tumbled together to the warm grass and she laughed as the puppy jumped onto her chest and licked her face. Agnes, her eyes dancing with merriment, heard a soft thud and gurgle behind her and turned her head back, laughing as her puppy nibbled at her chin. She saw the bowl lying up-side-down on the ground, thick bread dough clumped in the dirt. She heard another gurgle and looked up to see her mother still standing in the doorway, her entire apron bright red. Her mother fell to her knees and Agnes screamed when she saw her mother reach up and almost caress the feathers of the black arrow shaft lodged in her throat. Blood gurgled from her mouth and Agnes had screamed again.

Agnes jerked upright on her horse, coming out of her memories when the animal neighed softly.

Her Haissan angled over to her and its whispered voice brought her fully out of the dream, "You screamed."

Embarrassed, she nodded curtly. "I am fine."

The Haissan didn't question her further and turned away without pausing.

Agnes wiped her brow, which was damp with sweat. It had been some time since that dream had come to her. It was a memory that had haunted her for many years, but as she had gotten older, it had faded to a distant pain.

She had been taken that day by the man who had killed her mother and had not seen any of her family since. She had been raised by the man. The first years had been difficult and she had tried to escape many times. But eventually she had stopped trying to run. The man, whom she had eventually come to call father, had treated her decently but had never shown her love or affection.

Every morning he had come to her room and taught her mathematics, starting with the basics, then progressing to more advanced math as the years passed. And the thing that had surprised her was that she loved mathematics, considering she had never heard of it before being abducted. When she had turned seventeen, her father had sat her down and told her about the Oblate and the Korpor. He told her about the Proofing and when she had shaken her head that she didn't want any part of it, he had slapped her. Through her tears, she had watched him leave the room.

And then she had felt pain worse than any she had ever felt before as a huge creature with giant blue eyes entered the room and stared at her. The agony had made her lose consciousness and when she had woken up, the pain and creature were gone. Her father — no, the man who had abducted her, for she refused to call him father after he had beaten her for failing the Proofing, had delivered her to the Oblate and ridden away without a word, as if she were dead to him.

With her astounding mathematical abilities, she had become a Blue Robe of the inner circle within a single year of arriving at the Oblate. To her surprise, she found she liked it there, that she had a purpose in life.

Agnes slapped at another mosquito and came out of her reverie. She couldn't seem to stop her mind from wandering and realized that she was exhausted. Riding had taken more out of her than she had expected. She waved frantically as more mosquitoes whined around her head. "When will we reach Vorllindo?"

The Haissan hissed back to her without turning its head, "Before the sun sets."

Gritting her teeth at the pain in her thighs and back, she groaned, unsure if she would make it. To take her mind off of the pain, she thought back to her orders from the Black Robe.

Just the idea of riding into the Masteen's domain, much less approaching the man whose name caused grown men to go weak in the knees, made her wonder again what she had gotten herself into.

She believed in what the Oblate stood for. It was a force for good in an often chaotic land, working behind the scenes to guide kings and queens, merchants and politicians, and almost all others in positions of power to make the right decisions to benefit everyone. The fact that she now had more gold coins available to her than she had ever thought possible was something that had bothered her at first, for she wondered why she should benefit so grandly. But the old Black Robe had spoken to her many times in his quavering voice, quietly reassuring her they had gained the wealth over the millennia to ensure the Oblate was beholden to no one. They had to be above the petty wants and needs of others so they could guide others without envy or greed.

But with this new Black Robe, she felt uncertain about the Oblate for the first time. She had experienced just how cruel the young man was, and combining this with the fact that he was more powerful than any Black Robe in the history of the Oblate, made her worry that the organization she had pledged her life to was no longer something she could support.

She had gone on this mission because she had no choice. She firmly believed that the Black Robe would have killed her if she had refused.

The Haissan put up its hand and Agnes pulled back on her reins, forcing her horse to stop. They sat silently for a long time, not even their horses made a sound. Agnes trusted her Haissan's abilities, so she kept quiet, knowing there had to be a reason for it to stop them.

The Haissan sat very still on its horse, staring into the forest to their left.

Agnes scanned the area around her. To her left was the forest, thick with birch and poplar trees. She turned her head to her right and studied the swamp that was the breeding ground of her flying tormenters. She didn't see or hear anything out of the ordinary.

She was about to ask the Haissan what the problem was when it hissed to her, "Quietly get down from your horse, go to the swamp, and lie flat on the ground in the reeds."

Her heart beating faster, Agnes slowly swung her right leg back over her horse and slid to the dry gravel of the road. She carefully made her way to the edge of the swamp, her feet soon squishing into soft, wet mud that smelled of rotten vegetation. She knelt in the tall reeds and then lay flat, her body settling into the cold, black water. The mosquitoes instantly swarmed over her. She slapped at them, but no matter how many she killed, there were a dozen more landing on her, sinking their proboscises into her flesh. Their constant whine drove her crazy and the rotten smell overwhelmed her.

She was about to stand up in an effort to escape from the swamp's edge when a scream echoed from the woods. It was strangely pitched, deep yet shrill as it rose in volume. It sounded unlike any animal she had ever heard, like one that was in both pain and in a rage. The scream seemed to reach deeply into her psyche, to the areas where the deepest fears she had ever known resided.

Her Haissan leapt from its horse and edged closer to Agnes, its sword out and held up in a defensive position toward the treeline. The first scream faded and a second scream immediately replaced it, angry and wild, the echoes bouncing through the trees from some distance away. The horses whinnied and took off at a gallop down the road. Agnes put her hands to her ears, trying to block out the terrible sound.

The scream faded away and from the woods across the road Agnes now heard the sounds of breaking branches, coming closer as if someone or something was running at full speed toward them. She couldn't even think straight. Fear clouded her thoughts and her adrenaline pumped hard, making her entire body shake uncontrollably. She didn't even notice the mosquitoes biting her anymore.

The crashing grew louder and more violent until a huge brown grizzly bear burst from the forest. Its eyes were wild and foam bubbled and flew from its mouth as it ran on all fours. It didn't slow down as it crossed the gravel road and plunged into the swamp, splashing through the black water and reeds close by Agnes and her Haissan, not even noticing them as it passed. Agnes could see bloody gashes on its head and shoulders from crashing through the brush and branches.

From the woods, another scream rang out and grew in volume, closer now, and she could hear more branches breaking. Agnes wanted to run, but her Haissan suddenly dropped to the ground next to her and reached its hand to her mouth. It shook its head slowly from side to side for her not to move.

The crashing grew louder and louder until another brown grizzly bear burst from the trees. It was even larger than the first one, easily three times the size of her stallion, with thick muscles that undulated beneath the long fur as it ran. The scream changed pitch and Agnes was startled to realize that it wasn't coming from the bear. The huge animal came to a stop not five paces from Agnes and her Haissan, its huge front paws sliding in the gravel and sending up a cloud of dust. It spun around, reared up on its hind legs, and roared, its jaws opening wide, filled with sharp teeth almost as long as Agnes' own hand. Foam and saliva flew from its mouth.

The scream from the forest grew in volume and the ground shuddered as something gigantic approached. Agnes felt her bladder release but she didn't care. With a crashing of timber, she caught movement coming through the trees, which were being pushed aside as if they were nothing but small branches. The crashing grew louder until a creature smashed aside two trees and stepped through the treeline.

It stood on two heavily-muscled legs, humanoid in shape but with gray skin filled with red pustules that leaked a foul fluid Agnes could smell from across the road. It stood almost twice as tall as the grizzly, with arms that hung low, and hands that each had three triple-jointed fingers. Its thumbs had thick, black nails that stuck out like pointed spears. The face of the creature was literally impossible for Agnes to understand. It was as if it had melted like candle wax, the skin running down so it was difficult to see any actual features.

The creature's mouth split apart, revealing sharp, blackened teeth. It opened wide and Agnes, unable to look away, watched a long, black tongue flutter out as it screamed again, turning its head back and forth. It was so loud that Agnes thought her eardrums were going to burst.

The creature leaned forward as it screamed and charged the grizzly.

The bear dropped to all fours and charged the creature in turn, rising up on its back legs just as they collided. The impact was so powerful that Agnes felt the ground itself shudder.

As they collided, the bear wrapped its immense arms around the creature and with jaws wide open, sunk its teeth into the creature's chest. The giant grizzly jerked its head viciously back and forth in fury, and the creature roared at the pain.

The creature swung its right arm at the bear's head and struck so hard that the bear was knocked sideways, tumbling twice across the road.

The grizzly slowly got to all four paws, shaking its head before it charged the creature again, hitting it at full speed. The collision pushed the creature back two steps, and the bear rose up and slashed with a giant paw, its long claws gashing into the creature's stomach, causing black blood to burst forth.

The creature raised its head to the sky and screamed in anger.

The grizzly lunged its head forward and clamped enormous jaws on the creature's arm, and for a moment Agnes thought the giant bear might actually have a chance against the creature. She knew the grizzly could have easily killed her stallion with a single swipe of its paw. But as she watched, the creature grabbed the snout of the bear with its free hand and twisted upward with a violent jerk. The bear's snout broke with a sickening snap of bone and the creature twisted hard again, ripping the upper jaw clear from the bear's head.

The bear let out a howl of pain that quickly turned to a gurgle as blood poured into its throat. The creature dropped the bloody snout, raised its hand, and smashed down on the bear's head with such force that the animal's skull shattered.

The bear instantly went limp and fell to the ground with a hard thud, dust rising up in a plume.

The creature raised its head and screamed in victory at the sky, spittle flying from its mouth, its black tongue moving back and forth angrily. Then it bent down and plunged both hands into the bear's stomach and pulled hard in opposite directions, tearing open the flesh as easily as parchment. It reached inside, pulled out the heart, and stuffed it into its mouth, blood running down its face as it chewed. When it finished, it bent down and picked up the massive grizzly and threw the carcass over its back.

It stood for a moment then, turning its head in all directions, sniffing loudly. When its gaze passed by the spot where Agnes and her Haissan were hiding, it stopped and stared hard in their direction.

Agnes lay perfectly still deep in the reeds, unable to move. The creature took three long strides forward, towering over them, and sniffed again, a deep, wet sound. The smell of pus leaking from the open sores made her eyes and nose sting and she wanted nothing more than to stand up and run as fast as she could into the swamp. But she knew if she even so much as twitched a muscle, she would be killed instantly. She only hoped that the smell of rotten vegetation was masking her own scent and keeping her from being noticed by the creature.

The moments stretched until Agnes didn't think she could handle it any more. Then the creature raised its head to the sky and screamed once more, this time for so long and so loudly that Agnes began to lose consciousness. But just as she felt darkness descending upon her, the creature stopped screaming and turned and ran into the woods, carrying the bear like a sack of potatoes.

After some time, her vision slowly cleared. She rolled over to her back and stared at the sky, her ears ringing and her head aching. The Haissan next to her didn't move and she feared that maybe it had been stepped on. She turned her face toward the Haissan and saw it staring at her through its hood.

It calmly hissed, "Let's go find our horses," and smoothly got to its feet and put out its hand to help her shakily to her feet.

Her knees wobbled and she had to lock her legs to keep from collapsing.

The Haissan cocked its head at her. "Can you walk?"

"Yes, just give me a moment."

The Haissan led her a little distance away to dry ground. "Sit here and rest. I will be back shortly with our horses."

Agnes nodded, too weak and exhausted to argue. She pulled her knees to her chest and hugged them tightly as she watched the Haissan sprint away, as light on its feet as a deer. Soon it disappeared from view and Agnes was alone. It was so quiet that the ringing in her ears seemed very loud. She tore a piece of her shirt and used it to wipe inside her ears. The cloth came away with a spot of blood on it, but she didn't think she would have permanent hearing loss.

She lay back on the ground until her heartbeat slowed down and she got her breathing under control. She couldn't believe that they were still alive. She had no idea what kind of creature that had been. She had never heard of anything like it, not even in stories. The ringing in her ears began to fade and the sounds of the forest were a welcome relief. She watched a black and green bird land on a branch above her, its head quickly twitching from side to side. But it fluttered from the branch when, from very far away, another scream echoed. Her heart instantly started beating more quickly and chills ran up her entire body.

She couldn't stay here, the creature could be back at any moment. She got to her feet and stumbled in the direction the Haissan had gone. She fearfully looked to her left, into the trees, and before she knew it, she found herself running and staggering, her breathing coming hard until she lost her footing and fell to her hands and knees, skinning them on the gravel. Her chest heaving, she pushed herself back up and continued down the road in a daze, her sight blurred from tears and sweat, until hands suddenly grabbed her, holding her steady. She flinched and started to fight until she realized that it was her Haissan holding her. She cried out and let herself be lowered to the ground.

Its voice hissed next to her, "Drink this."

She felt cool water trickle down her throat and she greedily gulped at it. The Haissan wrapped her hands in soft cloth, and then she felt herself being picked up and placed on her own horse. The Haissan set the reins gently into her left hand and hissed again, "We need to keep moving. Can you ride?"

Agnes, ashamed for her weakness, nodded and straightened her back.

"Good, we don't have far to go."

The Haissan jumped up on its own steed and tapped her horse on the rear to get it moving.

The jostling of the horse quickly brought Agnes out of her shock. She took control of her horse more fully and they rode, side-by-side, until the sun disappeared behind the horizon.

In the half-darkness of dusk, they approached Vorllindo. Lights from windows brought Agnes a sense of calm for the first time since the battle between the creature and the bear. The main street of the small village still had quite a few people on it, so they guided their horses carefully until they came upon a series of taverns. The Haissan motioned to one and they angled over to a narrow alleyway that led to the back of the building where they found a fairly large stable.

A young man heard their approach and came out of the three-sided structure holding a brightly lit lantern. "Evening, Lord and Lady. Please leave your horses with me. I will take good care of them." He gestured with his free hand toward the building. "You can enter 'The White Horse' through the back door."

The Haissan slid from its horse and handed the young man the reins and a copper coin, then reached up to help Agnes down from her horse, but she pushed its hands aside and slid her leg back and gingerly let herself down to the ground. As her feet touched the gravel though, her legs buckled and she quickly tightened her grip on saddle to stop her fall, then slowly straightened up. Her joints cracked and popped as she started toward the back of the tavern and the Haissan quickly got ahead of her to open the old wooden door.

Light spilled through the doorway and the smell of cooked meat caused Agnes' mouth to salivate. She stepped into the tavern and, with her Haissan by her side, made her way to the bar.

A middle-aged man was at the end talking to a rough-looking customer. He turned his head, and when he saw Agnes, he said something to the customer, who nodded and laughed. He approached them and smiled. "How may I help you?" But his smile faltered when he saw her torn clothing and dirty face. "You've had some trouble, let me get you the captain of the watch!"

Agnes shook her head. "No, I just want a room, a hot bath, and food."

The man eyed her warily. She knew that coin usually helped, so she took his hand in hers and then let it go.

He looked down and saw a large gold coin sitting in his palm and quickly closed his hand and put it into his pocket. "Of course, my lady." He didn't even speak to her Haissan, the look in his eyes showing that he thought it nothing more than a servant. He motioned to someone behind Agnes. "Get room number four ready for the lady with a hot bath."

Agnes turned and saw two young women hurrying into the back servants' quarters.

The man smiled. "Your room will be ready shortly. Until then, let me get you and your servant some food and ale."

Agnes nodded curtly and walked to an empty table. Her Haissan pulled the chair out for her, then sat down next to her. Food was immediately brought out for them, along with two large mugs of a black ale with foam dripping over the rims. Agnes looked at her plate and her stomach rumbled at the sight of a thick stew of potatoes, carrots, onions, and large chunks of browned meat in a thick brown gravy.

She and the Haissan quickly picked up their forks and began eating. Food had never tasted so good to her as it did at this moment. She took a large swallow of the black ale and wiped foam from her lips. With the hunger pains lessening, she slowed down and ate more deliberately and with more decorum. Soon the stew was gone and she sat back, satisfied and very tired.

The man approached their table with a smile. "Your room and bath are ready, my Lady." He motioned to two lovely young women. "Gertrude and Sally will guide you to your room."

Agnes and her Haissan stood and followed the young women up the stairs to a long hallway. They opened a door about halfway down and held it open for Agnes, but her Haissan stepped into the room first. It stepped back out very quickly and hissed, "It is safe."

Agnes stepped into the room, and when the young women tried to enter behind her, they were stopped by the Haissan's arm across the door opening.

"Leave," it hissed.

The two young women backed away in fear and quickly ran down the hall. The Haissan softly shut the door and stood silently with its back to it.

Agnes knew her Haissan would not let anyone through and feeling safe for the first time since the encounter with the monster, she tiredly removed her riding clothing, letting it drop to the floor. Naked, she knelt down, leaned her head over the side of the tub, and dunked it under the hot water. She grabbed a chunk of soap and making a thick lather, she washed her hair and rinsed it. Her hair clean, she stepped into the steaming water of the bath and settled slowly down until her chin was just above the water.

The heat instantly penetrated her sore muscles and stung the cuts on her knees and palms from when she had fallen to the gravel. She picked up the chunk of dark soap and a soft brush and began scrubbing her body, paying close attention to the cuts, getting out the small pebbles that had lodged under her skin. Here arms were covered in bug bites, so she gingerly scrubbed at them, then she reached back and worked at her shoulders and neck.

When she was done, she got out of the water and wrapped a large but coarse towel around her, feeling clean but tired. She took another towel and dried her hair, then made her way to the bed and climbed under the covers. She blew out the candles and was asleep in moments.

She didn't see the Haissan enter the room and collect her dirty clothing and just as quietly leave the room.

Chapter 11

Prennia stretched her back and rolled her neck painfully, the sound of cracking joints seeming louder than it had been the previous day. The extended period of time she had spent in the Raith world with Melinda had taken its toll on her. A young girl brought her a cup of water. The cup was made from the leaves of the Wilden tree woven together with such complexity that not a single drop of moisture leaked from it. The cool water gave her strength and she thanked the girl who knelt at her feet, then said, "Goris, please gather everyone."

The girl rose fluidly and nodded, before bounding away with the unlimited energy of youth. Prennia so wished she had that kind of energy again. But that was a foolish wish; she had lived a long life and was ready for the end whenever it chose to come for her. She didn't have long to wait before members of her clan stepped into the clearing one at a time, coming from all different directions.

Prennia waited until all 38 of them were present. Each knelt down on one knee and waited for her to begin. She let her eyes pass over each one, then sadly looked down to the ground. Their numbers had decreased during her lifetime from a peak of 62 when she had been a child. Fewer of them were able to have children, although they had been blessed with four children in the past seven years. But the powers of the Zranh had also decreased with each new generation, to the point where the new children could not maintain their hold on the Raith world for more than a few moments at a time. She hated to admit it, but she feared that soon they would be extinct as a race.

Which was why she needed to ensure Melinda's safety, for Melinda had the blood of the ancients in her veins, blood so pure that she could stop time almost completely. As the elder, Prennia had memorized the history of the Zranh. The oldest stories, thought to be more myth than history, spoke of the ancients being able to completely stop time. No one had truly believed in them though, and to be honest, she hadn't believed in them herself. That is, until she had met Melinda. The full power of the Zranh existed inside the young healer, power that had been fading in their race for thousands of years.

The official oral histories told of the Zranh being able to enter the edge of the Raith world, to slow down time to a small degree. But Melinda's mother had shown brief glimpses of the ancients' power, even if it had been sporadic. Prennia had hoped she would marry and the power would show up in her child, but Melinda's mother had left in the middle of the night and never returned. Prennia knew how abusive Rollien had been, but what had happened between them had been none of her business. Privacy was the one thing they all respected. Because they had the ability to move unseen at any time, it would be too easy and tempting to spy on the most intimate moments of someone else. So their law was absolute when it came to respecting privacy, with banishment from the clan the only punishment.

They had let Melinda's mother leave, although Prennia had to force the issue when Rollien had flown into a rage, promising to hunt her down and kill her for abandoning him. Some of his closest relatives had agreed with him, and Prennia had to threaten death to any Zranh who would harm her. Her word was law, so Rollien had stormed off. He had never truly been the same since, always filled with anger and rage. But he had obeyed her.

Now Melinda had appeared, a gift that could change the history of the Zranh forever. But instead of a happy reunion, the poor young woman was filled with anger, something that the Zranh, as a race, had suppressed to the point where emotion of almost any kind was rarely shown. Anger, combined with their power, was a recipe for disaster. Rollien had been the first Zranh to lose complete control and let his anger rule his life. Melinda must have gotten the gene from him. She thought about it and wondered if maybe it had mixed with the power of the ancients in Melinda's mother, opening the way to creating a child with the old blood.

Prennia put the thought out of her mind, for she was no philosopher. However Melinda got the blood of the ancients didn't matter. The fact that she could save the Zranh did matter. She cleared her throat and took another sip of water from the leaf cup. "My children, I have some sad news. Rollien no longer walks this earth. He has merged with his Krypen blade."

No one moved or spoke. Merging with one's Krypen blade was an inevitability. They all carried the essence of their dead ancestors in their own Krypen blades and would one day join with them.

Prennia took another sip of water, saddened by what she had to say next. She pointed three times, each time a young man stood up proudly. She hesitated, then pointed a fourth time. A young woman stood up and held her head high. She had short hair that framed a narrow face with high cheekbones and deep brown eyes.

Prennia spoke, "Saulian, Nren, and Oeth, you will join with Pronni, who will be the Gorepeth." They nodded respectfully at Prennia, then turned toward the young woman and bowed slightly, replying in unison. "We will serve you."

Being selected as the Gorepeth, or literally translated in their language as, 'one who leads down the path,' was a great honor.

The young woman didn't respond to the men, which was proper protocol as the Gorepeth of the Quadrant, the traditional assassination squad sent on missions. She faced Prennia and spoke in a high, singsong voice, "Command me."

Prennia hardened her eyes and spoke, "You will follow the woman who just left here. Her name is Melinda, and you must ensure that no harm comes to her. If she succumbs to the Raith world, you must bring her back here as quickly as you can."

The young woman didn't flinch or react in any way. She merely nodded and said, "We will do as you command."

"There is one more thing." Prennia hesitated briefly, then continued in a quieter tone, "Melinda is special in a way we have not seen in thousands of years." She paused again, letting the importance of what she would say next build amongst the clan. "Melinda can enter the full Raith world. You will not be able to follow her where she goes."

The young woman asked a question for the first time, "What do you mean? We are Zranh."

The old woman nodded. "You are Zranh, but Melinda is something more." She stopped briefly, then whispered, "She has the blood of the ancients inside of her."

Shocked whispers broke out amongst the other Zranh, and Prennia raised her voice. "That is right. The old blood can save us, which is why we must ensure her survival."

Pronni stood tall. "We will protect her with our lives."

Prennia sat back, exhausted. "My final command to you is the most difficult for me to issue. If Melinda enters the Raith world too often, she may begin to fade away. If this happens, you must do whatever you can to bring her back here. This may mean you will have to stay in the Raith world for longer than you have ever done before, even if it means giving your lives. She must be kept safe."

The three young men swallowed hard but nodded. Pronni held her head high and didn't show any emotion as she answered, "We will gladly give our lives."

Prennia closed her eyes. "Go with grace and speed, and may you all return to us."

The four young Zranh bowed, then came together and disappeared into the trees. The remaining Zranh also stood, then faded away into the forest until Prennia was alone.

A tear rolled down her cheek.

She had just sent her great-grand-daughter on a mission from which she might not return alive.

Chapter 12

When Melinda and Crowdal had returned from deep in the woods and the strange people had melted away into the forest, Sid was relieved they were all safe, but he immediately knew something was wrong with Melinda. Outwardly she looked fine, unharmed. But when he looked into her eyes he saw a coldness and distance that he couldn't read. Crowdal kept his distance from her, not even attempting to talk to her.

They all walked in silence for the rest of the afternoon until they came upon a narrow dirt trail that crossed their way. Writhgarth held up a hand and they all stopped. He looked to his left and right and saw that the trail curved out of sight not far away in both directions, tall grass swaying in the slight breeze. He faced the group, sweat glistening on his forehead as the afternoon had become quite warm. "This is the Grang Trail which leads to Undaluag. We could take a chance and follow it, since it is rarely used." He looked at Crowdal, then at the rest of the group, waiting for them to make a decision.

Crowdal wiped his sleeve across his own forehead, then dropped his pack and sat down with a loud sigh. "I have to say, following a trail would be a welcome change."

The rest of the group followed his lead, removing their own packs. Mrs. Wessmank almost dropped to the ground, she was so tired, and Sid quickly knelt down next to her, asking if she was all right. She nodded, although her face was flushed red. He handed her his water skin and she took a small sip, smiling tiredly up to him at the same time. "Thank you, Sidoro, I'll be fine. I just need to rest these old bones for a spell."

Sid settled down next to her and took a drink of the water, too. He listened to the birds twittering above him, their songs filling the air with life. He was quite tired, also. Making their way through the thick woods had been much harder than following a trail or road. If he were by himself, he wouldn't have had any trouble, he was used to spending time in the wilderness. But with Mrs. Wessmank, they had to find the easiest route, which took time. He was worried about her. She was just too old to be on such a long journey by foot. He turned to Writhgarth. "How much further do you think it would be to Undaluag if we took this trail?"

The little man thought for a few moments before answering, "I'm not entirely sure where we are on this trail, but I don't think that we could be much more than a day or two from Undaluag."

Sid nodded. "Then I say we should take the chance and follow the trail."

Crowdal was about to respond when he cocked his head slightly and sniffed the air. He quickly stood up and peered intently down the trail toward Undaluag. Writhgarth also stood, followed by the rest of the group. Crowdal hissed quietly, "Quickly, I want you all to cross the trail. Writhgarth, stay with them and watch for mercenaries. They are coming."

The little man nodded and whispered to the group, "Let's get moving."

They all crossed the path and entered the woods again, trying to be a quiet as possible. Crowdal stayed behind and Sid was going to say something, but Writhgarth shook his head and whispered, "Crowdal will be fine. Keep moving."

* * *

Crowdal stood in the middle of the path facing toward Undaluag, his sword in his hand. The swaying grass that covered most of the trail confused the eyes and made it difficult to see far ahead. It was a beautiful spring day, but the birds had stopped making any sound, as if they knew what was coming. Then from around the corner, a group of five men appeared, all dressed in mismatched leathers and the occasional armor chest plate, some wearing old and tattered helmets of various designs.

They saw Crowdal standing in front of them and stopped about fifty paces away. As if unsure what to do, they just stood there for a few moments until finally the leader, a man who may have been good-looking at one time but now had teeth missing, as well as a nose that had been broken too many times, made a small motion. Two of the men raised bows and released arrows in a motion so smooth and fast that one moment they were still and the next moment arrows were whistling through the air at their target.

Crowdal stood still and the two arrows whistled past his head, so close that his hair moved from the passage of each shaft. He faced the mercenaries, unmoving, his eyes locked on those of the leader, until with a small nod toward Crowdal, the man motioned with his hand and the five men turned and moved away, back the way they had come.

Watching them disappear around the corner, Crowdal put his sword back in his scabbard, but remained where he was. He got a bad feeling as he thought back to the attack on their camp by the mercenaries. They had concentrated their arrows on Sid, but had not struck him, even though Sid had been standing still. He saw, just a few moments ago, how the two men had raised their bows, pulled out arrows from the quivers on their sides, nocked them, pulled the mighty bowstrings back and released them in one smooth motion. They were men who did not miss. Yet they had missed both him and Sid. He realized with a sinking feeling of certainty that they were not being hunted by the mercenaries. They were being kept from going to Undaluag. He turned, entered the woods, and quickly caught up with his friends.

Writhgarth turned as Crowdal came up behind them, relaxing only when he saw that it was the big man. "What did you find out?"

"Mercenaries, five of them."

The little man nodded, his face serious, knowing there was something more.

Sid, Melinda, Mrs. Wessmank, and Maelon also looked to Crowdal questioningly, who motioned them all to keep moving as he quietly spoke, "I think we are being kept from going to Undaluag. When I confronted them, they only shot two arrows at me and then went back the way they had come, a clear message that we were not going to easily go in that direction."

Sid slumped his shoulders.

Mrs. Wessmank saw his reaction. "What's wrong, Sid?"

Instead of answering, he angled over to a tree and slid down, resting against his pack. He looked defeated and exhausted. The rest of the group stopped and came over to him.

* * *

Mrs. Wessmank sat down next to Sidoro and as she touched his hand an image instantly flared in her mind. She gasped and closed her eyes as more images flowed quickly, like a dam that had finally burst; images of dark-skinned and hideous men surrounding Sidoro, of darkness and cries of pain, blood and screams, of men missing their heads. Then the images stopped and she sat back, shaking and cold, despite the warmth of the sun beating down on her.

Sidoro touched her shoulder and spoke in a soft voice, "You felt it too, didn't you? The darkness."

When she opened her eyes, she could see the pain and fear on his face. She nodded slightly, then looked up and around at the small group of people whom she considered a gift from the gods, for they were all tied into this together, each one of them an important piece to the overall outcome of what would happen to Sidoro. Their strength was in their unity, she had felt it from the moment she had met them in the cavern. But the vision she had just experienced was the strongest she had felt in ages. And it wasn't a good one. She snorted to herself. As if her visions were ever good ones. She motioned for everyone to sit down to her level. "We need to talk."

Melinda sat next to Sidoro, and Crowdal and Writhgarth knelt down on one knee, their swords still out and ready to defend them if needed.

The old woman sighed contentedly as Maelon settled by her side and rested his head on her thigh. She lovingly stroked his head and looked at each member of the group in turn before finally speaking in a tired voice, "We are not meant to go to Undaluag, no matter how important I thought it was to reach the Anderom. They simply cannot help us anymore. We have to go back south, as fast as we can."

"What do you mean south, I'm not going back that way," Melinda cried out in alarm.

Crowdal nodded. "Melinda is right, we just spent two days coming from that direction, and I've no wish to face those... people in the woods again. They may not be so hospitable a second time."

"Nonetheless, we cannot go north," Mrs. Wessmank said vehemently. "We are being driven in that direction by someone who will try to take Sidoro's powers. This is one big trap and I see nothing but pain and destruction if we continue north."

Nodding, Writhgarth spoke reasonably, "Then we should go west."

Unable to see anything wrong with that option, Mrs. Wessmank nodded her head. "West would work also. Anywhere but north or east," she finished with a shudder.

They were about to stand up when Melinda shook her head and whispered, "We can't go west."

"Why not?" Crowdal asked.

Melinda shook slightly. "We've been shadowed by three large men to the west of us for a few hours now and there are more of them out there, a force radiating darkness and evil."

Crowdal and Writhgarth immediately looked into the trees, embarrassed they had not seen anyone out there.

Crowdal turned back to Melinda. "How do you know?"

Melinda looked down to the ground. "Just trust me on this."

Crowdal studied her for a few moments, then shrugged his shoulders in acceptance. "Great, we can't go south, east, or west unless we want to fight our way through unknown numbers of mercenaries, or people who appear and disappear at will. And we can't go north, which seems to be the only way open to us. It seems we are in a nice little trap, indeed."

* * *

Sid had kept quiet during the exchange, for his numbers had suddenly grown restless, appearing in bursts and bouncing around in his mind. He watched their chaotic motions, losing himself in the beauty of their complexity until he reached the calm center of his being. Letting out a long breath, he let the power of the Black Numbers manuscript flow through him and he felt an erection grow in his trousers. He pulled the power into himself, letting it fill the numbers, making them pulse and vibrate in odd frequencies. Astonished again at the power available to him, Sid concentrated his efforts on one particular dark area where the numbers refused to touch, an area in his mind he had not noticed before now. It sat just behind and to the right of where his numbers usually spilled from, and it was here where the power from the Black Numbers manuscript seemed to be drawn, yet also pushed away from.

Trembling with barely contained eagerness to explore that area, he drew near to it and knew that if he touched it, he would have an orgasm. He wanted nothing more than to do it, he ached to touch it, but he held back, and as he did, he felt the darkness bubble out of every crevice of his mind and spread across his vision like a blanket of cold air. It swirled in one direction, then shifted and spread thinly with little pops here and there as if something worked its way from its depths to the surface. Sid concentrated on it, wanting instinctively to calm the surface.

He felt the numerical makeup of the blackness; it was made up simply of five numbers repeating in random order. Without thinking about it, he started rearranging the numbers, moving from one to the next slowly at first, then picking up speed as he started to understand the order he wanted. Soon he was shifting entire groups of numbers at once, reordering them as he shifted them until soon all of the numbers were ordered 1, 2, 3 ,4, 5, 4, 3, 2, 1, 2, 3, 4, 5: repeating the sequence thousands of times. He mentally pulled back and saw that the surface was smoothed out, and images swirled in it. He locked the numbers and leaned forward to look into the darkness... and gasped.

A clearing surrounded by a forest of dark and colossal Miq trees, so tall that he couldn't see their tops, slowly appeared in the numbers. The scene spun in a circle and he saw the sun setting to the west, and to the south rose high mountains, black and ragged, dominating the sky.

The spinning stopped and he saw himself lying on his back in the center of the clearing, and standing over him was the most beautiful woman that he had ever seen, with shoulder-length black hair and green eyes that sparkled with intelligence and sensuality. She stood over his prostrate body and held his Rissen blade in her hand as if to strike him, the beautiful blade gleaming in the light, but for some reason that he couldn't understand, he got the sense she was protecting him. Just behind her, Sid saw a man shrouded in darkness who emanated a power greater than any he had ever felt before.

The image faded and swirled into a bird's eye view of the clearing. Scores of evil-looking men wearing black armor surrounded them all; and paced evenly around the edge of the clearing stood two Murder of Haissen. At the front stood one man who was as tall as Crowdal, but where Crowdal was slender, this man was hugely-built. He wore a helmet shaped like something out of a nightmare. The man laughed, then pulled out a black sword and strode toward Sid's friends who were back-to-back in a circle, unable to reach Sid who lay at the feet of the green-eyed woman and shrouded figure.

He sensed a new type of power and shifted his view to see a large obelisk standing in the clearing, and from it he felt a power of numbers that both frightened and called to him, almost with a real voice. Instinctively, he knew it was the key to Black Numbers. His breathing quickened, but then time seemed to shift and he heard a loud crashing come from the deep forest at the edge of the clearing. When he looked, he saw movement as something gigantic made its way toward them through the trees.

Sid felt a sense of hopelessness fill him and he wanted nothing more than to end this nightmare vision. But then he saw the figure of a woman approach his prostrate form in the clearing. He couldn't see her face, but he felt a sense of peace fill him at the sight of her, almost like he knew her. He wanted to get closer, to see her face, but then the clearing began to fade into swirling darkness.

He grasped at it futilely, but the surface of the darkness itself started to jump around and Sid couldn't hold it together any longer. He cried out in frustration, but he was exhausted and couldn't stop the numbered sequence from falling apart. The darkness flowed back into the part of his mind where the numbers wouldn't touch. Soon his thoughts were clear once again. But just as the darkness completely disappeared, he thought he heard a soft woman's voice reach out to him, breathing his name, floating from the west. He listened for more, but nothing else came to him except complete silence.

Sid opened his eyes and saw his friends staring at him. The images from his trance stayed with him, powerful and still pulling at him even with his eyes open. When Crowdal raised his right eyebrow questioningly, Sid sat up straight and flipped his mop of sandy brown hair from his face. He knew now that they had to go west first, to find the woman in his vision, but that ultimately they had to travel north, to find a mountain range and a forest of Miq trees beyond it. He had to find that clearing and confront the power of numbers in the obelisk.

He turned to Mrs. Wessmank who seemed much older than he had ever thought possible. Her eyes were sunken in as if she already knew what he was going to say and dreaded hearing it. He stood up and situated his pack more comfortably on his back before speaking with a strength he didn't feel, "We have to go west for now."

Mrs. Wessmank sunk into herself at the words and Sid had to swallow before continuing, "I can't ask all of you to travel with me any further. It will be dangerous, and I don't know for sure what we will find. But there is someone whom I need to find, and she is to the west. Once I find her, then I need to travel north to a mountain range."

The group looked from one to other briefly, before Crowdal said, "It seems that things just keep getting more and more interesting when we are around you, Sid."

Sid was about to speak, but Crowdal held up his hand for him to hold his thought. "I don't know who is to our west, but if you say we must go in that direction, I believe you. As for finding the mountains to the north, that sounds a bit cold to me, and I hate the cold. But I'll travel with you."

Crowdal turned to Writhgarth and Melinda, who both nodded their agreement, and Sid released his breath, not even realizing that he had been holding it, so great was his relief to know his friends would travel with him.

Crowdal continued, "I think we should travel until it gets dark, then in the middle of the night, we can quietly move north a ways and then angle west to see if we can slip away from our mercenary followers."

The others nodded in agreement, except for Mrs. Wessmank, who still sat against the tree, her head bowed, absently stroking Maelon's furry ear between two fingers.

Sid knelt down next to her and lifted her chin. "It is the only choice we have. I must meet a woman, she is the key to everything. You know this as well as I because you've seen it, haven't you?"

The old woman looked into his eyes and finally nodded. "I have, although..."

"What, Mrs. Wessmank?"

She looked like she was about to say something but then changed her mind. She merely smiled instead and patted his hand. "Never mind me, Sidoro. Your plan is sound and I will follow you."

Sid stared into her eyes unflinchingly and she touched his cheek softly before struggling to her feet. He helped pull her up, then looked around the forest to pick out the easiest path for her.

Shifting her pack to a more comfortable position, Melinda spoke softly, "It is not long till dusk. Let's keep moving so we don't attract any attention to our plans." She turned and started walking away from them.

Crowdal watched her walk away into the woods and he grinned at Sid and Writhgarth. "Looks like we are in for some fun, at least. It has been kind of boring lately."

Grunting, Writhgarth put his sword back in its scabbard, turned away and muttered under his breath, "Trith…"

They cut through dense brush and thick woods until dusk settled on them. The air had grown cool in the late spring evening, and as they made camp, they each felt a chill deep in their bones. When Crowdal began to gather wood for a fire, Writhgarth asked him if that was wise. Crowdal looked at the trees around them, then down and nodded. "It seems everyone knows where we are, so a fire won't hurt, and it will be a cool night so we might as well be comfortable and eat a warm meal. If whomever is out there sees a fire, they will assume that we will be staying put tonight. We can quietly slip away when the fire burns to coals."

Writhgarth nodded, agreeing with the logic. "I'll get the pot out and make my special Writhgarth stew."

Crowdal groaned.

"What, you don't like my stew?"

"Stew? You call it stew?"

Looking hurt, Writhgarth spread his hands wide. "What do you mean, I use nothing but fresh ingredients. Potatoes and rabbit. It is good for you."

Crowdal looked quickly around, pretending to be outraged. "Poor bunnies! Run, bunnies, run." He turned back to Writhgarth and winked. "Aside from my not eating meat, haven't you heard of the word 'spices'? Perhaps some Wilden tree leaves, Miq cone hearts, Salin root? Good gods, even onions would help!"

Shaking his head, the little man turned away and left the camp with his knife to gather what he could for the stew.

Crowdal chuckled.

Sid looked up at Crowdal as he laid out the thick blankets for everyone. "You sure like to needle him, don't you?"

Crowdal turned serious all of a sudden. "He is a good man, one of the best I've ever met, and I would trust him with my life. But he is too serious. I just like to lighten things up a bit."

A corner of the blanket was bunched up, so Sid reached over and flattened it out as he spoke. "I wish every day that this was all over with."

"I know, but what will happen will happen. All we can do is try and tilt the odds in our favor." Crowdal looked over at Melinda as she checked on Mrs. Wessmank, his face radiating worry.

Sid glanced over to where Crowdal was looking. Aside from her recent comment, Melinda hadn't spoken all day and her eyes were darkened as if from lack of sleep, although he knew she got sleep whenever the group stopped for rests. Something was wrong with her. "Is she all right? She hasn't been the same since we left that group of people who surrounded us in the forest." He looked up at Crowdal. "What happened to her, do you know?"

Crowdal shook his head. "I'm not sure. But I think there is more to her than any of us can imagine." He looked down at Sid. "Come on, let's get some more wood and build a large fire. I'm cold."

Sid could tell that his friend was more worried for Melinda than he let on. He followed Crowdal away from the small camp to help gather fallen branches for the fire.

Chapter 13

The Haissan squeezed the pommel of the saddle a little harder as she listened to the Red Robe sigh. The occasional soft sounds from the human were irritating. She closed her gills in disgust. Humans were noisy, weak, and they smelled bad. And worst of all, they couldn't stop making noises for one moment it seemed.

She hissed quietly at the thought of the humans that she had served for so many hundreds of years, at how they looked at her in fear, how they referred to her as an 'it'. But that didn't bother her in the slightest. They were beneath her, not worthy of her anger.

Saleth flicked her eyes to the green-eyed woman. But at least this one was a little different. She treated Saleth with respect, albeit with fear, too. But it wasn't only this that made Saleth's heart beat quicker. It was the fact that their plans were coming to fruition.

For her entire existence, there had always been one inscrutable fact: the Aleph Null had to be found, for the Aleph Null was the only being who could save the Haissen species from extinction.

Saleth let her mind wander back to her early years, of sitting cross-legged on the soft and shiny wooden floor of the sacred Meisasiura chamber, where all Haissen spent seven days meditating on their history before the sword ceremony. Only after sixty years of training with the sword was a Haissan allowed to truly call themselves a Haissan. Until that time, they were nothing, they had no standing, no purpose.

Saleth remembered those final seven days of meditation, of reliving the 5000-year history of the Haissan. For 3000 years, the Haissen had inhabited an island far off the Northern coast. They numbered in the tens of thousands, living both in the sea and on land with equal ease.

Then they had started to die from a strange illness. Births became more and more rare, and when they found themselves down to just a few hundred in total, their Saikon, or leader, had awakened one night in a sweat after having a vision of a human who would be born with the power to save them; a human with mathematical powers so great that it could change their molecular structure and destroy the sickness gene within them.

The Saikon had called this human the Aleph Null.

So the Haissen had come to the mainland and searched for humans who had mathematical ability, a search they found to be very difficult amongst the primitive human race. It had taken the first few hundred years to gather even just a small number of humans with mathematical ability, but the Haissen were not mathematicians themselves and couldn't advance the humans in that area. So the Haissen formed a secret society called the Oblate as a way to build a self-fulfilling prophecy among the concentrated group of humans who had mathematical ability. They taught the humans the basic prophecy of the Aleph Null as a way to make them take control of their training, of the search for the Aleph Null, but omitting any reference to the true purpose of the Haissen.

Saleth felt the barely-contained power of the Aleph Null, even from such a distance. The power was like a living force bubbling inside of the young man, ready to burst out at any moment. Saleth could sense it as easily as the smell of the grass all around her. The power was truly awe-inspiring, nothing like the paltry power that the Black and Red Robes of the Oblate thought they had wielded over the millennia.

Within a few generations after the Haissen had established the Oblate, the humans had gained a false sense of power and self-importance, until finally they thought of themselves as the rulers, forgetting the history of the Haissen entirely. Saleth almost smirked inside of her hood. It had all been according to plan by the Haissen, and when the humans were ready, the Haissen offered themselves as protectors to the Black Robes of the Oblate. By doing this, they would never be considered a threat and they would always be invisible because of the superiority complex inherent in all humans.

But over the thousands of years since, the Haissen had fractured as a race. They had forgotten their own history and had come to believe in the Oblate as the only purpose for existence. Only a small group had remained who still worked toward the day the Aleph Null would appear and save them. They were driven into secrecy, forced to outwardly agree with the majority that protecting the Oblate was their only calling.

This small group had a newer, secondary objective. Their current leader, Tierre, had a vision only a few hundred years earlier that, one day, a Red Robe would come who would be very important in the final battle. While the Korpor was a simple creature that the Haissen had bred thousands of years earlier to be the catalyst to awaken the power of the Aleph Null, it was this aberrant Red Robe who would be the chaos-binding force that would open the sexual pathways enough for the Aleph Null to fully access the power of Black Numbers.

Saleth thought back to the day she had been ordered to replace Bornif when he had been killed by the sickness during his service to a Red Robe. Back then, there had been two hundred Haissen serving the Black Robe of the Oblate and only twenty three serving in secret for the Aleph Null.

Over the years, Red Robes had come and gone, and Saleth had despised them all. But then, a few weeks ago, this new one named Agnes had ascended, and Saleth had immediately known she was different from all the rest, that she would be the one who would help the Aleph Null.

Now Saleth was just one of fifty two Haissen left in existence. Only a few days ago, four Haissen had been killed by the Trith and thirteen more had been killed by the Aleph Null in an awesome display of power in the cavern under the city.

Saleth was saddened because the four Haissen killed by the Trith were, apart from her and Tierre, the last of their small group of believers.

As she rode now with the Red Robe called Agnes, she accepted with finality that the future of the Haissen race was on her shoulders.

She would protect the Aleph Null and the green-eyed Red Robe against all the forces gathering against them.

The Haissen prophecy would be fulfilled, even if Saleth had to die in the process.

Chapter 14

The horses had thick sheens of sweat as Agnes and her Haissan pulled back on their reins, coming to a stop in a cloud of dust. She swung her leg over the saddle and stepped down to the ground, surprised that she was no longer sore after a day's ride. The journey had toughened her up. She had thought that she had always been in good shape, but she had been soft, where now her muscles were harder, tighter. She liked the feeling of having more energy.

Two dark-skinned men, one with an ugly scar across his forehead, silently took the reins of their horses and led them into a large stall, the soft nickering of other horses greeting them.

Agnes immediately turned and walked toward a high-gated arch built of sandstone that was carved with figures of men and women in various stages of dying.

Her Haissan walked in front of her, casually looking left and right, but Agnes knew it was aware of everything around them. Six huge, dark-skinned men, each wearing blackened-steel chest plates and black helmets with horns sticking out of them, stood at arms in front of the opened gate. They moved aside as she approached, not saying a word. She craned her head up and shuddered as she studied the arch and stylized carvings, and she realized she was looking at the infamous 'Arch of the Dead', the entrance to Masteen Vorn Maghuur's inner domain. Few people deliberately passed through this arch.

Agnes squared her shoulders and passed through it with steady, unhurried steps.

They had entered Masteen Vorn Maghuur's territory after a four-day journey through some of the roughest country that Agnes had ever seen, and now, in the early morning darkness just before dawn, they had arrived at the fortress of Masteen Vorn Maghuur. They had ridden hard and fast after their first stop in Vorllindo, only stopping for short rests during the day and leaving early each morning. When they knew they were getting close to the Masteen's domain, they had decided to ride through the night.

Agnes had slept for short periods each time they had stopped for a rest, but in the past four days she had not slept for a total of even a single night, especially after her encounter with that monstrous creature on the road. She still had nightmares about it every time she tried to sleep. She was exhausted, but her Haissan didn't show even a hint of fatigue, as usual. She wondered, not for the first time, what the Haissen were and where they came from. Why they served the Oblate, she had never heard. It was a mystery she would like to solve one day.

As she entered the courtyard, the temperature seemed to drop, and she put the thought of the Haissan out of her mind.

She heard distant moans of pain.

In front of her, randomly scattered throughout the courtyard, stood at least twenty pockmarked and blackened wooden posts, each three-times the height of a man and sharpened at the end. On six of them, men were impaled, five of them through the groin, or initially through the groin, for their body weight had caused them to slide down the wood, forcing the stakes to tear through to their chests, leaving a blackened trail of blood and intestines on the wood above their heads.

As Agnes looked up at the post directly in front of her, she stopped and stepped back a few paces involuntarily, for to her horror she saw a man impaled through his rectum. She swallowed with a suddenly dry throat, wanting nothing more than to turn away from the grisly scene, but she forced herself to look at him to remind herself of the character of the man she was about to meet. She had heard rumors that this was the torture reserved for those whom Masteen Vorn Maghuur felt needed special treatment.

She had heard that people often lived for more than a day, writhing in agony, suffering a lifetime of pain with every heartbeat, but the heartbeats never seemed to end. Most had their eyes plucked out by crows well before succumbing to death.

As she looked up at this man, she realized he was one of the few untouched by the crows and she watched in guilty fascination as he lifted his head slightly and turned to look over his shoulder and down at her. The pain that radiated from his eyes was palpable to her even from the ground. He tried to speak, his eyes imploring her to help him. Agnes felt sick to her stomach. She nodded slightly to him and then put her head down and continued walking, but as she did, she created a numbered equation and sent it into the man's heart without turning. She heard him gasp, and then a bubbling sigh reached her. She knew that he was now hanging lifeless on the post, at peace and free from the pain at last.

Shuddering, Agnes put her head down and followed her Haissan across the courtyard to another gated arch, this one smaller but even more heavily-guarded. They stopped when a large man dressed in black armor holding an ugly and scarred helmet in the crook of his arm stepped forward and leered at Agnes, totally ignoring the robed and hooded Haissan.

His breath reeked of old meat as he breathed on her, then he spoke in a low, gravelly voice, "What do you want here, whore..."

She ignored him and coldly strode past him.

The man, startled and angry at being ignored by a woman, reached out a huge hand and grabbed her arm, spinning her around. "You will not..."

He didn't get out another word because the Haissan's sword tip had lightly punctured the skin of his throat. The man turned slowly, eyes blazing with anger at the Haissan, ignoring the sword at his throat. "Remove that sword... right... now."

Agnes nodded slightly at her Haissan and it smoothly returned the sword to the scabbard at its side. She didn't want any violence here. Seeing the Masteen Vorn Maghuur was too important. She spoke to the large man who still held her arm. "You will kindly remove your hand. We are here to see Masteen Vorn Maghuur, and if you keep me from him, you can be assured that you will suffer a fate worse than that impaled man out there."

The large guard coldly glared at her, then slowly released her arm. He looked at the Haissan coldly, then back to Agnes, fighting a battle inside of himself, as if he wanted nothing more than to kill her Haissan and rape her. But he took a step back. Her commanding tone had obviously told him that she was no common whore and the speed with which her Haissan had brought its sword to his neck caused him to pause. Shaking slightly in anger, he nodded curtly to another man and in the same gravelly voice said, "Bring them to the Red Room but do not awaken the Masteen. They will wait for him." He lowered his voice even further and leaned slightly toward the Haissan, "You and I are not finished."

Agnes didn't hesitate. She followed a guard through the gate, then through a thick double-door into the building. They entered a dark chamber lit only by a single torch. The man turned to his right, opened another door and motioned them inside. Her Haissan entered first, and she followed. The room was small, with a dozen wooden chairs situated randomly throughout it. A chill went through her when she saw that the walls, floor, and ceiling were a dark ruby-red color, the same color as blood, she realized. The door shut behind her and she heard the lock turn. Knowing it could be a long wait, she crossed to the far wall and lay down on the floor. She was asleep in moments.

Her Haissan stood next to her, unmoving.

Dark fragments of dreams plagued Agnes as she slept on the cold stone floor, and when the door opened, she sat up stiffly and just as tired as before she lay down. She pushed hair from her face and slowly got to her feet, her knee joints popping.

A well-dressed man with long, black hair stood in the doorway and nodded to her. "The Masteen will see you now."

Agnes started when she realized that the man's nose had been cut off, a gaping hole where it had once been. Air sucked in and out of it, and snot slowly ran down to his lip, which the man casually patted with a dark cloth.

When he saw her staring, he smiled and his eyes burned into her. "I would not keep the Masteen waiting."

Quickly pulling her eyes from his face, she nodded and crossed the red floor and followed the man out. Her Haissan walked behind her, and she felt grateful having it close by.

The three of them walked single-file across the chamber, which was still dark even though she knew it must be at least mid-morning. How long she had slept, she wasn't sure, but it couldn't have been too long. The air grew warmer as they climbed a broad staircase which had at one time been made of white marble but which now was blackened and pitted. Same with the walls. The whole place was gloomy and foul-smelling.

Not for the first time, she wished she could turn around and leave. But she steeled herself and followed the man in front of her. The stairs ended at a large landing area. The man turned right and led them down a long, dark hallway lit by only a few torches, the ceiling blackened from soot. They soon came to a cross hall and the man turned left without pausing and Agnes wondered just how large this building was, but just as she thought this, they arrived at a set of enormous double doors guarded by four of the largest men Agnes had ever seen. They didn't even look at her as they stepped aside and opened the doors. The man with no nose half-bowed respectfully to them before entering the room beyond.

She glanced at the men as she passed them and quickly looked away, feeling her bowels loosen at the sight of their faces partially hidden by hideous black helmets. They were the most fearsome-looking men she had ever seen.

That is, until she entered the room and took her first look at the Masteen Vorn Maghuur as he sat eating at a large table. He was not only the largest and ugliest man she had ever seen, she realized she was looking at pure evil. His eyes, black and lifeless, bored into her, crowned by bushy eyebrows and sunken eye sockets.

She took in his whole visage in a moment and she knew that it was burned into her memory and would haunt her for the rest of her life. His forehead protruded far out, as did his large chin, which was covered in coarse, black hair that did little to hide it. He had black hair that hung to his shoulders, as well as thick, pelt-like hair covering his arms. But it was the scars that she knew she would never forget. They covered every available area of his face, arms, and hands — some crisscrossing, others deep and wide — puckered red and white. Other scars were raised and blackened, including one that went from the top of his head, down between his eyes, then continued down his left cheek and disappeared beneath his tunic. She had no idea what sort of man could survive a wound like that. As she looked back up into his eyes, Agnes suspected it would take a lot to kill this man.

The Masteen Vorn Maghuur turned back to his food, ignoring Agnes and the Haissan as he calmly cut a piece of meat from a large steak and delicately placed it in his mouth, chewing slowly. When he finished, he patted his mouth with a black cloth and sat back with a sigh. "Please, sit down and eat. You must be hungry."

Prepared for a voice to match the man's visage, Agnes almost stopped breathing at the sound, for it was beautiful and melodious, yet so deep and powerful that chills of pleasure coursed through her. As she stepped forward, he turned to her again, and she marveled at the power emanating from his eyes as he studied her. She felt weak and flushed with excitement at the same time. Against her own judgment, she found herself wishing to do anything to please him, and she now knew how he had gained and held power. While he was the most fearsome and ugly man she had ever seen, the power in his eyes and voice was beyond anything she had ever experienced, and she knew that anyone would follow him, or even die for him.

She frantically reached for her numbers. They moved sluggishly and she had to concentrate to make them come forth into her mind, and even as they did, she struggled to control them. She felt the power of the Masteen and realized he somehow negatively impacted her control of numbers. She let her numbers fade away and instead reminded herself that he was just a man, an evil and twisted man, but still a man. Feeling like she was at least partially in control of herself again, she nodded slightly to him as sat down and filled her plate with an assortment of meats and vegetables. Her Haissan reached over and took a large leg of mutton and stepped away, eating quietly, apparently unaffected by the Masteen.

Agnes was very hungry, and she ate heartily until she finally pushed the mostly empty plate from her. She had eaten more than she had planned, but she never passed up a meal. Sitting back, satisfied, she dabbed at her mouth with a black cloth and looked again at the Masteen, who she noticed had barely touched the rest of the food on his plate. He was sitting back in his chair studying her with mild curiosity, his dead eyes looking slightly bored.

Raising a metal goblet of ale, he took a sip and carefully set it down. He spoke and Agnes again felt the power in his voice, but she was able to suppress the feelings it invoked. Mostly, that is.

"So, how is the Oblate doing in this current political climate?"

Agnes almost spit out the sip of ale that she had just taken. She recovered quickly, but the Masteen's eyes lit up in amusement. "Oh, come now, you Robes in the Oblate don't honestly think you could keep your secret from me, now, do you?" He put down the goblet of ale and coughed lightly into a piece of cloth. "Excuse me. Now, why don't you tell me what you require from me."

Knowing this man was formidable in both strength and intellect, Agnes decided that the best thing she could do would to be honest. She set down her goblet and folded her hands on the table, although her thumbs moved in circles on each opposing hand in nervousness. "I come with a request from..." she hesitated, but knew it was foolish to worry about secrets with this man, so she continued, "The Black Robe."

The large and ugly man smiled and nodded. "Go on, I'm listening."

"We require the use of one of your death squads. We will pay you a large sum."

The Masteen laughed, a deep, booming sound that reverberated off the walls of the room. "So the Black Robe wants to capture the Aleph Null and he doesn't have the... special resources to do it on his own." He put his hands together, elbows on the table, and pressed his fingers against his chin, staring directly into Agnes' eyes.

She stared back, unflinching, waiting for his answer. The fact that he knew about the Aleph Null surprised her, but she understood that he probably had spies everywhere. Right now, though, she couldn't show any weakness. This man respected only strength.

The silence stretched for a few moments longer and then the Masteen leaned forward slightly. "No answer, then. Interesting." He leaned even closer, his eyes hard and cold. "There is something you are not telling me, something you haven't even told the Black Robe. Tell me what it is and I just may agree to help."

He gazed into her eyes unrelentingly, and she stared back, although her heart raced. She couldn't tell him the truth, but she knew that she had to tell him something. So she took a deep breath and whispered a half-truth. "I was sent here to request your help in providing one of your famous death squads." She hesitated, then continued. "But as you most astutely could tell, I also want something else." She looked away briefly, then down at the floor and whispered, "I want the Black Robe position, and. . I hope the current Black Robe will die when he faces the Aleph Null. If that happens, I will remember this meeting and your support." She didn't voice the fact that she hoped the Masteen's death squad could kill the Black Robe before he killed them.

The Masteen leaned back and laughed out loud again, the sound frightening. "Now, that kind of thinking I can understand." He paused for a few moments, then nodded toward the darkness of the back corner of the room. The man with the gaping hole where is nose should have been stepped forward. Agnes started, not aware that he had been there the whole time. The Masteen nodded toward Agnes. "So Norloc, what do you think of our little guest's proposal?"

The man wiped the black cloth against the hole in his face and looked at Agnes before answering, "I think she hides something still, but this could be a chance to do what we talked about earlier. I say yes, we should provide the death squad." He paused, then said, "But I think we should both accompany them." He looked directly at the Masteen as he said this last part, and a silent discussion happened between them that Agnes found intriguing.

The Masteen finally nodded. "Make it so. Prepare a death squad."

Norloc bowed and quickly left.

Agnes felt like she had lost control of the situation, and then she sighed. Like she ever had a chance to control this situation.

Sliding his chair back, the Masteen stood up, and as he did, the door to the room opened immediately and an old man appeared. "Teel will see you to a room. I suggest you get some sleep, for we will leave tomorrow morning at dawn."

Agnes turned to the old man and realized that she had been dismissed like a servant. Her face flushed slightly but she stood her ground. She secretly exulted in knowing the Masteen would accompany her, as he might be the only person who could present a problem for the Black Robe, perhaps even destroy him. But she couldn't let the Masteen know, so she spoke sternly, "Now, wait a moment, I didn't agree to have you and... your aide accompany me. That is not part of the plan."

Looking down at her, the Masteen smiled and it chilled her to the bone. "Stop trying to play me, woman. We both know you think I may serve your own purposes in getting rid of this Black Robe." His voice lowered and she could barely hear the words through the rumble, "I have been... gentle with you so far because of your beauty. But make no mistake, I would be just as happy impaling your body on one of the stakes outside and watching your guts slide down the wood." He arched a bushy eyebrow. "Do I make myself clear?"

Swallowing, Agnes nodded. She knew he was not making an empty threat.

"Good, now leave me."

She turned and it took all of her inner strength not to hurry her steps. She stepped through the door, her Haissan by her side, and when she heard the old man close it behind her, she let her shoulders slump and she breathed deeply. She had never been so scared in her life, not even when she was with the Black Robe. This man was animalistic, violent, and powerful, and struck fear into her that she could not push away.

The old man was already walking down the hall, so Agnes hurried her pace and stayed behind him until he opened a door to a chamber and motioned for her to enter. Her Haissan stepped in first, as usual, and checked it quickly before coming back out and motioning her in. She stepped across the threshold and her Haissan closed the door behind her. The room was bare except for a straw bed, a wash pan, and a chamber pot. Feeling more drained and tired than she had ever been, she walked to the pan and splashed her face with cold water, then crawled on top of the straw. But even though she was tired, she found herself staring at the rough stone ceiling for a long time, wondering again what she had gotten herself into.

When sleep finally came, she tossed and turned as nightmares of impaled men ravaged her mind.

She slept through the day and following night, and woke grudgingly when the Haissan touched her shoulder. She could tell it was just before dawn and was surprised she had slept straight through a full day and night. She felt somewhat more refreshed and rested, despite her anxiety. She saw a tray of dark bread, cold meats, and cheeses next to her bed, so she sat up and ate until she was full. Then she got out of bed, splashed her face in the pan of water, and relieved her bladder and bowels in the chamber pot, not even caring that the Haissan was in the room with her.

Soon after she finished getting ready, the door opened and Norloc motioned to her. "Come, it is time to leave."

She quickly left the room and followed the man through the halls and down the stairs to the main floor, then out into the cold, dark morning. Fog rolled across the courtyard and through the gate, and she could see the slight lightening of the sky to the east and knew the sun would rise very soon. She followed Norloc through the gate and across the courtyard, and as she came to the post of the man she had helped cross over to death, she looked up. At first she just saw him as a shadowed figure on the post, but then his head moved. She started briefly, a small gasp escaping her lips, but then she realized it was just a crow perched on his head. The large bird flapped its wings angrily, then settled back and continued pecking at the man's face.

Norloc chuckled and she turned away, slightly embarrassed. They soon passed through the 'Arch of the Dead' and she saw a group of men on horses waiting for her.

Her horse was brought forward and she slid easily into the saddle. After spending so many days on the horse, she had gotten a lot of practice. Her Haissan also mounted its horse beside her.

From out of the darkness a massive figure appeared and approached her on the largest horse she had ever seen. She shivered as the Masteen glared down at her through a blackened helmet shaped out of a nightmare creature's skull.

His voice rumbled from within the helmet, even deeper than their previous meeting, if that was even possible, "Tell me where we are going."

Swallowing slightly, Agnes nodded. "We need to force the Aleph Null toward the Srithian Wood."

"And how do you propose we do that when we don't know where he is located?"

For the first time she half-smiled "Leave that to me." She closed her eyes and formed the communication equation that the Black Robe

had taught her, then removed the Alpha symbol. The equation
wavered, then started to break apart. Agnes struggled to hold it
together but failed. Just as she was about to let it go, it suddenly
solidified.

"*Tris?*"

She jumped slightly when he spoke directly in her head, his voice
clear and loud, sounding irritated even through the connection, "*You
sound like you didn't expect the equation to work.*"

Agnes wasn't sure what had happened. One moment she couldn't
keep the equation solid, and then the next moment, it stabilized. She
voiced her question to him, and he replied condescendingly, "*Maybe it is
because you are weak and need my superior ability.*"

She ground her teeth together, but didn't answer his taunt.

"*Are you finally ready?*"

Agnes nodded, forgetting that she was speaking to him in her
mind. "*Yes, we have a death squad at our disposal.*" She didn't tell him that
the Masteen accompanied her. She wanted to keep that information
from him for as long as possible. "*Do you know in which direction we need to
move?*"

Tris' voice dripped sarcasm, "*Of course I do. Head south until you get to
the Branstal Wood, then head east. The Aleph Null and his friends,*" this last
came out in a sneer, "*are now staying off of the road and moving north, but will
soon try to turn toward Undaluag. I have... other resources converging on them from
the west to keep them from turning. You and the Masteen should meet up with the
Aleph Null on the Grang Trail. Send scouts ahead so they know you are there, but
do not engage. Once you know where he is exactly, make sure they continue traveling
north.*"

Agnes nodded, even though the voice was in her head. "*We are
leaving now and should be there in a few days.*"

"*Very good. And whatever you do, make sure you do not confront the Aleph
Null just yet. Just make sure he keeps going north toward the Srithian Wood. And
Agnes... do not screw this up.*"

She spoke sarcastically, before she could stop herself, "*Oh, I
wouldn't dream of it.*"

There was a pause and Agnes thought maybe he had closed the
communication. But then she heard him speak softly in her head, his
voice low and promising pain, "*We will have some words when next we meet.*"

The obvious threat in the tone made her swallow slightly, then she
removed the Alpha symbol from the equation and let it fade away. She
turned to the Masteen and pointed. "We need to move south to the
Branstal Wood, then head east to the Grang Trail until we find the
Aleph Null and his small group of followers. We then need to ensure
they are forced to head north, toward the Srithian Wood."

The Masteen stared into her eyes for a long time, then spoke to
the same man who had accosted her at the gate. "You heard the

woman. Move out, standard formation."

The man gave a brief glare of hatred toward her, then turned his horse away and barked a single order. The group of fifty men all began moving as one, three abreast, down the road, silent and orderly. The only sounds made were the clinking of armor chest plates against steel scabbards, and the soft clip clop of the horses hooves on the damp ground.

The Masteen spurred his horse to the front, leaving Agnes and her Haissan to find a spot in which to ride amidst the group.

She looked around her at the Masteen's death squad, men whose appearance alone would cause even the most hardened of men to loose their courage in battle. She thought back to her childhood, of her parents telling her that she could be anything she wanted.

She shook her head and smiled humorlessly to herself. Never in her wildest dreams had she ever thought that she would be in the middle of a Karillon death squad on a mission to force the Aleph Null into a trap set by the Black Robe of the Oblate.

Chapter 15

Tris finished the communication with Agnes and angled his horse to the right of the narrow, muddy road, avoiding a large puddle of brown water. His two Murder of Haissen surrounded him protectively as they traveled, all twenty-six of them riding in silence and fully dedicated to his safety.

They had passed through the Funglewood Pass and were descending to the harbor, no more than a few leagues from Grundenheilm, a dark and filthy city, and the only one with a harbor for hundreds of leagues, which was therefore the starting point for all traders of foreign goods. It was a lawless city ruled by the Taigro, a violent and merciless organization that controlled all commerce that came into the port. If a ship wanted to trade its goods, it had to pay the Taigro, who specialized in everything illicit and illegal, including selling intelligence and weapons to factions within most of the royal houses across the land. It also controlled all opium distribution to the pleasure houses, and even restricted the food and wool supply that came from the large and wealthy trading ships.

The royal houses had tried to break the Taigro, but Grundenheilm was a port surrounded by mountains with the Funglewood Pass being the only road that led through the mountains, so no army could make it through without being destroyed in the bottleneck. So the Taigro had grown powerful and rich over the past thousand years.

'Just my kind of city,' Tris thought.

Vapor streamed from his mouth as he exhaled in the cold morning air. The city spread out before him, a stepped layering of ramshackle buildings built almost on top of each other down the descending grade to the sea. Most had trails of dirty smoke curling up from simple rusty pipes in the roofs. The road they descended snaked back and forth down the hill with switch-backs that were so sharp, there was little room for error while navigating them. While the road was fairly wide, enough to let travelers going up and down the mountain pass each other, a spooked horse could still easily send one over the edge.

The horse that Tris sat upon was a huge animal, one bred from the best lines, and it made its way steadily and calmly down the muddy path. The Haissen, as always, seemed unfazed by the possible danger.

Tris thought about his Red Robe. She believed she was hiding her true motives, and he wanted her to think she was succeeding, but what she didn't know was he could see through her eyes when she actuated the equation, not just hear her thoughts. He knew that even if she did suspect, she didn't have the skill to de-construct, much less understand, all of the variables of the equation that he had planted in her mind. It was a sight and sound equation, the variables for each spectrum of communication tied together in such a convoluted way that it looked like a single equation.

Things were going exactly according to plan. The Masteen and his death squad would maneuver Sid and his pathetic group toward the Srithian Wood, and the Masteen would dull his control of numbers, weakening him considerably. The mercenaries that he had hired out of Yisk would continually harass them and keep them from going to Undaluag. They would be forced to continue north, and when they reached the Srithian Wood, Sid would be trapped between the Masteen and his death squad, the mercenaries, and himself and his two Murder of Haissen.

One thing did concern him, and that was the dark and unknown forces within the obelisk. Despite the vast amount of research he had performed, he could only find bits and pieces of information about the obelisk. He didn't know who had constructed it, or even whether it still held any power. But from the information he had found about it, the obelisk was the original source of the power of Black Numbers. While Tris didn't require the obelisk to trap Sid in his mathematical array, he wanted to be close to the structure just in case he could tap into its power to help rip Sid's power of Black Numbers from his mind. It was his insurance that events would transpire according to plan.

Tris would offer the Masteen double the amount of coin to have his death squad attack Sid and his group when they got to the obelisk, and while Sid was expending his energies against the death squad, Tris would trap his old friend in the powerful mathematical array he had constructed and seize the power of Black Numbers.

Then Tris would execute the Masteen and his death squad, as well as whomever else remained. There would be no witnesses, except for his trusted Haissen..

Tris chuckled dryly and spurred his horse to a faster trot, anxious to get to his destination. The final weapon he would use against the Aleph Null was held prisoner deep within the city, the last piece of the trap that would ensure Sid would not use his power of numbers to his fullest potential.

He focused on the final stretch of the mountain pass. The closer they got to the bottom of the hill, the worse the road became, until the horses were kicking up black mud with each step they took. Finally they rounded a switch-back in the road and the gates to the city rose before them, made of ancient timbers from giant Miq trees, each one as wide as six horses. Tris looked up and even he was impressed with the height of the gate, stretching upward at least ten times the height of a man.

They came to a halt before the closed gate. A guard house, large enough to house at least twenty men, stood to the side. Five large and menacing guards stepped out to block their way, each casually holding well-worn pikes with wickedly curved blades at the ends. Tris and his two Murder of Haissen sat on their horses, not offering to get down.

One of the guards stepped forward. "What be your business here?"

Tris looked down at the man, then pointed at the gate. "That is none of *your* business. Let us through."

The guard took another step forward, his face turning red with anger. "That is not how things work, and if you want, we can show you how we like to do things around here." He lifted his pike and held it forward, pointed directly at Tris. "So, one last time, what be your business?" His fellow guards tightened their grips on their own pikes, eager for violence.

Sighing, Tris controlled his temper. Now was not the time to get into a pissing contest; it would waste too much time, which was short in supply as it was. So he nodded to the man. "My apologies, kind sir. It has been a long ride and we are tired, which is no excuse for my rudeness to you and your fine men."

The guard eyed him for a few moments, then relaxed, setting the end of his pike back on the ground, holding it casually with one hand. "Aye, fair enough, I know what long marches can be like. But, I still need to know your purpose for coming here"

"My men and I are here to settle a debt and acquire a piece of property, that is all. We would like to first find a tavern for the evening and have some food, drink, and women. Not necessarily in that order."

The guard grinned and nodded his head. "Now, that I can understand." He turned and lifted his head in a short nod to someone in the gatehouse, though to whom, Tris couldn't see.

The gate slowly opened toward them, groaning as it swung on giant metal hinges. Tris could see four gears of graduating size just inside and to the right of the gate, each at a different angle and driving the larger one next to it. Two large men turned a crank, neither wearing shirts, the prominent muscles in their arms bulging as they leaned into each turn.

Tris nodded down to the guard. "Thank you, kind sir. May you have a woman warm your bed tonight."

The guard spit to the ground and wiped black tobacco juice from his lips. "Aye, that be my plan."

Slapping the reins against his horse, Tris led the way through the gate, his Haissen surrounding him protectively.

Just inside the gate was a large open yard with a street stretching ahead of them, wide and lined with shops of all kinds. To their immediate left and right were guard houses that probably held a thousand soldiers, weapons, and machines of war. Tris and his Haissen were ignored as they trotted through the yard and entered the muddy street.

The air stunk like human waste, burned meat, and urine. Hundreds of people walked up and down the street, most wearing rough-spun woolen clothing. Tris led his group briskly forward, causing people to hastily step aside, some cursing and spitting. One woman didn't get out of the way in time and was bumped by one of the Haissan's horse, causing her to fall to the muddy street. She got up angrily and threw a clump of mud at the Haissan, cursing at it.

The Haissan stopped its horse and backed it up until it was beside the woman. She looked up at him defiantly, shaking her fist. The Haissan tilted its head down at her, its hood covering its face completely. Then, in a move so fast that the woman didn't even see it, the Haissan pulled its sword and sliced the woman's still muddy hand off. It fell to the ground with a splat, and the woman didn't even react, unaware of what had happened until the pain hit her a few moments later. She held up her arm and started to scream as she watched the blood squirt out of the stump. The Haissan returned its sword to its scabbard just as quickly and started its horse moving forward, already forgetting the woman.

Tris glanced back and smiled. He loved his Haissen. No better masters of the blade existed in the land, and they never questioned his orders. They were merciless and efficient, and he wished he had more of them.

They came to a cross street and Tris turned left. After quite a long way he turned right, then left, then right again, turning corner after corner, each street getting narrower and darker as they rode. Most of the buildings were three stories tall and leaned toward the road, blocking out most of the light.

The air was thick with smoke because it had nowhere to go, and pedestrians became more scarce as they rode. At one point they passed a small shop just as the proprietor stepped to the door. He was covered in blood, with pieces of fat and meat sticking to his sleeves. He threw a large bucket of blood onto the street. Dozens of dogs and cats immediately began lapping up the fresh blood. Tris looked down and then back the way they had come and saw that the entire street was red from flowing blood, layer upon layer of it probably dating back hundreds of years. The man barely glanced at the riders going past him as he re-entered his shop, kicking at a little bloody-whiskered cat and just missing it as it leapt backward, before he slammed the door shut behind him.

The sunlight was mostly gone when they turned a final corner and Tris raised his hand to stop. Before them was an open courtyard leading to a nondescript building that rose up three stories and surrounded the space on all three sides. It had no windows and just a single door. Tris heard a clang behind him and he turned to see that a gate had been closed by a man wearing a brown robe, blocking them in the small courtyard. Tris slid from his horse, as did five of his Haissen, and he simply waited. The courtyard was bathed in shadows, and the open sky above them was dark with black clouds. It looked like a storm was approaching.

After a few moments, the single door opened inward, though no one appeared. Tris shrugged his shoulders and walked toward the door, five of his Haissen following behind him. The rest waited on their horses, silent and still. He stepped through the doorway and entered a long, narrow hallway lit with torches spaced ten paces apart, making shadows dance along the walls and ceiling.

He saw no one, and as he started forward, he built a simple wall of numbers in front of him as a shield. He didn't trust anyone except his Haissen. He soon came to a corner and turned it. Directly in front of him was an open door. He stepped through into a small room. The floor was made of rough, unpolished wood, the walls the same. Other than that, the room was bare save for a single door directly opposite and a dark figure in a black robe, not unlike the one Tris wore when at the Oblate, standing next to it.

Tris moved forward until he was three paces from the figure and he dropped his number shield without thinking. His five Haissen fanned out around him. He raised his hands, palm outward toward the figure. "In the name of the Oblate, I am here to see Xavitandar to claim ownership of the prisoner."

The figure stepped forward and removed his hood. His skin was black and he was disfigured beyond recognition. His nose and skin had been burned off at one point and the new skin was stretched and scarred. The man's lips no longer existed, so his teeth were permanently visible. He nodded once. "I am Xavitandar. We have completed our task and relinquish ownership of the woman. Final payment is to be made now."

Tris motioned to a Haissan behind him and it stepped forward, set a small chest onto the floor, then backed away.

The man didn't even look down at the chest. He produced a large key from within his robe, fit it into the lock on the door, and turned it. A loud clunk echoed through the room as the latch disengaged. The man stepped aside.

Tris turned the door handle and stepped into a small room perhaps ten paces squared. The room had a bed, a chair, and a nice rug on the floor. He ignored it all, focusing instead on a woman who stood in the exact center of the room facing him. Her hair was long and black, though streaked with gray at the temples. Her eyes were beautiful but tinged with sadness. Her lips were thin and unsmiling. She stood, her back straight, and held her hands clasped in front of her. She wore a simple white blouse and a blue skirt with riding boots.

Tris just stared at her for a long moment. It had been ten years since he had last seen her.

She looked at him, head cocked slightly. "Who are you?"

Tris raised an eyebrow. "You don't recognize me?"

She studied his face for a few moments, then whispered, "Tristian, is that you?"

He smiled. "In the flesh. I'm here to take you away from this place."

Confusion washed over her face. "But... why you?"

"You honestly don't know, do you?"

"All I remember is waking up here, so many years ago. I remember you were friends with Sidoro. Oh Tristian, have you seen Sidoro? Is he all right?"

Tris smiled what he knew was his most calming smile. "Of course he is. I am here to take you to him."

Relief washed over her face briefly, but then her eyes hardened and she balled her fists tightly. "You are lying. I can see it on your face."

Tris grinned. "Bravo... cousin. Yes, of course I'm lying, you twit. Now, I could leave you here to rot, or you can come with me now, and I promise that if you behave and do as I tell you, that you will see Sid soon."

Her eyes burned with pain, hatred, and fear, then she slumped her shoulders and let out her breath. "I will do whatever you say if I can even get one chance to see Sidoro."

Tris smiled broadly. "Wonderful. Well, with that, how about we leave this place?" He stepped aside and waved his arm toward to the open door.

Lorielle paused for a few moments, as if she didn't quite believe that she were leaving, but then she squared her shoulders and strode across the room. She stopped next to him and without warning, slapped him hard across the face.

He didn't flinch or try to block the blow. She glared at him for a moment, then exited the room without turning back. She stopped by the disfigured monk and caressed his disfigured face, whispering something to him before kissing his cheek and continuing down the hall.

Tris rubbed his cheek and grinned. She still had fire inside of her, which is what he needed from her. She would play perhaps the most important role in what was to come.

He walked out of the room and followed her and his Haissen out of the building. It was fully dark outside and the air was cool. Two of his Haissen held torches, which provided some light, but also caused flickering shadows to fill the small courtyard. Bats swooped erratically overhead, attracted by the light. Tris motioned to a horse and Lorielle mounted it smoothly and sat with her back straight, her hair fluttering in the slight breeze. He saw her take large gulps of air into her lungs as she looked around. It was her first time outside in ten years, and he imagined she was still in some shock at the events that had so quickly transpired.

He swung onto his horse and started toward the gate. As he approached, a shadowy figure opened it and they all rode through, the clopping of the horse's hooves on the cobblestones loud in the darkness of night.

Chapter 16

Crowdal gave Writhgarth a little shove, causing the diminutive man to stumble.

"What the hell! Why did you do that?"

"Oh, sorry Writhgarth, I slipped."

The little man punched Crowdal in the stomach, having to reach up to do it. "You're lucky I reached high, I didn't have to."

Crowdal feigned horror and immediately put his hands across his crotch. "Point well-taken, my friend."

Writhgarth chuckled. "We've been walking all morning, I'm hungry."

"For such a small man, you are always hungry."

"You're right, so let's stop then and have something to eat."

Crowdal realized he needed nourishment also, so he held up his hand for them all to stop. "Let's rest here and have some food and water. Apparently Mr. Writhgarth can't go another step or he will pass out from hunger."

Mrs. Wessmank chuckled and looked at Writhgarth. "Any time you are hungry, young man, please speak up, my old bones will be happy for the rest breaks." She swatted at a large hornet that zoomed in to check her out, making it angry. It buzzed at her again and slammed into her neck. She let out a yelp and slapped at it, killing it. But the damage was done and a red welt grew where she had been stung.

Melinda stepped forward. "Let me look at that." She tilted Mrs. Wessmank's head gently to the side and examined the area.

"I've been stung hundreds of times in my life from working in the garden, I'll be all right."

"Well, just the same, let me get the stinger out and put a poultice on it to get the swelling down. Crowdal, let me have your knife please." He handed it to her without question and she started lightly scraping the skin in one direction, then held the blade up. "Got it. Nasty little bugger. It was still moving, trying to work its way deeper into your neck." She wiped the stinger onto the ground, handed the knife back to Crowdal, then looked around. She exclaimed happily and stepped over toward an old, fallen tree. She reached under it and returned shortly with some wet moss and mud. She applied the mud to the large welt, then put moss on top of it. She took Mrs. Wessmank's hand and placed it on top of the moss. "Hold this in place until it dries out."

The old woman sighed. "It already feels better. Thank you, Melinda."

Crowdal watched Melinda work and marveled at how calm she

was when tending to people. Nothing bothered her. Luckily, they hadn't had any major wounds since Sid had almost lost his ear in the attack earlier. He turned to Sid. "By the way Sid, how is your ear?"

His friend reached up absently and touched the bandage. "I think it is healing well. It only throbs occasionally now."

Melinda stepped over to him. "Let me take a look at it." She unwound the bandage until the last layer was visible. She slowly pulled it away. The bandage was red from the bleeding, but she nodded. "It looks good, no infection. In fact, I don't think you even need a new bandage. The air will do it good, help it to heal." She put a finger in his face. "But keep it clean."

Sid nodded. "I will, thank you." He reached up to touch it and she slapped his hand back down.

"And don't touch it!"

Looking sheepish, he kept his hand down.

Crowdal bent down to look at it and was amazed at how well it had healed in such a short time. A nice scab had grown over the large cut. He slapped Sid lightly in the shoulder. "I think that cut makes you look distinguished and dangerous at the same time. A man of the world, so to speak."

"Gee, thanks, Crowdal."

"Hey, no problem. Who knows, maybe you'll find yourself a half-eared woman some day and have half-eared babies."

Sid rolled his eyes and walked away, muttering under his breath.

Crowdal was glad to see him in a lighter mood. Sid had always been the quiet sort, really only speaking when spoken to. He had too many pressures weighing him down.

A branch cracked and everyone turned to their left, peering into the trees. Crowdal noticed Writhgarth had his sword out of his scabbard as quickly as he did. Leaves crunched and he saw movement through the trees. His senses sharpened as they usually did when danger presented itself. He stepped forward and yelled out, "Show yourselves."

The crunching of the leaves ceased for a few moments, the silence in the forest oddly eerie. Then the leaves began crunching again and Crowdal saw two half-hidden figures make their way toward them.

He spoke quietly, "Everyone, get behind me."

Writhgarth stepped along side of him, his sword held steadily in his hands. "You aren't going to have all the fun by yourself."

Crowdal grinned. "Welcome to the party." The grin fell from his face, though, when he got his first glimpse of who was approaching. He spoke quietly but urgently, "Writhgarth, do as I say. Get behind me."

The little man looked up quizzically at first, but the tone in Crowdal's voice made him step back.

From the forest, two huge figures approached, weaving around the many trees until they were fifteen paces away, where they stopped.

Crowdal heard Writhgarth curse under his breath and he didn't blame his friend, for he faced two Trith for the first time since he had left his home.

One of them was about the same height as Crowdal, but the other one was at least another hand-span taller yet. They were older and thicker, their arm muscles corded and bulging. One of them had a thick beard that hung down to its chest. The other had a beard, but only on the right side of its face. The left side of his face was bare of hair but covered with puckered white scars. They both wore bear skins over their shoulders, making them look even larger than they were.

Crowdal gestured with his sword, his voice controlled but cold, "Boren, Athgar, so nice to see you."

The two Trith stood silently, surprise clearly evident on their faces. Then the one with the half-beard stepped forward. "What are you doing here with," he looked at everyone standing behind Crowdal, "humans?"

Shifting his sword to his left hand, Crowdal stepped forward until he was two paces from the Trith. "I don't want any trouble with you, Athgar."

The Trith hardened his eyes. "Have you already grown so weak that you beg to avoid a fight?"

Crowdal shrugged and raised his sword to point at the Trith's face. "Perhaps you would still have a full beard if you had not challenged me over that mug of ale."

Athgar growled, "We can finish that fight now, pup."

They glared at each other, the tension so thick that no one even dared to cough.

Then Crowdal stepped forward.

Athgar growled and did the same and they each slugged the other across the face.

Crowdal looked up, rubbing his chin. "You've still got quite a punch. It is good to see you, Athgar!"

The Trith nodded, rubbing his own chin. "Aye, and you too."

The other Trith merely glared at Crowdal, disgust evident on his face. Crowdal nodded to him. "Boren."

The Trith didn't even acknowledge him, instead turning away.

Crowdal turned back to Athgar, putting his sword back in his scabbard. "So, what are you doing so far from the Trith Nation?"

The Trith put his own sword away. "Just got bored I guess. Needed a good fight or two with someone other than a Trith."

Crowdal raised an eyebrow. "Any takers?"

Athgar spit. "No, not a one. I swear this world has grown too soft." He looked behind Crowdal. "So, what have you gotten yourself mixed up in now?"

Turning to glance over his shoulder, Crowdal shrugged. "Just having a little fun is all."

Athgar studied him, waiting for more information, but when it was apparent that Crowdal would say no more, he spit to his side and motioned toward Boren. "You could join with us, we are heading toward Undaluag, maybe we will find some action there."

Crowdal shook his head. "Sorry, I have business elsewhere."

"Suit yourself." The Trith started walking away but stopped. "Don't stay away from the Trith Nation for too long, you will grow soft." Then he continued on without looking back. As Boren stepped past Crowdal he leaned closer and whispered, "Coward!"

Crowdal glared at him, then laughed.

Boren's face turned red and he stalked away.

The two Trith made their way through the forest and were soon out of sight.

Crowdal slumped his shoulders and turned to the group. "Now that was... not fun. I need some food."

Chapter 17

Agnes rode at a steady pace in the middle of the Masteen's death squad all day and night. They only stopped briefly to rest the horses a few times until they came to the Grang Trail, which they had now been following all morning. They made their way down the trail until the sun was high in the sky and the Masteen suddenly raised his hand for them to stop.

He growled in his low voice, the rumble so deep that it was hard to make out the words, "Make camp in that clearing over there. And dig a pit."

His men didn't hesitate and immediately got off of their horses, their armor clanking and jingling as they stepped heavily to the ground. He turned in his saddle to his captain. "Send out the scouts, I want to know exactly where this group is located."

The captain motioned his hand and three men, wearing soft leather clothing colored with patches of brown and black to blend into the woods, dismounted and silently faded into the trees, leaving their horses with the group.

Agnes took the opportunity to eat and lay down. She was exhausted and knew she had to rest when she could. Even though she had gotten used to riding a horse for long hours, she was still an intellectual who had spent her whole life studying mathematics, so her muscles were not fully hardened for long days of physical exertion. The scouts returned all too quickly and reported they had spotted a small group that matched the description of their targets in the woods not far off the trail. They also reported seeing two groups of mercenaries shadowing the group to the west and south.

The Masteen listened to the report, then walked over to Agnes. He roughly nudged her with a dirty black boot and smiled cruelly down at her. "Get up, woman."

Agnes quickly got to her feet, swaying slightly from fatigue, but was fully alert in the huge man's presence.

Grunting in disgust at her weakness, the Masteen rumbled, "The group you spoke of is not far away, but there are also mercenaries shadowing them. Explain."

She squared her shoulders, not wanting to look weak in front of the Masteen. "They are there to keep the Aleph Null from going to Undaluag."

The ugly man grunted, not liking it. "Then why did you need my death squad if you have... mercenaries?" His voice dripped contempt when he said this last word.

Agnes spoke quickly, "They are merely there as blocks. Your

death squad will be the ones to finish this, for only you have the strength to handle the Aleph Null."

The Masteen eyed her coldly, not believing a word she said. He leaned toward her, his voice a deep growl, "I will make you and your little Black Robe suffer if you are lying to me."

Agnes leaned back slightly, but held his eyes with her own. "When we get the Aleph Null to the Srithian Wood, you and your men will be paid enough to support your kingdom for the rest of your life. The Oblate has resources beyond anything you can imagine."

"That had better be the case." He grinned suddenly, which sent chills down her body. "And what will you pay if I kill the Black Robe, for that's what you're hoping I will do, isn't it?"

Standing tall, Agnes remained silent for a few moments, then nodded and spoke quietly, "If you do that, I will give you anything you want in return."

He laughed then, outright. "I'll hold you to that." He turned from her and strode back to his men who all stood tall and ready, and spoke to Norloc quietly.

Agnes watched the Masteen and his aide for a moment longer and finally sat back down. She put her head against the tree, closed her eyes, and began to tremble.

She was playing a dangerous game and knew she wasn't the only one playing it.

Chapter 18

Lorielle breathed the fresh mountain air deep into her lungs and when she released the breath, her eyes filled with tears at the beauty that surrounded her. They had just passed over the peak of the mountain and were descending toward Undaluag. Her cousin rode slightly ahead of her.

Wild flowers, white and yellow and blue, filled a meadow to her left, and butterflies and bumblebees fluttered and buzzed between flowers. She turned to her right and gazed again in wonder at the small bubbling stream that followed the path down the mountain, its crisp and clear water flowing over granite rocks, reflecting the sunlight in bursts of constantly-changing colors. Brown speckled trout swam lazily against the current, staying in one spot with a casual and constant back and forth movement of their tails as the water flowed over them.

It had been ten years since she had been outside, seen the sun, felt fresh air on her face. She had been held prisoner by the Faussian monks, her mathematical powers as well as her mind trapped in a complex and unreal world designed and maintained by the Black Hypnotic Arts that the monks had mastered over the past millennia.

She knew her mathematical powers had once been a part of her life, but no matter how hard she tried, the block the monks had implanted deep within her psyche was not something that she could remove, much less find. They had simply made it so that when she thought of mathematics, it was just a bunch of numbers and letters to her, making no organized sense. She had been turned into nothing more than a simpleton as far as her knowledge of math was concerned. It frustrated her so much because she could faintly remember that she had been brilliant at mathematics, but it felt as if she were remembering someone else's life.

She glanced covertly at her young second cousin as he rode just ahead of her. He was slightly older than Sidoro and she remembered when he had shown up in town with his 'family'. No one in the village had known they weren't his real family, but she had known. Her mother Elenora, Mrs. Wessmank to the townsfolk, had raised her with full knowledge of the Aleph Null prophecy and her aunt's treachery.

She had almost been the Aleph Null herself. She was the most powerful mathematician to ever be born. She could do things with her numbers that had never even been thought possible, but despite her exceptional intelligence, she didn't have the special ability to create Black Numbers. But she had also not felt pain at the sight of the Korpor.

She was the first person to ever manifest that strange ability, and no one, neither in the Anderom, nor the Oblate knew what it meant. It did, however, cause the Oblate to be fearful of her, and they orchestrated her marriage to an Oblate agent in the hopes that they would create a child that could be the Aleph Null.

She had married Danicu, also a brilliant mathematician, though nowhere near her level, and they had conceived their son, Sidoro. She was so happy, and even when Sidoro had been inside of her, she had known that he could be the Aleph Null.

She had spent six glorious years raising Sidoro, and she had loved him more than life itself.

Then she had been betrayed by Danicu.

One evening he had slipped her a drug to knock her unconscious, and she had woken up in a windowless room surrounded by chanting monks who wore robes so black that they absorbed all light, making them appear as voids in the room. She had immediately reached for her power of numbers, but at that exact moment, the monks had all clapped as one, the sound like thunder in the room, and her vision swam. When her sight cleared, she had no clue what mathematics was. She faintly remembered that it had been a part of her life, but it quickly faded from her grasp, and the harder she reached for the memory, the further it sank from her consciousness.

They had locked her in a bare room then, with no bed, no furniture, and no light. She remembered how she had screamed in the blackest depths of that room, of how she had run in panic and slammed into a wall so hard she had knocked herself unconscious.

When she had woken up, she hadn't even been sure she was awake. She couldn't hear anything, see anything, and it was only the texture of the rough wood beneath her that told her she was alive. She had carefully crawled around the room, only to realize it was empty of everything but a chamber pot. She crawled into a corner, pulled her knees to her chest, and hugged them tightly, rocking herself and whimpering.

Time passed. She was brought food, although how it appeared she had never been certain. Her chamber pot was cleaned out daily, and again she had no recollection of it happening.

She soon came to suspect they were masters of hypnotism, that they could make her forget anything that happened to her.

Time passed.

Slowly.

She had learned to listen for the faintest of sounds. A distant scuffle of a footstep on the other side of her door. The dripping of water far away. The creak of the building as it settled.

Then one day she had heard something make a scratching sound in the corner of the room. She had held her breath because it was so loud to her. The scratching stopped and soft padded footfalls approached her hesitantly. When she sensed the creature was close to her, she had stuck out her hand, palm up on the floor. She heard a soft footstep, and after what seemed a long time, she felt something tickle her hand. She forced herself to remain motionless. Then a cool wetness touched her index finger, pushing into her skin softly and she heard a sniffing sound. Then two small paws touched her finger, cool to the touch, followed by two more paws. She held her breath as the small creature crawled up her hand, then her arm and came to a stop on her shoulder. She turned her face toward the creature and felt the soft tickle of whiskers, then two paws gently touched her cheek. She pursed her lips and the creature pushed its wet nose against her mouth and squeaked softly. Tears fell down her cheeks, and she moaned as she put her hand up and the mouse crawled onto it. She felt a surge of joy and love overwhelm her and she cried for a long time as she caressed the little creature.

The mouse became her closest friend, spending all day and night with her. She fed it small morsels of her food and gave it small sips of her water. It was so soft and she could feel its quick heartbeat with her fingers as she held it. Its whiskers tickled her face when she kissed its nose good night, and she had talked to it for hours, calling it simply, 'Mouse'.

Years passed, at least she thought it had been years, when one day she had woken up and Mouse wasn't next to her. She had called out its name and listened, expecting to hear an answering squeak, but only silence greeted her. In a panic she had moved carefully about the room, her hands in front of her, and when she got to the other side of the room, she smelled something sickly sweet. She had carefully felt around until she brushed against a small furry body. She had carefully picked Mouse up and started to caress the little creature in relief when she felt a sticky wetness. In horror, she had realized that Mouse's head was gone.

She had wailed and put Mouse against her cheek, hot tears falling down her face, sobs wracking her body until she could cry no more.

Time no longer mattered to her then, she just sat in the corner, not thinking, not caring about anything.

Until, one day, the door opened and light poured into the room. She immediately closed her eyes in blinding pain and backed up to the farthest corner of the room. She felt hands pick her up and carry her out of the room. She had been bathed, and after a full day, she had finally been able to handle the light. She was put into a comfortable room with a soft bed and warm covers.

A man wearing a robe came into the room and tried to speak with her, but she would have nothing to do with him.

More days went by, and each day the same man came into the room to speak with her, asking her simple questions like whether she was comfortable, or if she wanted reading material.

Finally, after a few fortnights, she gave up and answered one of his questions.

Every day after that, the man came to her and they talked. After a while, she was told that she had only been in the dark room for a few days. They had implanted every single memory, every single experience she had felt, the sense of years passing. She didn't believe it at first, but she looked into a mirror and saw that she didn't look any different, that her hair was exactly the same as she had remembered it.

She had looked at the man then and simply asked, "Was Mouse real?"

He had stared at her for some time before finally nodding. "Yes, Mouse was real."

A small cry had escaped her lips then. "Why? Why did you kill it?"

The man sat back and removed his hood, showing her his face for the first time. She cried out at his visage and shrank back from him, for his face had been burned almost completely off. He had no eyelids, and the skin of his forehead and cheeks was stretched and scarred white and red. But it was his mouth that had caused her to shrink back from him, for it had no lips or skin to cover it. His teeth and jaw were fully visible, glistening in saliva.

He whispered, "Because, I wish you to fully know your situation."

The shock of his face lessened, and Lorielle, realizing she was being rude, sat up straight and said in a trembling voice, "Which is?"

"That you are here as my guest, but you are fully in my control. Everything that happens to you is because I wish it to happen. To know that is to make our stay together more pleasant. There is no escape for you, there is only this life now. For both of us." The monk smiled, although his lipless mouth couldn't complete the gesture, so his gaping mouth just opened slightly wider, his teeth gleaming in the light. He had then reached inside his robe, and after taking something out, held his closed hand out to her.

She had looked in confusion at him until he opened his fingers and Mouse sat in his palm, its whiskers and nose twitching toward her. She had cried then as she reached out for her friend, afraid it would simply be another illusion. But as she had held out her hand, Mouse had crawled quickly onto her palm. She had brought the tiny animal up to her face and kissed its nose, tears falling down her cheeks. She finally looked up at the man and said in a small voice, "Thank you."

He nodded and waited quietly until, after a few long moments, she had asked him his name.

"Samuel. It is... Samuel."

Lorielle had smiled then. "It is nice to meet you, Samuel."

Ten years had passed. Her life had been comfortable, if boring. She had never left the building, and she had never met any of the other monks. She grew to love Samuel as a brother, and his disfigured face had become a comfort to her every morning as he appeared in her doorway.

She had tried to escape only once during the first month. She had waited for Samuel to open her door and had hit him over the head with her chamber pot, the urine and feces splashing all over both of them as he fell to the ground. But as she ran through the door and into the hall, she had blacked out. She had awakened in her room again, still covered in her own excrement. Samuel was gone and her door was locked. She had spent five days in her room, filthy and hungry, until Samuel opened the door.

He didn't look at her as he told her to follow him.

She had slowly gotten to her feet, weak from hunger, and followed him to a room where they had bathed her.

Samuel didn't visit her for several weeks. She sat alone in her room until Samuel had walked in one morning as if nothing had happened. She smiled hesitantly at him and he reached out a hand to help her to her feet. As she stood up, he leaned in close to whisper into her ear, "Never try that again. If you do, you will sit here, alone, for the rest of your life."

She nodded, tears flowing down her cheeks. He pulled his head away and she saw that he had been crying too. Her heart melted and she leaned her head against his chest.

He would become her whole world, her only friend for that ten years. She had missed Sidoro greatly, and had only hoped he was being allowed to grow up as a happy child and free from danger. The fact that her husband had betrayed her weighed heavily upon her, but she had taken solace in the fact that her mother was there to watch over him. She also knew that since Sidoro could be the Aleph Null, he would not be harmed by the Oblate.

As the years passed, she often lay in bed at night and dreamed of what Sidoro would look like as he grew. But no matter how much she tried to visualize him, she always saw him as the same little boy she had seen as she had put him to bed that final night before she had been drugged and taken away from her home.

Then, only the previous day, Samuel had knocked at her door and opened it. She looked up as she worked on a cross-stitching, surprised because they had just had breakfast together. He looked sad, and she could tell he was close to tears. She put down the fabric and needle and slowly stood up.

He took a step back, set down a bundle of clothing, and quietly said, "Prepare yourself, you are leaving here." He then turned and walked out the door without another word.

Puzzled, she just stood there for a few moments, then crossed to the pile of clothing and saw they were travel clothes. Her heart beat quicker as she bent down to touch them. They were real. Could she really be leaving? Did she want to leave? She was comfortable here and she loved Samuel. She had hesitated for a few moments, then an image of Sidoro appeared in her mind. He was a young man with tousled brown hair covering his face. It was the first time she had been able to visualize what he might look like now at age sixteen.

She took it as a sign and had quickly pulled off her dress and put on the travel clothing. She looked around the room that had been her home for the previous ten years and realized she had nothing to even take with her. So she had just stood in the center of the room, facing the door.

She had heard footsteps approach, the first time she had heard multiple footsteps since she had been there. Her heartbeat quickened as the door opened. A young man stood there and she thought it was Sidoro at first, but when he stepped into the room she saw it was a stranger. Then, to her surprise, she had realized it was Tristian, the childhood friend of Sidoro, and he had offered to free her. She had accepted the offer with the promise to see Sidoro again. As she entered the hallway, she stopped by the man with the burned face and reached up to caress his cheek, then leaned forward and kissed him lightly on the cheek and whispered softly, "Goodbye, Samuel."

Samuel looked lovingly at her for a few moments, then turned away.

Lorielle let her hand drop to her side, then she strode down the hall and never looked back.

She trembled now at the possibility that she might see her son again. He would be ready for the Proofing soon and she ached to be there to protect him, but she knew, deep inside her heart, that she was too late. Events were in motion that far exceeded her ability to control. She didn't expect to live through whatever would happen in the coming days, but she hoped that whatever her cousin Tristian had in store for her, she would get one last chance to speak with Sidoro, to tell him that she was sorry for leaving him. But deep down, she was worried he wouldn't remember her, that he had been turned against her by her husband and the Oblate.

Lorielle closed her eyes and took a deep breath. She couldn't let herself think these thoughts. She had to believe that there was a chance. After the past ten years, even just a chance that she would be with Sidoro again was more than she could have hoped for, and she would take that hope and never let go of it.

She listened to the sound of the horse's hooves as they made their way down the mountain trail, and she breathed in the sweet mountain air again, marveling at the multitude of fragrances mixed together.

To not be around Samuel was a strange feeling. She missed him. He had been a gentle man, even though he was her captor. But she also could never trust him or her experiences there. He could make her feel anything with the soft lull of his voice and a snap of his finger. In fact, there were times over the past day and a half where she had pinched herself to see if she were really here. Of course, even in doing that, she couldn't be sure she was really free. She would never forget her experience in the dark room. Samuel's mastery of hypnotism and illusion were total. But now, she chose to accept that she was indeed free. She wanted to believe it. She had to believe it.

Tristian turned his head slightly. "Do you have any questions for me? You must be dying to know how Sid is doing."

Lorielle didn't answer, knowing she couldn't trust anything he said. Her cousin chuckled and turned away, enjoying himself. She rode with him now because she would do anything to see Sidoro again.

Tristian knew this and had made it very clear that she had no choice in riding with him. He had narrowed his eyes slightly that first day and she felt raw pain burn in her veins.

He had smiled and said, "That is just a taste of my power. You will ride with me and cause no trouble. And if you do as I say, you will see your son again, I promise you that."

That promise, however empty it may have sounded or been, was enough for her.

The trail came to a sharp curve with the mountain and stream to her right. Tristian put his hand up and started to slow his horse. Lorielle did the same. They were alone. He had sent his Haissen ahead to the Oblate. She remembered the way that he had turned to her and smiled before saying, "Now we can have some time alone to get to know one another again after so long." She had shuddered at the look in his eyes.

She sat up straighter in her saddle as three men rose up from the tall grass and stepped onto the road in front of them. They were tall men with pale skin, wearing weathered and worn leather over ragged clothing. They held weapons, though they were varied and in bad shape, the steel rusting and nicked from rough usage. A tall man stepped forward and raised a long sword for them to stop.

Tris pulled his reins and Lorielle did the same, coming to a stop five paces from the men.

The man spoke, his voice strong and mean, "Throw down your coin and jewels and you might live through this."

Tristian raised his hands, his frightened face making him look very young. His voice squeaked, "Please don't hurt us."

Lorielle looked at her cousin strangely, wondering what he was up to in acting so scared, for he held a power of numbers that was at least equal to what she had held, before it had been taken from her. He could have killed these men with a single thought.

The man stepped forward, grinning nastily. "I said you might live,

I didn't say I wouldn't hurt you."

Tris backed up his horse, looking around wildly, but the man lunged forward and grabbed the bridle, yanking the horse to a stop. He yelled to his men. "Take them from their saddles."

The other two rough-looking men stepped forward. The tallest man grabbed Lorielle, pulled her from the horse, and dropped her to the ground at his feet. She started to protest but he slapped her hard across the top of the head. "Speak again and I will hit you so hard your face won't be so pretty anymore."

The other man yanked Tristian from his horse and her cousin cowered as he lay on the ground. "Please, don't hit me. Do whatever you want to the woman, but please don't hurt me."

The man grinned down. "We have a little prissy boy here don't we? Well I like prissy boys, so I think you and I will have a lot of fun together." He leered at Tristian as he rubbed his crotch, a huge bulge growing as he touched himself.

The leader stepped forward. "You can have your fun with the boy after we search their packs." When the man didn't stop rubbing his crotch, the leader smacked him across the back of his head. "I said search these packs now!"

The man whipped his head around to glare at his leader, his eyes smoldering with hatred. But he did as he was told, grumbling the whole time under his breath. The other man looked through Lorielle's pack.

Lorielle couldn't believe what was happening. She started to reach for her numbers but stopped when she remembered they were not there for her. She often found herself trying to manipulate them before realizing she had no idea what mathematics were anymore. Reaching for her numbers was just a habit she remembered doing. She pushed her hair away from her eyes and looked around, searching for an opportunity to run away. She glanced over to Tristian, hoping he would do something with his numbers, but she only saw terror in his eyes. Maybe he wasn't as powerful as he had tried to make her believe.

The leader of the thieves looked down at her and his eyes softened slightly. Lorielle felt some small amount of hope flare within her. She pleaded to the man with her eyes and she saw he was attracted to her.

The two men finished going through the packs on the horses and the shorter of the two held out a small sack of coins that he had found in Tristian's pack. He tossed it to the leader who caught it with a loud jingle. He pulled the string apart and emptied the contents into his hand, his eyes widening when a dozen gold coins filled his palm, overflowing to the ground.

He looked up at his men and motioned at the two on the ground. "Do whatever you want to the boy and then kill him. Same with the woman." He turned away and spoke over his shoulder, "And make it quick, we have some coin to spend."

The two men grinned at each other. They had just found more coin than they had in years, and now they had just gotten permission to rape and kill the two rich people. The day couldn't get any better for them.

Lorielle stood up and faced the filthy and evil-looking man who approached her. She lashed out and scratched the man across his face. Blood welled instantly from the scratches and he struck her hard across her chin. She cried out from the pain and almost fell to the ground.

The man reached a finger to the cuts and licked the blood from his fingers. "For that, bitch, you will suffer." He ripped her blouse from her in one savage motion and angrily twisted her bare breast with his dirty hand. She cried out again as he pulled her head back by her hair with his other hand. His breath smelled like rotten meat as he violently kissed her, forcing his tongue into her mouth.

Lorielle gagged on the stench in her mouth. Then anger pushed the fear away and she opened her eyes. She felt the tongue twisting inside her mouth and she bit down with all her strength. Warm blood filled her mouth as she ground her teeth through the man's tongue.

He screamed and tried to pull away from her but she locked her hands around his head and pulled him harder against her mouth. She finally severed the man's tongue then bit down on his lower lip and twisted her head to the left and right until she heard flesh ripping and more hot blood spurted into her mouth. The man pushed her so hard that she flew backward and fell to the ground.

The man tried to roar but it came out in a liquid gurgle. The horses whinnied and side-stepped away in agitation.

Lorielle spit his lip and tongue in a bloody glob to the ground at her side.

The man looked wildly down at the dirt, then screamed a gurgled sound and lunged at Lorielle, intent only on killing her. But before he could strike her, he stopped, then stood upright. His eyes bulged out impossibly until they burst from the sockets in a shower of viscous liquid and blood. He gurgled once more, then fell backward. He landed hard, his head bouncing sickeningly on the ground.

The other two men stood gaping at what had just happened, then the leader ran forward and knelt by the body, the look on his face radiating disbelief. The man's mouth was torn from his face, and his eyes had exploded outward with such force that the bone around the sockets had even shattered. The leader stood up shakily and stepped back as the man on the ground took one final gasp of air, shuddered, and died.

Lorielle got to her feet and noticed Tristian standing casually not far away. But when she looked into his eyes, she saw they were wild and filled with violent ecstasy.

The leader pulled his sword out and turned to Lorielle. The other man, face white, pulled his own sword and approached Tristian. But before they could take two steps, they yelped and tried to drop their swords as the metal started to glow, but they couldn't open their fingers. Soon they began to scream as the metal of the swords turned bright red and their hands started to sizzle on the hafts. Flames soon burst around their hands and Lorielle watched in sickened wonder as the fire raced up the men's arms.

The leader looked around wildly and saw the stream. He ran toward the water, his entire arm in flames. He made it to the edge of the stream, his toes actually in the water, when he came to a sudden stop. He struggled, but he couldn't move. The flames caught on the rest of his clothing. He stopped screaming and fell to the ground. His head fell into the water while his body burned. He tried to lift his head but couldn't. He struggled, his body thrashing in the water, until he finally lay still.

Lorielle watched in horror as the leader both drowned and burned to death. She didn't even notice the other man fall to the ground in flames. She closed her eyes and tried not to breathe in the smoke, but she couldn't help it. She gagged and threw up the contents of her stomach. When she was able to open her eyes again, she saw Tristian casually picking up his gold coins and putting the sack back into his saddle pack.

He turned his head back to her. "Now that was fun wasn't it?" He breathed in the acrid, burnt odor and chuckled. "Now, if you are done being sick, we really should get going again. It will be dark soon and I don't want to sleep outdoors like an animal. We are not far from Undaluag."

Lorielle looked around and saw that the fires were completely out and the bodies were nothing but charred remains. Except the leader's head, which was under water and unburned. She looked again at Tris and realized fully what kind of a monster he truly was. While the men deserved to die, and she had inflicted much damage upon the one man, she felt sickened by the casual violence Tristian had inflicted with his numbers. He was the embodiment of evil and she knew now that she would do anything she could to ensure he didn't harm anyone else. Especially her Sidoro.

Shaking and filthy, Lorielle got to her feet and stumbled over to her horse. Her meager belongings were scattered on the ground, including a spare blouse. She reached down, picked it up, and shook the dirt from it before putting it on. She gathered up the other items and put them back into her pack. Tris was already on his horse, waiting for her. She slipped her foot into the stirrup and slid into the saddle.

They began to trot down the remaining part of the mountain and were at Undaluag before dark. Tristian led them to a beautiful travel lodge on the edge of the city. "We will stay here tonight, have a little bath and some relaxation, then tomorrow we will travel through the city to the Oblate."

Lorielle gasped. She had never expected to learn the location of the secret Oblate headquarters. Then a chill swept through her. If she was being shown the Oblate, that meant she would not live through what was to come.

Tristian saw the understanding on her face and smirked at her. "Don't worry, cousin, you may yet live through this and see your son again. That is, if you continue doing as I say." He had a livery boy take their horses to a stable around back. He pressed his hands down his shirt, smoothing it out, before he opened the door to the travel lodge, holding it for Lorielle. She walked past him with her head held high. He got them a room and paid the clerk a gold piece, which was more money than the entire lodge would make in a fortnight.

With wide eyes, the clerk snapped his fingers and two young boys rushed forward and picked up their travel packs and led them to their room. It was large, with two copper tubs in the corner, separated by a tall screen. Two young girls, no more than fifteen years old, were pouring the last steaming bucket of water into the tubs. They were about to leave when Tris stopped them. "You will stay here and wash me." They curtsied and helped him remove his clothing. Word had already spread around the tavern staff of the rich man who freely spent his coin.

Lorielle looked away as she stepped behind the screen and removed her clothes. There was a bucket of hot water and she scrubbed the majority of the blood from her face and hair before stepping into the steaming hot tub of water. She sighed contentedly and settled into the water until just her face was above it. She could faintly hear a few giggles from the other side of the screen, even with her ears under water. Then the giggles turned to soft splashing and low moans of pleasure. Lorielle tuned it out and was almost asleep in the water when a loud shriek of pain startled her awake. She sat up in the tub, the water now cool, and heard soft sobs and whimpering sounds from the bed.

She stood up and grabbed a large towel to dry herself, the air cold on her wet body. She stepped from the tub and peeked around the screen and gasped. What Tris was doing to the two young girls on the bed made her immediately turn away with disgust. She put on a clean set of clothing and without looking at the bed, walked silently to the door.

"You will not go far now, will you, cousin?" Tris' voice was low and throaty, yet sent a chill down her spine.

Lorielle paused at the door then opened it and slipped out. She closed the door with a small click and made her way to the great room downstairs. She took a table by the fire and ordered some food and ale.

She put her head into her hands and sat that way until the food and ale arrived at her table. She knew she had to stay with her cousin because he told her they were going to meet up with Sidoro very soon. There was nothing she could do to him. She only hoped that when the time came, she would be able to sacrifice herself to give Sidoro even the smallest chance to kill Tristian. She would die willingly for that opportunity.

She ate the food, even though she had no appetite.

She had to stay strong. For her son.

Chapter 19

As Crowdal and Sid disappeared into the trees to gather some firewood, Melinda cracked the bones of her back as she turned from checking on Mrs. Wessmank. She had overheard them speaking and she tiredly walked over to her bedroll and lay down on her back. It bothered her that she had pushed her friends away, but she had to. She had to deal with this alone. They wouldn't understand. She put her right arm back behind her head and closed her eyes, so tired that she wanted nothing more than to sleep. But she resisted, for when she slept she heard the whispers of her father, accusing her, beckoning to her.

So she stayed awake. She had felt the pull of the Raith world since she had killed her father, and the urge to enter it was difficult to resist. She had entered it, slowed down time, purely by reflex in her confrontation with her father, but since then she now knew that time itself was a constant flowing of force moving by like a river. It was physical to her, she could see and feel it. As a Zranh, she was able to reach out with her mind and slow its forward movement, what her grandmother called entering the Raith world, similar to putting a log across a small stream to hold back the water.

When her father had slowed time down in their confrontation, he could only slow it down a little bit, a fraction of what she could slow it to, and instinctively, she had known that she could stop it entirely if she had chosen. Although for some reason, she had been scared to try this, unsure of what would have happened. How she was able to do any of this was beyond her understanding, but the experience beckoned to her. The power that flowed through her veins was almost a need, intoxicating now that it had been awakened within her.

As they had traveled over the past two days, she had experimented with the time shift and had been amazed when the group around her had slowed down to the point of almost looking like they were standing still, while she could move around them at a normal pace. Each time she had brought time back to its normal flow, she had returned to her exact starting point so they wouldn't suspect anything. After two days of experimenting, she could slow time at will and she found herself having to fight the temptation to stay in the Raith world permanently. When she was in the time shift, she felt the power fill her, warm her, the silence of that world providing a comfort. And each time she had only reluctantly let the time shift return to normal.

Recently, she had slowed time and left the camp because she had gotten the feeling they were being followed. She had moved through the forest in silence for some distance and had come to the edge of a long valley. Far below she saw a large group of men traveling on horseback, now frozen in place. Even from a distance, she got the feeling they were not there by accident, exuding a sense of evil.

She had returned to camp and was surprised that each member of the group was in a slightly different location or position. She realized she had been away long enough that a handful of moments of time had passed.

She saw a look of concern on Crowdal's face, as if he was just starting to register that she was missing, and she realized she had been by his side when she had entered the Raith world and left the camp on her reconnaissance, a mistake on her part because she had been gone longer than she had planned.

She wasn't sure how to join them without their knowing she had been gone. The only thing she could think of was to go a few paces into the woods, let the time shift return to normal, and re-enter the camp as if she were returning from relieving her bowels.

She did just that, and as she let the Raith world go, the sounds of the forest assaulted her. She pushed her way through the brush into the camp and Crowdal spun around toward her.

"Where were you, Melinda?"

She tried to look innocent. "I just had to relieve myself. Is that all right with you?"

Crowdal studied her for a moment, then a look of embarrassment came over his face. "Sorry, you were gone and no one saw you leave. I was just about to go and look for you." His face turned red. "I'm, ah... glad that I didn't."

Melinda slapped him playfully on the arm as she walked past and sat down against a tree. She was glad he didn't suspect anything. She had to be more careful the next time she entered the Raith world.

She leaned her head back against the tree bark and closed her eyes tiredly. The return to the normal world had weakened her this time more than ever, and she felt so tired that she wanted nothing more than to sleep. As she leaned against the tree, she opened her eyes and stared at the darkening sky above her, drifting in her thoughts. She hadn't forgotten her grandmother's warning to beware the Raith world, she just felt that she was strong enough to control its effects on her body and mind, so she didn't realize how dark the skin around her eyes had become, or how pale the rest of her skin had turned.

But Mrs. Wessmank did notice and she frowned as she studied the young healer from her bedroll not far away.

Chapter 20

After the semi-darkness of the night settled on the woods, a raccoon nosed through the brush looking for a meal when it stopped and sniffed the air, its whiskers twitching as it raised up on its hind legs. In front of it, a white creature with huge blue eyes stepped from behind a tree and the raccoon immediately scurried away.

In the near darkness, the Korpor lifted its head toward the west and sniffed the air, then knelt down and moved slowly until it got to the tree Sid had sat against earlier in the day. It lowered its head to the ground and licked the dirt once before straightening up to a fully upright position. It savored the taste of the boy and would soon have him to itself again. But first, it had to give a report.

"They are moving north, like you wanted. The boy is growing more powerful."

The voice of the Black Robe filled the Korpor's head, dripping sarcasm, *"That is of no concern to you. Follow them and make sure no harm comes to Sid. That is your only goal, do you understand?"*

The Korpor tilted its head slightly, then slowly blinked its left eye, followed by its right eye. *"Of course, Master."*

It ended the contact, then bent down and licked the bark of the tree where Sid had leaned against it, relishing the taste. Smiling savagely, the Korpor loped into the darkness of the forest, following the trail as if it glowed in the darkness.

Chapter 21

Athgar and Boren stepped into a small clearing and decided it would be a good place to set up their camp for the night. The sun had set and dusk was quickly encroaching upon them. They didn't require much, just a space in which to build a fire and lie down. They didn't care about getting rained on or any other discomforts. As Trith, they were hardened from years of battle.

Earlier in the day, they had come across a shallow gully with a stream running at the bottom and had surprised a large buck as it drank from the pristine water. Without hesitating, Boren had leapt from the top of the embankment onto the deer before it could bound away, grabbing the long antlers as he landed. He had twisted hard, the snap of the buck's neck loud in the gully. With practiced ease, he had drawn his knife from its sheath and quickly sliced open the belly of the deer and pulled out the guts. He had then thrown the deer over his shoulder, the animal's head dangling down his back, and had carried it for the remainder of the day as easily as a small child.

He dropped it to the ground with a thud. "I'll cut us some steaks, you make a fire."

Athgar nodded and left to gather some dead branches from near their camp, along with a few chunks of larger wood. He carried a large armful back and dropped it to the ground, making Boren jump as he cut and peeled the skin from the buck.

Boren looked up angrily at Athgar. "Did you have to do that?"

Athgar rolled his eyes. "You're a little jumpy tonight."

Boren muttered as he continued skinning the animal.

Athgar saw a Birch tree close by and stepped over it. The white bark was peeling away in thin strips. He pulled a few long strips from the tree and returned to the middle of the camp. Birch bark was the most flammable material one could find in the forest. One spark could easily ignite it, so it was perfect for starting a fire. He stuffed it under some small sticks and then struck his flint near the dried bark. On the second strike, a spark caught in the bark and it smoldered for a few moments before the delicate bark burst into flame. The fire soon caught on the sticks and started to burn hotly. He kept adding twigs, working his way up to larger pine branches, then chunks of wood.

Soon he had a nice fire going, the wood sparking and spitting sap as the flames boiled the sticky fluid inside of the wood. He stared into the glowing embers of the fire, which were flickering from orange to white and back to orange as if they breathed. He never got tired of staring into a fire at night.

Boren laid the deer hide across a bush, causing the branches to bend down from the weight. He then cut two large steaks from the hind quarters of the buck and spit them on sharpened, three-pointed sticks that he carried in his pack. He handed one to Athgar, then sat down and put his steak over the flames.

They didn't speak as they cooked the meat.

Trith rarely spoke.

Soon the meat was sizzling and turning brown as they occasionally turned their sticks, the smell making their stomachs grumble in hunger. Darkness filled the forest until the fire in the little clearing cast a small circle of light. The whisper of the trees as they swayed in the breeze was comforting, and the temperature of the air was perfect for them. When the meat was darkened enough, they each took their steaks from the fire and blew on them briefly before ravenously tearing into the meat. Bloody juice ran down into their beards as they ate, and they occasionally wiped at their mouths with dirty hands.

It took them a while before they noticed the ground shaking softly at regular intervals, and as they turned their heads to the darkness surrounding them, they both heard the distant crash of a tree falling to the ground. They immediately dropped the meat to the ground and stood, pulling their long and well-used swords smoothly from their scabbards, the ring of steel causing their blood to pump quicker.

Another crash sounded and they knew whatever it was, it was approaching them quickly. They had never before heard or felt such a disturbance in the forest. Athgar glanced at Boren. "What do you think that be?"

His partner shrugged his shoulders. "I have no idea. Whatever it is, it's big."

The ground thudded harder and a tree crashed to the ground not far from them. They edged apart so they could each have room to fight, setting their feet wider apart. They peered into the darkness, trying to see what was out there.

The ground shook again, then again. Athgar felt his skin break into a slight sweaty sheen, and for a brief moment he felt fear, something he had not felt since he had been a small boy.

Another loud thud sounded and a tree crashed forward into their small camp, making them jump to the side to avoid it.

Athgar saw a shadowy presence fill the night in front of him. He tilted his head back and looked up slowly as a creature at least three times his height leaned forward into the light.

It screamed, its mouth filled with long teeth opening wide as it raised its face to the night sky.

He had never seen a creature like this and part of him exalted at the upcoming battle, for he faced a creature that he very well might not defeat. Adrenaline surged through him and he grinned at Boren.

They had found the fight they had been searching for.

He roared loudly and leapt forward, swinging his long sword at the creature with all of his might, a blow that would have cut a small tree in half, but the creature swiped its long arm and knocked him sideways before he could connect. He flew into the darkness of the forest and slammed into a tree.

He rose to his hands and knees, feeling blood run down his face from the impact. He knew his nose was shattered, but he didn't care. He turned and looked back into the clearing and saw Boren engage the creature.

Boren let loose a blood-curdling yell as he leapt forward and swung his blade at the creature. He connected with its leg, chopping into it like a tree trunk. Pus and blood drenched his face and dripped into his mouth, the taste making him retch as he tried to pull his blade free. He looked up and saw the creature's fist coming down at him, so he let go of his sword and dove to his right.

The ground shook as the fist hit where he had been standing.

He rolled back to his feet and ran around the back of the creature, which bent at its waist and twisted its body to follow him, its head swinging back and down. It screamed and swatted back at Boren.

The Trith punched the creature's hand mid-air with all of his considerable strength, the impact loud in the night. If he had punched a human as hard, he would have killed him instantly, but as he connected with the creature's hand, every bone in his own fist shattered, some pushing up through his skin in white shards covered in blood. He was thrown back by the creature's momentum, landing hard on the ground.

The creature screamed and swung around to face him fully.

Boren stood up, his arm hanging limply at his side, and charged back toward the creature, roaring as he ran. The creature smashed down with its fist and crushed the Trith to the ground, his body exploding outward in all directions. The creature screamed again and turned its head, searching the forest.

In the darkness twenty paces away, Athgar staggered to his feet and stared into the light of the camp. He saw bits of blood, guts, and bone lying everywhere, all that remained of his partner, his friend, and his secret lover.

He scooped up his sword and ran toward the creature, his blade held high, and leapt, flying through the air with a scream. He connected with the beast and rammed his blade into its stomach. It sunk in to the hilt, a blow that would have killed a grizzly bear. But the creature just lowered its head and screamed directly at him, the exhalation of air blowing his hair back and the sound so loud that he felt his ear drums burst. He hung from his sword, his feet dangling just above the ground.

The creature spun around and Athgar lost his hold and fell to the ground. He looked up and saw that his sword was still buried in the flesh of the beast, so he jumped to his feet and wrapped his mighty arms around the creature's leg and heaved backward with all his might, hoping to make it fall on the blade and drive it completely through its body. But despite his great strength, he couldn't throw the colossal beast off balance.

He let go and rolled between the creature's legs, coming up behind the beast. He pulled his dagger, the blade almost as long as a normal human's sword, and spun around, slashing at the corded muscle of the creature's leg, hoping to cut the tendons and make it fall to the ground. But the flesh only parted slightly, the skin of the beast so tough that it seemed nothing more than a deep scratch.

Athgar rolled to his left as a giant fist crashed to the ground next to him. His heart pumped strongly and he grinned without knowing it, enjoying the fight more than any he had ever experienced. He had fought dozens of human warriors and even a few of the Masteen Vorn Maghuur's feared guards, but he had never once been fully challenged in battle. He laughed out loud as he jumped up to sink his dagger into the stomach of the creature, hoping to pull it down enough to spill its guts to the ground.

But as he jumped, the creature reached down and grabbed him in mid-air with one massive hand. Boren felt his body being crushed and knew this was the end. He repeatedly stabbed down at the creature's hand with his dagger, roaring in both anger and joy, reveling in the knowledge that he was going to die in a great battle beyond anything a Trith had ever experienced. His name would be remembered forever.

Athgar thrust down violently one more time before the creature reached with its other hand and ripped his head from his body as easily as a flower from a stem, silencing the Trith's voice forever.

The Unnamed One raised Athgar's bloody head, dangling sinew and torn flesh, to its mouth and ate it like a coconut, crunching through the skull easily and slurping out the brains. It then angrily ripped the clothing from the headless body and devoured the Trith in a bloody orgy of flesh.

Finished, the creature reached down, pulled the little blade from its stomach, and dropped it to the ground.

No trace existed of Athgar the Trith, other than his sword lying discarded on the ground and a few torn shreds of clothing.

No one would ever know of his final epic battle, one he had searched for his entire life and finally found.

The Unnamed One scraped up whatever flesh remained of Boren from the ground and ate that also, then scooped up the buck and devoured it, too.

It was enough to fill its stomach and it screamed at the sky again.

Finally it settled to the ground and rested its head against a tree, exhausted. It had been traveling without stopping since it had escaped its prison, and it had just had its first real battle in millennia. And not even back when it had faced entire armies of the thickly-armored men of the north had it faced warriors such as these.

Chapter 22

The decaying tree had fallen hundreds of years earlier from old age, landing with a crash in the darkness of night. Now, leaning against its moss-covered rotting wood sat five hardened men, each wearing mismatched pieces of leather and steel armor blackened with age and heavy use. Except for one man, each of them had hair that hung to their shoulders, greasy and filled with lice that jumped back and forth from strand to strand. The fifth man was completely bald.

One of the men took out a leather wine skin and drank sparingly, then put his head back and looked at the clouds that raced by in the night, illuminated by a mostly full moon that occasionally appeared between them. He turned his head to the right and looked at Ulff, the largest of the five. "Do you think we are getting paid enough for this job?"

Snorting softly, the large man tilted his head to look at him and then grunted before leaning his head back against the tree trunk and closing his eyes; he was a man of few words.

Nik, the man to the far left, laughed. He was smaller than all of them but also possessed the quickest wit. "I second that! Well said, Ulff. And why do you keep asking that question, Richard? We are never paid enough for any job we take, so why don't you just shut up about it for once?"

Richard angrily stood up and glared down at Nik. "If I kill you now I will get even more of the payment."

Nik shook his head. "Richard, you couldn't kill a pig in a pen."

Richard flipped his knife and it landed between Nik's legs, the handle vibrating for a few moments after impact.

Nik looked down at it with wide eyes, then yanked it from the ground and stood up. "Now that's just not right. You never mess with a man's balls like that."

He approached Richard with the knife held before him. "Just for that I'm going to..." but before he could advance, the bald man to the far right said quietly, "Sit down, Nik. You too, Richard. I'm tired of your games." His voice was smoothly modulated, but it was the calm promise of death carried in the undertones that made both Nik and Richard quickly sit down, glaring at each other.

Nik tossed the knife to the ground next to Richard and glared at him. "When this job is done, I'm going to make you even uglier than you are now."

"Anytime, just name the place."

Nik snorted loudly. "Right, you'll never show up, you'll be too busy banging some filthy whore to face a real man in a fight."

"At least I like women and not goats."

The little man rolled his eyes. "Screw you."

"No thanks."

Nik balled his fists. "Oh, now you're going to get it."

The bald man stood up and glanced down at them with resignation, and the two men instantly shut up, although Nik muttered angrily under his breath. The bald man reached down and grabbed his neck in a powerful hand and squeezed. Nik's eyes bulged and he croaked as spittle came from his mouth.

The bald man dragged him to his feet and spoke quietly and without anger, almost like a father speaking to an errant child, "Now, I said that will be enough."

Nik dangled in the air, his toes barely touching the ground, and his face turned purple, mottled with white splotches.

The bald man glared into his bulging eyes. "I take it I've made myself clear, Nik?"

Nik managed to nod his head.

"Good, now let's have some quiet for the rest of the night." He lowered the little man down to the ground and casually said, "I'll watch over our quarry for the remainder of the night," and then turned and disappeared into the trees as if nothing had happened.

Nik lay on his side, dry heaving and trying to take air into his lungs. Richard, knowing that the bald man could have easily killed Nik, reached over and helped him to a sitting position, then handed him a wine skin. "Here, take a small sip, it will help."

Nik took a few more gulps of air, then took a small sip of wine before handing the skin back to him. Despite their constant bickering, he and Richard were best friends, whereas their captain was a man who was as mysterious as anyone they had known. Nik nodded and whispered his thanks.

Richard half-smiled. "Don't mention it." He leaned toward Nik and whispered with a wink of his eye, "And I'll still meet you anytime, anywhere."

Nik grinned and felt the tension go away. He nodded and whispered back, "And you're still ugly."

The fifth mercenary sitting next to Richard spoke quietly, "You better watch yourselves. Tulman is dangerous."

Leaning his head sideways, Nik whispered, "You think so, Harri? Gee, you're smart."

Harri merely closed his eyes and put his head back against the tree trunk.

They all settled in for the remainder of the night, trying to get some sleep.

Tulman returned later in the night, pushing a bush out of his way as he entered the small camp. He looked down at the four men as they opened their eyes. "They are on the move, trying to lose us, so let's get going." He pointed at Richard and Nik. "The group has turned to the west, so you two take point and make sure that we move parallel them. Do not engage them until we get in front of them. We want them to turn back north, not start a fight." He looked directly at Nik. "So don't go off half-cocked again and start shooting arrows at them like you did a few nights ago. We don't want to reduce our numbers any more."

Nik swallowed, remembering that night when he had gotten bored and fired a few arrows into the camp to scare the skinny kid. He hadn't expected them to fight back so viciously. And then that idiot Raiyme had gone and tackled the kid and was killed, along with two others. It had been a bad night and he still felt the pain in his thigh from where the small man had nicked him with a sword. He was lucky it had only been a scratch. The little man had been ferocious and Nik had barely escaped into the night, unprepared for such a difficult fight. He wouldn't make that mistake twice, so he nodded with downcast eyes. "That won't happen again, sir."

"Good. Now get ready. The rest of us will be following a ways behind, just like before, to make sure they don't try getting behind us." Tulman looked at each of them before nodding slightly and turning away.

The four men began putting on their packs and checking their weapons. Richard and Nik checked their bows carefully. They were the only two who were adept at the bow, which made the bond between them that much stronger.

In the silence that only comes late in the night, Nik and Richard chewed on dried deer meat as they moved quietly into the forest, followed a short while later by the remaining three mercenaries.

Chapter 23

T he fire had burned down to red and orange coals that flickered and smoldered. The tree branches above swished back and forth in the darkness, and the air had turned cold again during the night. Crowdal sat hunched against a tree ten paces from the camp, keeping watch. He had neither seen nor heard much all night, although he had once heard a faint clank of steel against steel and he was fairly certain that a large group of men were camped not far to the west.

He looked back through the trees to their camp and saw that the light from the fire was almost gone, so he worked his way back to the small clearing and bent low over Writhgarth, who instantly opened his eyes. Crowdal whispered quietly. "It is time."

Writhgarth immediately got out of his bed roll. The rest of the group heard him and also sat up and began getting ready. Sid rubbed his eyes, trying to get the cruddy buildup out of them. They had packed up everything except for their bedrolls before dark and none of them had really slept well. Within moments, they were ready and with a motion from Crowdal, they silently left the camp and entered the trees heading northwest.

They moved as slowly and quietly as possible until the sky started to lighten in the east. Crowdal put up his hand and motioned to his left. They all turned to the west and made their way carefully through the brush and trees, silently picking their way until the sun rose directly behind them, a deep red color in the wet, misty air. The red hue made the trees seem sickly, and their unease mounted as they continued, ducking under low branches and skirting around thick brush. The breeze had died out and the still air became damp and sticky. None of the chill from the previous night remained and soon sweat started dripping down their faces, their clothing sticking to their skin.

Crowdal held up his hand and they all stopped. He studied the trees in every direction, listening carefully. It was so quiet he could hear the breathing of each member of the group. He stayed still and continued to cast his senses out. Something felt wrong, but he couldn't tell what it was. Finally he took a step forward, thinking the blood-red sun had spooked him for no reason, when from the trees about thirty paces in front of them stepped the five dangerous-looking mercenaries. Two of the men had bows pulled back with long, black arrows aimed directly at him.

Crowdal immediately ordered his friends to get directly behind him. He didn't want them to be easy targets. He was angry and tired of being forced down a path not of his choosing. No matter how hard he tried to temper his anger, he was a Trith, and Trith were never forced to do anything that they didn't want to do. He pulled out his sword and started walking forward, his face set in stone, eyes flashing angrily. "I suggest you gentlemen leave us be and move along. I've had about enough of you."

The two bowmen looked sidelong at the large bald man, who nodded slightly to them and they immediately released their powerful bow strings simultaneously. The two arrows streaked forward, but Crowdal casually slapped both arrows out of the air with his sword. The look on the two men's faces showed amazement and fear.

Crowdal smiled darkly. "I don't happen to like bows, they are cowardly weapons. Is that the best you can do?" He was no more than twenty paces from the five mercenaries.

The two bowmen looked at their leader again, but he shook his head no so they didn't reload with new arrows. The bald man strode forward, taking his sword out at the same time, and Crowdal stepped forward until they were five paces apart. They stopped and eyed each other curiously. Although the bald man was large, he only came up to Crowdal's shoulders.

They stood like this for a few moments until Crowdal broke the silence. "I know you have been paid to keep us from going where we want, but I grow tired of this game and we are traveling west whether you like it or not. If you want to earn your money, you can try and stop us, but I wouldn't recommend that action."

Crowdal watched the leader glance up at him and twitch briefly as he recognized that Crowdal was a Trith. But the man recovered, showing no fear.

The man casually spat on the ground between them and looked into Crowdal's eyes. "I have no interest in a fight, although you are welcome to one if you like."

Crowdal raised an eyebrow, intrigued by the casual response, and felt his anger draining away to be replaced with curiosity. "Why are you keeping us from going west?"

"I don't know the reason why, just that I'm to prevent your party from moving in any direction but north."

Crowdal waved at the men behind the leader. "I don't think your little group would be much good in stopping us. Why don't you just step aside and be on your way?"

Scratching behind his ear, Tulman chuckled. "While that is very kind of you to offer, and I do appreciate that you could probably kill us, although with a bit more difficulty than you seem to think, I can tell you that even if you manage to get by us, there is a contingent of strange and violent men not too much further to the west. I'm not even sure that you can fight those men, and I have no interest in getting any closer to them myself. So I suggest you turn north again, for both our accounts." He spat to the side and looked calmly but intensely at

Crowdal.

Crowdal met the mercenary's gaze and realized that he faced an intelligent man who was used to leading. The man wasn't boasting, nor was he looking for a fight. He simply stated the facts and Crowdal respected him for it. He let a his lip curl into a half-smile. "Well, that makes things a bit interesting doesn't it? I don't suppose you want to tell me who hired you?"

The bald man shook his head no.

"I didn't think so. And do you know who is camped to our west?"

Again, the man shook his head, although Crowdal could see wariness in the man's eyes, and perhaps a hint of fear. "Well, since we are at an impasse and have to work things out somehow, I suppose introductions couldn't hurt." He stepped forward and stuck out his hand. "I'm Crowdal."

The man took his outstretched hand and shook it firmly. "Tulman."

Crowdal waved at his friends behind him. "We are about due to break our fast, as we've been walking since before dawn, hoping to get around you, which you so adroitly blocked. I imagine you are hungry also and are welcome to join us."

Tulman thought about it briefly before nodding. "I suppose it couldn't hurt." He turned and motioned his men forward, and Crowdal did the same to his group. They all met in the small clearing, both groups eyeing each other suspiciously.

When Writhgarth looked up at Crowdal with a questioning look, Crowdal smiled. "We might as well be social while we figure this out." He pointed to the group of men. "This is Tulman, who has kindly agreed to join us for some food this morning."

Writhgarth regarded Crowdal like he was crazy, and kept his hand on the hilt of his sword.

Crowdal shrugged. "I know, it is a bit strange, but there is no reason not to be pleasant to those who are just doing their jobs."

Writhgarth grunted. "Jobs? Mercenaries don't have jobs." He looked at the mercenaries. "No offense."

The mercenaries looked just as uncomfortable, standing nervously and shifting back and forth.

Tulman motioned to his men. "Don't be rude, sit!"

The two bowmen looked at each other and shrugged as they leaned their long bows against a tree and sat down cross-legged. The two other rough-looking mercenaries settled down to the ground too, careful to keep their swords ready to draw.

Mrs. Wessmank carefully pulled out her blanket and prepared to sit next to the smallest of the mercenaries, smiling at him. "Do you mind? My old bones are not meant for all of this walking."

The small man stood up and helped her to sit down, then looked embarrassedly at his friend as if expecting a biting comment, but his friend only smiled. He settled back down next to the old woman who leaned over and patted his leather-clad knee.

"Thank you, dear, that was kind of you. You may call me Mrs. Wessmank."

Maelon padded over and lay down next to her, resting his head on her lap. The small mercenary grimaced, looking like he wanted nothing more than to stand up and leave. He finally mumbled his name to her and she nodded kindly at him. "It is nice to meet you, Nik. Could you introduce your friends?"

Nik glanced around and then smiled hesitantly. "Sure. This ugly guy is Richard. And those even uglier guys are Harri and Ulff. And you already met Captain Tulman."

She nodded a greeting to each of the men, then glanced up to Crowdal. "Could you please bring me the pack of food?"

Crowdal took off his large pack and untied the flap, then pulled out a smaller pack and set it down next to her.

Mrs. Wessmank smiled a thank you and took out another small blanket and spread it out on the ground in front of her. Then she set out some dried deer meat, hard cheese, thick bread, and even a few dried apples.

They all began to eat, hesitantly at first, eyeing each other. But soon they chewed with gusto and quickly finished the food.

Ulff sat back and belched loudly. He smiled and shrugged, not embarrassed in the least, then looked down curiously as a long, black arrow punctured his throat, splattering Melinda and Sid with thick blood, who were sitting opposite him. He looked up in surprise, then slumped forward, dead.

Another arrow hit Harri in the neck at almost the same time and the group merely looked at the two dead men for a moment before they all dove to the ground. Two more arrows whistled over where Crowdal's and Tulman's heads had just been a moment before.

Crowdal looked over at Tulman. "I take it those aren't your friends out there?"

Tulman shook his head, sliding his sword out at the same time and scrambling around next to Crowdal, facing the direction from which the arrows had come. He spit to the side and grunted. "I imagine it is the unknown group to the west. They appear to be a little upset that we are sitting with you."

Crowdal turned his head and caught Writhgarth's eye and whispered, "You go left, I'll go right, and we'll flank them.

Tulman told Richard and Nik to crawl to their bows and look for targets. They nodded and crawled with their elbows to their bows.

Nik glanced sidelong at Richard. "Hey, think of it as good target practice."

Richard felt an arrow part his hair and stick in the tree in front of him. He glanced at Nik. "You want to reach up for your bow first?"

Nik grinned. "Sure, no problem, since I am always the brave one anyway."

He counted to three and then lifted his hand to his bow.

Chapter 24

Melinda had been startled when the arrows had started flying, killing two of the mercenaries in a matter of moments. Panic had initially frozen her, but when an arrow had thudded into the tree next to her, she dove to the ground. She felt for that familiar heat inside of her, the comforting warmth she had felt when she entered the Raith world. She was still tired; in fact, since she had been experimenting with time shifts and entering the Raith world over the past few days, she had not been able to get her strength back. She felt empty inside, drained of all her normal energy.

But the heat infused her as always, filling her veins with power, and she exalted in the energy that flowed through her. The heat built, expanding until the world around her stopped moving. She stood up and looked around the small clearing. Mrs. Wessmank was sitting not far from her, her hand half-raised, a look of sadness on her face. Melinda reached up and pulled away an arrow that was touching her cheek, leaving a small drop of blood where the tip had just started to enter her skin.

Melinda started to shake, realizing just how closely she had cut it in entering the Raith world. Even another heartbeat would have been too long and Mrs. Wessmank would have been dead. She dropped the arrow and looked quickly at every one of her friends. They were all safe and no additional arrows were on a trajectory toward them.

The heat coursed through her as she made her way in the direction from which the arrows had originated. She only had to walk fifty paces, stepping over small, dead branches and mossy rocks in the silence, before she found the first of the men. He was kneeling next to a birch tree with his bow fully pulled back, a deadly black arrow notched and ready to fly. He was an ugly man with filthy black hair hanging to his shoulders. She leaned closer and saw a flea in mid-leap from one hair strand to another. Disgusted, she pulled out her Krypen blade from its special sheath and felt the power inside of it fill her with hate. She grabbed the man's hair, and yanking his head back, sliced his neck open from end to end with one vicious pull of her blade. She then knocked his bow from his hands with a kick.

She scoured the forest around her and quickly found five more men, killing them the all in same way. Four of them were holding bows like the first man. One of them had just released his arrow and it hung in mid-air three paces from him. She swatted it to the ground before she killed him.

The fifth man was obviously the leader, quite large and mean-looking, his eyes glittering with pleasure as he leaned around a tree to witness the carnage his men were unleashing upon the unsuspecting group without having to put himself in danger. Melinda loathed cowardly men like this and the heat within her pulsed even more. She removed his helmet and slowly cut his eyes out, followed by his tongue. She then stabbed down with her Krypen blade and severed his spinal cord just above his shoulders.

Melinda looked around her and made sure there were no more attackers left alive, then looked down at her blade. It dripped blood and she smiled. It was a strange sight as she watched the blood fall in thick droplets when everything around her was still.

She bent down and wiped her blade on the tunic of the dead leader, then put it back into its sheath as she started back toward her group. She was very tired and stumbled over a tree root, and as she did, she lost her concentration and came out of the Raith world.

The world came back to life with a rush of sound, scents, and chaos.

She saw Crowdal's eyes go wide as he saw her catch her footing. He jumped up and ran to her. "What happened? Are you hurt?"

She just shook her head and walked past him, hoping he wouldn't suspect anything.

Every member of the group lay still for a few moments, but when no more arrows flew into their midst, Tulman turned to Richard and Nik. "Go check it out and report back immediately."

The two men jumped up and grabbed their bows before fading into the trees.

Tulman ambled over to Crowdal's side, still scanning the trees around him.

Melinda sat against a small birch tree, exhausted almost to the point of losing consciousness. She watched the people around her as if from a distance.

Richard and Nik soon walked back toward the group and up to Tulman, both a little white in the face.

Tulman spoke sternly, "Well, report!"

Richard visibly swallowed, then spoke, "Six men... were out there." He glanced sideways at Nik, then continued, "They are all dead, sir."

"Dead? How were they killed?"

"Most had their throats cut." He hesitated.

Tulman slapped the side of his face. "I said report!"

Nik hesitated briefly then spoke up to save his friend any more embarrassment, "They all died, sir, without even trying to fight. The leader, he... he had his eyes gouged out, his tongue cut out, and his spinal cord severed." Nik's face went even whiter as he whispered one word, "Zranh."

The word hung in the air, and everyone turned as one to look at

Melinda as she sat by herself against a tree.

Tulman turned to Crowdal and for once there was an edge to his voice. "Who is she?"

Crowdal stood up tall. "She is a healer, not a killer. I suggest you stop looking at her like you are."

Melinda felt guilty but thankful for how Crowdal stood up for her. He was a good man, but he was wrong. She was a killer. Perhaps the worst kind, for the men whom she had just killed hadn't even had the chance to defend themselves, or even know they were being killed. She saw suspicion clearly etched on the three strangers' faces.

Crowdal looked at Melinda as she slumped against the tree, then turned back to Tulman. "The important question is, what do we do now? It appears that your friends out there didn't much like the fact that we were being friendly toward one another."

Tulman eyed Crowdal for a long moment "Aye, we are in a situation, no doubt about it. Perhaps I made a mistake. Maybe we should have avoided all contact with you people. That was the job I was hired for." He spit to his left. "Now things are all messed up and I have only myself to blame." Pointing at Richard and Nik, Tulman spoke harshly, "Go strip everything of value, then bury the bodies, leave no trace that this occurred."

As the two men turned to leave, Writhgarth stepped forward. "I'll help." They nodded to him, accepting him as a strong man despite his small size. The three of them disappeared into the trees.

Tulman turned to Crowdal, and Melinda could tell he assumed Crowdal was the leader of their group. "I don't know what is going on, but I don't like it. We were hired to keep you moving north. I know politics usually plays a part in what I am hired for, but I didn't sign on to be killed just for talking to you." Rubbing his thumb across the hilt of his sword, he looked up unflinchingly into Crowdal's eyes, and when Crowdal started to speak, he held up his hand to stop him. "I don't care what your group did, or who you are fleeing from. When those two arrows killed my men, my contract was terminated. I now work for no one."

His face reddened slightly and he narrowed his eyes. "I'm going to find out who hired me, and I am going to kill the son of a bitch, and I don't mean that cowardly middle man who hired me. I mean the guy behind all of this." He spat again. "I believe that means that we are in the same shit."

Crowdal raised an eyebrow. From where she sat against the tree, Melinda could tell that Crowdal liked the man, despite his being a mercenary. Crowdal turned back to Sid. "Sid, what do you think?"

Melinda smiled slightly as Tulman's eyes widened when he realized that Crowdal was asking Sid what to do.

Sid stepped forward and spoke quietly, "As far as I'm concerned, you and your men are more than welcome to travel with us, but I need to talk this over with my friends, first. And, quite honestly, I am not sure you should travel with us, for reasons I can't go into now. I'll let you know our decision in a few moments."

Tulman nodded. "I'll go help my men bury the bodies." He walked into the trees without another word.

Melinda felt more tired than she had ever been. She watched Sid approach her and kneel down, concern on his face. "Are you all right, Melinda?"

She nodded weakly. "I'm fine. Just a little tired, is all."

Sid touched her shoulder then stood up. "So, what do you all think? What should we do?"

Crowdal towered over them all but spoke quietly, "Tulman has apparently been fired, if his two dead men are any indication. I think we should let them join up with us for a bit. They seem like good men, even if they are mercenaries." Crowdal pushed his long, black hair from his face as he looked down at them.

"I think we can use all the help we can get." Melinda tiredly said.

Sid turned to Mrs. Wessmank. "Do you trust them?"

The old woman nodded immediately. "We can trust them." She slowly got up from the ground. Sid immediately gave her his hand and she nodded her thanks. She brushed a few leaves from her butt. "They may have their flaws, but they will not harm us."

Sid looked over his shoulder into the trees where the mercenaries and Writhgarth were burying the men who had attacked them, then back to Crowdal. "Then it's settled. I trust her judgment with my life. I need to continue going west, but I can't ask you all to continue on with me. It is too dangerous."

Crowdal shrugged. "I think I speak for everyone when I say you are stuck with us, Sid. Where you go, we go."

Melinda slowly got to her feet, although the effort seemed to take what last reserves of energy she had and she slumped against the tree.

Crowdal immediately stepped to her side. "Melinda, what is wrong?"

"Nothing. I... just need to walk it off. I'll be fine." She lifted her head and straightened her shoulders. "See, I'm fine."

"Yeah, well you don't look fine." He glanced over his shoulder at Mrs. Wessmank and Sid, then back to Melinda. "What happened a few moments ago? How did you..."

Her eyes flashed and she spoke angrily. "Nothing happened, Crowdal. Now leave me alone."

Crowdal was about to retort when crashing sounds came through the trees behind them and he turned, pulling his sword at the same time.

From out of the trees came Writhgarth, Richard, Nik, and in the rear, Tulman, all running as fast as they could. They slid to a stop with a clatter of armor and weapons, breathing hard.

Writhgarth spun around and faced the way he had come. "We are about to have some company."

Crowdal cocked his head and was about to speak when he heard the trees rustling from the direction the men had come. The entire group turned to face that way and Writhgarth spoke out of the corner of his mouth, his eyes never leaving the trees that surrounded them. "I would suggest we run, but that doesn't appear to be an option, as I think we are surrounded."

The trees stopped rustling and silence settled on them all.

Melinda felt a chill go down her spine. She turned to her left, feeling a... presence. Her face turned even whiter as she watched ten men step into view, wearing black armor that sucked in all light, helmets shaped like living things from her worst nightmares, and swords as long as she was tall; but it was the man in the front who caused the breath to catch in her throat, for he was the largest and most fearsome man she had ever seen, a full four hand-spans taller than the other men around him.

She heard more men coming out of the woods all around her but she didn't take her eyes from the man in front of her. His helmet looked like evil incarnate, horns rising above it, and was made out of, unbelievably, the snout of a Kraagiquazz, its long teeth still intact.

The man stepped forward from his men and stared directly at Melinda, causing her to stop breathing. She felt a tingling sensation deep inside and she tried to force it away in disgust. But she couldn't lie to herself, she felt a sexual charge emanating from him unlike anything she had ever felt, and a wet warmth pulsed between her legs. She took in a ragged breath, then two, three more. Finally, she forced herself to turn away and she felt the true warmth of Crowdal next to her, and she thanked the gods he was there with her. She watched her friends turn in a circle, taking in all of the men around them.

The nightmarish figure strode forward and stopped in front of them. He slowly lifted both of his hands, one of them still holding the giant, blackened sword, and carefully pulled the helmet from his head. Long, black hair fell to his shoulders, and Melinda breathed in and held it, for she couldn't take her eyes from the man. His nose was large and bent, and scars crisscrossed every available part of his face. His teeth were blackened, but it was his eyes that held her, for they looked exactly like those of a corpse, dead and empty. A shudder of fear raced through her, as well as an increased sexual excitement. He was a man who emanated a maleness she couldn't ignore.

She covered her reaction quickly by turning away, pretending to ignore him. She closed her eyes and thought of death and blood and pain, and the warmth between her legs faded as quickly as it had come.

She felt nothing but disgust, hating herself even more then she had when she had killed those men.

The man smiled cruelly, as if he knew what she had just gone through. He tucked his helmet under one arm, his sword laid casually back over his shoulder. Then he turned his head and focused on Sid. When he spoke, his voice rumbled, so deep it was almost beyond hearing, "Hmm... interesting. You are just a pathetic boy, yet you have caused all of this fuss. I wonder why that is." He spit sideways. "If you are the great Aleph Null, I am disappointed. I think I should just kill you now and be done with it."

The man's dead-looking eyes were those of someone who was accustomed to inspiring fear in all whom he met.

Melinda turned to Crowdal, who was kind and gentle. She looked into his warm eyes and leaned against him. The feeling of being dirty and ashamed left her at his touch, and she realized for the first time that she had true feelings for the Trith.

But fear filled her when Crowdal pushed her gently behind him, then pulled Sid back also.

Crowdal smiled belligerently at the nightmare of a man and said in a calm and causal voice, "I would like to see you try that."

Chapter 25

The chamber was damp and cold even though it was late spring and the weather outside was turning warm. The room was fitted with beautiful tapestries that hung on all four walls, and thick carpets, intricately woven into amazing images of historical battles, covered large portions of the floor. A large fireplace, almost as tall as Lorielle herself, burned with a hearty fire; but still, nothing could ever completely make her feel truly warm in this room. She pulled a coarse blanket from the bed and wrapped herself in it as she waited.

It was now late afternoon and she was tired. She and Tristian had left the White Horse tavern not long after the sun had risen over the roof tops of Undaluag. It had taken almost the entire morning to reach the Oblate, for they had to stop constantly. The city was large and crowded, people pushing and yelling constantly as they bartered for food, goods, pretty much anything that could be bought or sold. It seemed like total chaos to Lorielle after spending the past ten years in almost solitary captivity. Her head had throbbed in pain and her vision often swam, making her dizzy. She had thanked the gods when they had finally reached the Oblate. She tried to memorize the location as best she could, but she admitted to herself that she was totally lost and would probably not be able to find it again, much less reveal to someone in the Anderom how to find it.

To all outward appearances, the building looked like a wealthy private residence. It was built from chiseled stone blocks fitted perfectly together. As she had walked through the main door, she had entered a standard great room. An angry-looking boar's head was mounted over a large fireplace, which warmed a cozy room richly appointed with overstuffed chairs and ornate tables. But the place was empty and had the feeling of never being used. She had realized that it was just the facade the Oblate portrayed to anyone who came calling, that of a rich man. She had been led straight through the room to another door.

Beyond this door everything had changed. She had come into a large room occupied by at least thirty Haissen. They had apparently been waiting for them, for they were standing calmly at attention. Tristian had ignored them as he led her down a long hall to her left. They had passed many doors until they reached the second-to-last one. Ushered inside of the room, she was pushed toward the bed.

Afraid she was about to be raped, Lorielle resisted, but Tristian rolled his eyes. "Oh please, cousin, don't flatter yourself. I don't rape old women." He stared at the wall for a brief moment and a set of gears rumbled inside the stones until the bed swung sideways to reveal a large opening. She realized he had used some kind of equation to open it and marveled at the security. Only a member of the Oblate would be given the equation to master, and only they would be able to use it to open the door.

Tristian stepped aside and held out his arm. "After you."

Lorielle followed a stairway that wound downward, the steps unevenly spaced, until she came to another door. She waited for Tristian to open it, and he laughed. "I think even you are capable of opening this one. It isn't difficult. Just push down on the handle and, mysteriously, the door opens."

Lorielle shot him a scathing look, then pushed down hard on the handle and pushed the door open. Tristian chuckled behind her and took her arm. "Come, cousin, let me show you to your room." He led her down a series of hallways until he came to one that had a Haissan standing with its back to it. As they approached, the Haissan reached back and pushed the door inward.

Tristian gestured toward the room. "Make yourself comfortable. If you need anything, pull the cord and a servant will get you what you want." He turned to leave, but stopped. "Just so you know, orders are to cut your tongue out the first time you try to escape." He paused as if he were going to say something else, but then just walked away. Lorielle had entered her room and the door had clicked shut behind her.

She had taken a nap but now she was hungry. She walked over to a braided rope that hung from the ceiling and pulled it gently. Nothing happened, so she pulled harder. Still nothing happened and she was about to pull it again when her door opened and a young girl, probably no more than fourteen years old, entered the room. She stood there without saying a word.

Lorielle walked over to her. "Hello, dear girl."

The girl opened her mouth and pointed.

Lorielle gasped when she saw that her tongue was missing. "Oh, my poor dear, I'm so sorry."

The girl smiled hesitantly and shook her head, her meaning clearly saying it was all right.

Lorielle put her hand on her shoulder. "Could I have some food, dear?"

The girl nodded and immediately left. While she waited, Lorielle walked around the room, examining the fine artwork of the tapestries. One caught her eye that depicted a cottage in a small clearing. Smoke spiraled out of a chimney and snow covered the ground. Trees surrounded the clearing, including a large Miq that towered over the rest of the trees. She saw something at the base of the tree and leaned forward to get a closer look, then gasped and pulled away from the tapestry, her skin going cold. A creature was painted there, leaning around the corner of the large tree, its huge blue eyes seeming like they were staring at her.

The Korpor.

A chill ran through her and she quickly stepped away and sat on one of the overstuffed chairs. She didn't have long to wait before the door opened and the serving girl brought in a tray and set it on the table next to her. The aroma of grilled meat filled her nostrils and she smiled. "Thank you, my dear."

The girl bowed and left the room.

Lorielle picked up her knife and fork and cut a piece of meat, slicing away a piece of fat before getting to the pink and juicy flesh. She put it to her mouth, chewing with relish. She took her time with the meal, and when she picked up the mug of ale to wash it all down, she saw a piece of parchment under the mug. She set the mug back down, forgetting about her thirst, and carefully picked up the note. She opened it and read.

"I am a friend. Tonight, before the moon rises past its zenith, I will come to you."

Lorielle read the note twice more, then walked over to the fireplace and set the note in the embers on the edge. Spots of black soon appeared, and then the parchment burst into flame. She watched until it turned to ash, then sat back down and drank her ale. Who the note was from, she didn't know. But for the first time she felt a sliver of hope.

She was tired again, so she lay down on the bed and closed her eyes.

* * *

Lorielle heard a soft scrape behind her. She opened her eyes and saw the room was dark. The fire had burned down to just a few red embers. She sat up in the bed, swung her legs over the edge, and gasped softly when she saw a Haissan standing in an opening in the wall.

The Haissan put a finger to its mouth and motioned to her to join it.

Lorielle didn't hesitate. She slipped her feet into her shoes and entered the dark space in the wall, which shut softly behind her. Immediately, a light flared in the darkness and the Haissan turned and led the way, holding a smoking torch above its head.

They made their way silently through very narrow passages that often turned at right angles. Lorielle figured they were behind the very walls of the building and surmised the passageways had been built as a way to either escape if attacked, or to move about without anyone knowing. Since she was in the Oblate, she figured both purposes could be valid.

They soon came to a stairwell that led downward. It was very narrow, the walls so close that her shoulders brushed them as she began her decent. She had to keep her arms at her sides, for if she lifted her elbows away from her body even a little bit, she would scrape them on the rough, pockmarked stone walls. They descended for a long time, curving in a tight circle. The steps were uneven in height, some so deep that she had to put her foot carefully over the edge until she touched the next step. She became dizzy after a while, but kept going until they reached a small door at the bottom, only half the height of herself.

The Haissan put a key in and twisted the latch. The door opened silently and the Haissan stooped down and stepped through. The stairwell instantly darkened to shadows as Lorielle stepped through the small opening.

The Haissan shut the door and motioned her to follow it down a short hallway. They didn't have far to go before the Haissan stopped at a single door, this one full-sized. It put the same key in the latch and twisted it. It stepped aside and motioned her inside, setting its torch in a holder by the door and extinguishing it with a steel cup.

Lorielle stepped through and gasped.

The room was well-lit with tripod stands that held burning torches. Lorielle walked far enough into the room so she could turn to take it all in. The room was circular and huge, with walls that were covered from floor to ceiling with small stone cubby holes, and each cubby hole held a number of scrolls. She saw a long ladder on wheels that reached the ceiling. She smiled in appreciation when she noticed the top of the ladder also had wheels that sat inside of a track which ran along the entire parameter of the room. A person could climb the ladder and simply push in either direction to move around the whole chamber.

She turned back to the Haissan and spoke hesitantly, "What... is this place?"

The Haissan pushed its hood back and smiled at her. She hadn't known that a Haissan could smile.

"Welcome, Lorielle."

To her surprise, Lorielle noticed the Haissan sounded female. During the time she had spent with the many Haissen as of late, she hadn't thought of them as male or female. Curious, she said, "I don't mean to be rude, but are you... female?"

The Haissan spoke in a voice more like the hiss of a snake than the rich timber of most humans. "Yes, my name is Tierre."

Lorielle half-bowed to her. "It is a pleasure to meet you, Tierre."

The Haissan bowed back.

Lorielle looked about the room, studying it carefully. She had never seen such wealth before, neither in knowledge, nor the value of the parchment itself. She turned her head back to Tierre. "Who are you?" The question was simple, but her inflection indicated she was asking about more than Tierre personally.

The Haissan glided over to a table that sat in the middle of the room. It was an immense table, perhaps fifteen paces squared, obviously made to accommodate long scrolls and large maps. It was solidly built of worn but well-cared-for Miq wood, the hardest and heaviest type of wood in the land. Resting on the table was a small, plain, wooden box.

Tierre pulled out two simple, three-legged stools and motioned for Lorielle to take a seat, doing the same herself. The Haissan looked around the room slowly, as if she were seeing it for either the first time or the last time. Finally she concentrated fully upon Lorielle. "You are sitting in the Gairium chamber." The Haissan spread her arms wide. "In here exists every manuscript, every scroll, every bit of knowledge that has been written about the Aleph Null, the Haissen, the Oblate, as well as all fields of mathematics." She stopped speaking, giving Lorielle time to digest what she had said.

Lorielle didn't speak for some time as she moved her eyes along the rows of scrolls. She trembled slightly at the thought of so much knowledge. She had joined the Anderom for just this reason: to gain knowledge about the Aleph Null prophecy, and hopefully to be a part of it all. But she had never, in her whole life, thought there would be a place such as this.

She turned back to the Haissan. "This is amazing. Truly. But I still don't understand why you brought me here."

The Haissan stared at her with lidded eyes. "We only have until dawn, so I will have to give you the abridged version. Myself and one other Haissan named Saleth, who travels with the Red Robe at the moment, are the last two surviving members of the original Haissen who created the prophecy of the Aleph Null, and the Oblate itself."

Lorielle broke in, scoffing outwardly, "You created the prophecy of the Aleph Null and the Oblate? I find that hard to believe. You have blindly served the Oblate for a millennium, killing anyone and anything in its name. And just today I saw many Haissen here in the Oblate, so you are not the last two."

"That is correct, there are, to be precise, fifty-two Haissen left in existence. The other fifty serve the Oblate, having abandoned the original goals of the Haissen that were set forth more than two thousand years ago. It is now down to Saleth and myself to ensure the Aleph Null survives."

Scratching at a small ridge on the table with her fingernail, Lorielle had a difficult time understanding such vast numbers. She had an idea of what the number fifty two meant, but it was at the very limits of her ability to count. When the Faussian monks had removed her mathematical abilities, she could no longer count beyond ten without feeling nauseated, and only if she pushed herself could she count higher. She pulled her hand back and dropped it into her lap and straightened her shoulders. "How can I help?"

Tierre spoke calmly. "You are the mother of the Aleph Null. Your role appears to have become important for the Black Robe to have brought you here. I believe he is going to find a way to use you to weaken the Aleph Null, perhaps by threatening your life to make the boy hesitate, or even do as the Black Robe commands. For two thousand years we have been working toward this time, and now events are unfolding at a rapid rate."

Lorielle raised her hands in despair. "But what can I do to help you? I've had all of my mathematical abilities taken from me. I am useless."

"Ah, that is the heart of the matter isn't it? I can help you regain that which you lost."

Lorielle leaned forward. "What do you mean?"

Tierre opened the wooden box that sat in front of them and removed a small scroll. Heavy ivory handles were inserted in the ends of the scroll. She offered one handle to Lorielle. "Could you please carefully hold this?"

Lorielle did as the Haissan asked, and Tierre pulled her end away, unwinding the scroll with a soft cracking of parchment until it tugged to a stop. The Haissan set her end on the table and Lorielle did the same.

The parchment was yellow and filled with a spiderweb of cracks. The writing was in a language Lorielle had never seen before, slightly faded but still legible, done in beautiful brush strokes. She looked up at the Haissan in wonder. "What is this scroll? I've never seen anything like it."

Tierre carefully pushed a bent part of the scroll down to the table and spoke in her hissing voice, "This scroll was written long before the Haissen came to this land. The information in this scroll can restore your mathematical abilities. While I am not a mathematician and cannot help you directly, by reading the words out loud, your buried mathematical abilities will activate the power within the verses themselves."

The Haissan spoke so calmly that it took Lorielle a few heartbeats before her words registered. She gasped and grabbed the sleeve of Tierre's cloak and twisted it, not even realizing that if she had done that to any other Haissan, she would have been killed instantly. But Tierre calmly removed her hand, the skin of her hand dry, but smooth. Lorielle felt embarrassed, but she still leaned forward, her eyes glinting in the light of the torches. "Can such a thing be done?"

The Haissan nodded intently. "Yes, it can. But it will be... painful for you."

"I will do anything you ask."

Tierre nodded slightly. "Then let us begin." The Haissan put a finger at the top of the scroll and moved it down as she read to herself. Finally she glanced back up at Lorielle and slipped a piece of steel from her sleeve, holding it out.

Lorielle took it and turned it in the light. It had a short, round handle, and the end had a tiny hair-width blade. She looked up in question.

"When I read the verses, you will begin to feel a tingle in your left temple that will move around the back of your head to your right temple. At this point, you will feel pain, but you must not let it affect what you must do next."

Not liking the sound of that, Lorielle lifted the small blade. "I take it I will have to do something unpleasant with this?"

Tierre nodded. "This is the key part of the ordeal and you must do it at the precise moment. As soon as you feel pain flare in your right temple, you must make a small incision in the corner of your right cornea, enough to release fluid but not so much as to blind yourself."

Lorielle felt a flicker of fear jolt through her, but pushed it away and nodded acceptance. She would do whatever it took if she could have her mathematical abilities back and be able to help her son. "I will do it. Please begin."

The Haissan stared at her. "You are a strong woman. If more humans were like you, the world would be a better place for us all." She immediately put a finger on the first word of the scroll and began speaking in her hissing voice.

The words meant nothing to Lorielle, but as she listened, she felt a tingle appear behind her left temple, just as the Haissan told her would happen. The tingle began to slowly move around the back of her head, but not on the outside, it felt like it was moving through the tissue of her brain itself.

She gritted her teeth, wanting nothing more than to scratch at her head, to make the tingle stop. But it continued moving slowly around her brain as Tierre spoke. As it approached her right temple, she lifted the narrow blade and held it to her right eye. Her hands shook slightly and she felt nauseated at what she would soon have to do.

The tingle reached her right temple and pain exploded in her head, feeling like a red-hot branding iron had been pushed into her eye. She gasped and her vision grew dim. She faintly heard the Haissan urgently hiss, "Do it now!"

Through the pain, she forced her hand to her right eye, the blade blurry through her tears. She wanted nothing more than to shut her eyelid, but she opened it wider instead, set the cold steel of the blade against her eyeball, and slid it lightly across to the corner. Pain flared anew and she cried out and dropped the blade. She felt pressure release from her mind and flow out of her eye along with a warm, sticky fluid. The pain increased and she screamed, putting her hands to her head, feeling like it was going to collapse upon itself. The pain continued to build until she lost her balance and fell to the rough stone floor. Tierre caught her before she struck it and gently lowered her down.

Just when she felt she couldn't take any more pain, it began to fade away, as if it streamed out of her eye in a rush. Then... nothing. She cried out in relief at the absence of agony, and sobbed as she curled into a ball, hugging her knees to her chest. She felt a hand lift her right eyelid, then heard the Haissan as if from far away, "You did it, Lorielle."

She stopped sobbing at the sound of Tierre's voice and slowly pushed herself to a sitting position, keeping her eyes closed. Her right eye throbbed and still leaked fluid.

"Let me put some liquid into your eye to help it heal. Tilt your head back please."

Lorielle nodded and did as was asked. She felt the Haissan pull her eyelid back. The light of the torches was blurry and excruciating, then she felt cool liquid drip into her eye. The Haissan let go and she closed her eye again.

"Now, roll your eye in a circle a few times."

Lorielle did as she was told and the discomfort lessened. She then felt a piece of cloth being tied around her eye and head. "Keep this on until we return to your room. Your eye should be healed enough by then to remove it, although your vision will likely be blurry for a few days."

She nodded and felt hands under her arm, helping to pull her to her feet. She was guided back to her stool and she sat down gratefully. "Thank you, Tierre."

"Of course. Now I want you to think of a mathematical problem. Any one will do."

Lorielle hesitated. For the past ten years she had not been able to even think of a simple math problem like 100 x 200 = 20,000. She had known what math was, but any time she even tried to think of math it was like looking into a void. She remembered how she had wanted to count the 248 tiles in her room, or the 190 short, narrow wooden boards that made up her floor, but always got sick by the time she got to twenty.

She gasped, realizing what she was doing. Numbers. They made sense to her again. She jumped up from her stool, crying out in joy, and lost her balance. Tierre steadied her and she grabbed table's edge to make sure she didn't fall.

She concentrated and numbers bubbled out of the recesses of her mind that had been closed to her for ten years, numbers so great that they trailed back and disappeared into the darkness. Symbols, letters, equations, and formulas spun and twisted and turned in her mind, and she tentatively tried to manipulate them.

They moved!

It felt like she was physically reaching out and grabbing them. A smile grew on her face as she mentally examined the damage to her right eye. She built a formula based on her left eye that replicated the healthy tissue and examined it for a few moments before attaching it to her right eye. Her eye began to itch and she wanted to reach up and rub it, but she forced herself to remain still. As soon as it began, the itch faded away, and she examined the equation. It was identical to her left eye, so she carefully reached up to untie the cloth from her head.

Tierre hissed, "Do not do that yet, you need to give it time to heal properly."

Lorielle ignored the Haissan and pulled the cloth away from her face. She carefully opened her eyes. The right eye was sticky and she gently rubbed the residue away. The light hurt and she blinked rapidly a number of times until she was used to it. The room was blurry so she gently rubbed away the rest of the sticky residue and when she opened her eye again she could see perfectly.

She smiled to the Haissan, who merely nodded to her, not showing any surprise. "I take it you have your power of numbers back."

"Yes, I do. Thank you, Tierre. Thank you from the bottom of my heart." She reached out and hugged the Haissan, who remained stiff. Lorielle let go and sat back down. "You have given me a gift that I never thought I would receive again. How may I repay you?"

Tierre carefully rolled up the scroll, the parchment cracking pleasantly, then placed it into the small box and stood up and carried it to the wall to her left and climbed the rolling ladder. She placed the box into one of the cubby holes at the very top, then climbed back down and rejoined Lorielle at the table, but remained standing. "It is getting close to dawn, we must make our way back to your chamber before you are missed. I will give you a short explanation of our history, as well as what you must do in the coming days."

Lorielle stood up and nodded. "I will do what needs to be done to save my son, and to help repay you for what you have given me here."

Tierre glided to the door and pulled the unlit torch that she had set down when they had first entered the chamber. She relit the torch from one of the existing torches, then strode around the room extinguishing the rest of the torches until she stood next to Lorielle again. She motioned Lorielle through the door, closing it securely behind them.

As they walked down the short hallway to the half-door that opened to the long stairwell, Tierre began telling Lorielle the history of the Haissen.

The climb was agonizing for Lorielle. She absently counted the steps as she climbed, listening to the Haissan tell her story. By the time she reached the top of the stairs, huffing and puffing, she had counted 354 grueling steps. This had given the Haissan enough time to tell her the abbreviated history of the Haissen, the Oblate, and the Aleph Null, and she almost couldn't believe it. The fact that the Haissen had created the prophecy of the Aleph Null and the Oblate itself, all so the Aleph Null would some day save their race from extinction, made her feel small and insignificant, and guilty for how she had always thought of the Haissen as nothing more than mindless killers.

She was thankful that she could play even a small role in their prophecy, and that her son, her beautiful boy Sidoro, was the one who could save them. She shivered, and not from the dampness of the stairwell, when she learned of the malevolent forces all converging on her son. The odds were not in his favor and she almost wept at the thought of him out there, alone against such evil.

They reached the hidden door to her chamber and Tierre stood perfectly still for a number of moments, listening, until she silently opened the door and motioned Lorielle through.

As Lorielle stepped through the opening, Tierre put a hand on her arm. "We will meet again. Stay strong."

Lorielle touched the Haissan's hand. "I look forward to that day. Thank you, Tierre."

The Haissan turned without another word and closed the hidden door.

Lorielle stumbled to the bed, more exhausted than she had realized. Within moments she was asleep.

She dreamed of numbers.

Chapter 26

The air instantly thickened with tension as the Masteen Vorn Maghuur slowly shifted his gaze from the Aleph Null to his tall friend for the first time. He studied the skinny man who had stepped in front of him, recognizing him as a Trith but not impressed by their legendary status as warriors. He merely saw a dead man, for no one spoke to him like that. He growled deeply and took a menacing step forward, expecting the Trith to fall to the ground in fear. Even the most battle-hardened men often pissed themselves and fell forward when caught in his cold glare.

But, to his shock, he had to stop mid-step because the Trith had stepped forward to meet him, leaning his face forward threateningly until they almost touched noses, locking his eyes on the Masteen. No one had ever done this to him; in fact, it had literally never occurred to him that it could happen. He froze for a moment, unable to process the situation.

Not even the Masteen's men dared move. They had never even dreamed someone would dare stand toe-to-toe with the Masteen, and they all held their breaths. From their point of view, the stranger was as tall as the Masteen, but lean, where the Masteen looked to be made of steel with arms that rippled with muscle. They waited, knowing the Masteen would soon reach forward and destroy him. Most of them couldn't wait for this to happen, for it would be a tale they could tell for the rest of their lives.

The Masteen's eyes grew wide, and then he started to tremble from his need to kill. His mouth twisted into a scowl and his hand gripped his sword hilt so tightly that it creaked. He knew the effect his size, his face, and especially his eyes had on people. But here stood this young Trith, glaring at him as if expecting that he, the Masteen, should back down. Another growl escaped his throat, deeper this time, almost beyond hearing, and everyone in the clearing took a step backward, the hair rising on their arms and necks.

Except for the Trith facing him, who smiled mockingly, then winked and said, "So, are you going to fight, or are you just going to stare at me with those pretty eyes of yours?"

The Masteen roared, death his only thought, but before he could move, the Trith shot his head forward with blinding speed, smashing into his face so hard it shattered his nose. Pain exploded through him and he felt blood splatter across his cheeks. Stunned, he didn't see his opponent spin around and sweep his legs, and he suddenly found himself on his back, staring into the mocking eyes of the Trith standing above him.

Four of his guards rushed the Trith, who spun around and punched one guard so hard in the face that his iron helmet caved into his face, cutting into his skull and brain, killing him instantly. He fell backward with a crash and didn't move. The other three crashed into the Trith, knocking him to the ground. He struggled but they pinned him securely. They were all huge men, heavier than he was and well-armored. One struck the Trith across the face with a iron-clad glove, stunning him.

The remaining guards rushed forward and held their swords against the chests of each member of the small group before they could move.

The Masteen slowly got to his feet. He reached up with one hand and squeezed the crushed cartilage and bone together, ignoring the pain, until his nose was somewhat back into place, the crunching of bone nothing more than an irritation to him. He licked the blood off of his fingers, then motioned for his men to lift the Trith to his feet.

The three guards violently flipped him over and pinned his hands behind his back before jerking him to his feet.

The Masteen spit a mouthful of blood to the ground, eyeing him coldly. "For what you just did, I will not kill you."

His adversary groggily raised an eyebrow. "Is that so?"

The Masteen sucked blood loudly through his nose and spit a thick red globule into the dirt. "Oh, yes. I am going to torture you in ways that you can't imagine. I will not let you die, but you will wish every single moment that you were dead."

The Trith did not show any fear, which angered the Masteen, sent his heart racing, and the need to inflict death overcame him. He reached out his hand and closed his fingers around the man's throat and began squeezing, glaring at him with cold hatred.

With a burst of strength, the Trith broke his hands free from the men who held him and reached up to pry the Masteen's fingers from his neck, but it was like trying to break iron shackles. The Trith made small grunting noises, his face turning red, then he stopped trying to pry the Masteen's fingers away and slammed both hands together against the Masteen's ears.

It felt like his brain had been stabbed with a dagger and he immediately let go of the Trith and roared as he put his hands to his ears.

His enemy stepped back to get some distance and drew his sword, but before he could do anything, the Masteen, face purple from rage, jumped forward and swung his fist into the man's forehead, dropping him instantly to the ground unconscious, so great was the power behind the blow.

He stepped forward and towered over the Trith as he lay on the ground, spittle dribbling down his chin as he breathed heavily, still not believing someone had dared to touch him, much less strike him. He kicked the Trith viciously in the side with his steel boot, and was about to kick him again when he felt a tickle inside of his head. He looked at the others around him, then focused on the Aleph Null who stood close by, his eyes closed, and the Masteen knew the Aleph Null was trying to use his power. The Masteen began to worry and berated himself for spending time on the worthless Trith at his feet before taking control of the Aleph Null. He stepped over the unconscious form and was about to strike the boy, when suddenly the pressure eased and the boy opened his eyes in defeat.

The Masteen realized with a start that the boy could not control his power, the look of defeat emanating from him absolute.

He spit more blood to the ground and glared at the Aleph Null. "Nice try, boy."

* * *

Sid stared at the Masteen in frustration and defeat. He had closed his eyes and brought his numbers forth, planning to kill the evil men. But his numbers had refused to obey his commands. They were there, but they bounced around in his mind chaotically and he couldn't keep them still. As soon as he stopped one number from moving and went to the next, the previous number would start vibrating away in a blur. He had concentrated harder and made every single number stop moving as one. But as soon as he tried to manipulate them, they began to vibrate away from him in clusters. It was like trying to catch a hundred flies with just two fingers. As soon as he caught one, he had to release it to catch the next.

Sid felt the chaos emanating from the Masteen and knew that the giant man was somehow blocking his numbers. He slumped his shoulders in defeat.

* * *

Melinda had been watching Sid, waiting for him to do something with his numbers, but she saw the frustration in his eyes and then the slump of his shoulders. Somehow, the giant man must be affecting Sid's power of numbers. With a start, she realized it was up to her to get them out of this situation. She did not want to enter the Raith world again, for she was exhausted, and knew the extensive amount of time she had spent there over the past few days had been a mistake. Her pride and curiosity had made her think she could handle the Raith world, but in reality it had weakened her to the point where she didn't think she had even the smallest amount of strength left to enter it now when she needed it the most.

But she had no choice.

Sighing, she reached for the familiar heat, hoping she could enter the shift just long enough to kill the men who surrounded them, and especially the enormous man who had just knocked Crowdal to the ground, unconscious. But instead of the heat growing and spreading within her like normal, just a trickle of warmth filled her now. She tried to phase into the Raith world, and for a few brief moments, time slowed down, but then it sped up again in jerky starts.

She concentrated harder, and time only slowed down in a stop-start motion, making her dizzy. What little energy reserves she had before she started, dissipated quickly and time went fully back to normal.

She breathed shallowly and fell to her knees. She had failed them.

* * *

The Masteen saw the woman fall to her knees, and at the same time, the strange three-legged animal leapt away and streaked into the forest. One of his men raised his bow and was about to shoot, but the Masteen pulled the bow down. "Don't waste your arrows on the mutt." He motioned to the prisoners. "Shackle them in irons and let's get back to camp."

He glanced down at the huge man on the ground. "Shackle that one tightly, then throw water on him to wake him up. We aren't carrying him."

His men immediately brought out a number of iron shackles and they ordered each member of the small group to put their hands behind their backs. They roughly secured everyone's hands tightly into the iron clamps, then did as the Masteen ordered with the large man on the ground. They latched the clamps around his hands behind his back and then threw water on him. He woke up gasping and spitting water and they laughed at him as he briefly struggled when they yanked him to his feet. One man punched him in the stomach and grinned when the tall man doubled over with a grunt.

The Masteen put his helmet back on. He would have some fun with that man back at camp, and then he would get the secrets out of the Aleph Null. The rest of them would be nothing more than a way to control the boy with threats against their lives.

As for the woman at his camp, the so called Red Robe, he no longer needed her. He smiled inside of his helmet. He would use her body up and throw her away. And if the Black Robe came against him, he would just have to destroy the upstart. There was not a man alive who could match him, not in strength, cunning, or with the sword.

He turned and made his way back toward camp, his men leading the small group of people behind him.

He grinned viciously.

It was going to be a fun next couple of days.

Chapter 27

Maelon peered out from his hiding space underneath a rotting tree that had fallen long ago. He had escaped from the evil men, although it had hurt him to do so. But his mother had spoken sharply to him, telling him urgently to get away when the Aleph Null had failed to control his power of numbers. He had hesitated at first, but she had grown angry, telling him not to be foolish. And strangely, when the healer had collapsed to her knees, his mother had actually yelled at him to run.

So he had run.

That had been only a short time earlier. He had circled around them and gotten ahead of the group. He watched the tall, evil-looking leader of the men who had captured his friends approach through the woods. He wanted nothing more than to leap out and kill the man, but his mother's warning for him to remain hidden kept him still.

Soon he saw his small group of friends march slowly past his hidden location, pushing through tall ferns and brush with their heads and shoulders because their hands were bound behind them in black irons. He watched his mother pass by and his heart dropped at the way her shoulders were slumped in exhaustion.

"Mother, are you in pain?"

Her thoughts floated over to him, *"No, I am fine, Maelon. Just the normal aches that an old woman like me has every day."*

Maelon knew she was lying so that he did not do anything stupid. She was the most selfless woman he had ever known. He twitched an ear as a mosquito buzzed inside of it and watched the kind mercenaries who had joined their group pass by in shackles, heads held high in pride. They were followed by the remaining evil men who wore blackened armour and helmets designed into shapes out of one's worst nightmare.

He could smell their unwashed bodies from where he hid, the smell hanging in the air like a foul evil. Soon, the last of them disappeared, the clanking of steel armour slowly fading away.

"Mother, I will come for you."

Her voice came back to him, though it sounded weaker, *"No, Maelon, whatever happens, I want you to stay safe. There is nothing you can do for us right now."*

He whimpered. *"But mother, there must be something I can do. Distract them, lead them away from you."*

"I know you think so, but these men are professionals and merciless, they will not leave us to chase you, or they may just send a few out to hunt you down. But it won't help us in the end. If anyone can save us, it will be the Aleph Null."

"*All right, mother, but I will be close by. I will never leave you.*"

Her voice caressed him with a sense of total love, "*I know that, dear. I take great comfort in your presence.*" Her voice grew stern. "*Now, stay back and unnoticed. Things will all work out fine.*"

He lay quietly underneath the fallen tree, hating himself for listening to her and doing nothing. It was the hardest thing he had ever had to do, even worse than putting himself into the clutches of Father Mansico for so many years. There was nothing that he could do to help his mother, or the Aleph Null and his friends. A sense of helplessness descended upon him, and he wanted to howl at the sky in frustration, but he held his voice, not wanting to announce his presence, even though the group of men were probably out of hearing distance.

Mosquitoes swarmed thickly around him, landing on his snout and in his ears, biting him everywhere he didn't have thick fur. He shook his head and the mosquitoes flew up in a small cloud, only to immediately land on him again. He crawled out from under the tree and listened carefully, then turned and followed behind the group, staying in the thickest parts of the woods to keep hidden.

After a short while he began to hear the clanking of metal on metal again, so he slowed down, slinking from tree to tree like a ghost.

Suddenly, a bolt of pain shot through him, burning through his mind unlike anything he had ever felt before.

He shot forward at a full run, panic blinding him.

Chapter 28

The daylight filtered weakly through the tall trees, and the air was thick and heavy. The forest was quiet, the ground covered with detritus from the previous winter. The leaves were starting to get thick and full on the trees, and insects of all kinds filled the air with a quiet hum. A small deer reached its mouth up and nibbled on a leaf, pulling it from the branch and chewing the succulent morsel quickly before reaching up to pull another leaf.

It stopped, the leaf hanging half out of its mouth. It angled its ears to the side and stayed perfectly still, the white spots on its brown fur making it blend into the forest perfectly. It stayed this way for a long time. It knew that predators were always close by, so staying perfectly still was its best defense.

Then it felt it.

The ground trembled slightly, and it heard a very distant crack of a branch. The deer began to tremble in fear, having never before felt such power traveling through the ground. It wanted to run away, its instinct strong, but the fear it felt rooted it to the spot. The ground trembled again, then again, and the deer now heard more branches breaking, growing nearer. Birds fluttered away in all directions, and small animals scuttled through the brush, running as quickly as they could. But the deer stood there, shaking, unable to move.

A tree crashed down and the ground shook over and over. The deer rolled its eyes upward as a colossal creature pushed aside a tree and loomed over it. The deer saw a hand come down and it was carried upward, high above the forest floor. It didn't struggle as the creature opened its mouth wide, then the deer felt nor heard anything more.

The Unnamed One finished eating the deer, but it was still hungry. It could never satisfy its hunger, no matter how much it ate. After a thousand years of starving in the cavern, its strength had diminished greatly. Now it was building it back up, but it needed protein constantly. It wavered between its need to consume flesh and its desire to follow the trail of Black Numbers, the scent intoxicating, fueling a need born from deep within the creature.

It raised its head to the sky and screamed, letting its frustration out. The deer had given it a little more energy and it began loping through the forest, pushing branches and small trees out of its way rather than going around them. It ran like this for some time when it suddenly stopped, moving its head back and forth and sniffing loudly. It caught a strange scent, one that it had never smelled before.

The forest was quiet, the trees all very old and tall. The creature stepped forward, directing its senses outward in all directions. It stopped when, from behind a tree not more than twenty five-paces in front of it, a creature stepped out and faced it.

Pain assaulted the Unnamed One, more pain than it had ever before felt. The pain flashed through its head in waves, white hot bursts that felt like fire. It put its hands to its head and screamed, its black tongue flickering in anger.

It charged the small creature, half-blinded, its need to destroy the offending thing overpowering the pain that assaulted it. As it approached the creature, the pain increased, almost completely blinding it.

But it kept charging.

The creature didn't back down, merely kept staring, its white fur and blue eyes almost glowing in the light. At the last moment, just before they impacted, the creature dove around the tree, and as it did, the pain lessened inside of its head and the Unnamed One screamed as it slid to a stop and peered around the tree.

Physical pain seared it again as the little creature leapt and quickly sliced long claws down its leg in a blur of speed and power. Before it could even respond, its leg was shredded with a number of deep bloody gashes.

It screamed to the sky in anger and pain, and swept its hands at the creature. But it hit nothing but air. It bent down and peered between its legs only to have pain assault its head once again as it looked into the large blue eyes of the creature standing not far away.

* * *

The Korpor released every bit of its power of pain into the giant creature as it looked between its legs. The Korpor had never seen this creature before, had never even known of its existence, but it knew that it was deadly, maybe even more dangerous than the Aleph Null.

The creature screamed, and the piercing sound, combined with the rank smell of its breath and open sores, assaulted the Korpor, causing it to lose concentration for a moment.

The creature spun around and charged the Korpor, screaming as it ran. The Korpor ducked and leapt forward, rolling between the creature's legs, swiping its claws as it passed by, cutting another gash in the fetid flesh.

The creature grabbed at a large tree and used it to swing its momentum around, surprising the Korpor with its agility. Before the Korpor could step back, the creature swung its long arm, connecting with the Korpor's shoulder, sending it flying back at least twenty paces. The Korpor tumbled through the leaves and brush, coming to a rest with a thud against a large tree. It fought the darkness that threatened to overcome it and cleared its vision just as the creature swung its hand downward. The Korpor dived to its right, the smash of the creature's fist on the ground throwing the Korpor off-balance.

Putting a paw to the ground to steady itself, the Korpor leapt onto the creature's leg and scrambled up its back, sinking its long claws into the rank flesh as an anchor to pull itself up. The Korpor heard the creature scream in pain and felt it spin around trying to reach behind it. The Korpor sunk its claws deeply into the shoulder of the creature to hold on, its feet flying out as the creature spun. The pus leaking from the open sores covered the Korpor's pristine fur, and as the creature stopped spinning, the Korpor reached up to sink its claws into the neck, hoping to kill it.

But the creature backed quickly toward a large tree, and the Korpor knew it was about to be crushed and abandoned its plan. It released its claws from the flesh and pushed away to its left as hard as it could just as the creature slammed into the tree, narrowly avoiding certain death. It landed lightly on the ground and took off running as fast as it could, zigzagging around trees in a blur of white fur.

The Korpor heard the creature scream behind it, then the heavy pounding of the ground as it gave chase. The Korpor had never run from anything in its life, but it ran as fast as it could now. Ducking under a large fallen tree, the Korpor turned left, slid down a gully, and leapt over a shallow stream, landing in the soft, loamy soil on the opposite side.

It jumped back into the stream and ran, hardly splashing any water, downstream. It heard a heavy thud far behind as it turned a sharp corner in the gully. It leapt from the stream to the shore and scrambled up the steep embankment and paused, its breath coming in short gasps. It turned to face the way it had come and heard the heavy pounding of the creature crashing through the trees in the opposite direction.

It stayed perfectly still even after the crashing of the creature faded completely away.

After a long time, the Korpor stretched, then slid down the embankment and lay in the cool water, letting the liquid wash most of the pus away. It stood up and shook itself violently, causing water to spray out in all directions until it was almost completely dry. The Korpor narrowed its eyes and started back the way that it had come until it found the spot where it had first met the creature.

It sniffed around the ground until it found the unique scent again, then melted into the forest, following the Aleph Null's trail.

Chapter 29

Tris paused, the quill raised just above the parchment as he felt the Korpor open their communication link in his mind. He set the quill back in its holder and sat back in his chair.

"What is it? You aren't due to report yet."

The voice of the Korpor had a strange quality that Tris had never before heard.

"A new development has presented itself."

Tris sighed. *"Well, what is it? I don't have all day."*

There was a momentary pause, as if the Korpor were carefully choosing its words. *"I had a rather... unpleasant confrontation."*

Intrigued, Tris waited for the Korpor to continue.

The Korpor began speaking after a short pause, *"A creature, at least three to four times my height, two-legged, gray-skinned, with a face that I am unable to describe fully, attacked me in the forest a half day back from the Aleph Null's position. I was forced to do battle with it, but was only able to scratch it a few times before barely escaping with my life."*

Tris was silent but his mind was spinning. He had never thought he would hear the Korpor say it had run from a fight, much less that there was a creature anywhere in the land that could even challenge the Korpor in a fight. Even though he controlled it, and would never admit this to anyone, he thought of the Korpor as the most frightening being in existence. What kind of creature could not only battle the Korpor, but also win, he had no idea.

He suddenly felt bumps rise along his arms.

The array he had accidentally released, of course! This creature must have been the thing that had been held prisoner inside of it.

He swallowed, his mouth suddenly dry. The Korpor had stayed quiet, waiting for him to respond, so he focused on his servant. *"Were you able to gather any information on its purpose, of what it was doing?"*

The Korpor immediately responded, *"We met on the trail of the Aleph Null. I don't think it was coincidence we met there. It is also following the boy."*

Tris nodded, even though he was speaking to the Korpor in his head. *"Well, this is a new variable to my equation, one that I need to think on for a bit. Continue following the Aleph Null's trail."*

"Yes... master."

"Oh, and one more thing. If this creature attacks Sid, I expect you to do everything you can to protect the Aleph Null, even if that means giving your life."

Tris waited, silence extending for a half-dozen heartbeats, before he heard the Korpor reply.

"Of course."

Then the link was broken.

Tris leaned his head back and stared at the ceiling.

What had he unleashed?

A knock sounded at the door of his chamber. "Yes?"

A Haissan entered the room and shut the door, then glided over to stop before his desk.

"Report."

The Haissan nodded, then hissed, "A Haissan came for the Aleph Null's mother during the night."

"And... ?"

"I do not know where they went. During one room check, the mother was sleeping. When I checked again, she was gone. I smelled a Haissan's lingering scent in the air. I immediately located a hidden door but didn't have the key with which to open it, so I waited until I heard footsteps approach behind the wall just before the sun rose. I left the room but listened at the door and heard the woman enter the room and say a few words, though I couldn't make them out. After a short while, I opened the door a crack and saw her asleep on her bed, the room empty of anyone else."

This was the most detailed report Tris had ever received from one of his Haissen. They rarely spoke more than a few words. He rearranged two other pieces of parchment on his desk as he spoke. "Interesting. Now I wonder where she was taken, and which of your mighty race has betrayed me." He pulled open a drawer in his desk, set the pages carefully inside, and slid it shut again.

The Haissan waited silently, not offering any guesses.

"Take the Aleph Null's mother from her room for the rest of the morning. I don't care where you take her."

"Of course." The Haissan immediately turned and left the room.

Tris struck his desk hard, then swept his arm across the wooden surface, viciously knocking the ink and quill across the floor, staining his ancient and irreplaceable rug black, although he didn't even notice. Two surprises had hit him back-to-back this morning, two things he had not planned for or foreseen, making his hands shake with rage. He pushed himself back from the desk and stood up.

He would just have to see where Lorielle was taken.

He left his chamber and made his way to her chamber, opening the door without pausing. It was empty already... his Haissen were very efficient. He immediately found the spot where the hidden door was located and studied the stone. It apparently could only be unlocked from the other side, so he sent his numbers into the stone and moved them around until he sensed the locking mechanism. He nudged numbers against it but it was a complex series of gears that couldn't just be physically nudged open with his numbers. Fortunately, he didn't need to do that.

His numbers moved around the lock and gave him a three-dimensional view of how it worked. The equation needed wasn't that difficult and he put it together almost without thinking. With the final variable, he glided the equation into the slot on the other side of the door. It fit perfectly and the gears turned silently until the door clicked open. A whoosh of cold air passed over him, but he ignored it and pulled the door open wider. It was dark beyond it, so he created a simple spinning equation that lit the space with a blue light.

He followed the turning hallway until he came to a steep set of curving stairs and descended them without hesitating. At the bottom, he quickly opened the half-door with the same equation he had used on the first door and bent down to step through. The short hall ended with another door. He sent the same equation into the locking mechanism, but it didn't turn.

He furrowed his brow and tried to send his numbers into the stone to see the lock, but they bounced back at him. He had never before experienced something like this.

Anger filled him. He had never been one to be denied anything. He closed his eyes and created the equation that Agnes had thrown at him during the challenge of ascension, one of nothingness. It instantly appeared in front of him, a swirling vortex of darkness. He violently threw it at the door, intending to dissolve the stone itself.

As the equation contacted the stone of the door, it began to eat the very stone, spreading across the door like a cold, colorless flame eating parchment.

Tris smiled cruelly and watched in satisfaction as the stone disappeared before his eyes. It would only be a few more moments before he was able to step through, although even waiting this short period of time made him impatient. He tapped his foot on the stone floor and was about to sigh with impatience when he heard a sizzling inside the stone as the void equation contacted the equation that had been protecting the door. He grinned, knowing there was nothing that he could not do.

A change of pressure blocked his ear drums and he looked around him to see what had caused it but didn't see anything. Then, from behind the door he heard a loud whump sound, followed by another change in air pressure. His void equation had just about eaten completely through the stone door in one spot, when he got a bad feeling.

As the equation dissolved the last bit of stone away he saw fire shoot through the opening. Without thinking, he put up a wall of numbers as quickly as he could blink. The fire was so strong, though, that he and his wall of numbers were blown back against the wall, the flames white hot in front of him. He was not burned, but his head hit the stone hard.

Through stars he saw the flame grow as his void equation

continued to eat at the door and open the hole wider. He turned and ran down the short hall as fast as he could and dove through the half-door, slamming it shut behind him. Flames shot around the edges and then were cut off. The wooden door began to sizzle on the other side and Tris leapt up the stairs two at a time, stumbling on a few and skinning his knees. He turned his head and created a wall of numbers across the stairwell behind him just as the door far below blew open.

Flames raced up the stairwell and slammed into his wall of numbers. He concentrated on the wall, keeping it solid. After a few moments the flames turned orange, then yellow, and then finally flickered and dissipated until he saw nothing but smoke behind his wall.

Shaking, Tris sat down on the step and put his head into his hands, catching his breath. He had underestimated whomever had placed the equation traps inside the room behind the door and it had almost gotten him killed. The fact that he had never before come across an equation trap didn't matter, he was still angry at himself for not seeing the trap before he triggered it.

The smoke started to dissipate behind his wall of numbers so he released them. He held his breath as the remainder of the smoke shot past him and up the stairs. Within moments, the stairwell was relatively free of smoke so he made his way back down the step and through the opening where the half-door had been but was now just a blackened hole, still smoldering. The short hall was blackened from soot and the stone floor was covered with deep grey ash, causing his shoes to puff with each step, covering his clothing as he went.

He approached the large hole in the wall and saw that his equation was still eating away at the stone, and was just about to start eating at the stone ceiling. He dismantled the equation with barely a thought. He didn't want the ceiling to give way on top of him.

He peered through the hole and his eyes widened slightly at the sight before him. The chamber was large, with cubbyholes covering every bit of every wall. But whatever had been inside of them had been completely incinerated by the fire. Ash covered the floor, the walls were blackened, and in the middle of the room he could see the charred remains of what had once been a large table. The room had obviously been a repository of thousands of scrolls, manuscripts, and who knows what else. The amount of ash that covered the floor mocked him at the knowledge that had been lost.

There was nothing left.

Tris grew angry all over again and turned away from the scene in front of him. He looked down at his soot-covered clothing, hands, and most likely his face, then stomped back the way he had come, growing angrier the further he climbed.

He was going to have an interesting conversation with Lorielle.

Chapter 30

The early morning dawned blood-red, and the air was sticky with moisture as Agnes threw back her sweat-soaked blanket and crawled to her feet. The camp was already active, with small fires burning all over with metal spits holding various animal carcasses being roasted for breakfast. She could hear the constant sizzle as fat dripped into the fires and the smell made her mouth water, but she would eat later. Agnes turned and squinted toward the Masteen's tent, then spun around to take in the camp. Something seemed wrong. There were fewer men lying around, standing, or talking, than normal. In fact, it was eerily quiet.

She didn't know what was going on, so stretching her back, she set off to the Masteen's tent to find out. Her Haissan walked behind her and slightly to her left as always. She was still not entirely used to having the creature always so close to her, but she had learned to appreciate having it around to protect her. She had once briefly caught a glimpse of the creature's face inside of the hood and the pale, alien-looking image had burned into her memory, one that she wished she could forget.

When she approached the Masteen's tent, she was stopped by three of the nastier-looking men in the death squad, his hand-picked inner guards.

She put her chin up and squared her shoulders, trying to look confident, but next to these men she felt small and weak. "I want to speak with the Masteen."

The men didn't even look at her, which made her angry. "I said, I will speak with the Masteen right now," and she tried to push past them, but she stopped immediately when the point of a sword touched her throat. She looked up at the man and he wasn't even looking at her. She was nothing but an irritation to him.

Agnes was about to step back when the blade slowly lowered from her throat and she saw the huge man's eyes grow wide in surprise. Then she saw the Haissan's blade against the man's neck, a thick trickle of blood slowly welling up against the steel.

She saw the other two men pull their swords out, each of them grinning in anticipation of a fight, which was not something she wanted to happen. No matter how good the Haissan was, it would not defeat everyone in the camp before they were both cut down. She glanced at the hooded figure next to her. Well at least she thought it would not be able to kill everyone in the camp, although the deadly stillness the Haissan emanated made her wonder what would actually happen.

She backed up and motioned with her hand for the Haissan to

lower its sword. She needed the Masteen and his men to kill the Black Robe. The Haissan whipped its sword in a circle so quickly that the air whistled as it returned it to its scabbard. It faced the group of men as if nothing had happened.

The man with the bloody neck stood still for a moment, rage boiling in his eyes. Before he could decide what to do, Agnes turned around and walked slowly toward her bedroll. The Haissan shadowed her steps. She expected the men to chase her, but she kept walking without looking back. She breathed a sigh of relief when she reached her blankets. That had very nearly turned into a blood bath.

Agnes sat down on her blanket and faced the Masteen's tent. Two of the guards ignored her, but the one with the bloody neck glared at her Haissan, his face still twisted in barely controlled rage. He was trained too well to leave the Masteen's tent, which she now knew was empty.

For some reason, the Masteen must have left in the night, taking with him a large number of his men. What he was up to, she didn't know, but there was nothing she could do, so she got up and went into the woods to relieve her full bladder and bowels, then returned to her bedroll and washed her hands with some of her water. Then she walked to one of the fires and cut a chunk of meat from the blackened carcass of what had once been the hind-quarters of a deer, ignoring the nasty comments some of the men made as they leered at her, then returned back to her bedroll to eat and wait.

By mid-day she was anxiously pacing around the area, slogging through mud that had been turned up from the soldiers and horses. She saw a large group of men working by the edge of the camp so she made her way over to them and saw that they were digging a deep pit. It was already at least three times as deep as she was tall and about eight paces across. The men were bare to the waist and digging furiously, while other men hauled muddy dirt out in buckets tied to lengths of rope. She remembered the Masteen ordering the pit to be dug, and the only thing she could think of was that it was a primitive prison.

Soon the men finished and pulled themselves out hand-over-hand up a rope ladder. She got a bad feeling as she made her way back to her bedroll. Something was going on that was not part of the plan, and she knew the Masteen was a devious and merciless man.

Suddenly she heard a commotion from the other side of the camp. She turned her head and saw the Masteen and at least thirty of his men enter the camp on foot. She angled over in that direction, coming to stop in front of them as they approached from the opposite direction. Agnes was about to ask him where he had been when she saw the small group of people being escorted behind him, and she could only stand there, speechless.

What had the Masteen done?

First she saw a man as tall as the Masteen, but young and good-looking, although his face was now bloody and bruised. When she finally took her eyes from him, she locked down and saw an old woman with wispy red hair hobbling slowly along, a pained look on her face, and next to her was a younger woman with darkened eyes and pale skin who didn't look very well.

Behind the two women strode a small but burly man looking quite stern and tough, and she started when she realized that he was a Vringe. She had never seen such a hard-looking Vringe, they were always soft and weak.

Trailing the Vringe was a thin young man with his head hung down, long hair covering his face. And behind him followed three tough-looking men, their heads held high and eyes bright with anger. She knew they were mercenaries from their gear. Why mercenaries were chained up with the others, Agnes did not know.

As the group came to a stop in front of her, the young man pushed his way forward from the back of the group and stopped next to the tall one, his head still down. As Agnes watched, he lifted his head and casually flipped his hair back, and they locked eyes immediately.

She took an involuntary short breath and her heart suddenly felt like it was vibrating in her chest.

Something happened to her as she looked into his eyes. She felt strength fill her, entering her all at once, and she immediately felt like she had known this young man her entire life.

Chapter 31

Sid trudged behind the group, surrounded by the foul-smelling men who had captured them. For some reason, his numbers felt sluggish when he was near the Masteen, like they were mired in mud. And as soon as he tried to control one number, it would chaotically fall away when he reached for another number. He couldn't do anything to help his friends, nor see any way out of their situation.

Sid glanced over at Tulman and smiled slightly, remembering how the man's eyes had shown brightly with respect and awe when Crowdal had smashed the Masteen to the ground, and Sid had a feeling that Tulman would now follow Crowdal anywhere, even to his own death. Sid shook his chained wrists behind his back, although it was a perfunctory gesture than anything.

Despair descended fully upon him. When they finally came to a stop, he kept his head down, not really caring what was happening. But when it appeared that they would not start walking again, he pushed forward to Crowdal's side and lifted his head, flicking his hair from his eyes to see where they were. But before he could take in the area around him, he felt a pull in one direction so he immediately focused to his left, and all of his breath escape in a rush.

There she was, her green eyes flashing, standing only a few paces in front of him. It was the woman from his vision and she was beautiful beyond belief. A force struck him with a power that almost buckled his knees as their eyes locked on each other. Everything around him, all sound, all senses faded away as he stared into those amazing green eyes of hers. Sid felt his power of numbers escape from the dulling frequency that had kept him from accessing them. Now they were so clear in his mind, he felt he could do anything.

His trance was broken by the sound of the Masteen's deep voice.

"Take them to the pit." The huge man glared at each of his men and rasped, "and do not be gentle with them."

Sid was punched in his lower back and he stumbled forward, having to take a few quick steps to keep from falling. He turned in time to see each of his friends get punched in the back also, and he seethed in anger when he saw one of the guards put all of his weight into his blow to Mrs. Wessmank's back. She arched at an impossible angle and then slammed hard to the ground, face first. When she didn't move, the large man stepped forward and kicked her viciously in the side with his steel boot and laughed as he ordered her to get up, but she just lay on the ground, unmoving.

Sid screamed and tried to go to her but was held back by one of the ugly guards. The Masteen merely chuckled as he turned away and marched to his tent, his footfalls so heavy that the ground vibrated slightly with each step.

The large man bent down, picked Ms. Wessmank up, and threw her over his shoulder like a sack of potatoes. Filled with rage, Sid was about to call his numbers when he was punched again in the back and he fell to his knees, his mind spinning with pain.

The guard who had hit him pulled him up by his hair and dragged him across the muddy ground to the edge of a large pit. It was at least twice as deep as Crowdal was tall, and the sides were sheer. Before he could catch his balance, he was shoved forward and fell heavily to the muddy bottom of the pit, landing hard on his side, unable to break his fall due to the chains around his wrists. He lay there for a few moments, trying to get his breath back, then pushed himself up into a sitting position.

He heard six more impacts around him as Crowdal, Melinda, Writhgarth, and the three mercenaries were pushed in. Sid looked up and saw the last guard flip Mrs. Wessmank from his shoulders and hold her body over the edge, a twisted smile on his face. Then, with a wink to Sid, he threw her like so much garbage into the center of the pit.

Sid struggled to stand up, but because his hands were bound by chains behind his back, he couldn't get leverage. He closed his eyes and formed the equation for steel, taking into account the different metals that made up the alloy. With a mental flick, he sent the equation into the links and they burst apart with a small flash and pop, freeing his hands. He sent the same equation into his friends chains and heard them fall to the ground with a metallic jingle.

Sid quickly scrambled over to Mrs. Wessmank. Her face was white and her breathing came in short, ragged intervals as she lay on her back. Two ribs stuck through her chest, piercing her shirt where her lungs were, white bones covered in white, viscous flesh and dark blood. Tears welled up in his eyes as he bent down and stroked her wrinkled face, still so soft to his fingers.

At his touch, Mrs. Wessmank cracked open her eyes and looked up at him with pain and sadness. She reached up a trembling muddy hand and caressed his face, then rasped in short breaths, "Sidoro... I... am... sorry... I... will not... be... here... for you... any... longer." A cough wracked her body and she started to sob like a child. Then she coughed violently again, the movement causing a third rib to slip through the hole in her chest and she began to shriek from the pain.

Sid held her down to keep her from moving and he gasped when a fourth rib cut through her chest and shirt. Every rib in her side must have been shattered by the kick, and he knew that when the guard had dropped her into the pit, her lungs and many of her organs had probably been shredded by the broken bones.

A soft, sucking sound escaped her lips and a bubble of blood popped as she opened her mouth. Her eyes became wild and unfocused. Then she arched her back one more time and rasped out a hoarse scream of pain that lasted for many moments before it faded and her back settled to the ground. Mrs. Wessmank took one last shallow breath and held it as she locked her eyes on Sid. She moved her lips, trying to speak, but then her eyes lost all focus and her face fell slack.

She stared up at him, unmoving.

Sid smelled the release of her bowels and the finality of her death hit him like a punch to the gut.

He squeezed his eyes shut for a few moments, then reached forward and gently caressed her eyelids one at a time, shutting them. He bent down and kissed the birth marks that looked like eyes on her forehead, then caressed her frizzy red hair back from her face. She looked calm now, free from pain. He hung his head for a brief moment and then stood up.

He saw Crowdal, Melinda, Writhgarth, and the three mercenaries stand up also, not even aware that they had been kneeling next to him the whole time. He saw the sadness in their eyes and Melinda reached out to comfort him, but he turned away.

Crowdal put a hand on Sid's shoulder. "Sid, I'm so sorry."

A chuckle drifted to them and he glanced up to see the guards looking down at them, grins on their faces. The one who had kicked Mrs. Wessmank and thrown her into the pit, laughed outright, the sound dark and cruel.

A darkness filled Sid, a wall of quiet rage that calmed his mind. He locked his eyes on the laughing guard and walked to the glistening muddy wall of the pit and just stood there, staring up him.

The guard kicked clumps of wet dirt over the edge and laughed harder as it struck his face, but he just closed his eyes until the last of it had fallen.

When Sid re-opened his eyes and again locked his gaze on that of the guard, the man's laughter quickly stopped. Confusion and fear spread across his face, then his eyes started to bulge out and the skin on his face started to bubble up like it was being burned. He put his hands to his face and when he lowered them, bloody skin hung from his fingers.

He screamed, the sound full of terror.

Spittle flew out of his mouth as the scream turned into a shrieking wail. Blood started to seep from the man's eyes and nose. He put his hands up to his eyes, trying to stop the bleeding, but it quickly turned into a spray of red as his eyes blew out of his head into his own hands. He reeled back, flailing his arms like a madman. Then, with one final, ear-piercing screech, his head exploded in all directions at once; brain, bone, and blood showering all of his fellow mercenaries, who all stared at him in horror.

The headless body swayed, then tumbled forward, landing with a thud at Sid's feet.

Sid calmly looked down at the body, then lifted his eyes up to the men standing around the rim, who quickly stepped back out of sight.

Sid continued staring up at the rim, not moving, waiting for someone else to appear.

Writhgarth ran shaky hands through his hair, and his voice cracked slightly as he whispered, "Good gods!"

* * *

Not far away, just past the treeline, Maelon felt the death of the woman who had been like his mother hit him with a force unlike any he had ever felt. He reached out to her, whimpering softly when he could not find her presence anywhere. He cast his mind out in all directions, searching in a panic for her loving essence, but all he felt was a cold emptiness pressing back against him.

He howled at the sky, feeling truly alone in the world, as if half of him had been ripped away. It was a pain worse than any beating he had taken at the hands of Father Mansico.

His legs buckled and he fell to his side, his head striking the ground hard.

He closed his eyes and lay unmoving, hot tears running down his soft fur and dropping to the cold ground.

Chapter 32

The numbers swirled in the darkness as if alive, mixing together to form long formula that grew until they stretched away like tails of a shooting star. Lorielle rejoiced at the ease with which she manipulated the mathematical equations. The past ten years seemed like a bad nightmare of how she had been unable to even understand the concept of mathematics. It had been like a piece of her had been ripped out and the gaping hole where her mathematics knowledge had been roiled in a dark void that she had dared not enter.

Now she reveled at how easy it all was. Even the most complex mathematical formula now seemed like an old friend whom she had gotten to know again after many years. She reached out and lifted the cup of tea, took a sip of the steaming liquid, and glanced around her. She sat at a table in a communal dining room. It was large and filled with many simple tables, each with six chairs. It was empty at the moment, although not too long ago six Haissen had finished eating, not even glancing at her as they left.

She picked up a chicken leg, took a small bite of the white flesh, and set the greasy meat back down in distaste.

She had been taken from her chamber by a Haissan without being given any reason and brought here. She hadn't argued because there was no use arguing with a Haissan. The food was welcome, and she used the time to practice manipulating her numbers and reflect on what Tierre had told her.

She still had a difficult time believing the Haissen were responsible for everything that had happened over the past two thousand years: the origination of the Oblate, the Aleph Null prophecy, the creation of the Korpor. She shuddered at the thought of the creature. It was almost too much information to digest properly, so she put it to the back of her mind and thought of Sidoro. He was out there, enemies were converging on him, and she was stuck here in the Oblate. But she felt a renewed sense of hope. She now had control of her mathematics again, and she would bide her time until she could help her son.

The door opened behind her. It was probably more of the Haissen coming to get something to eat. But instead, she heard only a single set of footsteps directly approach her. Just before she turned her head, she caught a whiff of charred wood and before she could move, she felt a hand on her shoulder.

"So nice to see you here, cousin."

She looked up into Tristian's face. His hair was damp and his robe was crisp and fresh-smelling, but she caught the slightest scent of burned ash.

"You don't mind if I join you, do you?" He sat down next to her and casually crossed a leg over the other.

Lorielle shrugged.

"Have you been comfortable here so far?"

She sighed. "What do you want, Tristian?"

"Please, call me Tris. Tristian sounds so... formal."

She shrugged, not caring. "All right, what do you want, Tris."

He spread his hands. "What, can't we have a nice talk like family?"

"We may be related, but I do not consider you my family."

Tris shrank back in mock horror. "You wound me, cousin. Fine, if that is how you want to play this, that is all right with me. I never have been one for family, anyway. They are always a disappointment, aren't they?"

She looked directly at him. "Yes, they are."

He chuckled quietly. "I had the most interesting morning."

Lorielle raised her left eyebrow. "I'm so happy for you. Now if you don't mind, I am in the middle of my meal." She turned away from him and picked up her chicken leg, but before she could take a bite, she yelped and dropped it back on her plate. It sizzled and turned black in front of her.

"I don't like rudeness. Now, if I can have your undivided attention, I will continue."

Pushing the plate away from her, Lorielle sat back and faced her cousin with another sigh. "Fine. I'll repeat my question. What do you want?"

He leaned back and picked at a fingernail. "Oh, I was just wondering who contacted you last night and where they took you."

A chill ran through her and she forced herself to remain calm, to keep her expression unchanged, although she was not shocked that he had knowledge of her rendezvous the previous night. She only hoped he didn't know the details. She had to count on this and give enough truth to ensure he believed her. So she spoke calmly, "Apparently you have some reason to bring this up so I won't play games and say something inane like, 'I don't know what you are talking about.' I was met by a Haissan who wanted to talk to me."

Tris looked up at her, picking at a nail. "Is that so. Interesting. And who was this Haissan?"

"How should I know? They all look alike to me."

"What did this Haissan have to say?"

She shrugged her shoulders. "It wanted to tell me that it was on the side of the Aleph Null, that we had friends who wanted to help us."

Tris leaned forward, giving up the charade that he wasn't that interested. "There is more to it than you are telling me, so don't think you can tell me half-truths and I will be satisfied."

Lorielle had expected him to say this, he was very smart. So she lowered her eyes to her lap, looking guilty.

"Tell me, Lorielle, or I will hurt you."

She shook her head. "I won't betray the creature. Even though I dislike the Haissen, this one was trying to help me. I can take the pain."

Tris smiled. "Oh, I'm sure you can. But it isn't you that I will hurt. When I catch Sid, I will make him suffer and make you watch while I do it. So again, I'd like to hear the entire truth now, if you please."

She picked at her robe for a few moments, then sighed heavily and let her shoulders slump. She was sure he knew about the chamber, he was too powerful not to have figured it out. She only hoped that Tierre had expected this to happen. The smell of burned ash that emanated from him told her he had been involved in some kind of fire, and the fact that she had been taken from her chamber meant that he had been told of the secret door and had followed it to the secret library. She felt sickened at the thought that Tierre had destroyed the entire library to keep him from such amazing information. That was dedication that gave her strength.

She spoke haltingly, "It... took me to a chamber underground that was filled with scrolls. We only had a short time so it showed me a scroll that mentioned Black Numbers, that the Aleph Null would save the world from darkness. It wanted me to not give up on my son."

Tris studied her for a long time. Then he probed her with his numbers. She had been ready for it and kept all of her defenses down, hiding her numbers behind complex walls that were impossible to see. It was difficult to let him inside of her and not fight him, but she pretended that she didn't know what he was doing.

The numbers withdrew from her and he sat back, seemingly satisfied. "Well, isn't that nice. I shall have to find this Haissan and have a talk with it. I am sorry to say that what it said was just fantasy, but if it makes you feel better, then by all means, believe what you want." He stood up. "Now, if you'll excuse me, I have business to attend to."

Lorielle watched him leave, and as the door closed, she sat back and clenched her hands together to keep them from trembling. That had been one of the most difficult things she had done. His touch had been vile, feeling like a slimy slug moving through her brain.

She thought of Sidoro and would give anything right now to see him, to know he was safe. And unbidden, she thought of her mother Elenora, wondering if she were still in her tobacco and tea shop in Orm-Mina. She had not seen her mother in ten years and missed her greatly.

A sharp pain struck her then, causing her vision to briefly go black. She cried out, putting her hands to her head. After a few moments the pain flared again, causing her to fall to the floor. She curled into a ball and rocked back and forth as the pain increased.

A Haissan immediately entered the room and checked her pulse. It then picked her up and carried her to her chamber.

She didn't notice the smell of smoke lingering in the room, she couldn't concentrate on anything except the pain of loss.

The Haissan lay her in her bed and checked her pulse again. She opened her eyes and managed to tell the creature that she was fine. It didn't question her and immediately left.

As the door closed, she sobbed out loud.

Her mother was dead and her death had been brutal and painful.

She cried into her covers, the sobs wracking her body for a long time.

Chapter 33

Agnes had watched in horror as the old woman had been kicked, probably a death blow, and then saw the small group of people get thrown into the pit, including the young man who had taken her breath away.

She didn't know what to do now. Everything had changed, the Masteen was not supposed to have interfered with the Aleph Null. The Black Robe's plan was quickly unraveling and she knew that she should contact him to tell him what had happened. But as she thought this, she realized with a clarity beyond anything she had ever known before that she wanted to help the Aleph Null no matter what happened to her.

Just as she realized this, she heard a scream come from the pit that sent shivers down her spine. She instinctively knew it was the old woman. Sadness filled her, for even though she hadn't known the old woman, she had the distinct feeling that she had been an amazing person.

When the scream turned to a wail, tears fell from her eyes. She looked toward the Masteen's tent, but he didn't emerge. She focused on the pit. It was ringed with guards who leaned over the edge to watch the spectacle. Anger filled her at the inhumanity of the situation. The wailing stopped and she knew the old woman had succumbed to death.

Agnes heard the guard who had dropped the woman into the pit start to laugh, a deep and evil sound. She started forward, to yell at the guard, but she only got half-way there when she saw him grab at his face and start to scream.

She stopped, her mouth open. The guard's scream turned to a shriek of pain, and then to her horror, his head just flew apart in all directions. Blood, bone, and brain landed with a squish all around. The man's headless body stood up for a moment, then toppled forward into the pit with a crash of armor. She had no idea what had just happened. The other guards quickly backed away from the edge, and she saw fear in their eyes. She sprinted to the pit and slid to a stop at the edge. Her Haissan shadowed her so closely that she didn't even notice it.

She wasn't entirely sure what she was going to do, but she didn't hesitate as she leaned over the edge. She immediately saw the Aleph Null standing directly below her and when their eyes locked, she was sure of her path. She quickly looked around the top of the pit and saw a rope ladder piled on the ground not far away, two of its ends attached to thick wooden posts. She ran over to it and kicked it over the edge, then leaned over and yelled out, "Hurry, climb out now!"

The guards saw her kick the ladder and they immediately lunged forward to grab her. The closest to Agnes was cut down by her

Haissan, and as the others thundered to a stop near the pit's edge, they fell to their knees grabbing their heads, screaming in pain. One by one their heads exploded, blowing backwards. Thankfully, Agnes and her Haissan were spared being splattered with the blood and gore.

She looked into the pit and saw the calm but unfocused look in the Aleph Null's eyes. The remaining few guards fell back again, not wanting to show themselves to the monster in the pit.

Agnes watched the tall man push the beautiful but exhausted woman to the ladder, then the short man followed her up, as well as the three mercenaries. The tall man then ran to the Aleph Null and spoke to him quietly. She couldn't hear what he said but it worked; the young man's eyes cleared, he nodded curtly, and quickly climbed out of the pit, followed closely by the huge man. They all stood facing the guards, who weren't sure if they should attack or run away.

A horn started to blow from somewhere in the camp, which broke the hesitancy in the guards and they charged. Agnes turned to the group. "Quickly, we have to get out of here." But even as she said this, the remaining guards fell to the ground as one, screaming in pain. Agnes saw the Aleph Null's eyes glint with a mixture of anger and joy.

The tall man grabbed the young man by the shoulders. "Sid, that's enough. We have to go now."

The young man nodded and turned away from the guards, and as he did, the foul men all fell silent and looked around, stunned at their luck to be alive. Then, as one, their heads exploded and their bodies collapsed to the ground in a clatter of armor. The Aleph Null didn't even glance back. He had just killed twelve of the Masteen's men, something that, up until a few moments earlier, Agnes wouldn't have believed was possible.

The tall man turned to Agnes. "Can you tell us where the Masteen's horses are located?"

Fortunately, the pit was near the edge of the camp, and the horses were in a make-shift corral made of brush not far away. Agnes nodded quickly and pointed across the pit. "Come on, follow me." She sprinted around the pit toward the treeline.

The group followed her and they slid to a stop just as she was pulling aside the large branch that blocked the entrance to the primitive corral. Fortunately, many of the horses still had saddles on them because the Masteen's men did not take good care of their animals.

Agnes climbed onto a gray horse, and watched as the tall man helped the Vringe, who was too short to reach the stirrup, onto the saddle of one of the smaller horses. The other woman climbed onto a horse, and the Aleph Null and three mercenaries slid comfortably into the saddles of the horses closest to them.

Agnes turned back to face the trees and saw her Haissan sitting on a horse right next to her. She was momentarily startled that she hadn't even noticed it by her side, but she immediately ignored it and faced the group. "We can cut through the forest that way to reach the trail." She pointed behind her toward the thick forest.

The large man, still standing on the ground, nodded and then chose the Masteen's huge stallion and leapt onto it. The warhorse stomped, but the man got him under control and yelled, "Come on, ride!"

He led the charge out of the corral and immediately turned to his left and pounded through the brush and around trees. The rest of them quickly followed and they ducked their heads to keep from getting whipped in the face by branches.

Agnes could hear angry shouts behind her. Over all of the din, the loud and deep voice of the Masteen bellowed orders, and even as she rode away, Agnes could hear the rage in his voice and the pounding of men as they raced toward the corral.

The branches continued to whip at them until they came upon the trail that stretched north and south. They pulled on the reins and the horses slid to a stop, stomping and neighing in agitation from the fast ride through the woods.

The large man spoke calmly, "Which way?"

They all turned to the Aleph Null, or Sid, as she had heard the tall man call the young man.

Sid looked around, ignoring the question. "Where is Maelon? Has anyone seen him?"

Agnes had no idea who he was referring to.

The tall man shook his head. "I haven't seen him since we were captured. I think he is safe. But we have to ride now!"

Sid looked around one last time, then turned his horse north. "This way."

Agnes didn't hesitate as she followed them at a gallop, racing north.

Chapter 34

The Korpor hid behind a large tree not far from the trail, watching the dust settle from the horses as the Aleph Null and his small group galloped away. It turned its head slightly, then blinked its left eye followed by its right eye. It didn't like the change of events. Things seemed to be out of control, and it was worried. Strange and powerful forces were at work.

First it was the Zranh who had done something to the young woman, something that made the Korpor nervous. Then it was the encounter with the violent and ancient creature in the woods. And now it was the arrogant Masteen who had captured the group instead of just shadowing it like he was supposed to do.

The Black Robe had told the Korpor about how the Masteen had a strange power to dull the Aleph Null's control of numbers. It was why the Black Robe had chosen the Masteen to shadow the Aleph Null. But somehow, there was a connection that the seemingly inconsequential Red Robe sparked with the Aleph Null, releasing the boy's numbers from the nullifying effect of the Masteen. It knew that not even the Black Robe had expected that to happen. The Korpor had been about to contact the Black Robe with this latest news when the old woman had been killed. The creature had felt the shift in the boy's psyche, an almost physical blow to the link they shared through the *Ringing*.

Where before the boy was timid and scared to use his powers, the woman's death had destroyed any hesitancy the boy had about killing. That was a problem. The Black Robe wanted the boy to remain weak and unfocused.

The last of the dust settled back to the ground along the trail, and the Korpor stepped further back in the trees as the remaining Karillon death squad, the giant Masteen leading them, thundered past and charged north down the trail. As the last of the men passed, the Korpor stepped from behind the tree and watched the group until it disappeared into the horizon. A large bumblebee buzzed by its face and the Korpor sliced it in half with one claw without even looking.

It closed its eyes and made the connection to the Black Robe.

"Things have changed, master."

The dark voice of the Black Robe filled the Korpor's mind and the creature was again amazed by the power of the young man who called himself the Black Robe. *"Changed? How so, my pet?"*

"The Masteen tried to capture the Aleph Null and failed."

The Black Robe was silent for a few moments, then spoke in a tightly controlled voice, *"I suspected the Masteen might try this. What happened? Tell me everything.*"

The Korpor told the Black Robe everything that had happened since the capture, ending with the Aleph Null's escape, the suspected change in the Aleph Null when the old woman had died, as well as his connection with the Red Robe and her defection.

The Black Robe was silent for a long time and the Korpor began to wonder if he had broken the connection, when he finally said, "*They are still traveling north, so all may not be lost. But this does change my plans.*"

There was silence again for a long moment, and then the Black Robe continued, his voice sounding a little excited even to the Korpor, "*Send me your coordinates. I will join you now, much earlier than I planned. I had wanted to avoid the long trek to the Srithian Wood, planning to use your location once you made your way there before creating my transport equation, but it looks like things are about to get interesting, and I need to be there.*"

The Korpor shivered slightly, not wanting the Black Robe to join it yet, but it had no choice. It opened up its mind fully and showed the Black Robe the entire path it had taken to this place, letting the Black Robe see exactly where it was. It was a special bond they shared that allowed the Black Robe to open a physical doorway between them.

The Black Robe broke the connection and the Korpor waited patiently. The area was quiet now and the Korpor relished the silence. It really didn't like being around so many humans, they were noisy and smelled terrible, and their minds were chaotic and dull. The sun hung directly above the Korpor, warming it almost to the point of being uncomfortable, and the creature began to grow sleepy as the wait dragged on.

* * *

Lorielle was shaken awake but she pushed the hand away. She didn't want to leave the warmth and darkness. She had dreamed of seeing her mother while she had been held prisoner by the Faussian Monks. Their relationship had been rocky after she had married Danicu. Her mother hadn't wanted her to, but never told her why. But after Sidoro had been born, they had grown close again, although Danicu had never been even remotely friendly with Elenora. She had chalked it up to Danicu just being Danicu. He had never been one to show much emotion, but he was handsome and brilliant with mathematics. She had never met another man who could talk so intimately with her about equations and formula. And then came that fateful day when she had woken up in the prison, alone and without any knowledge of mathematics anymore, wondering what Danicu had done with Sidoro and her mother.

Her mother!

She sobbed.

Her mother was dead!

The realization hit her hard and she wanted nothing more than the blackness of sleep to take her once more, to dull the pain.

The hand shook her harder and she felt cold water splash her face. She sat up, sputtering and cursing, only to see a Haissan calmly standing next to her bed as if it had all the time in the world. She wiped water from her eyes. "Why did you do that?"

The Haissan didn't even look at her. "Get dressed in travel clothing, we are leaving now."

She was tempted to hurl a single number to blind the creature, but she held back and pushed the thick blanket away and swung her legs over the edge of the bed. The cool air against her wet skin made her shiver as she stood up. A fresh set of clothing was laid out on the table. She angrily picked them up and stepped behind a screen to change into them.

She spoke over the screen. "Where are we going?"

Her only answer was silence, as she had expected. She buttoned her shirt up and stepped from behind the screen.

The Haissan was holding the door open, so she walked out, her head held high.

The Haissan led her down the hallway, up some stairs, and through a series of doors until they finally stepped outside. She saw a large courtyard, and to her right a stable that could house at least a hundred horses. It was after midday and the air was crisp and clean-smelling after the dampness of the building. She inhaled deeply and let it out, feeling the sun on her face for the first time in days. She heard a horse neigh and stomp its feet, causing the harness to jingle. Lined up were twenty-eight horses. Twenty-six Haissen stood calmly by their horses, holding their reins. At the lead, standing next to a large black stallion, was Tris, glaring at her impatiently.

"Any time now, cousin."

Lorielle approached the gray stallion next to Tris. It turned its head toward her as she approached and neighed softly. She ran her hand along its nose, the hair coarse but clean. Its huge black eyes rolled upward and it neighed again and stepped sideways away from her.

Tris chuckled. "It appears he doesn't like you."

She grabbed the bridle. "I can't imagine how badly you treat him, it is no wonder he doesn't like people."

Tris chuckled again. "Only you would care about something so insignificant as a horse. They are dumb animals I'd just as soon boil for their fat as ride. Unfortunately, that is what we have to do now."

He then turned away from her, closed his eyes, and began whispering.

The courtyard grew quiet. Lorielle didn't know what her cousin was planning to do, but she held her tongue and watched. Nothing happened at first and she grew impatient, anxious to finally be traveling again, hopefully toward her son. She reached up and pushed a strand of black hair streaked with gray away from her eyes and tucked it behind her ear, then felt the air change in front of her. She resisted using any of her mathematics to examine it for fear that her cousin would sense her abilities. So she just watched, fascinated despite her hatred for the young man.

About five paces in front of Tris, the air turned dark and crackled as it coalesced into a shape. The air hummed as the shape formed a square large enough to walk through.

Tris opened his eyes and turned to her. "Hold the reins tightly as you lead your horse through. It won't like this much." He then walked toward the strange opening and disappeared as he entered it. His horse pulled back at the last moment, but its head was jerked hard by the reins that disappeared into the opening, forcing it to step forward.

Lorielle watched, fascinated as the horse seemed to slowly melt into the doorway, its tail the last part to go through with a slight pop of air. She stood, rooted to the spot in awe. Never in her entire life had she heard of anyone having such control of mathematics as to build an equation so complex as to transport a person or beast. She hesitated until she heard a hiss behind her, "Move forward, please."

She forced her legs to move, then tugged on the reins when her stallion refused to move. She heard a slap and her horse jumped forward with a whinny. She glared back at the Haissan who had slapped the flat of its blade against the rump of her horse. Then she was at the opening and she felt the charge of the air as it hummed in front of her. Without stopping, she stepped through. Pain filled every nerve of her body for the briefest moment but was then gone as she stood in a small clearing. Tris was already mounted and waiting. She pulled her horse hard until it appeared behind her, and she angled it away from the opening.

The Haissen quickly followed through the space behind her, one at a time leading their horses.

She felt a presence that she had not felt in some time and turned to look into the forest. She gasped lightly when she saw the huge blue eyes and white fur of the Korpor, standing half-hidden behind a tree. They locked eyes and the Korpor nodded slightly as if in greeting, then blinked its left eye, followed by its right eye.

* * *

The Sun had moved halfway toward the horizon before the air shimmered brilliantly not far away. The Korpor watched from some distance away, standing behind a tree so as not to damage the horses with its painful stare. The Black Robe stepped through the portal, leading a beautiful black stallion that side-stepped in agitation, snorting through its nostrils.

The Black Robe punched the stallion hard across its nose and the horse immediately stopped moving, its muscles quivering under its skin.

The Korpor smiled at the violence.

Then from the portal, a beautiful woman with long, black hair, tinged gray, stepped through leading a gray stallion.

Then, one at a time, two Murder of Haissen, twenty-six in all, appeared behind her, each leading a horse.

The Korpor studied the woman and felt the similarities to the Aleph Null. She immediately turned her head and glared directly at it even from the great distance. She didn't cringe in pain, and he remembered her Proofing, of how she failed the test, but like Tris, she didn't feel pain at his presence.

When the entire group was through the portal, the Black Robe spoke to it, his voice dripping inside the Korpor's mind, *"Come, my pet. Let's go hunting."*

With a slight pop, the portal closed and the Black Robe swung his reins and viciously kicked at the horse with his heels. The beast immediately started galloping down the trail, heading north. The woman and the Haissen followed closely, and the Korpor noticed that the strange creatures didn't seem to use any physical movements to direct their horses.

The Korpor blinked its left eye, followed by its right eye, then began to run after them.

Chapter 35

The dust had settled back onto the trail and a flock of black birds swooped in and landed in the upper branches of the tall trees. They cawed in the thousands as they struggled to find perches on which to sit. No sooner had they gotten settled, when as one they rose from the trees, blackening the sky, and turned to fly south.

Far below, four people seemed to appear from the air itself. They were dressed in brown tanned leathers that allowed them to blend in with the trees and they each carried only a single knife strapped to their sides in blood-red sheaths. They stepped through the trees onto the trail and faced north. The dust still hung in the air far down the trail and they could hear the distant beating of hooves, but they were fading quickly. A young man turned to the three Zranh around him. "I don't like this. Too many people are involved here. We should take Melinda back with us now."

The woman stepped forward and leaned against a tree, visibly tired after being in the Raith world so often lately. They had traveled in the Raith world for equal parts of their journey to increase their speed, but not so much as to completely exhaust themselves.

They had luckily been in the Raith world when they had come upon the Masteen's camp just after the Aleph Null had escaped. They prowled around the parameter and come across the strange white-haired, violent-looking creature hiding by the trail, watching the Aleph Null ride away, so they were able to find a good hiding spot that allowed them to monitor the situation without being seen, then come out of the Raith world to watch in real time.

They had studied the strange creature curiously and with some trepidation. It was a huge creature and exuded a sense of power, although they were not aware that they didn't feel pain from its stare, or that it even had such powers to inflict pain. The Raith world had protected them from its painful stare.

They then saw a man wearing a black robe appear out of thin air and the power and evil that he exuded made them tremble in fear, an emotion they rarely felt. The man was soon followed by an older woman and twenty-six figures they immediately recognized as Haissen. They had never seen a Haissan before, only knowing them from reputation. But even from a distance, they could tell how deadly the creatures were.

The woman turned to her three male companions. "No, not yet. I don't know what is happening, but Melinda is surrounded by powerful forces that I'm not sure even we can handle. Do you want to remain in the Raith world for the extended time needed to get by all of these different groups, take Melinda, and then get her away from them all? We would have to remain in the Raith world for possibly days and days. I'm not sure even we could survive that."

None of the men answered, knowing she was right. They had to conserve their strength and choose the right time in which to take Melinda back.

The young woman turned away from them and studied the trail again. "Let's get moving. We are at a disadvantage being on foot while they are all on horses. But if we enter the Raith world for short periods of time like we have been doing so far, we should be able to catch up to them while still keeping up our strength. Come, we have a long run ahead of us."

She took off at a run, light on her feet and swift as a deer. The other three men ran after her, not leaving even footprints behind them.

Chapter 36

When the last of the humans had left the Masteen's camp, Maelon stepped from the treeline and slowly glided across the muddy ground until he came to the edge of the pit. He looked down and whimpered when he saw the bloody body of the woman who had been like his mother lying on the muddy ground. The sight made his legs buckle and he had to force himself to stay standing, his will to live almost completely gone.

With what little energy he had left, he leapt into the pit, landing awkwardly in the soft mud. His middle leg hit a submerged rock though, and it shattered at impact, the snapping of the bone loud in the pit. He closed his eyes briefly at the pain, then put it out of his mind and limped to her body, having to pull his front and back legs out of the deep mud, each step causing his middle leg to shoot unimaginable pain through him. He only made it half-way before his legs gave out entirely and he fell.

He awkwardly dragged himself through the mud the final distance until he was able to press against her side. He lay his head across her chest, his mud-covered nose touching her cold cheek.

He licked her face and whimpered, then licked her face again when she didn't respond. He knew she was gone, but he couldn't stop himself from trying to wake her, as if by will alone he could bring her back.

Finally, he lay his head fully on her chest and just stared at her face, reliving the life he had spent with her.

He did not move for the rest of the day, not even when the flies began to swarm over her open wounds.

He would never leave her again.

* * *

The sun hung just above the trees to the west, casting long shadows on the empty camp. Mosquitoes crawled from underneath the leaves and mosses of the forest and took flight, hungrily looking for animals on which to feast.

A rabbit hopped along the muddy ground, not liking the strange smells. It scampered to the edge of the treeline and nibbled on a fresh green leaf that hung from a bush. Mosquitoes covered it, biting the exposed skin inside of its ears. The rabbit flicked its ears and hopped a

few steps away, but the biting insects followed it. The rabbit stopped
and raised its ears despite the mosquitoes that instantly covered them.
The ground trembled slightly, then again and again, getting louder. The
small animal hopped quickly away into the deep forest and burrowed
underneath a pile of detritus, shivering, its eyes wide.

The sounds of destruction approached until finally, along the edge
of the abandoned camp, two trees were smashed aside and the
Unnamed One burst into the clearing. It swung its head back and forth
and wetly sniffed the air. Pus ran down its gray skin, thick and yellow,
but a number of the pustules had healed, leaving red patches on its
skin. Its ribs were not showing as much anymore, and muscle now
made the skin of its body taut. It had eaten every animal it had found as
it followed the Black Numbers scent. But it was still hungry, for no
matter how much it ate, it always needed more.

A scent wafted on the breeze and the creature turned to its right
and pounded across the empty encampment. It filtered out the human
and horse smells that lingered, and stopped next to a muddy pit that
had numerous headless humans lying around the edge. Saliva dripped
from its mouth at the sight of all of the meat, but it ignored them for
the moment, more intent on the scent of the Black Numbers coming
from inside the hole in the ground. It leaned forward, trembling in
anticipation.

It saw a headless man lying at the bottom directly below, and in
the middle of the pit, a human female lay in the mud. Some kind of
animal lay next to the body, resting its head on her chest. The animal
raised its head and glanced up briefly, then closed its eyes and settled its
head back on the woman's chest and licked her face once, nestling
closer to her body.

The Unnamed One jumped down into the pit, which wasn't deep,
the edge coming no higher than its waist. The power of the Black
Numbers was strong inside the pit and anger surged through it.

The Unnamed One reached down and picked up the animal and
raised it to eye level. The animal didn't squirm or fight, it just hung
limply in its hand. The Unnamed One bit it in half, chewing the flesh
quickly before stuffing the second half of the body into its mouth.

It then bent down and sniffed the dead human. It licked blood
from the body, and when it got to the human's head, it jerked slightly as
it tasted the dried remains of tears laced with the power of numbers.

It sensed that the power had been released because of this dead
human, the pain and anger still heavy on the air. The creature raised its
head to the sky and screamed for a long time, then devoured the dead
body, including the red hair on the head. The flesh was not warm, but it
was freshly dead. Energy filled the creature, even though it had eaten
such a small morsel. It reached over and picked up the headless human
and tore the armor from the body, then consumed it also.

The Unnamed One jumped from the pit. It quickly ate the headless bodies that littered the edge, ripping off the armor as easily as if it were made from cloth. Finished, it sniffed around until it caught the trail of the Black Numbers. It screamed at the sky again and loped after it.

Chapter 37

As the small group rode north, they pushed hard until the sun had moved toward the western horizon. They finally slowed to a fast trot to keep from exhausting the horses. They rode warhorses bred to walk for long periods of time with occasional bursts of speed, but they weren't meant for such a hard, prolonged run.

Melinda brushed the side of her horse's neck, calming it down, but the horse was accustomed to being treated roughly and didn't respond to her soft caresses. She straightened up in her saddle and looked around at their surroundings for the first time since they had escaped the Masteen's camp. The trail had initially been lined with thick trees on each side but as they had ridden, the trees had begun to thin out until they had come over a large hill and had seen nothing but wild grassland stretching out in front of them. The wind had picked up and the grass moved like waves on water.

They stopped briefly by the final stand of trees so they could all relieve themselves and get a few moments of rest. Melinda slid from her horse and her bones creaked as she straightened her knees. She was not used to sitting in a saddle for so long. The others around her did the same, except for the mercenaries. They were experienced riders and accustomed to a hard life. She slumped against a tree. She felt empty of everything; energy, emotion, even her senses seemed dulled.

Crowdal asked Sid something she couldn't hear and then made his way back to her. She looked up into his concerned eyes.

"Are you all right, Melinda?"

She nodded. "Of course, just a bit stiff and sore."

The new, green-eyed woman who had helped them escape was standing beside her holding the reins of her horse, and Melinda shivered at the sight of the Haissan that never left the woman's side.

Crowdal turn to the new woman and extend his hand. "Thank you for your help. We owe you a debt of gratitude."

The woman nodded as she looked up at him, and Melinda could see that she was a little awed by his great height. The woman glanced quickly over at Sid and her face softened, then she turned back to Crowdal. "I made my choice, and believe me it was not a difficult one to make. The Masteen Vorn Maghuur is an evil man unlike any in this world, and he will not rest until we are captured again. We need to keep moving."

Crowdal looked grim as he glanced back down the trail. "I think you are right. But first, introductions are in order if we are to ride together. My name is Crowdal." He pointed at each person as he introduced them to her, coming lastly to Sid. "And this is Sid."

Melinda watched as both Sid and the new woman gazed into each other's eyes for a long moment before Sid finally said a quiet hello to her. The woman murmured a greeting back, her face flushed. Melinda raised an eyebrow and smiled for the first time in a long time at their obvious attraction to each other. Crowdal caught her look and winked back to her, clearly amused.

Melinda coughed and the woman looked over at her with a start. "Not to be rude, but who are you?"

The woman quickly got herself back under control. "My apologies. My name is Agnes." She motioned briefly to her Haissan. "And this is... my associate."

She paused as if she wanted to say more, but when she didn't, Crowdal touched her shoulder lightly. "Thank you, Agnes, for your help." He turned to the Haissan and extended his hand to it. "I saw you cut down one of the guards above the pit. Thank you, too, for your help. We are in your debt."

The creature didn't move for a few moments, and then, a bit awkwardly, it raised its arm and shook Crowdal's hand. A hiss escaped from its hood that sounded like "yes" although Melinda couldn't be sure.

Crowdal released the creature's hand and turned back to Agnes. "We are happy to have you both travel with us, although I don't think it is the safest option for you."

Agnes hardened her eyes. "It is my only option." She turned to the Haissan and spoke to it in a clipped tone, "As you may have guessed, I am no longer working for our... employer. You may leave if you like."

The Haissan, its face hidden in its hood, stood silently for long moments before tilting its head slightly. "I would... like to stay with you."

Crowdal was about to speak when Tulman whispered fiercely, "They are coming!"

Crowdal quickly looked back the way they had come. Melinda turned to look also and saw dust rising up in the distance.

Crowdal spoke calmly, "Quickly, mount up, we have to ride hard."

Melinda tiredly put her foot into a stirrup and slid into the saddle, pulling on the reins to keep her horse steady. She only wanted to sleep, but within moments, they were pounding down the trail again at a full gallop.

They road hard until the horses started to falter, so they slowed to a quick trot and continued until the sun set in the west, and when darkness fully settled on them, they slowed to a walk, the horses snorting loudly, flicking foam from their mouths.

Melinda spurred her horse to a trot and caught up to Crowdal and Writhgarth, who were at the front of their short column.

Crowdal glanced at her and Melinda motioned behind her. "We

have gained some distance on them, as they have to ride slower due to the weight of their armor. But we can't go all night. We have to figure out a way to lose them for good."

"I know, our horses won't last at this pace for much longer. But I honestly don't know what to do."

Melinda saw the frustration and exhaustion on his face and knew that hers looked the same way. The only solution she could think of was for her to enter the Raith world and kill the Masteen and all of his men. But, like earlier when the Masteen had first captured them, she was too exhausted and drained to enter the Raith world. In fact, it had taken all of her last physical energy reserves just to keep from falling off of her horse during their flight.

She set her lips in a thin line. It didn't matter if she would succeed or not. She was willing to try and enter the Raith world one more time. Melinda saw Crowdal's concern for her in his eyes and she realized just how much he mattered to her. She wouldn't let anything happen to him. She was about to tell him that she was a Zranh, what she would try to do to the Masteen and his men, when Sid spoke quietly from her left.

"I can hide us."

Crowdal turned to him. "What do you mean?"

Sid pointed toward the tall grasses stretching out in all directions. "If we ride into the grass and stay quiet, I think I can make sure no one sees us."

Tulman leaned forward in his saddle and spit to his side, and Melinda saw that he had a wad of tobacco in his cheek. She had never seen that done before. The mercenary crossed his hands on the pommel of the saddle. "How can you make sure they don't see us?"

They all turned back to Sid, who squared his shoulders and spoke tersely, "I can't explain to you how, it is too complicated and you will not understand. But you must trust me, and we are almost out of time."

Melinda heard the distant clamor of metal armor and the thudding of hooves. She turned back around. "He is right, whatever we do we must do it now."

Sid immediately turned his horse and rode slowly into the tall grass. He turned his head and said, "Follow me, single file, and try not to trample any more of the grass than you have to."

The grass grew to a great height, almost to Sid's saddle.

The rest of the group followed him into the grass, careful to follow directly behind the person in front of them. Melinda was about to enter the grass, with Crowdal the last to enter behind her, but before she did, Crowdal called her name softly. She stopped and turned to see what he wanted. He swung from his saddle and led the horse to her and handed the reins up. "Lead the horse, I will try to make our trail less obvious by straightening the grass as much as I can. I'll be right behind you."

Melinda nodded and moved into the grass without a word. She could hear Crowdal swishing grass as he tried to erase their trail. She soon reached the rest of the group. She didn't know how Sid was going to hide them. Their horse's heads and their own bodies stood well above the grass level.

Sid sat in his saddle and saw her questioning look. "These are warhorses and cannot lie down because of their great muscled legs and shoulders. Since we can't hide, I'm going to try and create an equation that will bend the light around us, which, theoretically, should make us difficult to see."

Melinda nodded, not understanding how he could do it, but trusting him completely.

Sid spoke to everyone, "Don't bother getting off of your horses, but please, keep them very quiet."

Everyone reached out and calmed their horses with soft caresses.

There was a swishing and Melinda saw Crowdal approach from the grass, completely bent over from the waist to keep his body from showing above it. When he saw them all still on their horses, he shot a questioning look at Sid, who responded quietly that he could stand up straight.

Melinda watched as Sid closed his eyes. She couldn't tell if anything was happening and was about to speak, when she heard and saw the approach of the Masteen and his men.

Chapter 38

Tris hunched over his horse as it galloped down the trail and he reveled in the chase. His blood pumped and he felt something as close to joy as he had ever felt. He looked to his left and saw Lorielle riding with her head held high, her long hair flowing behind her. She ignored him, as she had since they had left Undaluag. He glanced to his right and saw the Korpor running just off of the road, easily keeping pace with them on their horses but staying mostly out of sight so as to not debilitate the Haissen with its gaze.

He knew Sid couldn't be that far ahead of him. He could sense Sid's power as easily as he could smell the sweat and filth of the Masteen's men who were also not far ahead of him.

Tris ground his teeth together. If the Masteen harmed Sid during this stupid chase, then he would make the large man suffer pain worse than any ever before inflicted upon a man. It had been a risk bringing the Masteen into this, but the man's strange numbing effect on the power of numbers was key to weakening Sid enough for Tris to subdue him. Tris would just have to catch up to the Masteen and take control of the situation before it devolved into chaos. He had reached out and examined the Masteen's physical and metaphysical make up earlier and had developed an equation that removed the Masteen's effect on his own power of numbers.

Looking ahead, Tris caught the faint lingering dust on the trail. The Masteen and his men were only a few thousand paces ahead now.

Adrenaline coursed through his veins as he kicked his horse to make it run harder. Events were coming together much more quickly than he had expected, but that was just how things worked out sometimes. He couldn't wait to have Sid in front of him, to revel in the horror-filled look his old friend would have when he found out that he, Tris, was the Black Robe.

He chuckled softly, the sound lost in the wind on his face. Oh, how he longed to see Sid cry out in pain when he pulled Sid's mother from her horse and shoved her into the Masteen's arms. Sid would do anything to ensure she was not harmed. It was all so delicious to Tris when a plan came together like this.

He was so caught up in his thoughts that he failed to notice a strange warp in his vision, or the small prickly sensation run up his arms. It happened so quickly that he rode on, not even noticing the Korpor looking into the grass at the same time.

The dust from the Masteen's group grew thicker, so Tris spurred his horse harder to catch up with them.

Chapter 39

Sid sat in his saddle with his eyes closed. He called his numbers and they instantly appeared in his mind. The clarity with which he saw the numbers again amazed him, and he could feel the bond with the green-eyed woman named Agnes as if it were a physical connection. He could also feel the power of the Black Numbers manuscript flow out of Crowdal's pack, only now it was a comfort to him and didn't overpower him sexually. The effect it had on him had somehow changed when he had met Agnes.

Agnes, now she was another story. Just looking at her caused him to grow hard in his pants, the sensations of lust filling him with longing, his thoughts pulsing with sexual energy, his body trembling from need. The sexual energy flowing from her was so strong that he had to force himself to concentrate on their dangerous situation. He was also pretty sure that Agnes felt the same sexual power he did. He could see it in her eyes and feel her body react to his, even separated as they were on their horses.

During their flight from the Masteen's camp, he had thought about what the connection with Agnes might mean. He no longer felt the total sexual power of the Black Numbers manuscript take over him, nor the loss of control and overpowering sexual release when he had killed the guards with his numbers. In fact, he admitted to himself that he felt a combination of anger and joy when he had killed the man who had so brutally murdered Mrs. Wessmank. This change had occurred when he had met Agnes. There had been some kind of link forged between them as soon as they looked into each other's eyes in the camp. What it meant, he wasn't entirely sure.

Now, as he pulled his numbers together and heard the Masteen and his men approaching, he put all thoughts of Agnes aside and concentrated on the grass around him. He felt each individual grass blade moving around him, how the wind pushed and pulled them all against each other, and in just a matter of moments, he saw the pattern emerge mathematically. It constantly changed as the wind gusted and waned, so he created a variable for the wind in his equation that would mimic the changes of increased or decreased forces.

Sid cast his senses further out and saw the light rays of the rising moon and how they bent slightly as they passed through the moisture in the air, and he calculated the angle and refraction based on the air density.

As the sound of the Masteen's horses grew to a dull roar, Sid bridged the equation for grass, wind, and moonlight into a single equation so complex that he had to struggle to fit it together. The

Masteen was only a few hundred paces away when Sid completed the equation. The air in front of him shimmered, although he knew that only he could see the shimmer. He also knew that anyone on the other side of the equation would only see grass stretching out into the moonlit distance. He had replicated the shape and pattern of the moving grass and used the moonlight to bend the pattern around them all.

The Masteen rode by and glanced right at him, but Sid saw no recognition in his eyes as he thundered past, followed by the remaining forty-four men of his death squad. Soon the loud thudding of the horses and jingle of armor faded away.

Slumping his shoulders with relief, Sid was about to dismantle the equation when he sensed a power unlike anything he had ever felt before approaching on the same trail. He quested out with his senses and saw the strange power as a black void. Not far behind the void, he felt the unique presence of the Korpor. And then he caught the faintest sense of a strange woman who also seemed familiar to him. But he didn't have time to concentrate on her, for instinctively he knew that the black void would sense his equations and see the bending of the light. How he knew this perplexed him, but reason dictated that only a master mathematician could control the Korpor.

He needed to cloak the equation that was hiding them, but he didn't know how to do it. He only had a short time before whatever was in the black void was upon them. Sweat beaded on his forehead and soaked his armpits. He thought of every equation that his father had taught him, of every mathematical formula that he had created over the years, but nothing matched what he needed.

He couldn't do it. He didn't have the time to figure this out.

Sid started to shake with fear, for he knew that whomever—or whatever—was at the center of the black void would destroy him as easily as he had destroyed the men in the Masteen's camp. His numbers started to vibrate and he was close to losing control of his equations when he felt a cool hand close over his.

A jolt of sexual power entered him at the touch of her hand on his, and the warmth and pulsing of an orgasm began to build from deep within him. He turned his face and looked into the green eyes amidst the shadow of Agnes' face, marveling at their beauty and depth, the colors almost swirling around the pupil in the moonlight.

Sid felt her hand grip his even harder as she, too, began to shake. They leaned toward each other, their legs brushing as their horses bumped each other, and as their foreheads touched, a powerful orgasm ripped through Sid, the ecstasy filling every part of his body, the pleasure so great that he moaned, not wanting it to end. He felt Agnes also shudder violently in her own orgasm, letting out a breathless 'ahhh' sound. He felt his seed release in wave after wave in tune with the clenching and unclenching of Agnes' whole body.

But unlike a normal orgasm that subsided in a few moments, their mutual release only built and through the pulsing pleasure, Sid heard her voice gasp in time with her breathless release.

"Use this equation... it will... create a void and... eat... all matter." She had to stop for a few moments as she sighed in exquisite tones. Finally she breathlessly continued, "But you need... to add it to your equation and modify it... so that it doesn't destroy your equation." She moaned in deep-throated pleasure and briefly lost her concentration to the orgasm before finishing her sentence. "If done correctly... it will blend with the light refraction equation... that you just created."

Sid closed his eyes as his own orgasm pulsed harder. With difficulty, he studied her equation and was astounded by its beauty and complexity. His orgasm continued to pulse in exquisite release, and he didn't know for how much longer he could take the pleasure. He reached out with his mind and tweaked her equation slightly so that it would perfectly merge with his and then snapped them roughly together as his concentration wavered. The new equation pulsed in time with their orgasms, undulating sensually just as the black void and the Korpor approached them on the trail.

Sid watched the dark void coalesce into a man on a horse, covered in a robe with a hood tied tightly around the face so he couldn't see who it was, but he emanated a deep sense of death and destruction. A figure rode by his side, also hooded, but her essence felt calming, serene. The two figures were surrounded by twenty-six robed figures that Sid immediately knew were Haissen by the way they rode their horses so effortlessly. He couldn't see the Korpor yet, but knew it was following the group out of sight, probably to keep them from its excruciating pain.

The group passed and Sid waited a few moments longer and then, as he had suspected, the Korpor dashed past them, a white blur in the light of the moon. It glanced toward him as it passed, but turned back as if it saw nothing. The combination of Agnes and Sid's equations formed a void of nothingness that concealed his equation that hid them. It worked and Sid felt his orgasm grow even stronger, which he didn't think would have been possible.

Sid felt Agnes grip his hand harder and moan as she collapsed into his shoulder gasping for breath, shuddering and twitching, and he did the same, finally giving in to the finality of his own release.

After what felt like an eternity, but was actually only a few moments longer, Sid felt the pleasure subside and his breathing come back under control. He and Agnes sat like this for a few moments more until she finally lifted her face to his, completely covered in sweat. He knew that his face dripped sweat also.

They stared into each other's eyes and Sid softly touched her cheek, and as he did, she leaned into his touch. Finally, they heard a cough. Sid looked over and saw that every single member of their group was uncomfortably looking out over the grassy plains, each in different directions, anywhere but at them. Except for Nik, who had a huge smile on his face and was watching them in delight.

Finally Crowdal turned to them and whispered, still not risking loud sounds, "Sid, you did it! I don't know what you did, but you did it." He then winked. "And I take it that you rather enjoyed the process."

Sid merely nodded, still trying to get his breathing under control, too tired to be embarrassed.

Agnes squeezed his hand once more, her eyes slightly unfocused, then pulled away from him and sat up straight on her horse. She angled slightly away from Sid, looking embarrassed and confused by what had happened.

After a few moments, Sid found his voice, "Agnes and I have only hidden us for the moment. They will realize soon enough that we are no longer in front of them when daylight comes and they no longer see our trail. In fact, the Korpor has probably already noticed that it is no longer following our trail." Sid brushed a shaking hand through his thick hair. "I'm exhausted. I won't be able to create another equation like that any time soon."

Writhgarth eased his horse forward. "Then we must get moving immediately." He stood up in his stirrups and looked over the dark, grassy plain. "I think we should continue cutting across this plain, away from the trail. With any luck, it will take them well into the morning before they double back and find where we left the trail and start following us. That will give us a nice head start."

Crowdal and the others nodded in agreement and prepared to move out. But Sid held up his hand weakly. "I just need a moment." He slid from his horse and walked into the grass a few paces until he was alone. He quickly pulled his pack from his back and opened it. He removed his water bottle, a spare pair of trousers, and an old shirt. He pulled out the cork of his water bottle with his teeth and poured a small amount onto the shirt. He then pulled down his trousers, stepped out of them, and began to clean himself as best he could. When he finished, he pulled on his spare trousers, then rolled the soiled trousers and old shirt into a ball and threw it into the grass. He didn't know when he would be able to next clean them and he didn't want the strong smell of his seed inside of his pack. He poured a little bit of water onto his hands to wash them, then brushed them on the ground. He returned quietly and slightly embarrassed to the group, pushing the tall grass aside carefully.

Everyone was lined up and ready to move out, so Sid climbed up onto his horse and they all started forward without speaking, heading northeast. They cut through the tall grass in single file through the remainder of the night, and when the sky started to lighten in front of them, they saw a mountain range far in the distance. When Sid saw them, he felt a calming energy fill him, luring him in that direction.

Crowdal held up his hand. "Let's stop here for a while and rest and eat."

No one argued as they slipped from their horses. Even the mercenaries sighed softly when they stood on their own two feet.

Sid stretched his back and looked around. His little group had grown over the past few days. Where before it had just been the five of them, now there were nine of them, including the green-eyed woman named Agnes, whom he couldn't stop thinking about. As Sid removed some food from his pack, he realized sadly that someone important was missing. He turned his head and scanned the group, and the finality hit him so hard that his knees almost buckled.

Mrs. Wessmank was gone. Forever. She would never again caress him when he was hurt, or offer him tea and cookies. He would never again hear her soft sounds of complaint as she settled down to a sitting position, one hand on her back. He would never see her blue apron around her ample waist; and he would forever miss her frizzy red hair and those two birth marks on her forehead that looked like a second pair of eyes.

Sid felt tears run down his face and he quickly rubbed them away. He would miss the old woman, and he would never, ever forget her.

Chapter 40

The tall grass swayed in a light breeze, undulating as if alive. The four Zranh slipped between the long stalks without sound, somehow finding a way through them without disturbing even a single one. They had briefly run along the trail, but they didn't want to risk being spotted by the group of Haissen and the white-furred creature, so they had entered the grassy plain and run parallel to the trail a half league from it. They had slipped into and out of the Raith world at intervals so they could travel faster than the groups they were following.

The woman raised her hand and they stopped. She listened to the sighing of the grass around her and picked up the distant jingle of a horse's harness ahead and to her left. She slowly angled back toward the trail, her three companions shadowing her every move. When they approached the gravel trail, she entered the Raith world without pausing, and the Zranh behind her did the same. The movements of the weaving grass slowed down, looking like seaweed swaying in a slow current under water.

She glided between the grass and entered a small area where the grass had been flattened by horses, some of the stocks broken, others pushed to the ground by the hooves of the beasts. She bent down and touched the ground, feeling along the imprint of a boot.

"They are moving into the grass now, which makes it easier for us. Let's just hope we can catch up with them before the other groups who are chasing them do."

She stood and let the Raith world go. The sound of the real world was always a shock to her after the near silence of the Raith world.

They turned and followed the trail through the tall grass.

Chapter 41

As the Black Robe and his group, including the Aleph Null's mother, finally caught sight of the Masteen and his men, the Korpor, running tirelessly a half league behind them, suddenly sniffed and turned its head back the way they had come as it caught a faint scent in the breeze. It slowed to a jog, then it came to a stop and spoke to the Black Robe through their link, *"I will catch up with you later."*

"What is it? Why are you stopping?" The voice inside the Korpor's head was dark and dripping with impatience.

"I caught a scent. I will investigate and catch up with you shortly."

"Make it quick, we are very close now to catching Sid."

"Of course... master."

The Korpor ended the communication and loped back the way it had come until it caught a stronger scent on the air. It slowed to a walk, dropping to all fours as it sniffed the ground. Its white fur glowed in the darkness, ruffling lightly in the soft night breeze.

It stopped, one foot raised in midair, and breathed the air deeply into its lungs. The Korpor started to shiver with pleasure as it angled into the tall grass, not making a sound as it moved. It made its way deeper into the grass, the scent growing stronger as it did, until it finally stopped and lowered its head to sniff a rolled up bundle of clothing lying on the ground.

The Korpor smiled grotesquely as it looked at the Aleph Null's shirt and trousers. It inhaled deeply, smelling that they were filled with the boy's seed, still wet and fragrant. The Korpor's whole body started to shake uncontrollably and it moaned in pleasure as it used a claw from each paw to unroll the bundle of clothes. It bent down lower, reached out its tongue, and slowly licked the cloth. There was more seed than the Korpor had ever seen before, it literally filled the trousers. The Korpor licked up the salty liquid, its eyes closed and its body shaking harder and harder. It finally lifted its head to the sky and let out a loud wail as it had an orgasm.

The need to find the boy filled it with energy and the Korpor rose up and began running through the tall grass, following the trail of the Aleph Null. It cast out a quick message to the Black Robe, letting him know that he caught the scent of the Aleph Null, who was riding away from the trail through the grassy plain.

Chapter 42

Word from the back of his squad reached the Masteen that a group was closing in behind them, so he ordered his men to turn and face the threat. He pulled his sword from its scabbard and waited for the unknown group of riders to either approach or attack him. Either way, he didn't care. There was no one whom he feared, especially with his death squad behind him. They were the most feared men in the land and few men engaged a death squad and lived to tell about it.

The approaching riders pulled up on their reins and came to a stop no more than twenty paces from the Masteen, causing dust to roll over him. He prepared himself to attack, for no one approached him so carelessly, nor risked covering him with grit and dust. Just as he was about to charge forward, the leader of the group put up his hand.

"Oh, stop that, we aren't here to fight you." He spoke so casually and with such disdain that the Masteen actually stopped, not out of respect or obedience, but from pure stupefaction. No one spoke to him in that tone. It was the second time in the past two days that had happened. First the Trith, and now this young man. His blood pumped harder, his face flushed, and he roared so loudly that his men's horses side-stepped away from him. He slapped his horse's rump with such force that it reared up, neighing loudly and kicking its front legs before coming down to charge the boy.

The Masteen leaned to his right as he approached and held his sword high, ready to decapitate the man who had insulted him. But the robed figures that rode with the man quickly surrounded the coward, protecting him, and one of the robed figures pulled a sword and rode out to meet the Masteen.

The Masteen swung his sword down on the robed rider with such power that an ordinary man would have never had the strength to block it. But somehow, the man raised his own sword and met the descending blade of the Masteen at the perfect angle, deflecting it down and to the left, moving his arm in a fluid motion and giving a slight push at the end. It was a move that had to be precise, for just a slight difference in angle would have resulted in a shattered blade.

The Masteen's blade slid smoothly down the robed figure's blade and as he rode by, the man leaned forward and shoved the Masteen, causing him to lose his balance and topple from his horse in a crash of armor and dust, his sword clattering to the ground in front of him.

The robed figure leapt lightly from his saddle and stood between the Masteen and the Black Robe, sword held casually at a 45-degree downward angle.

The Masteen got slowly to his feet and bent down to pick up his sword. He towered over the robed figure by at least five handspans. He took two steps forward, swinging his sword around his head and then down in a hissing arc. The figure stepped quickly back, just out of reach of the Masteen's blade. A master swordsman himself, the Masteen didn't pause, but reversed the direction of the strike, using his great strength to his benefit.

His sword was wide, thick, and almost as long as the robed figure was tall, and coupled with the Masteen's height and extreme arm length, it was an advantage he had used to kill thousands of opponents, for no one could get inside of his sword's reach without being spit like a pig. But this robed figure was faster than any man the Masteen had before faced and managed to dance away from the killing blow. The Masteen calmed himself. He knew he would kill the man. The thought of losing had never before entered his mind. But he also realized that the man he faced was a master and just hacking at him was not enough.

The Masteen took a deep breath and set his feet at a strange angle, his right foot facing slightly inward, his left foot facing away and forward with his hips slightly turned away from the robed man. It was the beginning of the Shimtune attack, a series of moves so complex and secret that only a small handful of people had ever mastered it.

He leaned to his left, twisted slightly, then leaned right, angling his sword down and to the right, then upward and back left but at a different angle. He moved constantly, changing the angles slightly every time and varying the direction his feet faced as he approached the robed man. It was hypnotic and impossible to predict the movement of the sword and footwork. There was no defense and the Masteen's scarred face split into a grin as he attacked, anticipating the sweet feeling of his blade cutting through flesh and bone.

The ring of steel on steel shocked the Masteen and his grin froze on his face. His opponent had actually engaged him, blocking his strikes one after another without backing up. The Masteen increased the speed of his attacks, yet the robed figure blocked every single blow. Sweat began to bead on his forehead and his frustration grew until he abandoned the Shimtune attack all together and began hacking at the robed figure in a rage, just wanting to split him down the middle and see his blood and guts spill to the ground.

The robed figure spun and swept the Masteen's front leg out from under him. Off balance, the Masteen staggered and put a hand to the ground to keep from falling, and as he did, he felt the cold hard steel of his opponent's blade touch his exposed neck.

* * *

T ris had watched the confrontation with curiosity. He knew the savage reputation of the Masteen, especially as a fighter. He was interested to see how he would do against a Haissan. Size and strength against speed and skill. It was a match-up that could go either way, although if he were a betting man, he would have put his coin on his Haissan.

Now he knew.

This fight confirmed his suspicion that there was not a race alive who could defeat a Haissan with a sword. Well, except for the Trith, from what he had heard from the Korpor in the underground cavern, although he still found that story hard to believe. The Trith were great warriors and blade masters, but he didn't think they could defeat the Haissen. More probably, the Trith had received help from Sid during their battle with the Haissen and Father Mansico.

The Masteen's death squad began to move their horses forward, swords out of their scabbards as the Masteen knelt on the ground with the sword to his neck. Tris didn't want any actual bloodshed, he needed the Masteen and his men.

"Tell your men to stop, Masteen Vorn Maghuur. I do not want to kill them all."

The Masteen growled, then spoke, his voice deep and menacing, "Your man may kill me, but my death squad will destroy you."

Tris shook his head slowly. "Now that would be an interesting battle to witness. Your death squad against two Murder of Haissen and the Black Robe of the Oblate."

***

The Masteen's eyes grew large, even though no one could see them, bent over like he was. Haissen! He had heard rumors of that race, but he had never known for sure if they had truly existed. The tales were almost too outlandish to be believed, but it was said they were unequaled with the blade. Looking up through his long hair at the robed figure standing next to him so casually holding the sword to his neck, the Masteen now knew the tales were true. He had never before been defeated in battle. The shock of it had been great at first, but now he accepted it. What he wouldn't give to have some of those Haissen by his side.

And the Black Robe! Could such a young man really be the Black Robe? Deep down, he knew it was true, he didn't have to think about it any longer. He wasn't one to ignore the facts.

The Masteen chuckled. It began low down in his stomach, then grew into a loud, booming laugh. The blade left his neck and he stood up, brushing dust from his leathers. He wasn't surprised to see that the Haissan who had so effortlessly bested him was back on its horse as if nothing had happened. He bent down and picked up his sword again, this time sheathing it with a hiss and click into his black scabbard. The young Black Robe sat upon his huge stallion, looking for all the world like he was out for an afternoon ride in the countryside.

The Masteen nodded slightly toward the young man. "That was an interesting way to meet you, Black Robe." He nodded to the Haissan who had beaten him. "I have never had the pleasure of meeting one of the mysterious Haissen before, much less been able to spar with one. Thank you for the practice."

The Haissan nodded its hood-covered head slightly.

The Black Robe raised his right eyebrow. "The pleasure was all theirs, I imagine. Well met, Masteen Vorn Maghuur, I have been following you for some time now after hearing that you let the Aleph Null and his friends escape."

The Masteen stopped chuckling and stood up to his full height, at the same eye-level as the Black Robe, who sat on his stallion. His voice rumbled deeply within his chest, "Yes... the boy escaped from my pit. But I will have him again very soon. We are close on his trail and he and his... friends, will not outrun a death squad."

"Is that so? Then tell me, why are you riding down this trail when the Aleph Null is somewhere out there?" The Black Robe gestured to his right into the tall, unending grasslands.

The Masteen stared at the Black Robe for a few moments, gauging whether he was speaking the truth. He wiped a dirty clump of hair from his face, and didn't blink as he called his captain over. "Where is our scout?"

The captain, a man almost as large and mean looking as the Masteen, turned his head and yelled, "Get me Rand, now!"

A member of the death squad immediately kicked his horse in the side and they took off at a gallop up the road, dust flying from the horse's hooves. The captain turned back. "We will have him here shortly. He is due back for his report soon, so he can't be far ahead."

The Masteen nodded, then turned to the Black Robe. "I am hungry. Join us while we wait."

The Black Robe slid from his horse and casually glanced over his shoulder as he removed his riding gloves and motioned to a woman. "Get down, you will see your son soon enough."

The woman sighed softly and slipped from her saddle.

She was a beautiful woman, and one that the Masteen would enjoy having in his bed, and he was not a man to be denied.

Chapter 43

$\mathbf{A}$ shooting pain arched through her muscles as she stepped from her horse, and Lorielle groaned as she put her hand to her lower back. She had been inactive for so many years that her body now protested from all of the riding.

The Masteen rumbled deeply, standing not far from her. "Woman... I can show you what real pain feels like... in my bed."

Lorielle shot the man a look but quickly glanced away, the evil within the man palpable.

She heard Tris chuckle and respond, "Maybe I will give her to you when we are finished."

The Masteen's voice rumbled again, so deeply that she could barely hear him, "I take what I want, I do not wait for gifts."

The Masteen's men quickly broke out rations and ale, while the two Murder of Haissen simply stood around the Black Robe, unmoving, looking for all the world like they were not even aware of the Masteen or his dangerous men.

Lorielle accepted a portion of hard bread and a chunk of moldy cheese from one of the Masteen's men, saying thank you. The huge man, stubble covering his face and missing an eye, leered at her, looking her up and down. She turned away, stepped over to the edge of the trail, and sat down on the slight slope with another small moan. She hoped her show of weakness made her invisible as a threat to her cousin and the Masteen.

She turned the bread in her hand and wanted to throw it away. It was coarse, covered with large spots of green mold, and when she peered closer, she saw a clump of black hair sticking out from where it had actually been baked into the bread. It still had dead lice stuck to the individual strands. She tore that portion out and threw it away in disgust, then picked as much of the mold off of the surface as she could. She didn't have much bread left when she finished and was about to bite into it when she felt a hand on her shoulder and heard a hiss behind her, "Here, eat this instead."

She turned and looked up at one of the Haissen. It held out a portion of food, neatly wrapped in green leaves.

She accepted it. "Thank you!"

The Haissan didn't respond and glided back to the side of the Black Robe.

Lorielle set the small packet on her lap and opened the intricately wrapped leaves to reveal a small plum and a perfect cube of bread with varied seeds baked on top. She broke the bread open and saw that it was filled with delicately cut meat and white cheese. Her mouth

watered and she took a small bite. It was the most delicious thing she
had eaten in the past ten years. The Faussian monks ate nothing more
than simple bread and raw vegetables.

She set the bread back down, then picked up the plum and turned
it in her hand before she took a small bite, quickly bringing her hand up
to wipe away a bit of juice that spurted down her chin. It was sweet and
delicious and she chewed it with relish. She ate the plum slowly,
enjoying every bite and feeling the healthy nourishment coursing
through her body. When she finished, she tossed the pit into the grass
and wrapped the bread back into the leaves and placed it into a deep
pocket, as she didn't know what the future would bring and extra food
could be the difference between life and death.

Lorielle sat back contentedly and looked out across the grassy
plain that now stretched out as far as she could see in every direction.
The grass moved like waves across water, the swishing sound soothing,
although the constant gruff voices of the Masteen's men silenced most
of the sounds of nature.

She could sense that she was getting close to Sidoro, like she could
almost reach out and touch his essence. Time was getting short and
Lorielle had to prepare for the time when she would be needed. She
wouldn't let Tris use her as a pawn to entrap her son; she would rather
die now than let that happen. But if there was a chance she could
actually weaken her cousin, to break his concentration at just the right
time to give Sidoro the moment he needed, she knew it could be the
one thing that tipped the scales in her son's favor.

Lorielle closed her eyes. To anyone who may be looking at her,
she appeared to be resting. But her mind was working feverishly.

First, she compartmentalized her thoughts. It was a technique she
had learned from Samuel as a way to gain full control of her emotions
and thoughts, to separate them into their base parts. He had taught her
the deep meditation techniques of the monks over the ten years she
had been held there. She used that training now as she kept the
majority of her general thoughts at the surface—the soft sighing of the
grass as it swayed in the light breeze, the jingle of the horses' bridles as
they tossed their heads, the sounds of mastication from the Masteen's
men as they devoured their food. But deep down she visualized a small
room, hidden from everything, which she entered and carefully shut the
door. Inside this room she released the power of mathematics, letting
the numbers and existing equations she had built throughout her life
flow from her.

She didn't have much time before the men would be ready to ride
again, so she hastily pulled the required numbers and symbols to
construct the equation she needed. It was a formula she had never
before attempted, complex and dangerous. But she reveled in the
power of advanced mathematics that was again hers to control. It all

seemed so easy to her and she almost cried in joy as the numbers obeyed her commands.

She built the equation one number and mathematical symbol at a time, and it grew in complexity until she placed the final number and it clicked into place. The equation hung in front of her, slowly twisting as it spun on an axis. She didn't have to re-examine it; she knew it was 100% accurate. Satisfied, Lorielle locked the equation, preparing it for a quick pull from the room, then slipped from the door quietly and returned to full consciousness.

She opened her eyes and set her shoulders. She was ready for whatever would come. She heard Tris' irritating voice call to her, "If you are finished napping, cousin, it is time to find your son."

She stood up, brushed a few crumbs from her clothing, and turned. The Masteen's men were getting onto their giant war horses, black armor and helmets seeming to suck in the very sunlight. She quickly approached her own stallion.

Tris swung his horse around so he was facing back the way they had just come. The Masteen trotted up next to him on a horse that looked too small for his giant frame. He was the largest man she had ever seen.

The Masteen questioned Tris, "My scout confirmed that the Aleph Null is not in front of us. How do you know where he is?"

Tris glanced to the Masteen. "I have my sources." He slapped his own horse hard, and it reared up and took off at a gallop back the way that they had come.

The Masteen followed at a slower pace, shaking his head in annoyance.

Lorielle swung onto her horse and pulled the reins gently to turn the beast without hurting it, and followed. Her heart quickened its beating at the thought of seeing her son again.

The noise of the men and horses was almost deafening around her, with the armor rattling, horses snorting, and hooves pounding. Compared to the quiet Haissen, it felt like she had entered a maelstrom of chaos.

Chapter 44

The light of the fire flickered in the darkness, outlining the swaying grass that surrounded the small clearing they had made when they stopped for the night. Sid closed his eyes and rested his head against his pack as he lay on the soft grass they had tamped down. It had been a long three days. They had only stopped for short rests, moving by day and night. They had planned to continue through this night but the horses had started to slow down and stumble in exhaustion, so they had made the decision to stop for the entire night and let them rest up.

Sid tried to sleep, but he kept thinking of the Black Numbers manuscript. This was the first time since before their capture by the Masteen that he had time to himself. He opened his eyes and saw that everyone slept around the small fire except for the Haissan, who stood perfectly still at the edge of the firelight, facing the way they had come. Sid had yet to see the Haissan sleep or even rest. It was a strange creature, and no matter how much he wanted to hate it, he just didn't feel a sense of evil from it. It seemed to exist just to serve.

Sid turned his head and saw the large form of Crowdal lying further from the fire so he had more space to stretch out his long body. The Trith rested his head on his large pack, using it as a pillow. Sid got to his feet, walked as quietly as he could to his friend, and nudged him softly on the shoulder. Crowdal immediately opened his eyes and sat up, looking around for danger. Sit put his finger to his own mouth and whispered, "It's all right, nothing is wrong."

Crowdal relaxed visibly, then whispered back, "What is it, Sid? You should be sleeping."

Sid leaned forward so they could talk quietly without having to whisper. "I can't sleep. I need to read the manuscript some more. This might be my only chance."

His friend hesitated, then shrugged. "Let me get it from my pack." He turned at the waist, opened the waterproof pocket inside the large leather pack, and removed the manuscript. The cover was so black that it looked like Crowdal was holding a shadow in his hand as he set it on the ground in front of Sid. Crowdal started to open the cover when Sid put his hand out to stop him. "Let me try."

"Are you sure?"

Sid nodded. Since he and Agnes had merged their equations and had the 'event', as he thought of it, he had felt different. The power of the Black Numbers manuscript didn't seem to call to him with such sexual power. He lowered his hand until it hovered over the leather cover. Whereas before he had gotten an instant erection when he had gotten this close to the manuscript, now he just felt a warm and comforting sensation. His finger settled on the leather and he quickly pulled it back, but nothing happened. Feeling confident, he put his hand palm down onto the cover.

He looked up and grinned at Crowdal, who was leaning slightly away from him with an anxious expression on his face.

Crowdal leaned forward again and whispered, "Well, you didn't try to kill me, which is a good sign."

Sid grinned wider and grabbed the manuscript as he stood up, then motioned his head. "Get some sleep, Crowdal. I'll be all right."

His friend hesitated. "Are you sure?"

Sid nodded, looking down at the manuscript in his hands.

Crowdal laid back down and whispered, "Just yell if you need me."

Sid rolled his eyes. "I'll be fine." He turned and walked back to the fire so he could get more light, then sat down cross-legged with the manuscript in his lap. He leaned forward and sniffed the leather, enjoying the musty smell. He opened the cover, then turned the pages until he got to the spot where he had last read.

Just like before, power seemed to flow from the pages, warm and comforting. He felt the equation that had leapt from the pages the first time he had read the manuscript begin to pulse inside of his mind, quicker and quicker now that the pages were open again. He leaned forward and as before, the numbers seemed to shimmer and then turn to text, and as he read the thick script, they turned back to numbers. He got a half-erection that pulsed but didn't overwhelm him.

The words that turned to numbers formed a mathematical formula he had never seen before. But the equation in his mind seemed like the answer key to the formula in front of him now, the base structure that allowed him to understand everything written on the pages. The formula were mathematical representations that laid out the basis of the power of numbers. He let his eyes flow over the page and then quickly turned it. As he read, he no longer even noticed the transformation of numbers to text to formula.

The pages contained groupings of equations that grew in length until finally there were no breaks between them at all. He almost forgot to breathe as he studied the formula, and as he did, power continued to fill him, entering the nerves of his hands and moving through his arms, then into his spine and up to his head. He learned formulas that he knew would physically recreate almost any form of energy by manipulating the invisible forces that made up all matter. The information was so complex that his head began to ache, but he kept reading, hungrily absorbing it all.

And then he turned a page and saw the words, 'BLACK NUMBERS', stretched across the parchment in thick, blocky lettering. He felt a chill run through his body and his fingers shook as he held the page.

He read further and as he did so, he began to sweat. The initial equation he had absorbed hummed at a strange frequency and he again felt the total absence of mathematics. There was no way to manipulate what one couldn't touch, see, or feel. He understood what Black Numbers were not, but he felt anger and then despair fill him as he read, knowing that he only had one page to go before the end of the manuscript and he had yet to understand not only what Black Numbers were, but how to manipulate them.

He turned the final page and stopped breathing entirely without knowing it. The final sentence felt like a punch to the gut as he read it over and over, and didn't even notice that it didn't turn into a mathematical formula like the rest of the book. It stayed as text.

> *"The Aleph Null can only unlock*
> *The power of Black Numbers*
> *By spilling the blood*
> *Of the Birth Mother.*
> *Only then will the power that*
> *Is not*
> *Burst to life*
> *And fuse between them,*
> *Releasing the energy behind the energy."*

Sid's hands started shaking and he hung his head.

Not only would he never have spilled his mother's blood in the first place, his mother was already dead.

He shut the manuscript and threw it onto the fire. It just sat in the red coals, unharmed. He watched it for some time, then sighed, grabbed a stick, and pushed it from the fire pit. He reached out a tentative hand and was surprised that the manuscript was not even warm to the touch. He pulled it into his lap and looked up at the night sky, staring at the pinpoints of light and feeling like everything he was doing was in vain.

Chapter 45

With the sun lowering toward the horizon to his left, Crowdal stood up in the stirrups to get a better view over the tall grass that swayed all around them from the slight breeze. He felt a thrill of hope when he realized the mountains were much closer, although they had never seemed to be actually moving toward the majestic peaks. He turned to take in the land all around them.

Aside from the mountains in front of them, they were surrounded by a grassy plain that had no end in any direction. The grass hissed and swished as it moved in the breeze, the sound and motion enough to lull everyone into a dull sleep-like state as they sat atop their horses.

For twelve days they had ridden their horses single-file across the plain, resting for a few hours at night, but never long enough for any of them to get any good sleep, except for the third night when they had to rest the horses longer to keep them from collapsing.

He still couldn't get the look of anguish and despair that had ravaged Sid's face that night out of his memory. Through half-closed eyes, he had watched his friend read the manuscript and all seemed fine until Sid threw the manuscript into the fire. He had tried to get Sid to tell him what had happened, but he wouldn't speak of it. Since then, Sid had been withdrawn and uncommunicative.

He glanced to the rear of the group and saw Melinda slumped on her horse. To make matters worse, she had not said a word in days either. Her eyes were blackened from exhaustion, and her skin seemed to hang from her face. He wasn't sure what was wrong with her and he didn't know if she would make it much further.

Crowdal worried greatly for his friends, wishing there was something he could do for them. But they had to keep moving, they had no choice. Writhgarth had doubled back their trail a few times and had reported that they were being followed. He had never seen who was following them, but he had heard the distant sounds of a large group and had never dared venture too far and risk being captured.

Crowdal faced forward again to examine the mountains. He only hoped the group would reach them soon and be able to lose whomever was chasing them. The journey hadn't been that hard for him. As a Trith, he could keep going for another fortnight if need be before he even started to tire.

As they had traveled, they had come across small ponds and had refilled their water skins. The mercenaries Richard and Nik proved to be amazing shots with their bows as they took down pheasants they occasionally scared up in front of them. The birds would fly up, the fluttering of their wings almost sounding like a low whistle, and both mercenaries would pull their bows and release three or four arrows each in just a matter of moments, dropping as many birds. They rarely missed, so they had enough food to eat, except for Crowdal who wouldn't touch the meat. He subsisted from the Liret, the hard-pressed grain and bean-paste bars that he had in his pack. He had enough to keep him alive for another month if need be.

A few times they had crested low hills and startled vast herds of bison, sometimes in groups of several thousand. The beasts were not frightened by them, and they once had to ride slowly through the middle of a herd. Nik almost shot one of the beasts, but Tulman pulled his bow down, telling him there was no way they had the time to clean such a large animal and carry the meat. Nik had grumbled, his eyes bright with the desire to kill one of the enormous animals.

It had been days since they had seen the last herd, and Crowdal hoped that was a sign the landscape was changing. He sniffed the air and was sure it smelled different now. He caught just a hint of the pungent green smell of the long needles of the giant Miq tree, but it was so faint that he couldn't be sure.

It was enough to lift his spirits, though. The endless, grassy plain had made everyone short-tempered. His friends barked responses to each other, their tones clipped. Except for the Haissan; the creature just rode in silence, never complaining, and never straying far from Sid or Agnes. It seemed to be as protective of Sid now as it was of Agnes. Crowdal wasn't sure he liked the Haissan being so close to Sid, but he got the feeling that it would die for his friend, which was a strange development, one he could not quite figure out.

Crowdal sat back down in his saddle and turned back to the group stretching out single file behind him. "Good news, everyone. I think we are getting close to the end of this plain. We should reach the base of the mountains in a day or two." He motioned toward the snow-capped peaks in the distance. "Can you smell the trees?"

Nik, who was right behind Crowdal, slowly lifted his head, his eyes dull with exhaustion. But as Crowdal's words sunk in, he opened his eyes wider and stood up in his own stirrups to get a better look at the mountains. He sat down just as quickly though. "We aren't any closer to those damned mountains."

Crowdal sighed. "Just use that big nose of yours to sniff the air and tell me what you smell."

Nik glared at Crowdal but let the comment go. He made an exaggerated show of sniffing the air, moving his head in a full circle as he inhaled loudly. "Gee, I wonder why I don't smell anything other than this dusty grass? Oh that's right, it's because we aren't any closer to... ," he paused mid-sentence and sniffed again, this time more carefully. Then his eyes lit up. "I smell it! I can smell trees!"

Crowdal smiled and nodded.

Nik turned behind him. "Come on everyone, take a whiff of that sweet air."

Pretty soon everyone in line, even Sid and the Haissan, were standing in their stirrups and breathing in deeply.

The sound of hooves broke into the good cheer and grew louder until Writhgarth appeared behind them and rode up the line until he was next to Crowdal. "They are getting closer, not more than a half-day behind us and gaining."

Crowdal sighed loudly and looked back toward the mountains. He made some calculations, then turned back to the others, who had all ridden up until they were in a circle around him.

Nik spoke from his horse to Crowdal's left, "What should we do? Run for it or fight?"

Agnes shook her head violently. "We can't fight them, not the Masteen or the Black Robe. And the gods help us if they have joined forces."

Tulman nodded his head in agreement. "She's right, we can't fight them all. I say we make a run for the mountains."

Murmurs of agreement rose from the group until Crowdal raised his hand. He had become, without it even being discussed, the accepted tactical leader of the group. "You are right, Agnes, Tulman, we can't fight them."

Tulman's horse side-stepped in agitation and he brought it under control with a whisper to the beast's ear. He then spat to his right. "Then it's settled, we make a run for the mountains."

Crowdal shook his head no.

The entire group looked at him with confused faces.

Writhgarth grimly gestured behind them. "If we can't fight them, and we aren't going to make a run for it, then what are we going to do, just sit here and knit hats?"

Crowdal looked directly at Writhgarth. His eyes burned intensely but his face looked slightly haunted. "I will stay behind and try to slow them down while you all make a run for the mountains."

A chorus of confused voices rang out, everyone talking at the same time. Except, that is, for Sid, who had kept silent, staring at the mountains in the distance, his hair fluttering in the breeze. He held his chin high and his back straight as he sat on his horse.

Finally, he spoke quietly.

Everyone kept talking, not hearing him, until Writhgarth raised his and yelled, "Quiet!"

The horses neighed and side-stepped at the shout, and everyone turned toward the little man. The wind sighed through the tall grass all around them, and the sun's low angle stretched their shadows in long, ghostly patterns away from them.

Writhgarth nodded slightly to everyone in a terse thanks. "Sid has something to say."

Everyone turned to look at Sid, who still sat straight in his saddle, staring toward the mountains. He didn't speak at first, but everyone stayed quiet, waiting patiently, knowing that he was their true leader.

Just a fortnight earlier he had the countenance of a boy on the edge of manhood who was unsure of his place in the world, showing flashes of anger, but always deferring to his friends for the big decisions. But since Mrs. Wessmank's death, he had changed. His facial expressions always looked to be set in stone, and his eyes were hooded in constant thought. He rarely spoke to anyone, not even Crowdal, who always seemed able to get a smile out of Sid, even if it was just a slight up-turning of his lips.

***

Sid let out a small breath and his eyes lost their faraway look. He turned to the group and spoke quietly, his voice even and flat, "Crowdal will not sacrifice himself for us."

When Crowdal opened his mouth to speak, Sid glanced at him, and Crowdal shut his mouth as if he had been slapped.

Sid continued, "The Masteen has joined forces with the Black Robe and his Haissen." He paused and shuddered slightly, remembering the darkness he had sensed from them both. "The Korpor also runs with them. They are too powerful together, for even me to handle." He turned and glanced again at the mountains and spoke, his voice carried away on the breeze so that it sounded distant, "There is a forest on the other side of those mountains."

Nik snorted, breaking the silence. "How could you know that?"

Sid turned and looked directly at Nik, and when the mercenary gazed into his eyes, he looked down immediately.

Sid blinked his left eye, followed by his right eye and said, "I can feel the forest. The living essence is strong, it reaches out to me, a power that is mathematically complex and fills my head with numbers I have never seen before."

Crowdal spoke up, "And you can smell the forest too, right?"

Sid smiled slightly. "There is that, also."

Tulman and Writhgarth chuckled quietly, then the rest of the group joined in.

Sid nodded thanks to Crowdal for breaking the tension, something that only the big man could have done. "There is something about that forest that draws me, and I think if I can reach it, I will have a chance against our enemies." He looked directly at Agnes.

Writhgarth spat. "Those are the Kulkraken Mountains! No one, as far as I know, has crossed over them. Why don't we just turn and head east or west now?"

Sid shook his head, remembering the vision he had received while on the Grange Trail; of the clearing in the forest, of Agnes standing over him with a knife, and his friends surrounded by the Masteen's men. There was no way he was going to put his friends in that danger. If he could change it, he would at least try.

"No, Writhgarth. At least Agnes and I need to cross them. I've seen it all happen in a sort of dream. But the rest of you need to get as far from here as you can. I can recreate the same equation from earlier to hide your trail. Go east or west, it doesn't matter now. Our enemies will follow only me."

Both Crowdal and Writhgarth looked at each other, then back at Sid and spoke in unison, "Not a chance, Sid."

They smiled quickly at each other before Writhgarth continued, "We are not going to miss out on all the fun."

Crowdal spoke up then, "But I want Tulman, Richard, and Nik to take Melinda away from here. She is too weak to continue."

Melinda lifted her head, shook it tiredly, and whispered, "No, I'm coming with you."

Crowdal started to object but was cut off by Sid sighing loudly.

Sid raised his eyes to the sky. "It appears that nothing I say or do will change what I saw."

When everyone looked at him strangely, he pointed at the mountains. "From my vision, I saw us all there together. I guess what will be will be." He wiped sweat from his brow. "All right. Let's ride together until we are about a day's walk from the Kulkraken mountains, and then I want you all, except for Agnes and I, to get off of your horses and move carefully into the grass, single-file, and walk silently at a 45-degree angle toward the mountains. See that taller part of the mountain range over there with the twin jagged peaks? Walk directly toward it. We will meet up at the base there."

Tulman spit over the side of his horse. "And what about you and Agnes? Why are we walking and you are riding?"

Sid pointed northwest. "We will lead all of the horses in that direction to get our pursuers as far from you as possible."

"No, Sid, that is too dangerous!" Melinda moved her horse closer to him, her face haggard. "We can find another way."

Sid looked sadly at her, then continued. "We will ride at an angle away from you until we get close to the mountains, then Agnes and I will get off our horses and send them west by themselves. We will then walk along the base of the mountain until we meet up with you. We will create an equation similar to the one we created when we first entered the plain, which should be enough to block our trail. We will do the same for you. With any luck, our enemies will follow the horses west, away from us all."

Melinda shook her head angrily. "No, that doesn't make sense. Why don't you just send the horses off by themselves now and we all cut across this godforsaken plain together?"

"Because the horses will not run far enough by themselves to sufficiently lead our enemies away from us. They will likely stop and start grazing after only a short distance. We need more time than that to reach the mountains safely."

Melinda stubbornly continued, "Still, why don't we all ride together then? It honestly makes no sense to split up."

Sid sighed. "Agnes and I can move much quicker by ourselves after we let the horses go. This will give us the most amount of time to find a path over the mountains while putting as much distance between us and our pursuers." He softened his voice. "You are exhausted, Melinda. This way you just have to walk the last little bit and wait for us."

Crowdal nudged his horse over to Sid. "As much as I hate to admit it, that plan makes good tactical sense, but you and Agnes shouldn't go alone. Take Writhgarth and Tulman with you for protection."

Sid smiled coldly. "We do not need protection with swords or arrows."

"I am going with you." The soft hissing voice made everyone turn to the Haissan. "I never leave the Red Robe's side."

Sid stared carefully at the hooded Haissan, then nodded acceptance, glad for a reason he didn't understand that the Haissan would stay with them. "All right, the three of us will go with all of the horses."

Crowdal looked wary, his expression showing that he didn't trust the creature. But he did not protest, merely nodded brusquely, then turned to the Haissan. "You will do everything within your power to protect them, do you understand?"

The Haissan merely turned its hooded head slightly toward Crowdal.

Crowdal reached out and gripped Sid's shoulder. "It is a good plan, let's do this. If we are not at the base of the mountain when you get there, don't wait too long for us before you start climbing it. We can meet up on the other side if need be."

Crowdal looked around the group. "All right, take what you will need in your packs and leave everything else on the horses. It will be cold up in the mountains, so make sure you have heavy clothing, and food and water."

Everyone quickly got their packs in order, and then Crowdal said, "Get into single file, then toss your reins to the person in front of you and tie them to your saddle. It will be dark soon, but we will continue on through the night. By my guess, we should be close enough to the mountains by dawn to split up. When we do, slide off of your horses without stopping them and carefully step into the grass without disturbing it if you can help it. Then walk fifty paces into the grass before joining up with everyone." He spoke to Sid and Agnes, "Can you set the equation while riding?"

Sid and Agnes both nodded yes.

The Trith continued, "Good. If we don't stop, then we will not leave any extra disturbances that might be seen. Does everyone understand?"

They were all either trained soldiers or, in Melinda's case, a trained healer, and were used to following orders, so they all just nodded grimly and moved their horses into a line with Sid and Agnes at the lead, and tied their horses' reins together.

Sid looked behind him and when he saw that everyone was ready, he lifted his arm and brought it down. They all started forward.

Nobody spoke. The soft padding of the horses' hooves, the occasional jingle of a bridle, and the constant sighing of the breeze through the tall grass were the only sounds to be heard for the rest of the night. A sliver of a moon rose, casting an eerie and faint glow to the plain, but it was just bright enough to allow them to adjust their angle to keep the mountains in front of them. In the immense grassy plain, it would have been difficult to keep their horses going in a straight line if it weren't for the mountains to guide them.

They were all lost in their own thoughts as they rode.

***

Not far behind them, the Korpor, glowing white in the sliver of moonlight, pushed out of the grass and stepped onto their trail. It sniffed the air, turning its head in a half circle, then stared down the narrow trail. Its huge blue eyes blinked, first the left, followed by the right. It smiled grotesquely, then faded back into the grass and continued to silently follow them.

Chapter 46

The Masteen's horse stumbled and whinnied in pain. It had been slowing down over the past two days, and the Masteen had to kick it harder and harder to keep it moving. He wiped dirt and sweat from his brow, having taken off his helmet four days earlier. While he liked how the Kraagiquazz snout enhanced his image, the helmet was too hot and heavy for a long journey. He hadn't expected to waste so much time chasing the boy.

They had quickly found the boy's trail where he had entered the grassy plain, but that had been many days earlier. They had traveled hard, pushing their horses to their limits; but they were war horses, bred to carry tremendous weight and gallop in short bursts upon a battle field. They were not bred for long journeys. So they had to proceed at a slower pace than the Black Robe had liked, which suited the Masteen just fine.

He disliked the pompous and arrogant young man, wanting nothing more than to spit him upon his sword. But the boy had power, and it hadn't been dampened by the Masteen. Apparently, only the Aleph Null was affected by him. Why this was, he didn't know, and honestly didn't care.

The Masteen turned his head and gritted his teeth. He was tired of seeing nothing but tall, brown, unending grass in every direction. The monotony wore him down. He was a man who had little patience, wanting instant gratification in all things and usually getting it.

Turning his head to face forward, he at least took solace in the sight of the mountain range ahead of them. But they had been heading toward it for days and it didn't look any closer, which irritated him.

He looked up at the sun as it baked upon him, and cursed. It was hot for being so early in the spring, and it heated his armor until he was dripping sweat from every part of his body, which made him even crankier.

A bunch of grouse flew up in front of them and ten of his men instantly released arrows, bringing down 11 birds. One of his men let out a whoop and held out his hand to his riding partners who angrily handed over silver pieces. One of the men, angrily putting his bow away, muttered, "You were just lucky to get two birds with one shot."

The man put the silver pieces into a dirty leather pouch and chuckled. "Luck had nothing to do with it, Guunter."

Two of the men let out a harrumph at this boast and cantered away to gather the fallen birds.

The Masteen's horse stumbled again. He cursed and put his hand up for the men to stop. "Time to rest the horses."

The Black Robe sighed. "We need to keep moving."

The Masteen glared at the little upstart and gritted his teeth. "We won't get too far with dead horses. Either you go on ahead of us, or stop here and take a rest."

The young man looked like he was going to take the Masteen up on the offer leave the death squad behind, but finally just shrugged as if he didn't care. He pulled on his reins and jumped lightly from his horse. The Black Robe's Haissen followed suit, stamping down the grass to make a place on which to sit.

The Masteen felt his anger drain away as he watched the way the Haissen moved. He marveled again at the strange creatures. He had never thought a man could beat him with a sword, and he had been right. But these were not men and he would like to get his hands on one to bring back to his castle. There was much he could learn from one of them.

He swung from his horse and stepped to the ground, noticing that his horse was bleeding under its saddle. He missed his war horse, a beast he had bred to easily carry his great weight. He seethed at the Trith for stealing it, and vowed to run his sword through the Trith's body when he saw him next.

He turned to the man standing next to him. "Norloc, get someone to tend to my horse's wounds."

The man nodded, wiping at the discharge that leaked from the gaping hole in his face where his nose had once been. He turned and ambled over to the horse master of the death squad and spoke quietly to him.

The man nodded and removed a cloth and some items from his pack, then approached the Masteen's horse and removed its saddle. The horse whinnied in pain and relief as the man softly caressed the animal between the eyes. He was not a cruel man and hated to see the horses treated so harshly. He ran his hand down the side of the horse and when he got to the back, where the saddle had been, his eyes hardened when he saw that the hair was worn completely away and the skin was matted with blood from bearing so much weight for so long. The man poured water over the bloody skin, and the horse sidestepped and snorted as he carefully wiped the blood away. He spoke soft words to the animal and calmed it down, and as he did, he suddenly leaned closer to the horse's back. He wiped away more blood and saw there were deep cuts going all the way to the spine of the horse. He put his cloth away and walked over to the Masteen.

"Sir."

The Masteen wiped ale from his mouth with the back of his hand, after having just taken a long pull from his flask. He growled at the interruption. "What do you want?"

The man looked frightened as he spoke, "Sir, your horse is

finished. It must be put down."

Looking over the man's shoulder at his horse, the Masteen nodded and pulled his sword. He stepped to his horse and saw the damage to its back. The beast shook where it stood, hanging its head. The Masteen lifted his sword and swung down hard, severing the horse's head in one stroke. The beast shuddered and collapsed to the ground. He wiped the blood from his sword on the side of the horse and turned away. "Cut it up and let's eat well tonight." He motioned to Norloc. "Find me another horse, the next largest we have."

Norloc nodded, holding a crusty, stinking cloth to his face, and made his way through the death squad. He motioned to a man who stood by a large brown stallion. "Is your horse well?"

The man handed the reins over, "He is strong."

"Good. Find yourself a replacement mount from what we have left."

They always traveled with spare horses, although after the Trith and his group had escaped, taking the Masteen's war horse and seven others, only four extra horses had been left, and they were the least desirable, smaller and younger, and not as well trained.

Norloc took the reins and walked the large beast back to the Masteen, who looked up as they approached. The Masteen finished urinating into the grass, pushed his huge penis inside of his trousers, then briefly examined the new horse.

"This one will do."

Norloc staked the new horse's reins to the ground, then pulled his knife and stepped over to the dead horse. He stuck the blade into the stomach and pulled it in a sawing motion across the belly. Blood and guts spilled to the ground and Norloc stepped to the side to avoid getting it on his boots. He then made an incision in the hide and pulled up on it as he sliced along the flesh with his sharp knife, peeling it from the body. Two of the men joined him and they soon had the animal skinned.

Norloc cut huge chunks of meat from the body and handed them to a line of men who passed them to a large fire that had been built. They had carried a good amount of wood with them into the grassy plains, knowing there would be nothing with which to make a fire. The meat was stuck onto huge spits and put over the fire.

The Masteen's stomach rumbled as he approached the woman. She was still beautiful, although probably close to his age. He normally liked young women who were just beginning their monthly cycles, but this woman held a promise of experienced pleasure that excited him.

Her face paled when she saw him approach and she quickly turned away.

His voice growled, "Look at me, woman."

When she didn't respond, he grabbed her hair and yanked it back.

"Do not ignore me."

She reached up and tried to pry his hands free to no effect. The Masteen enjoyed her terror, like he did with every woman he took. He reached down with his other hand and cupped her breast. "You are old, but I will have you anyway."

She struggled and then stopped, her eyes looking past his shoulder. He turned his head angrily. "Leave me be or I will kill you." But when he saw the young Black Robe and four of his Haissen, he hesitated.

The Black Robe spoke casually but with a hint of threat to his voice, "You will let the woman be, Masteen. She is not for you to take."

The Masteen seethed, but let go of the woman's hair and pushed her to the ground at the same time. "She is an old woman, anyway. I won't waste my time." He glared at the young man who stood so calmly, then leaned toward him. "Don't you ever tell me what to do again or I will rip your heart out." He spit a thick globule of phlegm to his side.

The young man lifted his hand and casually picked at a finger nail. "Whatever you say, Masteen. Just leave the woman be and I won't have to have my heart ripped out."

Growling deeply within his chest, not liking the mocking tone but knowing he couldn't fight the Haissen, the Masteen turned from the young man and made his way toward the fire, back-handing one of his men who happened to be standing in his way. He grabbed a large hunk of sizzling horse meat and tore at it with his teeth.

He would kill this young Black Robe, like the woman Agnes had asked, and he would do it for free.

He finished his meat, then mounted his horse, his great weight causing the animal to stumble sideways a few paces before it found its balance.

His men scurried around to pack up the rest of the meat and put out the fire. Within a short time they were all ready to move out.

The Masteen led them, anxious to reach the mountains.

Chapter 47

The Unnamed One stared across the unending grass and screamed at the sky in frustration. It had followed the Black Numbers trail for days but it was growing weaker by the moment. It had not found an animal larger than a mouse to eat since it had entered the plain, the hunger burning so deeply that it found it difficult to concentrate on the scent of numbers.

It stood tall and scanned the horizon, then started forward again, the hunger making it struggle to keep going at a quick pace. It traveled for some time before it slowly crested a hill.

In front of it, stretching almost as far as it could see, was a great herd of shaggy, four-legged beasts. With a renewed burst of energy, it took off at a run, and the beasts scattered in all directions; but there were so many of them that the Unnamed One ran through them, smashing every animal it came across. Soon all of the animals had disappeared from view and it stopped, breathing hard before turning.

Behind it, scattered across the immediate area, were at least a hundred dead animals. The Unnamed One made its way back to the first carcass and ripped it apart. The animal was huge and the Unnamed One glutinously tore into it, ripping flesh from the body and stuffing the bloody chunks into its mouth. It soon finished and stepped to the next dead animal, repeating the process. It devoured four of the beasts before it had satisfied its hunger. Blood and flesh covered its face and chest, and the thick blood ran down its legs.

It spotted a shallow pond in the distance and immediately turned and made its way in that direction, kicking the numerous dead animals out of its way. It soon reached the water, dunked its head deep down, and drank its fill, then lay down in the pond to cool down, the water barely covering its body.

It rested like this until the sun descended to the horizon before it stood up, shaking water from its skin. It drank once more then stepped over to another of the dead animals and devoured it.

It then sniffed in every direction before catching the scent of the Black Numbers trail. It screamed at the sky, then took off at a run toward the mountains, scooping up two of the dead animals and swinging them over its shoulders without slowing down.

Chapter 48

Sid yawned and looked up at the sun as it hung, hot and stifling directly above them. He and Agnes nibbled on bread as they traveled, with the Haissan silently riding just ahead of them. They had split silently from the group just before dawn, his friends slipping from their horses and melting into the tall grass without even a whispered goodbye. It was as they had planned, not wanting to give any indication that they were separating, like a twisting foot print that might dig up the earth, or a broken stalk of grass.

Sid stood up in his stirrups and estimated they would reach the base of the mountains by dusk.

He turned to Agnes. She was so beautiful that he felt his breath catch in his throat. She rode with her back straight, staring at the mountains with a lost look in her eyes. Her shoulder-length black hair fell over her eyes and he had noticed that she had a habit of tucking it behind her left ear. He had attempted conversation with her a few times now, but the words kept dying in his throat before he could form them. He angled his horse closer to hers and cleared his throat.

She turned her head to him. "Yes?"

Now when he had her attention, the words again refused to come.

She seemed to notice his discomfort, for she rolled her eyes. "Sid, honestly, just say what you want to say."

He blushed, embarrassed that she was aware of his nervousness. "It's just, well... we haven't really had a chance to talk since... well, you know."

She flushed slightly, knowing exactly what he was referring to. "I know." The corners of her mouth turned up in a small smile. "It was pretty amazing wasn't it?"

He studied her, surprised at how forward she was. She was a lot like Melinda and Mistress Riana; very strong-willed and confident. Every girl he had met in his village had been demure, yet coy. Not one of them had ever spoken their minds, much less said anything that was of interest to him.

He shrugged. "I still have no idea what caused that to happen between us. We should probably be careful not to touch each other until we know what is happening."

Agnes looked like she was going to make a joke, but instead, she just looked at him for some time. "You are so serious, Sid."

"Well, it isn't like we are on a holiday right now, is it?"

She shook her head. "That's not what I meant. It is just that you don't have to always carry every little burden on your shoulders."

"*Little* Burden? You think the murder of Mrs. Wessmank is just a *little* burden to me? You think the torture of Melinda at the hands of Father Mansico is just a *little* burden, much less the danger that all of my friends are in because of the Oblate?" His skin turned blotchy. "This is life and death I am dealing with. You don't know what you are talking about, Agnes."

Her face fell slack and she set her lips tightly, then turned forward to stare at the mountains again, ignoring him.

Sid felt a darkness inside of him, bubbling deeply, threatening to wipe all emotion away. That part of him honestly didn't care if he had hurt her feelings. His voice came out clipped, "What, are you going to pout like a little child now because you can't handle a few harsh realities?"

She whipped her head back to him, her eyes flashing. "Reality? You think I can't handle reality? I'm just a pretty woman who has had everything handed to her, right?" Her voice lashed at him like a physical blow. "How about watching my mother get violently murdered in front of me when I was just a little girl? How about being abducted by her murderer and never seeing my family again? Or feeling the pain and power of the Black Robe ripping through every nerve ending of my body for his own pleasure, knowing there was nothing I could do to stop him? It's just you, the great Aleph Null, who is the only person in this whole world who has suffered, right? Oh, poor you."

She glared at him, and he glared angrily back for a few moments until the darkness within him seemed to push back a little bit and he lowered his eyes in shame. She was right. He was being selfish, but he couldn't bring himself to admit it.

Silence extended between them for some time as they rode. The air smelled sweet, although it was quite hot. Sid wiped sweat from his brow and turned his eyes covertly to Agnes.

She faced stiffly forward, her lips pressed tightly together. He let his shoulders slump. He didn't know why he had picked a fight with her. She was here, with him, because she had thrown away her entire life as she had known it. She was helping him, risking her life for something she didn't have to be a part of.

"Agnes?"

She didn't respond.

He felt a lump in his throat. He always seemed to hurt people. He wasn't a very good person and he didn't know why anyone chose to stick by him. Crowdal, Melinda, Writhgarth, Mrs. Wessmank, Maelon, even the three mercenaries who had joined with them, all deserved better. At the thought of Mrs. Wessmank, he felt his throat constrict. He missed her so much. And not for the first time, he wondered what had become of Maelon. He had hoped the three-legged animal would join with them again, but there had been no sign of him.

They rode for some time, not talking. The sounds from the

horse's bridles that he led jingled behind them as they cut through the tall grass.

He glanced again at Agnes without turning his head. There was so much tension in the air that he felt like there was a physical wall between them.

Finally, he sighed softly. "This is stupid."

"What did you just call me?"

He held up his hand. "I didn't say you were stupid. I just meant that we shouldn't be fighting."

Her voice was edged with hardness, "I didn't start the fight."

Sid nodded. "I know. It was me. I was being mean-spirited."

She spoke in a hard voice, but she couldn't stop a small grin from forming on her lips. "Well, then stop doing that."

He grinned, then turned serious. "I really am sorry, Agnes."

She turned her head and her eyes softened. "Maybe we put the cart before the horse, so to speak."

"I don't understand."

Agnes motioned to him and then herself "Us. How we… ah…" her voice trailed off as she struggled to find the right words. "I just mean, well… most people get to know one another for a long time before they consummate their relationship with… sex. We not only had a sexual experience beyond anything normal people can possibly understand, we had it before we had said more than two words to each other."

Sid grinned. "I didn't mind it."

Agnes had unconsciously angled her horse closer to him as they spoke and raised her hand to smack him on the arm playfully, but pulled it away at the last moment, as if remembering what had happened before when she had touched him. She shook her head instead. "You are a horrible man, Sid!"

He laughed. "That I am."

She turned serious. "I get the feeling you don't smile very often."

The levity left him and he felt the weight of the past few weeks fall upon him once more. He thought again of Mrs. Wessmank's death and a blackness welled up inside at the loss.

"I'm sorry, Sid, I didn't mean to ruin the mood."

He gave her a half smile. "No, that's all right. I was just thinking of Mrs. Wessmank. She didn't deserve to die."

"She must have been very special to you."

Sid nodded. "I loved her more than anyone."

Agnes pushed a strand of hair from her face. "Tell me about her."

Sid was quiet as images of the old woman flashed through his mind—her frizzy red hair, the two birthmarks above her eyes, her blue apron, her wonderful hot tea and freshly baked cookies. He smiled at the memories. "She was an amazing woman. She owned a tea and tobacco shop in my village. I remember as a little boy, my father would send me to town to get supplies. Every single time, without fail, she had cookies and hot tea waiting for me and we would sit at her rough wooden table and talk. Most of the kids in town were afraid of her and called her mean names, but they never tried to get to know her."

He smiled again. "You should have tasted her date cookies." He mimicked a folding motion with his hands as he spoke. "She folded dates inside of the cookies and baked them so that when you bit into one, the dates would be thick and sweet yet the edge of the cookie would be hard and crunchy. She had this blue apron that she wore every day for as long as I knew her." He smiled to himself, looking at the tall grass around them without really seeing it. "I remember feeling safe when I was with her, and happy. Even when she would chastise me for something or other, I knew she loved me."

He stopped speaking and looked at Agnes, who was smiling at him.

"What?"

She shrugged. "You looked so happy just now. Even in the short time since we met, you always seem to look angry, but just now you looked truly happy as you told me about her. Mrs. Wessmank must have truly been a special woman."

Sid nodded. "She was."

They rode for some time, each in their own thoughts, until Sid said, "Why are you a part of the Oblate?"

Agnes sucked a breath through her teeth. "It... is a long story."

"We have the time and I'd like to hear your story."

She was silent for some time, as if collecting her thoughts, then she started to tell him about her life. He listened quietly, interested in every word she spoke. She finally got to the point where they had met in the Masteen's camp and she stopped. "You know the rest."

Sid nodded. "What I don't know is why you chose to go with us over staying with the Masteen.

"As the Red Robe, I was sent by the Black Robe to ensure the Masteen played his part in your capture." She looked up at him. "You don't know what the Red Robe position is, do you?"

Sid shook his head no. "From your tale, I understand that it is a high position in the Oblate, but that is about it."

"You don't know anything else about the Oblate?"

"No, not really. I know a little bit about the Black Robe, and about the... Proofing by the Korpor." He sat quietly for a couple of breaths. "That is all I wanted to know... till now. Tell me more about the Black Robe."

Agnes shuddered. "The Black Robe rules the Oblate, usually very fairly. But the new Black Robe is... evil. The Oblate that I knew no longer exists now that he is in power."

"But the Oblate has always been evil, why would you ever have wanted to be a part of it?"

She eyed him coolly. "The Oblate wasn't evil, Sid. We have always been a force for good, working behind the scenes to ensure every noble house and kingdom in the land was kept in line and under control so as not to harm the innocent and powerless people. If it weren't for us, the world would be a dark place."

Sid scoffed. "You don't actually believe that do you?"

Her face turned red and her green eyes flashed at him. "You don't know anything about us so don't you dare insinuate that I am somehow gullible or wrong!"

He shrugged. "I just know that the Oblate controls the Korpor, and the Korpor is evil." She started to speak but he continued, overriding her, "Agnes, in the last few fortnights I have been betrayed by my father who set the Korpor upon me. I've fought the creature numerous times, and been attacked by agents of the Oblate at every turn. Father Mansico, who worked for the Oblate, tortured Melinda to get information about me. The Haissen tried to kill my friends." He hardened his voice. "And I've lost someone very close to me because of it. So don't even try to tell me the Oblate is some force for good. I will do everything in my power to destroy it, that I can promise you!" He stopped, out of breath and angry.

Agnes looked away, staring across the grassy plain, her mouth set in an thin line.

He was sorry for snapping at her, but he couldn't believe her ignorance.

They rode for a long time, neither one speaking to the other. He worried that he had pushed her away for good, and was about to apologize when he heard her whisper, "You are right."

Sid started to speak, but she turned to him and put up her hand.

"Please, let me finish."

Sid shut his mouth.

Agnes rode silently for a few moments, then brushed a strand of hair from her eyes and said, "You are right about how things are now. But you must understand that the Oblate hasn't always been a negative force in the land. I've seen the Oblate do some great things. Just last year we helped save thousands of lives during a devastating flood in Bildenhall, ensuring that money and resources were provided to the people and local businesses, that the town was rebuilt. We have saved hundreds of thousands of lives over the years by preventing unnecessary wars between royal houses because we have agents in powerful positions everywhere. Our work behind the scenes has ensured that goods are traded fairly all across the land. The list of positive changes we have affected is long. It is only recently, when the old Black Robe was killed, that everything changed. This new Black

Robe is the darkest soul I have ever met, and he wields power beyond any I've ever before imagined. I've seen him do things I can't even begin to comprehend. There is no one who is his equal in the control of mathematics."

She paused, staring directly into his eyes. "Sorry, I misspoke. I think you may be able to match his power, but to be honest, I am not sure if you can fight this man and win because he won't fight fair. He is... malignant, which means he won't hesitate to destroy anything or anyone who gets in his way."

Sid opened his mouth to speak but she continued, overriding him. "Don't you see? Because you are constrained by those you love, you are at a disadvantage. He will destroy without hesitating, while you will hesitate to save those around you."

Sid was stunned and angry. "You know nothing about me. People have died because of me."

"Yes, but they died willingly because they believed in and loved you!"

"No! They died simply because I couldn't save them." He choked up. "Mrs. Wessmank died by the kick of a normal man! Just a man, and I couldn't even stop it from happening."

She looked harshly at him. "Oh, stop feeling sorry for yourself."

He was about to retort, but shut his mouth instead, realizing that he sounded like a child, and he felt himself grin before he could stop it from happening.

She glared at him. "Why are you grinning like an idiot?"

"Because I am one."

Her eyes narrowed at him. "Don't mock me, Sid."

"I'm not. I just realized that here I am, riding with the most beautiful woman I've ever met, and I'm picking fights with you over things that are in the past for us both."

Her face darkened. "Then why don't you stop being an idiot?"

He chuckled. "I'll work on that."

Agnes smiled then, although she was obviously trying not to. "So, idiot, why don't we stop and have something to eat?"

Sid laughed out loud. "Sounds like a good idea to me." He pulled up on his reins and felt the horse that was tied directly behind him bump into the back of his own horse, causing his horse to whinny and rise up on its back legs. He tried to hold on but felt the leather slip from his hands and he fell backward, striking the nose of the horse behind him before hitting the ground hard. The air whooshed from his lungs and he looked up into the large eyes of the horse he had just hit as it lowered its head and nudged him.

Agnes giggled as she looked down at him lying on the ground.

Sid rolled to the side and pushed himself to his feet. "Thanks, I appreciate that."

Still smiling, Agnes slid from her horse, opened the flap of her saddle bag, and rummaged around before pulling out a half a loaf of hard-crusted bread and a chunk of cheese. "Looks like bread and cheese again. What I wouldn't give for one of Richard and Nik's birds right now, roasted brown and dripping grease."

Sid brushed dust and brown dried grass from his legs. "Thanks for your concern, I almost died just then and you are talking about roasted bird."

She glanced over her shoulder, her eyes dancing with humor. "Oh, you didn't almost die. Stop being so dramatic."

Sid pretended to limp over to her, putting a hand to his hip.

Agnes rolled her eyes. "Come on, let's push some of this grass down so we can sit."

The Haissan stayed on its horse, scanning their surroundings. There were times Sid had forgotten that it was even riding with them.

When they had a small patch of the tall grass stamped to the ground, they sat down side-by-side and started eating the bread and cheese. Her right leg was so close to his left leg that he felt their sexual energy again. He took a bite of the bread and as he reached for his water skin, he moved his leg over just a little, a part of him wanting to touch her more than anything and experience their sexual bond again.

He took a sip and handed her the water skin and as she reached for it, her leg lightly touched his, and even through their trousers, the sexual energy flared up and shot through them like a flash of light. They both gasped before jerking their legs apart.

She breathed heavily, staring at him accusatorially. "You did that on purpose!"

His heart pounded in his chest and he wiped his forehead and his hand came away with sweat. "I didn't, honestly."

Agnes whispered, "Somehow I don't believe you." She slid away from him then so there was some distance between them, and started eating again.

Sid cocked his head toward her, his hair falling over his left eye. "Who is this Black Robe?"

Agnes stared at the grassy ground as she chewed, then finally swallowed. She wrapped up the rest of her uneaten food and stood up. "I don't want to talk about him." She shuddered. "Just the thought of him makes me uncomfortable. Come on, we should get moving again."

Sid nodded, not pushing her. He gathered what was left of his own bread and cheese, then stood and handed it to her. She put it into her pack, then stepped up and slid into her saddle. He did the same and he lightly slapped the reins to his horse to start it moving, the horses tied behind nickering softly as they were jerked forward.

The Haissan moved ahead of them slightly.

They traveled for the rest of the afternoon without talking. The mountains were directly in front of them now, rising up and out of sight into a thick cloud cover.

Suddenly, they stepped from the tall grass onto bare ground. Sid looked behind him and saw that the grassy plain had ended as if a line had been drawn in the earth. On one side, the ground was thick with tall grass, but on the side where they now rode, it was bare ground covered with small rocks.

Sid pulled up on his reins and stopped. "Wow, can you believe that?"

Agnes looked around her in wonder. "It's the strangest thing I've ever seen. But I'm more glad than you could know to be out of that tall grass."

Sid smiled. "Me, too. If I never see another plain again, I'll be a happy man."

The sun was descending to their left now. Sid turned forward again and tilted his head back to take in the mountains, having to crane his neck back as far as he could to look all the way up. "That is the most amazing view I've ever seen."

She nodded, her head back the same way and her eyes wide in wonder. "It seems to go up forever."

Sid saw her slap at her neck and say "ouch." He felt a fly land on his own neck then and he slapped it without thinking.

Then another fly landed on him, followed by five more, which was strange.

He heard a buzzing sound, looked forward, and saw what looked like a dark cloud approaching them. He heard Agnes curse as she slapped at her head.

"Are you all right?"

She nodded and swatted at another insect. She looked at the blackness approaching them. "What is that?"

"I don't know. Looks like a storm cloud or something. Whatever it is, I don't like the look of it."

Her voice took on an edge to it. "That's not a cloud. It's a swarm of flies. Quick, let's get out of here!" She kicked her horse forward and pulled the reins to the left to angle away from it.

Sid did the same and they raced as quickly as they could away, but the horses that he led slowed him down.

But it didn't matter because the swarm turned and hit them like a wave of water, washing over them completely.

They both pulled up on their reins, not wanting to run blindly through the sudden darkness.

Sid waved his arms wildly and heard his horse whinny as the flies landed on and crawled over its body, biting the poor animal everywhere. Sid tried to build a dome of numbers around them, to protect them from the biting flies, but as he pulled his numbers together into an equation, he kept losing his concentration as more and more flies landed on him, biting every area of exposed skin.

The Haissan angled its horse back to them, ignoring the flies that crawled all over its body.

Agnes cursed and flailed her arms around her in panic. "We have to get out of here!" She kicked her horse and it took off at a gallop. Sid did the same and all of the horses tied behind him didn't object as they ran hard.

The Haissan followed without a word.

Sid slowly caught up with Agnes and was surprised that the black flies kept pace with them.

She looked over at him with wild eyes. "What are we going to do? I can't take this for much longer!"

The flies had lessened somewhat as they rode, but it was only a brief lull before they fully caught up to them again, so Sid concentrated on the dome of numbers construct, connecting the equations together in a hurry, activating the protective barrier around them, although it didn't protect them from the flies that were immediately around them.

As they crested a hill, he pulled his horse to a stop at the sight in front of him, and Agnes and the Haissan did the same. About thirty paces away, down the other side of the hill, they saw a pit filled with thick black liquid. A huge bubble rose up slowly in the center and then burst open, releasing a black swarm of flies. The whole area was thick with them, the constant buzz blocking out all other sounds.

Then, as if they had been spotted, a great blackness rose from the pit, the flies so thick that he couldn't see past them. They approached frighteningly fast and descended on them like a blanket, covering the numbered dome that he had created to protect them.

Agnes looked up in amazement. "What did you do?"

Sid shrugged. "I just created a numbered barrier around us. It should protect us but we still need to get out of here." As he said it, the flies that were trapped inside of the dome seemed to grow angrier now that they were so close to their apparent source. They crawled all over him. He opened his mouth to speak again when a number of flies climbed into his mouth. He spit them out and turned his horse, which was whinnying in pain and fear. He couldn't see anything around them because the flies had completely covered the dome so he created a simple fire equation and added it to the dome of numbers equation.

A loud whoosh sounded and light flared so brightly that he had to close his eyes. When he opened them, he saw a smoking ring of dead flies piled high all around them.

Agnes turned to him. "What did you just do now?"

Sid shrugged. "I just added an equation for fire to the dome of numbers around us." He pointed in the direction they had been moving. "Come on, let's put some distance between us and this pit."

They took off at a gallop to their right, descending the hill and pounded away from the pit, but also at a right angle to the mountain range. The swarm of flies that hadn't been on the wall of numbers when it burned stayed with them.

It wasn't difficult for Sid to keep the dome equation relative to their position. He just locked it to himself.

After a half a league or so, they turned their horses to approach the mountains again. The swarm had gradually fallen away, although they were still covered in biting flies. Sid brushed them away from the back of his horse over and over while doing the same to himself. The horses were lathered with sweat and starting to stumble, so he pulled back on the reins until they slowed down to a trot. His stallion was heaving as it tried to suck in lungful after lungful of air, and he could hear the horses behind him doing the same. He kept them walking at a good pace so they could cool down, knowing that if he brought the beasts to a full stop they could overheat and die.

Agnes and her Haissan did the same next to him.

Sid saw a small blue lake up ahead and to their right. He pointed. "Let's angle over there and water the horses."

Agnes nodded and pulled her reins to the right.

The horses smelled the water and increased their pace until they were stumbling over the rocks in their haste to reach the water. Sid noticed there were no longer any flies covering the numbered dome he had created, so he disassembled the equations. A fresh breeze immediately washed over them and he took in a deep breath of the sweet air. Most of the flies from within the dome flew up and buzzed angrily around them briefly before finally dispersing.

He tried to control the animals but their thirst was too strong a need and they ignored him. They soon splashed into the water, coming to a stop when the water rose to the horses' bellies. They immediately lowered their mouths to the water and drank greedily.

Sid gasped when the water covered his legs. It was the coldest water he had ever felt.

Agnes and the Haissan sat on their horses to either side of him.

Agnes lifted her feet out of the water, and looked comical as she held them straight out.

Sid snorted. "Oh come on, it isn't that cold!"

She shook her feet and water sprayed away from her. "Speak for yourself."

He let the horses drink their fill, then urged them forward deeper into the water until they were swimming. The flies fell from the horses and covered the surface of the water. Sid urged his horse to swim in a circle until they were heading back to the shoreline. The other horses that were tied in a line behind him followed without hesitating, anxious to get out of the cold water.

Agnes and the Haissan had done the same and were riding their horses up the rocky beach.

Not far from him, he saw a narrow creek bubble into the lake from the mountain, realizing now why the water was so cold. It was probably not much above freezing.

The Haissan immediately slid from its horse and started rubbing the animal down, so Sid and Agnes did the same. Before they finished with their own horses, the Haissan had moved on to the other horses in the line, quickly wiping them down one at a time. The horses were covered in bloody fly bites, but the icy water had stopped the bleeding and Sid thought they were going to be fine.

Agnes spoke as she wiped down the side of her horse's neck, her voice chattering from the cold water that had come up to the saddle, covering her to the waist. "I've never seen anything like that before. What was that pit?"

Sid didn't know and couldn't even guess. "Whatever it was, let's not go back in that direction." He grinned. "At least we can take comfort in knowing that the Masteen and Black Robe will run into the same fate as they follow our trail."

He felt a flare of pain, and pulling up his shirt, he saw two ugly black flies biting him. He squished them both and dropped them to the ground in disgust. "We should get out of these clothes and wash all the fly bites so they don't get infected."

Agnes glanced up at him, slapping at her shoulder and reaching inside her tunic to pull out a struggling fly. "Gods, I don't want to go back into that cold water again."

"I know, but we have to."

"I suppose. Let's get it over with then."

They tied the horses to a stunted tree not far away, then walked over to the edge of the lake.

Sid nervously unbuttoned his shirt. His skin was puckered from bites and he had to resist scratching at the red welts. He didn't look at Agnes but heard her removing her own clothing. He untied and removed his boots, then his trousers and let them fall to the ground, hopping as he pulled at the wet leather to get it over each foot. Finally he stood, naked, and entered the ice cold water until he was knee deep. He gasped and heard Agnes do the same next to him. He glanced over to her without thinking and his breath caught in his throat at seeing her naked body.

She didn't see him looking as she gazed out over the lake. He felt his face flush but he couldn't help but stare at her. Her green eyes flashed in the sun, and her skin, where it wasn't covered in small red welts from the fly bites, was pale white except for her arms, face, and neck which were tanned from the sun. Her breasts were small but perfectly round with large brown nipples. He stared at them in fascination, and when she turned to him, he turned away guiltily.

She laughed. "It's all right to look, Sid. Haven't you ever seen a naked woman before?"

He nodded slowly, remembering Melinda's bloody and battered body as she hung from chains in Father Mansico's underground chamber. "It... was not what you think, though."

Her smile quickly faded when she saw the look on his face.

Sid quickly walked forward until the water reached his waist, then dove under the surface and came up sputtering from the cold. The lake was still fairly shallow, so he turned and swam lazily backward and saw that Agnes was still standing knee-deep in the water, looking undecided as to whether she could do what he had done.

His eyes immediately lowered to the patch of black hair between her legs and he felt himself start to grow hard, despite the extreme cold.

Agnes took three deep breaths, slapping her hands together, then swore as she dove into the water, swimming just under the surface and rising up in front of him, the water only waist-deep. Her lips were slightly blue and her mouth trembled. "Good gods, let's hurry up and wash before we freeze to death."

Sid didn't need any encouragement and they both began scrubbing themselves until their skin was raw.

Agnes pointed at him. "Turn around, let me get your back."

Sid raised an eyebrow. "Are you sure that is a good idea?"

Her eyes widened as she remembered what their touch did to each other, but she nodded. "We can just quickly rub the bug bites and it will be over quickly."

Sid's heart raced at what was to come and he turned and waited, his erection now fully hard.

At first she didn't do anything, and he turned his head. "It's all right, you don't have to."

Agnes, her lips blue from the cold, shook her head. "No, it is fine." She reached out and tentatively touched his back and the sexual energy instantly flared up between them despite the cold water. She gasped, but didn't pull away as she quickly scrubbed his back hard and then pulled her hands from him.

Sid's erection was almost sticking up out of the water, and pulsing close to orgasm when he heard her breathless voice say, "Your turn."

He turned and saw her facing away from him. Her back was beautifully-muscled at the top, and curved in a sensual arch down to her buttocks, which were just under the crystal blue water.

His erection throbbed hard and he hesitated with his hands hovering just over her shoulders. Finally, he lowered them and the touch filled him with a deep, pulsing pleasure that seemed to fill every area of his body at once.

He quickly scrubbed her shoulders, then ran his hands down her back, the red marks from the bites looking angry. The touch sent more sexual jolts through him, and he heard her gasp.

But even over the sexual ecstasy that filled him, he reveled in the simple feel of her skin. He had never touched a woman before in this way, and he found himself slowing down, softly moving his hands up the middle of her back. She sighed and leaned back into him, making his hands push even deeper into her. She tilted her head to the side, her chest heaving in and out slowly as she took deep breaths.

He leaned forward, caught up in the feelings coursing through him, and as he did, he got a little too close to her and his hard penis pushed against her back side.

She gasped, pulled away from him, and spun around.

He stammered, "I'm sorry, I didn't mean for that to happen."

She looked angry at first but then grinned mischievously. "Watch where you point that thing."

She pushed him playfully and he took a step backward but there was suddenly no ground beneath him. It angled steeply down just where they had been standing, and he found himself plunge under the water. It had surprised him and he didn't have a chance to take any air into his lungs. He pushed back toward the surface and came up gasping. His erection faded quickly as he took in deep gulps of air.

She reached out to help him, concern on her face, then slipped over the edge herself, disappearing under the water in front of him. She came up sputtering next to him, laughing hard.

They were so close as they treaded water that he could feel her warm breath on his face. They stared into each other's eyes for a long moment, then Agnes, her blue lips trembling, splashed him lightly in the face and turned to swim toward shore.

Sid wiped the water from his eyes and laughed, then swam after her.

When they got to shallower water, they stepped carefully over the stones, and Sid watched her backside as she rose from the lake. Water trickled down over her buttocks, beading on the taut curves that were covered in small, raised bumps due to the cold. They were perfectly shaped, and he could see beaded water in the soft hair between her legs. He flushed and hung back as his erection came back in a matter of moments.

She turned and raised an eyebrow. "Why aren't you coming out?"

Sid felt his face turn red as he lay back into the water to cover himself.

Agnes laughed. "I see. Don't worry, I promise not to look." She turned around and carefully stepped on the stones toward the fire the Haissan had started while they had been in the water.

Even though they had only been in the water for a short time, the Haissan had already rinsed their clothing and had the various pieces hanging on sticks close by the fire to dry out.

Sid hesitated briefly, but the cold water was starting to make him shiver uncontrollably, so he stood up and walked toward the shore, his penis sticking straight up despite the cold. He only took five steps before Agnes turned her head and looked over her shoulder. She giggled when she saw his member sticking up, letting her gaze stay on it for a few moments before she turned back and took the blanket her Haissan held out to her.

Sid cupped his hands over his crotch. "That's not fair, you promised not to look!"

Her giggle floated in the air as he hurried on his tip toes over the rocks toward the fire and pulled a blanket around himself.

He put his hands toward the flames, trying to get some sense of feeling back in his fingers. Agnes leaned forward, too, shivering, her hair hanging down in wet strands across her face. She pushed it away and then wrung it to get as much water out as she could.

Soon, they stopped their shivering and relaxed in the warm sunlight. The Haissan offered them some bread and cheese, which they hungrily ate, not bothering to talk, content for the first time since their flight from the swarm. The sun was almost to the horizon and a chill filled the air by the time their clothing was dry.

Sid buttoned up his shirt and looked at the mountains that rose up impossibly high in front of them. He couldn't see the peaks because they were hidden in low-hanging clouds, but earlier he had gotten a glimpse of the two peaks to the east where they were to meet up with their friends. He estimated that it would be a full night's walk to reach them.

From where he stood, the ground rose up at a 33-degree angle toward the mountain itself, covered with sporadic clumps of pine trees intermixed with boulders that had tumbled from the mountain over the years, some twice as large as their horses. The gently rising slope ended at a cliff about five leagues up the mountain. It looked to be made of solid granite and rose vertically into the clouds. He had no idea how they could climb up and over such a mountain. He turned his head to follow the mountain range to his left and right and saw it extend as far as he could see.

Agnes sighed. "This seems to be an impossible task doesn't it?"

Sid nodded. "I honestly don't see a way up and over. I think all we can do is make our way east until we meet up with Crowdal and everyone. Maybe they will have some ideas. Speaking of which..." He stood up and began removing items from his saddle packs. "We need to send the horses west, so take whatever you think you will need."

Agnes walked over to her horse, pulled out various items from the saddle pack, and set them on the ground. The Haissan didn't use a saddle, so it had nothing to remove from its horse.

Sid led his horse, and the horses that were tied in a line to his, back to their original trail. The Haissan walked up, holding its horse by the reins and took Agnes' horse and tied both to the end of the line. When they were ready, Sid slapped his horse on the rump and it whinnied and took off at a gallop, leading the other horses as it went. They continued running until they were out of sight, the thundering of the hooves eventually fading away.

Sid turned toward Agnes. "I need to set that same equation to hide our trail. You two go back to the fire."

"Do you need my help again?" Agnes looked nervous as she asked.

"No, I think I can handle it this time. The equation is set in my mind already, I just have to activate it."

She nodded and turned to follow the Haissan back to the fire.

Sid closed his eyes and the numbers appeared in his head. He filtered through them until he found the equations he and Agnes had merged together. He marveled again at their complexity. Her void formula was a thing of beauty. He never would have thought of it himself.

He reviewed his equation for bending light, and satisfied, he was about to connect them when he cursed to himself. He looked back at the campfire and then the lake. The odds were that the group that followed them would also make for the lake, so putting the equation right here would not do any good. He turned and made his way back to the fire. The flickering glow cast out by the flames made him realize it was already starting to get dark. He hadn't noticed until now.

Agnes rose as he approached. "How did it go?"

"I didn't set the equation there. It is the wrong place." He pointed at the fire and then at the lake. "They will probably head over to the lake just like we did, discovering our tracks and the burned-out fire." He pointed toward the east, in the direction they had to go. "We have to go that way, so I need to set the equation over there to block any trail we might leave. Just in case, we should probably put this fire out and bury it so the smell doesn't give it away. Who knows, maybe they won't find it."

They both kicked rocks and dirt into the fire until it was out and fully-covered.

Just as they finished, the Haissan approached, dripping water. It slipped the wet robe from its shoulders and carefully folded it.

Sid stared at its body, the first time he had ever seen a naked Haissan. The creature was completely white and hairless, and its body was featureless except for a slit between its legs. It stood and turned as it pulled a fresh robe from its pack and slipped it over its body. Sid turned away, embarrassed for looking.

He and Agnes put whatever items they had removed from their

saddle packs into their own packs and looked around to make sure they had everything. Satisfied, he sent Agnes and the Haissan ahead.

He took a half dozen steps in their direction, then turned and concentrated on the equations. They hummed as they clicked together, the now single equation pulsing with energy. He spread it out to cover at least a twenty-pace length of ground in both directions so that anyone who found the fire pit would only see the tracks around the fire leading west, where they would find the trail from the horses leading off in that direction.

Where he now stood, the equation would make it look like undisturbed earth. He backed away and turned to catch up to Agnes and the Haissan.

As they walked in the dark, careful not to twist their ankles on the numerous rocks, Sid thought of his friends and wondered how they were doing.

Chapter 49

W rithgarth tripped over a rock that was hidden in the tall grass and stumbled forward a few paces before catching his balance, cursing the whole time. He heard Tulman chuckle from behind him and turned his head back at the mercenary with an embarrassed grin and pointed over his shoulder. "Someone should have that rock removed!" He winked at the large mercenary, who chuckled.

Writhgarth wiped at the beading moisture on his brow with the back of his hand, then rubbed his hand on his other sleeve to get the dirty sweat off. "Gods, this heat is bad. I hate horses, but I hate walking even more. Curse these short legs of mine."

Tulman chuckled again. "Aye, but at least if you do fall, you don't have far to the ground."

Writhgarth took the ribbing in stride. He had gotten to know Tulman quite well over the past fortnight and found him to be an honorable and good man despite having a rather short temper. Writhgarth normally didn't like mercenaries, for they were generally men who lived outside of the law and reveled in that. As a former captain of the city guard, he had dealt with many drunken and violent mercenaries who had come into the city to spend their ill-gotten coin. But Tulman, Nik, and Richard were all good men who took honest jobs, except for the last one.

He watched the ground more carefully as he walked, thinking of Sid. They had all been rather somber after the Aleph Null and the young woman named Agnes, along with her Haissan, had split from them. Crowdal had taken the lead, and they had walked in a straight line all day toward the mountain with the twin peaks. They were all exhausted, although the sight of the mountain looming above them gave them hope that they would soon meet up with Sid. Writhgarth figured they would reach the base of the mountain by the end of the day.

Two birds flew up to their right. Nik and Richard loosed two arrows. One bird dropped to the ground, an arrow through its left wing, but the other bird flew away untouched. Writhgarth heard Nik giving Richard a hard time for missing such an easy shot, and he smiled to himself. They acted more like brothers than fellow mercenaries.

Nik raised his voice, "Since you missed, you can go get the bird and your arrow, if you can find it, that is. Your shot went high and to the right."

Richard grumbled but didn't argue. He disappeared into the tall grass. The rest of them stopped to rest after the long march.

Writhgarth turned to say something to Tulman when he noticed that Melinda was nowhere to be seen. He pulled Crowdal's shirt where it hung past his waist. "Hey, big guy, where is Melinda?"

Crowdal looked quickly around and swore under his breath. He set his pack down and took off at a run, following their trail back the way they had come. Writhgarth knew he couldn't keep up, so he took his own pack off and sat down to rest his feet, worried about Melinda more than he let on. He had watched her weaken more and more each day they had traveled, the skin dark around her eyes. But it wasn't until they left their horses and had to walk on foot that she really seemed to tire quickly. Crowdal had asked if he could carry her and she had snapped at him. The Trith had left her alone then.

Writhgarth didn't have long to wait before he heard footsteps approaching. Soon Crowdal pushed his way through the grass, carrying Melinda in his arms. He set her carefully to the ground. "Can you get one of my shirts from my pack?"

Writhgarth nodded, scrambled over to the huge pack, and rooted around inside until he found a shirt large enough to be a blanket for most people. He rolled it up and placed it under Melinda's head. Her skin was gray and sagging on her cheek bones, and the area around her eyes was black and blue. She breathed so shallowly that her chest barely rose and fell.

Crowdal leaned down and lifted one of her eyelids, but her pupils didn't react to the light. He looked at Writhgarth, panic showing in his eyes. "I don't know what is wrong with her. I don't see any injuries. It is almost like she is dying of old age." The large man caressed her hair as he spoke.

Tulman stood close by, pity showing on his face.

Writhgarth handed his water skin to Crowdal. "Try dribbling some water into her mouth."

Crowdal opened her mouth, then tipped the skin and let a small stream of water pour into it. But it just quickly bubbled out and dripped to the ground. He whipped the water skin into the grass and leaned down close to her face, his voice angry, "Come on, Melinda, fight this! Don't give up!" He caressed her forehead, then her cheek, his voice changing to a whisper, "Please, don't let go."

Writhgarth looked away, unable to bear seeing such pain on his friend's face, then swore loudly, for in front of him stood three young men and a woman. He jumped to his feet and pulled his sword.

Tulman cursed and pulled his own sword out, followed by Nik.

Crowdal just looked up in anguish.

The young woman put her hand up in the universal gesture of peace. Her voice was soft but firm, "We are here to help."

Writhgarth eyed her warily and kept his sword out. "Who are you?"

The woman stepped forward, looking down at Melinda and

Crowdal, and replied in a stern voice, "We are Zranh."

Writhgarth backed up while hissing, "Get out of here, we want nothing to do with... your kind." His sword was yanked violently from his hands and he looked down in confusion, then back up. One of the young men held his sword, but hadn't seemed to move. Tulman and Nik hissed and Writhgarth glanced over and saw them also standing empty-handed.

The woman spoke without looking from Melinda's unconscious form lying on the ground, "Please, do not instigate violence. We have disarmed you for your own good." She stepped lightly forward and knelt down next to Melinda, reaching out to touch her forehead. "Melinda will die if we don't take her back home."

Crowdal pushed the woman violently away. "You will not take her!"

The young woman landed on her back. She instantly put her hands on the ground behind her head and arched her back, jumping to her feet in a single fluid motion, hissing at Crowdal, "We can save her, but we must return her to her home."

Crowdal looked up at her, his eyes wet, his face anguished. They stared at each other for long moments until Crowdal finally nodded. "Please heal her. That is all I ask."

The young woman's face softened slightly. "You have our word, we will do all we can for her." She motioned to the three young men and they handed the swords back to Writhgarth, Tulman, and Nik.

The largest young man then knelt next to Melinda, and carefully slipping one arm under her legs and the other under her neck, he picked her up as if she weighed nothing.

Crowdal stood up and put a large hand in front of the woman. "How can I find you again?"

The young woman pushed his hand slowly down and spoke in a soft but firm voice, "We will be in the same forest where you first met Prennia. We will stay there until the leaves begin changing color. If you do not come before then, we will leave for the lands far to the west." She hesitated, then spoke softly, "I urge you to come before the leaves change color, for you will not find us after that time."

Crowdal nodded. "I will be there. I promise."

The young woman turned and then she and her three companions simply disappeared in front of them.

Writhgarth turned in a circle but saw no tracks or indication that they had ever been here.

He heard grass swishing and then Richard appeared, holding five dead birds by their necks, a huge smile on his face. "I thought we could use a few more for lunch." His smile faltered at the looks on everyone's faces. "What's going on?"

Tulman gestured to Nik. "Build a small fire and get those birds roasting. Help him, Richard."

Richard looked around in confusion but did as he was told. As he and Nik stepped away to build a fire, Writhgarth heard him whisper to his friend, asking what was going on.

Crowdal looked like he was lost, so Writhgarth approached him. "I'm sorry, Crowdal."

His friend nodded and walked a short ways into the grass to be alone.

Writhgarth sat down again, wondering if Crowdal would be able to continue with their journey now.

The birds were cooking over a small fire made from grass by the time Crowdal reappeared, sitting down opposite him. He spoke in a detached voice, "We have to keep moving, Sid is counting on us."

Writhgarth shifted uncomfortably. "I'm sure Melinda will be all right. We had to let them take her."

The large Trith nodded, then took a deep breath, releasing it angrily. "Gods, how I hate this."

"I know. She is a friend to us all. We will find her again."

Crowdal stood up. "I'm hungry. Let's eat."

Writhgarth studied his friend, amazed by his strength. He stood up also and they stepped over to the fire.

Richard pulled one of the birds from the smoldering grass and blew on his fingers as he dropped it. He stuck his knife into it and held it out to Crowdal, who put a hand up. "No thanks, Richard, I don't eat meat, remember?"

The man shrugged his shoulders. "Hey, more for us then." He handed the bird to Writhgarth, who slid the bird from the blade and moved it back and forth between his hands, saying, "Ouch, ouch, ouch."

They all ate quickly, tearing the dark meat from tiny bones and eating it greedily. Crowdal nibbled on some Liret.

The meal finished, Crowdal pushed himself to his feet and stretched. "Let's get going. I think we can make the mountains before dark."

Writhgarth nodded, anxious to get moving too.

Nik stamped the fire out and they all trudged into the tall grass, the two peaks of the mountain looming over them.

Chapter 50

The moon hung low in the night sky and the air had cooled down dramatically since sundown. The light from the sliver of the moon was as bright as daylight to the Korpor as it glided to a stop next to an old campfire at the base of the mountain range. It saw the small lake not far away and loped over to the water's edge and bent its head to drink deeply from the clear, cold water. It shook its fur and dozens of black flies buzzed angrily as they were thrown from its body.

It had come upon the black pit and had been attacked by the flies, although it hadn't really been bothered by the biting insects. But it wanted to be rid of them just the same, so it stepped into the cold water and dove under the surface, holding its breath for so long that the flies all abandoned their bloody feasts to get to the surface.

The Korpor swam lazily under the water for many moments longer before it surfaced and made its way back to the shallower water along the shore. It enjoyed the cold water and stayed submerged for a few more moments with only its huge blue eyes breaking the water's surface.

It blinked its left eye, followed slowly by its right eye as it studied the mountain rising up above it. Finally, it stood up and stepped from the water, its fur glistening in the moonlight as the moisture beaded and rolled down its body. It shook itself violently, starting at its feet, its body turning quickly in an undulating motion. The water flew out in a twisting pattern until it was almost completely dry.

It bent down and took another long drink of water, then ran back to the old campfire and caught the scent of the Aleph Null. It then turned and carefully followed the faint trail into the darkness.

Chapter 51

The Masteen Vorn Maghuur didn't like the situation in which he found himself. The moon was not bright enough to easily see the land around him as they left the last of the endless, tall grass of the plain. He could see the shadow of the tall, ragged mountains that filled the night in front of him, so much blacker than the ground at his feet. He casually tilted his head to his left and gritted his teeth at the shadow of the arrogant young man riding next to him, who called himself the Black Robe.

The Masteen had never considered another man to be his better, and he didn't intend to start with the Black Robe, who had taken control of the mission. Even though he respected the young man's power, he would, nevertheless, relish the moment when he squeezed the life from the Black Robe's body.

He reached back and pushed his fingers into the back of his heavy steel helmet to crush a fly that had crawled up inside to bite his neck, pulling out the crushed insect and flicking it away. Soon another fly landed on him, followed by another. He heard cursing and saw his men waving their arms. They were hardened men and didn't care about insects or discomfort, but the air was suddenly thick with the black flies. His stallion stomped its front feet and snorted, its skin covered with the crawling insects.

This was unnatural. The Masteen cursed as he turned to his captain. "Tell the men to quickly head toward the mountains. Maybe we can outrun these things." He viciously kicked his horse in the ribs and it reared up, neighing, then took off at a fast gallop. The Masteen saw the entire group following him, and as he rode, the swarm of flies kept pace with him. He saw a hill up ahead and turned to make his way around it. His horse was breathing hard as it ran, its muscles and lungs laboring to carry so much weight.

The swarm lessened after what seemed like a long time, until finally he could breathe in without having the insects crawl into his nose and mouth. He saw a lake up ahead and pulled on his reins to angle over to it. He soon slowed his horse until it was trotting, and slowed it even more to a walk until he reached the water's edge. His men crowded around the area, followed by the Haissen and the Black Robe, along with the woman.

His captain sidled up to him. "Masteen, what are your orders now?"

He pulled his helmet from his head and a dozen flies fell out. He felt more of them still crawling through his long hair. "Send scouts out to see which way they went from here; the rest may break for food and to water the horses here by the lake."

The captain nodded sharply and immediately rode away, barking orders as he went. Two men took off on foot, searching the ground as they went.

The Masteen slid his massive frame from the stallion and stepped to the water, kneeling down to rinse his hair. It was cold and refreshing after the endless days of riding through the dry, grassy plain.

The Black Robe walked up to him as he stood up. The young man didn't appear to have a single bite on him and looked as refreshed as if he had just stepped from an inn after spending the night with a whore.

"Now that was interesting, wasn't it?"

The Masteen growled deeply. "Just a few flies, nothing that would bother my men."

The Black Robe nodded as if he couldn't have cared less about what the Masteen had said. "Yes, well, get your men ready, we need to continue the ride."

The Masteen clenched his fists, his knuckles cracking loudly as he did. Before he could say anything, the young man turned and calmly walked away, his hands held behind his back.

Oh, how he would will relish killing that man.

He heard approaching footsteps and turned.

Both of his scouts ran up to him. "Masteen, the trail leads west."

The Masteen climbed into his saddle, his great weight making the horse tremble as it adjusted. "Good, let's move."

The taller of the two scouts held up his hand.

The Masteen glared down at the man. "What?"

The man looked nervous, as if he didn't want to speak. The Masteen growled deeply in his chest, "If I have to ask you twice, you will regret it."

The man visibly swallowed, and when he spoke, his voice trembled, "There is something strange about the tracks."

"Well, what is it? Speak!"

"Masteen, the tracks, they seem wrong."

When the Masteen impatiently glared at the man, the scout quickly continued.

"I don't think anyone was riding the horses. I noticed this before but wasn't sure until now. Some of the horse tracks seemed shallower than the others, but I didn't know if it had to do with them being smaller horses. But now, all of the tracks are of the same depth." The scout trailed off, sounding unsure of himself.

The Masteen spoke sharply, "Show me."

The scouts immediately turned and jogged toward the west, coming to a stop not too far away. The Masteen walked toward them slowly and looked down where one of the scouts was kneeling.

The scout put his fingers into the slight hoof indentations. "See, here, all of the tracks lead west, but they are all the same now. I followed the trail for some time, but it continues on so I returned back here."

A horse approached behind him and the Masteen didn't have to turn to know it was the Black Robe sticking his nose where it didn't belong.

The Black Robe pulled up on his reins and stopped next to the Masteen. He didn't speak, though. Instead, he looked around until he finally focused on a spot facing east. He rode in that direction for a short distance and stopped. The Masteen watched curiously as the young man stood still, his eyes closed. After a few moments, the air shimmered in front of him and returned to normal so quickly that the Masteen couldn't be sure he had even seen the disturbance.

The Black Robe laughed. "Little Sid is getting more clever with his equations."

The Masteen walked over to see what the Black Robe was talking about. He studied the area and immediately saw footprints leading east.

The Black Robe glanced at him. "Gather your men, we need to set off in that direction immediately." He turned his horse without waiting for an acknowledgment and headed back to the group.

The Masteen found himself growling again, but motioned to the scout. "Gather the men and bring my horse."

The scout saw the dark look on the Masteen's face and ran back to the group of men as if death were chasing him.

The Masteen didn't have long to wait before the rest of the group thundered up to him, including the scouting leading his horse.

They set off east at a slow pace because the ground was covered with large rocks, making it difficult for the horses, especially at night. Finally, the way became impassable for the horses, so the Masteen ordered his men to dismount.

"Carry what you can, we go on foot from here."

Chapter 52

Sid was tired and shifted his pack for what seemed like the hundredth time since they had set out on foot After riding on a horse for so many days, he found it difficult to get used to walking again, much less carrying his own pack. It was amazing how quickly he had gotten used to letting the horse do all the work.

He glanced up and saw the sky was slightly lighter. Sunrise was not too far off. He heard a small curse from Agnes to his left. "What's wrong?"

She whispered back, "Nothing, just these small rocks. I swear I'm going to break an ankle before the sun comes up." She cursed again and kicked a small rock, then yelped in pain.

Sid chuckled. "Oh, come on, you honestly didn't know that would hurt?"

She hopped on one foot. "Oh, shut up." She put her foot back down and limped for a ways.

"I know this blue light isn't very bright, but the sun will be up soon and we will be able to see fully where we walk." He looked up at the spinning equation he used to lighten their immediate area. He didn't want to make it too bright and possibly give their location away.

Suddenly, a shadow rose up in front of them and Sid yelled in surprise. He was about to build a wall of numbers for protection when he heard a chuckle.

"Took you long enough to get here, Sid." From the darkness, Writhgarth stepped forward and stood with legs apart, his hand casually on the hilt of his sword. "We've been waiting here all night for you."

Sid laughed in relief. "Gods, you could have announced yourself, Writhgarth, you almost made my heart stop."

"Aye, although you wouldn't have been caught unaware if you had been paying attention to your surroundings instead of jabbering away incessantly. I heard you coming for the longest time."

Sid nodded, feeling a little sheepish. He saw that the Haissan stood calmly and hadn't been surprised in the least. He pushed hair from his eyes. "So, where is everyone?"

Writhgarth tilted his head behind him. "Just back that way. Follow me." He turned and faded into the darkness.

Sid and Agnes hurried to catch up, the Haissan staying slightly behind them. They didn't walk far when they came to a huge rock that rose from the ground, blocking their way. He looked left and right but couldn't see an end to the stone in the darkness until he saw the shadowed form of Writhgarth step out of the rock itself.

Sid stepped a few paces to his right and saw that Writhgarth stood beside a narrow crack in the boulder, waiting for them. The little man motioned to him. "Go on through. It is narrow in parts, but you can won't have any problems. I'll stick back here a few moments longer to ensure you weren't followed and will join you shortly."

Sid stepped through the opening, followed by Agnes and the Haissan. There was just space enough for him to fit. He crept through the gap for a few hundred steps, crawling up and over a few dead trees that must have been washed into the crack during floods, until he stepped into a clearing lit by a small fire. He immediately saw Crowdal jump to his feet. "Sid, there you are!" The Trith stepped forward and clasped Sid's shoulder. "It is good to see you, my friend."

Sid smiled. "And you, Crowdal." He looked around the camp and saw Tulman, Richard, and Nik and smiled at them. "It is good to see you gentlemen, too!"

Nik chuckled. "Gentlemen? Now that is the first time I've ever been called that."

Sid smiled and then turned as Agnes stepped into the clearing, followed by the Haissan. He shrugged out of his pack and sat down by the fire with a loud sigh, reaching out his hands to warm them.

Then it struck him that someone was missing. He looked around wildly, then back at Crowdal. "Where is Melinda?"

His friend sat down and hung his head. "She was... taken back to her people."

Sid's voice rose an octave. "What are you talking about?"

"She collapsed, unconscious, during the trek and was close to death. We didn't know what to do, and then four people appeared, as if from thin air. They were the same strange people from the forest back when we first started this journey."

Sid opened his mouth to speak but Crowdal cut him off. "They took her, Sid. They said that only they could help her."

"And you just let them take her? How could you?"

Crowdal's eyes flashed in the light of the fire, his face hard and tight as he glared at Sid, and for the first time since he had known Crowdal, he was afraid of the Trith. Sid leaned back and held up his hands. "I'm so sorry, Crowdal, I didn't mean that."

Crowdal slumped his shoulders and hung his head. Sid barely heard him mumble, "I didn't have a choice. She was dying."

Sid hesitantly put his hand on Crowdal's leg. "You did what was best for her."

The giant man looked up, tears streaming down his face. Then he angrily wiped them away. "I will find her if it is the last thing I do. But that is out of my hands for the time being. We must keep you safe until this whole thing is finished."

Sid held his gaze for some time, feeling guilty but knowing he spoke the truth. They couldn't help Melinda right now, and they were so close to their goal. It was just on the other side of this mountain. Images of the dark evil that followed him filled his mind, of being in a small clearing in a thick, ancient forest, of Agnes standing over him holding his Rissen blade. And most importantly, of the figure of a woman whose face he couldn't clearly see, but whom he felt he knew. He had to get to that clearing.

Sid gripped Crowdal's shoulder. "I promise you, I will help you look for her. We will find her!"

Crowdal pulled out a thick piece of cloth and blew his nose into it. "Thanks, Sid. Now, let's figure out how to get over this mountain. Any ideas?"

Sid looked up at the rocky peaks that were now visible in the first light of dawn. The gray light made them look impossibly high and inaccessible. The ground rose up at a 33-degree angle for a few leagues, but then a 90-degree cliff rose up, the granite smooth and stretching up for what looked like forever. There was no way to climb it and Sid let his shoulders slump. After all they had been through, he felt defeat filling him. He looked back down to Crowdal. "I don't think it is possible. There is just no way we can climb that."

A soft hissing voice spoke directly behind them, "I know a way."

Sid and Crowdal both turned their heads to the Haissan standing right next to them, looking up at the mountain. Sid saw the white, noseless face inside of the hood and, not for the first time, felt distrust and disgust at the sight of the creature. But he pushed the feeling away and spoke quietly, "What do you mean? How?"

The Haissan tilted its hood-covered head down to Sid. Its voice was soft as it hissed, "My... race comes from the oceans on the other side of those mountains. There is a path up and over the mountain directly between the two peaks." It stared at Sid. "How did you know to come to this spot?"

Sid felt hope flare up inside of him. Where just moments earlier he had felt defeat, he now felt energized. They could get over the mountain after all! He shrugged to the Haissan. "I don't know. Just luck, I guess."

The Haissan shook its head. "No, it was not 'just luck'. You knew to come to this spot. How did you know?"

Sid gazed into the alien face and sensed something deeper was going on with the Haissan. What it was, he had no idea. He noticed his friends staring at him also.

Writhgarth stepped through the crack in the boulder and sensed something was wrong. He set his feet wide apart. "What's going on?"

Sid turned around to face the group, knowing he had to tell them the truth, for they deserved it. He took a deep breath. "I've mentioned briefly before that my mathematical visions have shown me a clearing on the other side of this mountain that seems to contain the answers to my questions. For some reason that I don't understand, I seem to be on a path that can't be changed, both physically and metaphysically."

Nik looked at him blankly, clearly not understanding the large words. Sid shrugged at him. "I can't fully explain it, other than to say that my path has led me here, for better or for worse. None of you has to go any further. I wouldn't blame you if you chose to go your own ways."

When no one spoke or responded, Sid felt a lump in his throat at their dedication to him. Not for the first time, he felt he didn't deserve such friends. He turned back to the Haissan. "Does that answer your question?"

The creature nodded and hissed, "Yes. You are truly the Aleph Null."

Sid turned away, not comfortable with that label. "Let's eat now, and then you can show us how to ascend the cliff."

They ate quickly, then packed up their camp just as fast. Nik kicked dirt and rocks over the fire to put it out. Tulman rummaged in his pack and pulled out a thick fur cloak.

Sid saw him and raised an eyebrow. "What is that for?"

The mercenary pulled out some leather gloves. "It is going to be cold up there. I would put on whatever winter clothing you have before we set out."

Confused, Sid asked, "Why would it be colder up there than it is down here?"

Writhgarth spoke up as he put on a thick woolen coat. "I don't know why, but Tulman is right. The higher you go, the colder it gets."

Tulman nodded agreement and the group quickly broke out their winter gear, except for the Haissan who waited patiently wearing just its robe.

They were all ready, and with a nod from Sid, the Haissan turned and made its way up the shallow grade toward the base of the cliff some leagues away.

As they climbed, Sid felt anxious to move faster, but the Haissan set a steady, slow pace, and by mid-morning, they had reached the base of the cliff. Sid craned his head back and became dizzy as he looked straight up. The cliff rose so high that he couldn't see the top. He put a hand against the cool stone to steady himself, then turned to look behind him.

The view was panoramic and he could see for leagues. The sun was bright in the sky, illuminating the grassy plain far in the distance. The sight was so beautiful that he couldn't stop staring. Never in his whole life had he ever been so high off of the ground. In Orm-Mina, the land was mostly flat. There were occasional hills, but they were insignificant. Literally, nothing in his whole life could compare to the view before him.

He felt light-headed, and had noticed that the higher they climbed, the more difficult it got to take a full breath into his lungs. Around him, everyone else breathed harder also.

Sid looked up at the sheer rock wall and huffed, "So, how do we get up there?"

The Haissan turned its head left, then right, and making a decision, turned briskly to the right and quickly glided over the rocky ground.

Sid raised an eyebrow at Crowdal. "They sure don't talk much, do they?"

Crowdal nodded agreement. "I honestly don't care if it speaks much, as long as it knows a way up this cliff and over the mountain." He adjusted his pack to make it more comfortable and lifted his hand out in the direction the Haissan had just gone. "After you."

Sid turned and walked after the Haissan, followed by Tulman, Nik, Richard, Writhgarth, and Agnes, with Crowdal bringing up the rear. The ground was full of rocks ranging in size from ones as big as his fist, to boulders as large as a home. They picked their way slowly across the ground, careful to avoid twisting their ankles on rocks while conserving their strength. Every movement this high up seemed to take five times the energy as it did down on the plain.

Sid stepped over a rock and as his foot touched the ground he heard a cracking sound. He looked around trying to figure out where it was coming from. He didn't see anything and was about to take another step when Tulman grabbed him and pulled him violently against the cliff wall, shouting at the same time, "Take cover against the wall now!"

As he said this, rocks began to crash to the ground around them. The sound was deafening and Sid covered his head with his arms and cowered against the wall. A huge boulder the size of Crowdal smashed to the ground not more than an arm's length from him, the spray of crushed rock striking him as it hit. He felt pain in his arm but didn't look, afraid to even move.

After a few more heartbeats, the rocks stopped falling and Sid heard Crowdal anxiously call out.

"Is everyone all right?"

Sid lifted his arms from his head and widened his eyes at the sight in front of him. In the direction they had been walking, not more than fifteen paces away, there was now a pile of jagged rocks and boulders at least three times as high as Crowdal was tall. Sid felt pain in his arm and looked down at it. A sharp piece of rock had cut him but the cut was shallow. He heard each member of his group say they were fine, one at a time. He croaked out, his voice a little shaky, "I'm unharmed, too."

Crowdal sighed. "Thank the gods, that was close." He craned his neck upward, squinting his eyes. "We need to stay as close to the cliff wall as possible from now on. We may not get a warning next time."

Nik laughed sharply. "You call that a warning?"

Crowdal smacked the mercenary's shoulder with the back of his hand. "Hey, you're alive aren't you?"

Nik nodded. "You have a good point." He looked around and exclaimed. "Hey, where is that Haissan?"

Sid quickly looked toward the way that they had been moving. The cliff curved up ahead, but between them was the huge pile of rocks. Without the Haissan, they had no way of getting over the mountain. As he searched the rocks, looking for a piece of cloth or any indication of the creature, he felt hope slip away.

Then the Haissan's hood-covered head appeared over the top of the pile and it motioned as it hissed, "Come."

Sid felt his heartbeat settle down in relief. Even just a few days ago, he never would have thought he would be glad to see a Haissan. He pushed hair from his eyes and started to climb the rock pile, careful where he put hands and feet as he climbed to avoid any shifting or loose rocks. He heard a rock tumble down behind him and then a curse. He looked back and saw Nik sucking on his thumb.

The mercenary took it from his mouth and showed Sid that it was bleeding. He flexed his thumb and then shook his hand a few times. "Ouch, that hurt. Stupid rocks!"

From behind him, Crowdal chuckled. "Oh, stop whining like a little girl."

Nik glanced back at the Trith. "I'm not whining. That really hurt!"

Crowdal just shook his head. "Can we please continue, little girl?"

Tulman spoke gruffly from behind Crowdal. "Nik, move it!"

Nik immediately began climbing.

Sid continued up the rock pile until he reached the top. He was surprised that Crowdal was joking around after being so somber just a short time ago. He figured it was a coping mechanism, a way to keep going without falling into a depression..

On the ground on the other side stood the Haissan, patiently waiting.

Sid made his way carefully down the pile until he reached the safety of the ground. He brushed dust from his trousers as he waited for the rest of the group to make it over. Soon they all stood, huffing and puffing, ready to continue.

The Haissan immediately began to lead them around the curving cliff. Sid followed but didn't have far to go before the Haissan stopped with its hand up. It turned and hissed at them, "Here is the path."

Sid looked where the Haissan stood and didn't see anything different about the cliff wall.

The Haissan spoke, "Follow me up and do what I do. Brace your back against the wall and use your legs to push yourselves up each level.

Do not use your arms or you will not make it all the way up. Tie your packs with a short length of rope around your waist. As you climb, the pack will dangle below you. Move slowly, and precisely place your feet into each indentation before sliding your back up. Do not hurry or you will likely fall and kill yourself, as well as everyone below you." The creature stepped toward the cliff and disappeared into the stone.

Sid turned to glance at his friends, who looked as worried as he felt. He removed his pack and lifted his coil of rope out. He carefully cut a piece off just long enough that it would hang below him but not too far, and tied one end to his pack and the other around his waist, double-checking the knots to ensure they would not let loose. Agnes, the only one who didn't carry any rope, asked him if she could have a piece of his, so he quickly cut her a length and helped her tie it around her narrow waist, then to her own pack. She smiled in thanks.

He turned back and stepped tentatively forward, dragging the pack awkwardly behind him, and as he reached the spot where the Haissan had stood, he widened his eyes in surprise when an opening in the cliff appeared. It was narrow and impossible to see except from a direct angle.

The crack in the cliff was not deep and looked like a three-sided chimney. He reached in and could touch the back wall. It was just wide enough for him to fit into it sideways and touch the opposite wall with his arms outstretched. On one side of the chimney there were what looked like half-steps carved into the wall. On the opposite side there were small bumps of stone, extending out from the wall no more than the length of his smallest finger.

He craned his neck back and saw that the Haissan was far above him. The creature had its back to the wall and was inching upward by putting its feet into each shallow step and pushing with its legs, sliding its back upward. The Haissan repeated the process slowly and methodically.

Sid couldn't make out the top of the chimney, it extended to a tiny point as far as he could see.

Sid heard his friends crowd around the opening.

Crowdal looked up and sighed at the sight of the chimney-like opening and the Haissan far above. "Great. There couldn't be a simple path, could there? It had to be a straight shaft. Just great."

Nik reached up and smacked Crowdal on the back. "Now you're the one whining like a little girl."

Crowdal looked down at Nik, whose head barely reached his chest. "Just for that, you can go last, so in case I fall, I will take you out on the way down."

Nik grinned. "At least I won't whine on the way down."

Crowdal grinned back. "I like your style, Nik." He turned to Sid and was instantly serious. "Sid, you go first. The Haissan was right, take your time, place each step carefully and use your legs to push yourself up. Don't hurry."

Sid nodded and stepped into the opening. He saw that the opposite wall was polished perfectly smooth and actually felt slick to the touch, except for the slight bumps jutting out from the stone. He calculated that the bumps of stone would be enough to rest his butt against and keep from slipping down, but wouldn't project out enough to affect his ability to slide his back upward with each step.

He lifted his leg and put it into the first step. He braced his back against the wall and was able to get his second foot into the step, although it was a bit awkward. He straightened his knees and pushed up, surprised at how easily he slid up the wall. He put his right foot into the next step, then his left and pushed upward again. He repeated the process, feeling like an inchworm. It seemed effortless, and he began to think that the climb would actually be easy, although the pack hanging below him made it a little more difficult to climb when it lifted from the ground and the full weight pulled at him.

After pushing himself up one hundred steps, he was gasping for air and realized he was climbing too quickly, so he stopped, his chest heaving and his forehead wet with sweat. He looked down and saw Agnes climbing below him. He couldn't see past her.

She inched her way up until she was just below him and craned her head back. "Everything all right, Sid?" She was also gasping for air.

"Yeah, just catching my breath." He looked up and still couldn't see an end to the climb, nor could he see the Haissan anymore. He breathlessly said, "Looks like we still have a long way to go."

Agnes grumbled below him, "Great, I'm already exhausted."

Sid's breathing slowed down a little bit, so he pushed his back up and continued to step up, push, step up, push; the process seemingly unending. After every one hundred steps he rested; and at the twentieth rest he looked up and saw sunlight far above him. His back was aching and his legs felt like jelly. It was frightening to know that he was stuck and had to continue upward. There was no going back down.

No matter how long he rested now, he couldn't catch his breath and was constantly gasping for air. Sweat ran down his face and into his eyes, the salty sting making it difficult to see clearly. He heard Agnes wheezing below him and worried. One slip and he would fall, killing everyone.

After the thirtieth rest, he had to stop longer. He just couldn't seem to find any strength anymore. When he tried to slide his back up the wall again, he realized it had been a mistake to stop for so long. He wasn't gaining his strength back, rather he was constantly losing it the longer he paused because he had to support himself, causing his legs to cramp up.

From below he heard Agnes gasp out, "If we stop for much

longer Sid, I won't be able to start again."

Sid gulped air, unable to even respond. He steeled himself and pushed upward. His legs protested, shooting pain, the cramps threatening to make him lose his grip. He gritted his teeth and pushed himself upward with every bit of reserved strength he could find, and one small movement at a time he slid up the wall, his legs eventually straightening out and relieving the cramps. He didn't hesitate, immediately lifting his right leg to the next step, followed by his left, and pushed upward.

He got back into a shaky rhythm. This time, he kept moving after a hundred steps, making it to three hundred before his head started feeling light and he couldn't get enough air into his lungs. He stopped until he was able to clear his vision a little bit, and just as he felt his legs start to cramp up, he started climbing again.

He continued like this, stopping every three hundred steps until he knew it wouldn't be long before he would be unable to push himself up even one more step. He tilted his head back and almost cried with joy when he saw that the opening was not that far above him. He pushed upward, his legs protesting with every movement. He slid up, and through sheer willpower, kept his legs moving.

After two hundred more steps, his head cleared the top of the chimney-shaft and he felt the Haissan grip him under his armpits and pull him up and over the edge. The Haissan dragged him a few steps away until his pack cleared the edge.

Sid fell to his side, panting, his eyes closed in pain. He felt himself being dragged further backward but didn't care. Just being able to stretch his legs out and lay flat without straining was all that mattered at this moment.

As he lay on the stone, he heard Agnes cursing. He opened his eyes and struggled to a sitting position.

She was lying on the ground by the opening. The Haissan dragged her next to Sid, along with her pack. Her eyes were closed as she gasped for air.

Sid reached over and gripped her shoulder. "You made it."

She merely nodded, her face white.

Sid untied the rope from his waist, then from the pack, coiling the rope twice before putting it inside an inner flap of his pack. He stood up on wobbly legs, then opened his eyes wide at the view stretching out in front of him. He stood on a rock shelf that ended in a sheer drop, not more than ten paces from him. He turned around and saw that the snow-covered mountainside angled up at about a 50-degree angle toward the two peaks far above him, much farther than it looked from the ground.

He turned away and shivered in the cold air, crossing his arms to keep them warm as he walked to the edge of the cliff and looked down.

They were so high that he couldn't see any detail on the ground, it just looked like a flat piece of parchment from this height. He saw the grassy plain stretching out unending into the distance. Vertigo hit him and he started to lose his balance, so he turned and fell to his hands and knees to avoid falling over the edge.

He heard grunting and crawled over to the Haissan to help pull Nik over the edge.

The mercenary fell to his back and closed his eyes just like Sid and Agnes had done.

The Haissan dragged him away from the hole, so Sid hurried over and grabbed his pack as it reached the top, carrying over and setting it next to Nik.

He returned to the opening, peered over the edge, and saw Tulman making his way slowly up the chimney, maybe twenty steps down.

Agnes soon joined them at the opening, looking better.

As Tulman's head appeared over the edge, Sid leaned down to pull the captain up, but the mercenary swatted his hands away.

"I don't need your help." He strained upward until he was able to get his hands over the edge and push himself into a sitting position. He slowly swung his legs up and onto the stone and to Sid's surprise, he stood up. The man had strength and honor, impressing Sid greatly.

Tulman pulled his pack up hand-over-hand, lifted it from the edge, and walked ten paces from the hole before setting it down. He couldn't get the rope untied from his waist, so he pulled a knife and cut the knot. He put his knife away, then put his hands to his lower back and stretched, and even from where Sid stood, he could hear the cracking of the man's bones.

Nik made his way over, looked at Sid, and rolled his eyes, whispering, "I have never seen that man ask for help in all the time I've worked with him."

Sid nodded, awed by the show of strength. "That, I can believe."

He leaned over the opening and saw Writhgarth not far below. The little man was too short to brace his back against the opposite wall like the rest of them had done, so he had to climb the steps like a ladder. Sid gulped. The effort must have been extraordinary, not being able to rest the full weight of his body at any point.

Writhgarth's hands reached up and gripped the top edge of the chimney shaft and the Haissan grabbed the man's forearms and pulled him up and over the edge.

As the Haissan released him, the little man stumbled and fell to his knees, gulping for air, his face purple and sweating. He crawled a few paces, struggling against the weight of his pack still hanging down the chimney. Sid pulled at the rope and was able to get the pack over the edge. Writhgarth turned his head and heaved, his body convulsing.

When he didn't have anything more to throw up, he flopped to his back and just lay there, his eyes closed and his stomach rising and falling as he took huge mouthfuls of air.

Sid walked over and set the pack next to the little man, then took his waterskin from his belt and opened the stopper. He tilted Writhgarth's head up. "Here, drink."

Writhgarth opened his mouth and drank the water greedily without opening his eyes, spilling some down his chin. He finally stopped, lay his head back on the ground, and rasped, "Thank you, Sid."

Sid put the stopper back in and put the flask in Writhgarth's hand. "Here, if you want more."

The little man nodded but didn't respond.

Sid walked back to the hole, peered over the edge, and saw Richard just below. The Haissan leaned down and pulled the mercenary gently over the edge. Sid pulled up the pack and carried it as the Haissan dragged Richard some distance away. The mercenary was breathing just as heavily as everyone else had been, but he seemed to recover more quickly.

Sid heard Crowdal grunting, so he hurried over to see if he could help pull the Trith up and over the edge. He was worried about Crowdal because he didn't know how such a huge person would be able to climb the chimney. At almost twice Sid's own height, he didn't think Crowdal would be able to shimmy up the shaft like he had done.

Sid leaned over the edge and saw Crowdal not too far below, slowly making his way up. He was right, Crowdal couldn't lean his back against the wall and push himself up. He was so large that his back pressed against the wall even when he was in a vertical position. Instead, he had to climb the chimney like a ladder. But unlike Writhgarth, he was sandwiched so tightly that he didn't have the room to bend his legs to reach the next step. Instead, he had to pull himself up to each step using just his arms until his feet could find another foot hold. He then rested for a short time and repeated the process.

Sid sat back, stunned. The previous summer, he and Tris had bet each other a copper piece to see who could do the most pull-ups on a wooden beam. Sid had lost, but had still done sixty-five before trembling halfway up number sixty-six, then letting go in defeat. Looking down now, he realized that Crowdal had just done more than five thousand pull-ups. But his friend couldn't quit like Sid had done during his contest with Tris. If Crowdal quit, death was guaranteed.

The sun was getting close to the horizon before Crowdal reached his hand over the top edge, followed by his other hand. He strained mightily and Sid reached down to grab his arm. The Haissan, Richard, Tulman, and Nik all did the same and heaved up with all their strength until they were able to pull Crowdal over the edge. The giant just laid on his back, his legs still bent over the edge, gasping for air.

Sid let him rest, knowing he needed to catch his breath more than anything right now.

Nik and Richard took out some bread, meats, and cheeses and set them on the ground.

Crowdal sniffed loudly and opened one eye. He turned his head toward them and croaked out, "Ah, supper, wonderful." He pushed himself into a sitting position, swung his legs from the edge of the chimney, and stood up, swaying slightly, before he pulled up his pack and stumbled over to the two mercenaries.

Richard handed him a large chunk of black bread, which Crowdal took gratefully and immediately bit into, tearing the hard bread with a shake of his head.

Writhgarth leaned against a rock not far away and shook his head in amazement. "You could be dying with a sword rammed through your gut and you wouldn't turn down bread."

Crowdal turned and looked down at Writhgarth. "No. No I wouldn't."

The little man muttered, "Trith" under his breath as he accepted a piece of dried meat from Nik.

Sid sat down and took a piece of meat for himself, suddenly very hungry.

They sat, shivering in the cold as they ate. The sun fully set and darkness descended upon them.

They were all exhausted, so they took out thick blankets and wrapped themselves in them to keep warm. Soon everyone was asleep, snoring loudly. Sid moved the top of his blanket down and saw the Haissan standing by the edge of the cliff, its shadow darker than the sky. He wondered in amazement how the Haissan could keep going without needing sleep or rest. But he was grateful to have it with them. Soon his eyes closed and sleep overtook him.

* * *

At the base of the cliff, far below the sleeping group, a huge pair of blue eyes looked up the chimney shaft. The left eye blinked, followed by the right.

The Korpor sniffed, smelling the boy. It then closed its eyes and opened the connection with the Black Robe.

"They have ascended the cliff."

The dripping vileness of the Black Robe's thoughts filled the

Korpor's head. *"Really? Interesting. Send me your coordinates."*

The Korpor visualized the route it had taken, finishing with its current location.

"Good, we are not far away. We will be there before the sun rises."

The communication ended abruptly and the Korpor set out to hunt.

It was hungry.

Chapter 53

T he sun hung low in the eastern horizon as the Unnamed One stepped from the grassy plain onto bare rocky ground and stopped. It knelt and sniffed wetly, casting its head in different directions before standing back up. The scent of Black Numbers filled its head, the numbers swirling and eddying like tidal waters over rocks.

It raised its head to the gray sky and screamed in rage, its black tongue flickering wildly.

It started to run toward the mountains, now so close, and as it ran, the scent grew stronger. Black flies started to buzz around the creature as it ran, but the little insects quickly veered away as they got close, wanting nothing to do with the strange being.

It reached a lake but bypassed it, anxious to reach and destroy the carrier of the numbers and absorb them into itself.

The scent grew stronger as it ran, and as it reached a certain spot, it turned east without pausing, following the trail as if it glowed.

The ground trembled beneath its pounding steps.

It was close now.

It raised its head and screamed as it ran.

Chapter 54

The moon was descending to the horizon and a cold dawn was almost breaking when Tris looked up the three-sided chimney shaft. His old friend Sid was full of surprises, finding this route so cleverly hidden as it was.

The Korpor's voice filled his head, "*I am at the top now. They rested here for most of the night, only recently setting off for the peak.*"

His heart beat faster at this news. Everything was coming together exactly as he had planned. The fact that Sid had convinced his group to follow him to the Srithian Wood on the other side of the mountain was more than he could have hoped for. He had expected to have had to have forced Sid here, but for some reason, as yet unknown, Sid had chosen to come here on his own. This actually bothered Tris for some reason. It seemed a little too easy, and when things were easy, they rarely turned out well. But there was no way for him to know what Sid was thinking, or what the reasons were for him to travel to the Srithian Wood.

The most important thing was that he was close behind the Aleph Null and he would have the power of Black Numbers very soon. His palms tingled at the thought. To be so close after all this time.

The Korpor sent him a mental cough, waiting for his reply, which angered him. He sent a cold thought to the Korpor, "*Follow them as you have been, not letting them know you are there. And before you leave, send me your exact coordinates. I will skip this tedious climb.*"

"*Of course... master.*" The Korpor sent him the coordinates, then closed the communication without waiting for another word.

Tris turned to the Masteen. "This is the way up. I want one Haissan to go first, followed by Lorielle, then the rest of my Haissen. You and your men follow last.

The scarred giant of a man glared at him, his eyes glittering in the light of the moon. "And what of you?"

Tris turned away, already forgetting the Masteen, and formed the equation that would let him transport directly to the Korpor's location. He stepped through the metaphysical doorway and disappeared, stepping out onto the top of the shaft where the Korpor sat waiting.

He nodded to the Korpor and it quickly turned and loped away up the mountain. Tris sat down and made himself comfortable. After some time, he heard a primal scream far in the distance, and even from this great height, his skin crawled at the sound. It was the second time now he had heard that scream. Whatever creature was making that sound was following them for some reason. What it was exactly, he had no idea, although he instinctively knew it was the thing he had accidentally released from a mathematical array. Whomever had imprisoned it must have been very powerful. It worried him, the only variable in his plans that he did not fully understand.

Suddenly, from far below, he heard a different type of scream, one of fear, then a clatter of armor against stone, followed by a series of loud impacts. He edged closer to the shaft and looked down, but couldn't see anything. He heard the echo of yells and screams and then a very distant smashing sound as multiple bodies struck each other and fell down the shaft. The screams faded until he heard the faint impact of metal upon stone as the men hit the ground. Silence filled the shaft.

Tris wondered how many men had just died. He shrugged, not really caring. That is why he had the Masteen's death squad follow last. They were huge men, wearing heavy armor. One mistake by one of them would take out the men below.

He settled back and closed his eyes to catch a quick nap. Eventually he heard the first Haissan approaching the top of the shaft, so he opened his eyes and sat up. The Haissan put two hands on the edge of the shaft and pulled itself up in one motion, landing lightly on its feet.

After some time, he finally heard Lorielle approaching. She struggled for some time to raise herself the final few feet over the top edge. It was the hardest part because she couldn't slide her back up anymore but still had to work her legs up the shaft to force herself to the point where she could get her arms high enough to reach the edge and push herself the last final bit. He watched her, enjoying her struggle, until she finally heaved and fell to her back, gasping for air. Eventually, she pulled her feet from the edge and rolled away.

A Haissan immediately rose behind her and shoved itself up lightly into the air, landing on its feet with bent knees. It straightened up and stepped away from the shaft. Each Haissan followed, not more than a few moments between them, all vaulting from the shaft and landing on their feet. Even Tris was impressed by their strength and grace.

Soon all twenty-six Haissen were out of the shaft. Tris pulled out a piece of cheese and ate it, waiting for the Masteen and whatever was left of his death squad. Soon he heard a clatter of steel on stone and then the head of the Masteen rose from the shaft as he pulled himself up with a series of grunts and gasps. He stumbled a few paces and sat down, his head bowed as he tried to get some air into his lungs.

The sun was fully visible by the time the last of the Masteen's men climbed from the shaft. In all, the Masteen had lost nine of his men.

Tris could have transported them all to the top of the cliff and saved a lot of time and many lives, but moving that many people would have drained even him, so he had let them do it the hard way. He needed to conserve his strength for what was to come.

He didn't let the last men rest. He began walking up the steep, snowy slope, followed by Lorielle and his Haissen. The Masteen angrily bellowed at his death squad to form up and follow. They all trudged up the mountain in a single line, many of them cursing.

The peaks were far above them but the incline was manageable, much better than the climb up the shaft, and they made good time.

Chapter 55

It was late morning when the Unnamed One reached the base of the cliff where the shaft led upward. It could smell the numbers very strongly here, along with the reek of many other humans. It looked up, its eyes narrowing as it studied the shaft. There was no way it could fit inside of it. The creature walked along the edge of the cliff, studying the surface, and without hesitating, reached up and grabbed an outcropping and pulled itself up. It reached out for another far above it, its long arms able to find cracks and ledges that were spaced far apart. It heaved and pulled, climbing relentlessly.

It was soon so high up the cliff that it couldn't fully focus on the ground far below it. It was here that the Unnamed One came to a point where it couldn't reach the next ledge in the cliff. It looked to its left and right, studying the cliff face. It put its head back and screamed in frustration, the sound echoing off the hard stone. Then it spotted a ledge far to its right, about two full arm spans away. Without thinking, it let go of its right hand and hung by its left hand, then began swinging. Just as its fingers were about to slip from its grip, it let go at the top of its swing and flew across the cliff face and grabbed the ledge with its right hand. Its thick arm muscles flexed and strained as it hung by its three fingers. It gripped the edge and without pausing, stretched up to a crack at the limits of its reach and pulled itself up. It climbed relentlessly until it finally gripped the top of the cliff and pulled itself over the edge.

It breathed hard and hoarsely screamed, then began wetly sniffing. It caught the scent of numbers to its left and made its way along the cliff's edge until it found the spot where the humans had risen from the shaft. It saw the tracks leading up the snowy mountainside and immediately set off, its feet soon sinking deeply into snow, slowing it down.

But it didn't stop, the smell of numbers driving it to a frenzy.

Chapter 56

Sid's fingers and toes were numb as he pulled his left foot from the deep snow and took another step.

They had been climbing the mountain for two days now, the distance to the peaks deceptive as they climbed. The first day they had hiked slowly all day, making camp at night in a shallow outcropping of rock. Crowdal had taken out a few pieces of wood he had carried in his pack, Writhgarth commenting on how he was a lifesaver for thinking of bringing wood. They had huddled miserably around the small fire until it went out and they had pulled thick blankets tightly around themselves. No one really slept well, but at least the temperature was just above freezing so they hadn't been too uncomfortable.

Today though, the temperature had fallen dramatically as they had climbed. Sid wore gloves, but they were frozen solid after getting wet from the snow earlier in the morning. The sun hung brightly in a cloudless sky, painful to their eyes as it reflected off the snow crystals.

The Haissan had suggested they all cut a piece of cloth, poke two small holes in it, and wrap it around their eyes and head. Sid had been skeptical, but he had to admit that even though he could barely see through the tiny holes, they did reduce the glare enough that he wasn't completely blinded by the light.

They had followed the Haissan up the snowy slope in a back-and-forth path to more easily march up the incline. With the thin air, they had to move very slowly, placing each step carefully, resting, then placing the next step, and resting again. The mountain grew steeper the higher they climbed, and dark grey granite rock occasionally jutted out of the pure white snow, forcing them to walk further before they could turn back up the slope.

The sun would be setting soon, and the temperature was dropping even more rapidly as the light faded. Sid kept moving, afraid to stop, when he felt the wind pick up. He looked up and saw dark clouds flowing over the peak above them, roiling and bubbling angrily down the mountain.

The Haissan had been quite a ways in front of Sid the whole time, leading them unerringly, but now it came sprinting down toward him. Sid stopped to wait, marveling at the way its feet barely seemed to sink into the snow. The Haissan slid to a stop in front of Sid just as Agnes caught up to him from below.

Sid gulped the cold air and his teeth chattered, his lips so numb he could barely force the words through them. "What's wrong?"

The Haissan hissed, barely loud enough to be heard over the rising drone of the wind, "A storm is upon us." It pointed to a rocky outcropping above them. "We can shelter at the base of that rock. You must hurry." It turned and began ascending.

Writhgarth stopped behind Agnes and looked up, his face hidden in a furry hood lined with ice. "What did it say?"

Agnes turned. "Tell everyone to hurry, we must reach that rock up ahead before the storm hits!"

Writhgarth nodded and turned, passing the message to Nik, who passed it on down the line. They all began to hurry now, although even this accelerated pace was little more than a shuffle.

The clouds rolled over them, blotting out the last of the daylight, and hard icy snow hit them like a hammer.

Sid put his head down to protect his face and tried to follow the trail that the Haissan had left. But it was soon covered from the blowing snow and he couldn't see anything in front of him. He heard Agnes cry out behind him, so he stopped. He couldn't see her through the snow. He yelled her name as loudly as he could.

He faintly heard her reply, then her figure materialized out of the snow next to him. She had only been a few steps behind him yet he hadn't seen her till the last moment. Sid swung his pack off and pulled out his rope, then put his pack back on. He tied it around his waist, then handed it to her, yelling, "Wrap this around your waist then hand it to Writhgarth and tell him to do the same to those behind him.

Agnes fumbled with frozen fingers and was finally able to get the rope tied around her waist. Writhgarth must have appeared behind her for she turned and screamed over the wind. Sid could not see the little man's outline through the snow but saw Agnes hand the coil of rope into the whiteness behind her. Agnes gripped the rope tightly to keep it from sliding to her feet. He waited for some time until he felt Agnes touch his back and heard her shout through the storm.

"Writhgarth just told me we're all tied together now."

Sid didn't waste time answering. He immediately turned and trudged up the hill toward where he had last seen the rocky outcropping, hoping he was going in the right direction. He had only taken a few steps when the Haissan appeared in front of him and grabbed his hand, leading him upward.

The storm grew in intensity, the wind blowing so hard that Sid had to lean forward to keep himself upright. The temperature dropped even more and he closed his eyes against the painfully blowing snow and knew they wouldn't survive for much longer. It never occurred to him to create a mathematical dome around them all like he had done for the flies. He was just too tired and cold to make his brain work.

He felt a jerk on the rope behind him and was pulled to a stop. The Haissan lost its grip on his hand as Sid turned.

Agnes was lying face-down. He struggled through the deep snow and bent to pull her to her feet, but she didn't move. The Haissan appeared next to him and picked her up like a sack of potatoes. It pointed ahead and Sid had to force himself to start moving again. He was so cold that he wanted nothing more than to collapse to the snow and rest, to close his eyes and sleep. But he forced himself to move and had only taken a dozen steps when the black outcropping of rock loomed above him out of the blowing snow.

He came to stop at the base of the rock, and almost cried in frustration, for it wouldn't provide any shelter at all. In fact, the wind and snow swirled around him with even more fury. The Haissan pointed to the left and Sid moved along the base of the rock in that direction, not sure what the Haissan had been pointing at.

And then, out of the blowing snow, Sid saw a darkness. He reached his frozen fingers along the base of the rock and felt the opening. He pushed his way into it and the sound of the storm immediately lessened. It was pitch dark but he didn't slow down, knowing everyone needed to get inside. He slammed his forehead into a rock and swore. He touched his head and felt blood, then reached up to feel the rock. "Watch out, there is a rock hanging low right here."

He ducked down and continued into the cave until he came to a wall. Light suddenly flared in the darkness and Sid spun around to see the Haissan holding a torch. He looked down and saw Agnes sitting against the wall. She was conscious, though dazed.

Writhgarth, Nik, Richard, Tulman, and Crowdal all shuffled into the ring of light and sat down heavily in exhaustion. Crowdal awkwardly untied the rope from his waist, and everyone followed his lead. Sid coiled the rope back up and put it into his pack.

Crowdal pulled his pack from his back and opened the main compartment. He pulled out two more small chunks of wood and some kindling.

Writhgarth's eyes widened and his teeth chattered as he forced himself to speak. "How much wood did you carry in your pack?"

Crowdal looked inside the pack. "Sorry, that was the last of it."

The little man's teeth chattered. "I wish I would have thought of that. Thank you, a fire will feel good right about now."

Crowdal pulled out his tinder and flint and soon had a fire going. The warmth did little to fill the stone cave, but they were all able to crowd around the flame and at least get some warmth back into their extremities.

Soon Sid could feel his fingers and toes, and warmth had never felt so good to him before. He looked at Agnes and she had recovered enough to pass around some food.

The Haissan approached the fire, startling Sid, for he hadn't even been aware that it hadn't been there the whole time. It hissed, "The cave turns into a tunnel that continues for some ways. I believe it cuts right through the mountain."

Tulman stood up, his knees popping. White air puffed from his mouth as he spoke. "Then I guess we should get moving. I don't relish spending the night here or going back outside and continuing that climb."

Sid turned to Agnes. "Are you able to walk?"

She nodded and pushed herself to her feet. The rest of the group did the same and Sid was the last to rise, not looking forward to leaving the heat of the small fire.

Crowdal pulled out a handful of torches and handed one to Tulman, Nik, Richard, Writhgarth, Agnes, and Sid.

Nik stuck his torch into the fire and it flared, but Crowdal pulled it from him and stamped it out.

The mercenary yelped in surprise and anger. "What'd you do that for?"

Crowdal handed the now flameless torch back to the man. "We don't know how long this tunnel system is, so don't light your torch until it is needed."

Nik looked at the blackened torch in his hand. "Fine, but you could have just asked me to put it out."

Sid spoke up. "I can create a light for us." He concentrated on his numbers, looking for the equation he had created back under the House of Healing, but he was so tired that he felt his mind wandering. Finally he slumped his shoulders. "Sorry, I guess I'm just too tired to get it to work right now."

Crowdal touched his shoulder. "Don't exhaust yourself when we have good old-fashioned torches to use."

He turned to the Haissan. "All right, lead the way."

The Haissan immediately started forward. Sid felt like he could close his eyes and sleep for a week after the long trek across the plain, the brutal climb up the cliff face, and then the miserably cold struggle up the mountain. He stumbled a few times before he got his feet to work right again, wishing he could just lie down and close his eyes. But he pushed on, followed by Agnes, Writhgarth, Nik, Tulman, Richard, and Crowdal.

The blackness of the tunnel was absolute except for the small ring of flickering light from the Haissan's torch. The farther they walked into the tunnel, the warmer it got, until Sid began to sweat inside of his winter clothing. He removed his fur hood and opened his jacket.

The floor was rough and uneven. They often had to climb over boulders and slide down steep rock faces. Eventually, the Haissan's torch began to flicker so Sid handed it his torch, which it lit from the dying flame before tossing the spent torch to the side. They marched for what Sid estimated was a half a night. He stumbled and realized he couldn't go on. He needed to rest, so he whispered to the Haissan. "Let's stop for a while. I need to sleep or I won't be able to take another step."

The Haissan immediately stopped and turned back.

Nik spoke up from the semi-darkness, "Now that is a good idea." He flopped down to the stone floor and closed his eyes, instantly falling asleep.

Everyone else did the same, and Sid didn't even remember closing his eyes before sleep took him.

After too short a time, he felt the Haissan nudge his shoulder. It leaned down and whispered to him, "We should get moving again. It has been a half-day."

Sid sat up groggily, the muscles in his arms and legs aching badly from the climb. He spoke loudly, "Come on everyone, time to get up and get moving."

He heard groans and protests, but soon everyone was awake except for Nik, who snored away on the floor. Tulman kicked him in the leg and Nik yelped, sitting up and rubbing his thigh. "Fine, I'm up."

They continued on and time seemed to be irrelevant inside the tunnel. Sid often saw narrow passages leading off to his left and right, but the Haissan led them unerringly forward. The air was dank and stale, with an undercurrent that smelled like unwashed bodies and excrement.

His eyes began to drift shut, and he had to continually force them open, only to have them slowly close again. He tripped on a small ledge in front of him, stumbling forward with his hand out to stop his fall. But there was nothing to grab onto and he fell forward, banging his knees onto the stone and scraping the palms of his hands. Cursing, he pushed himself to his feet. He heard Agnes behind him asking if he was all right.

"Yeah, I'm fine. I think I actually fell asleep while walking and tripped on that ledge."

She nodded, her own eyes puffy and red-rimmed as she stepped up to the short ledge and stood by him.

They continued on, and after what seemed like another full day, they still hadn't reached the end of the tunnel and Sid motioned for them to stop again.

They all sat down heavily and ate a quick meal, this time just bread and meat. Within moments of finishing, everyone was asleep again.

This time when the Haissan nudged him awake, he felt a little more refreshed. He was finally getting his energy back. The sleep had done him good.

They were on their last torch—thankfully the Haissan didn't keep a torch lit while they slept—but as they entered a larger room in the tunnel system, it flickered and went out and they were plunged into darkness.

The Haissan stood perfectly still and hissed, "Quiet!"

Sid listened but only heard a distant dripping of water. He was about to ask the Haissan a question when he heard a faint sound, almost like an echo of an echo. He held his breath and cocked his head to listen. It was quiet for some time and he began to wonder if he had imagined the sound when, to his left, he heard a soft squishing sound, almost like wet flesh sliding along rock.

The quiet ring of steel echoed in the tunnel as the Haissan slid its sword from its sheath. Sid heard echoing rings as his friends pulled their own swords out. Sid desperately wished he had not given Crowdal the sword he had taken from the dead Haissan back near Father Mansico's chamber. But then he remembered how awkward it had felt in his hands and knew it was safer for him to not have it.

The wet sliding sound grew louder and now there were more sounds moving all around them. Sid strained to see into the gloomy recesses of the cave and then kicked himself for not creating a light. He felt for the equation and it was instantly there this time. He activated it and the spinning numbers faintly lit up the tunnel in a bluish tinge, but it wasn't bright enough to light up the back of the tunnel, making it impossible to concentrate on any single feature.

Sid closed his eyes and let his numbers form again. He remembered how he had replicated the flame of a torch and increased the heat to burn all the Haissen to death underneath Yisk. The equation appeared in his mind, only this time instead of compressing the heat, he studied the mathematical makeup of the light, separating it from the heat. It was a simple equation, he only had to remove three elements that would leave only the light left. He pulled those variables from the equation, then increased the values of the light portion of the equation a dozen times so the light would be even brighter; then he activated the equation.

The cave lit up almost as brightly as if it were daylight, the shadows all disappearing at once. Screams rose up all around them, and Sid saw at least forty creatures scattered around the tunnel, pure white of skin, glistening with slime, but somewhat human in shape. Their faces were flat, like that of a slug, and almost featureless except for small round mouths and eyes that were translucent. They put webbed hands up to block the light and slithered quickly back behind rocks and ledges to escape from that which caused them such pain.

The Haissan hissed, "Come, keep moving." It glided forward, holding its sword down.

Sid heard Nik behind him, his voice calm. "Here all this time we are using and conserving torches when he can do this?"

Tulman shushed. "Shut up, Nik, or I'll cut out your tongue."

Sid followed the Haissan, looking wildly left and right. None of the creatures were visible now, but he could still hear wet slithering sounds all around the tunnel.

They made their way more quickly now that there was so much light. Sid never saw another of the creatures, and soon the wet sounds had faded too. He began to relax and as he turned back to Agnes to see if she were all right, something landed on him, knocking him to the floor.

He looked up into the face of one of the creatures as it pinned him to the ground. It leaned forward and pushed its face onto his, and slimy skin covered his eyes, nose, and mouth. He couldn't breathe and felt a sharp pain as something hard pushed into his mouth and slid down his throat.

Just as quickly as it happened, the pain was gone and he could breathe again. He took in deep gulps of air, then retched sticky fluid from his mouth.

He heard a scream which was quickly silenced. Writhgarth and Agnes knelt at his side, and Writhgarth held his head as he spit the remaining sticky goo from his mouth. "What. . what happened?"

Agnes motioned her head to her left and Sid glanced to his side to see one of the white creatures, split open from stomach to sternum. He sat up. "Thank you for getting that thing off of me."

Agnes motioned to the Haissan. "Thank the Haissan, it pulled the creature from you and gutted it."

The Haissan hissed at them, "We need to keep moving, there are more of them."

Sid pushed himself to his feet and was glad that the light he had created had not faltered. Once he set the equation, it would stay without him needing to fully concentrate on it. He pulled more sticky slime from his face and flung it to the ground. "This stuff is disgusting."

Nik put his fingers to his nose. "It don't smell that great, either."

Sid pulled more of it from his hair and flung it to the floor, swiping his hand twice to get it to drop. "Yeah, try tasting it."

Nik grinned. "No, thank you, I'll take your word for it."

The Haissan hissed again, "Move!"

Sid turned and followed the Haissan, now looking up to ensure there were no creatures hanging from the ceiling. They continued at a fast pace, the tunnel turning and rising slightly before descending at a slight angle. It kept going downward until they came to a corner. As they turned around it, the floor of the tunnel leveled out and opened wider. In the distance, still far away, a bright opening beckoned to them. They all picked up their pace then until they were almost jogging.

And then they were there.

They stood at the edge of the tunnel opening and Sid's mouth hung open.

A valley opened below them, so green that the color almost hurt his eyes after the endless white of the snow followed by the grey monotony of the long tunnel. He heard gasps all around him.

The valley was so thickly covered with treetops that he couldn't see through them. He felt joy surge through him when he realized they were Miq trees, although even from this height, he could tell they were nothing like the Miq trees of his home. While the Miq trees near his home were the largest trees that he had ever seen, the Miq trees below him had canopies that were so wide, he estimated they were at least twenty times the size of the trees he had known.

The valley was shaped like a spear, perhaps only forty leagues wide, surrounded by mountains on all sides except toward the north, where it stretched out in a line. And in the far distance, Sid caught just a glimmer of blue water.

The Haissan spoke reverently, "This is the first valley that the Haissan set foot on when we came to this land. Welcome to the Srithian Wood!"

Chapter 57

The wind picked up and a hard, icy snow began to fall, blowing hard against Tris as he made his way up the mountain. He muttered under his breath, irritated by the weather, the snow, and the cold. And to top things off, the wind and snow were quickly erasing Sid's trail.

The voice of the Korpor drifted to him, *"The Aleph Null has entered a tunnel system far up the mountain."*

Tris nodded, even though he was speaking telepathically, something he did without thinking. *"Good, follow them carefully and notify me when you find out where they end up."* He paused, thinking. *"Who all is with Sid now?"*

The Korpor's voice whispered back, silky smooth. *"The Red Robe, her Haissan, the Trith, the Vringe, and three mercenaries."*

"Interesting, not only did they all make it up the cliff, but the mercenaries have stayed with him even when faced with death. He must be quite a leader, our little Sid." He chuckled, then turned serious in an instant. *"Remember, I don't want Sid to know that you are close."*

The Korpor replied in a throaty voice, *"It is difficult not taking the Aleph Null. I want him so badly that I can taste him."*

Tris hardened his voice. *"I don't care what you want. Do not touch Sid or the woman."* He formed the simple pain equation he had used on the Red Robe during her challenge and flung it at the Korpor. It traveled the great distance in just a moment, impacting the creature through their connection. He whispered to the Korpor, *"Do I make myself understood?"*

The Korpor's voice came shakily back, *"Yes... master."*

Tris cut the communication without another thought and put his hands up to block the snow from stinging his eyes. The storm was growing stronger and the temperature was quickly dropping. He had to make it to the tunnel without delay, they couldn't afford to waste time making some sort of camp during the storm. Not to mention that he couldn't afford to lose any more members of the Masteen's death squad. So he closed his eyes and visualized his numbers. The math was so easy for him that he barely had to concentrate as he quickly built a complex formula that mimicked the molecular structure of air. He adjusted the variables so he could compress the molecules until they were solid. He then replicated them, over and over, and as they connected with each other, the equations grew into one single formula that, in turn, grew into a substantial structure above him. He let it spread out for some distance, then pulled the edges down toward the ground around every single member of his group. As the equations touched the earth, they blocked all of the wind and snow from touching the members of his group.

He heard gasps from some of the men behind him and turned to look. Even the most hardened men of the Masteen's death squad were looking up and around them in wonder.

Tris set the formula to follow him, then let it go, not having to concentrate to maintain it. He started up the mountain again. Without the snow and wind, the effort required to take each step was so reduced that he was able to pick up the pace without expending any additional effort. He heard the Masteen bellow out in a deep rumbling voice, "Stop looking around like children and double time it."

The sun had set some time earlier, and the storm had blocked out all visibility, but the link Tris had with the Korpor guided him unerringly up the mountain slope. They had been traveling up the mountain for two days now, and he had considered creating his transportation equation to move everyone up the mountain to the Korpor's location, but after he had transported his two murder of Haissen and Lorielle, as well as the horses from the Oblate, to the Masteen's camp, it had taken him days to recover his full strength again. The energy required to move so much mass had drained almost all of his reserves, although he didn't let anyone know just how weakened he had been. He didn't want to waste that much energy now when they were almost to the end of the journey. While the climb up the mountain was difficult, it was purely physical and he was able to save his mental strength, which he would soon need more than anything else.

After a longer time than he had expected, the blackened, jutting rock finally loomed up in front of him. He found the entrance to the cave and stepped into the darkness without hesitating, followed immediately by Lorielle and then the Masteen. He kept his air equation activated outside until all of his Haissen and the Masteen's men were inside. He then disabled the equation and created a light equation in its place, which lit up the cave.

He turned and made his way back into the dark depths, and he almost trembled with anticipation as he entered the narrow tunnel. It was almost over now, and soon he would rip the secrets of Black Numbers from Sid's mind, taking control of mathematics so complex and powerful that they would make what he could now do now look like child's play.

Behind him, he didn't notice that Lorielle's eyes glittered in the light also, although there was pain in them, too.

* * *

Lorielle walked quietly behind the Black Robe as they marched through the tunnel system. The Haissen surrounded her and the Black Robe, and behind her strode the giant, beastly Masteen, the malevolence within him so palpable that she shivered whenever she thought of him. And following him was what remained of the legendary death squad of the Masteen. She actually felt safe having so many Haissen with her.

She stumbled and flailed her arms to stop herself from pitching forward but failed. She saw the cold, stone floor rushing up to her and put her hands down to keep herself from hitting her head. At the last moment, she felt strong hands around her waist, stopping her fall.

She was lifted upright and a voice hissed next to her, "Watch your footing, these stone floors are very uneven." The Haissan let go of her and continued walking next to her.

Lorielle brushed her long hair away from her face. "Thank you."

The Haissan did not acknowledge her.

They traveled the tunnel for what seemed a full day, until the Black Robe called a halt. "We will rest here. Get some sleep."

She lay down and was instantly asleep, not even caring that her stomach was empty. But all too soon, she was awakened, and after a quick meal, they continued on again. They marched for at least another full day, and while she walked, she occasionally heard soft squishing sounds, but she never saw anything that indicated where the sounds came from.

She grew tired of the tunnel, of how it pressed upon her, the air so stale and wet. She put her head down to concentrate on the uneven floor to ensure she didn't trip again, until, out of the corner of her eye, she noticed a somewhat brighter light and faced forward. Up ahead, the cavern grew lighter and she quickened her pace slightly, anxious to get out of the close, cold tunnel.

The air grew warmer, and she took a deep breath, enjoying the fresh, clean scent of Miq trees, slightly sharp and acidic as it filled her nose. It was a smell she remembered fondly from Orm-Mina.

Soon they came to a stop at the other opening to the tunnel and she gasped at the sight. It was more beautiful than anything she had ever seen. Stretched out in front of her, and far below, was a valley filled with giant Miq trees that created a green canopy that blocked out the ground itself. She breathed in deeply, filling her lungs with the fresh air, and as she did, she sensed a power emanating from the valley.

Tris turned his head. "Well, cousin, we are almost at the end of our journey. You will finally be able to see your son again. You must be very excited."

His voice dripped sarcasm, so she chose to ignore him. He

grinned, then looked past her. "Masteen, remember what we discussed. When we finally catch the Aleph Null, I want your men to kill his small group, specifically the Trith, as I don't want him getting involved. But I want you beside me as I confront Sid."

The Masteen's voice rumbled from behind Lorielle, "I know what is expected of me, little man."

Even though she couldn't see the Masteen, she felt goose bumps rise on her arms at the venom in his voice. How Tris could trust him was beyond her. Maybe they would kill each other and save her the trouble. She sighed, knowing that was unlikely.

Her cousin didn't acknowledge the threat in the Masteen's voice. "Good. Then let's get moving." He turned and made his way down the small trail that cut down the steep face of the cliff, zigzagging as it went.

Lorielle looked over the edge and shrank back slightly at the sight of the long drop to the ground. One misstep, one stumble, and death was guaranteed. She put it out of her mind, though, because she would risk everything to not only see her son again, but to do what she could to ensure he didn't fall into the Black Robe's hands. She didn't see much hope though. From what she had heard, Sid traveled with only a small group of people, and they would be no match against the Masteen and his death squad, much less two Murder of Haissen.

It seemed hopeless.

Chapter 58

The air had grown warmer and incredibly humid as Sid and his friends had descended from the tunnel entrance toward the floor of the valley. It took them most of the morning to make it just part way down the steep trail, and the sun was high in the sky as they finally approached the tops of the trees. They grew so thickly and closely together that they looked like the ground itself. The trees grew right up to the edge of the cliff and Sid had to climb over a thick branch that pushed against the stone, then duck under another branch.

The way appeared to be completely blocked and he and his group had to pick their way over and under a dozen more branches until Sid pushed a final branch out of his way and stopped, staring in wonder at the sight before him.

The sun was completely blocked out as he stood on the cliff trail just below the tops of the trees. But even though the sun was unable to get through, it was still light enough to see. They were so high that Sid could just barely make out the floor of the valley at least a thousand feet below. At this height, using the trees as reference, the height seemed much more dramatic than even being high up in the mountains. He was surprised to see that the Miq trees didn't grow thickly together. Instead, they were so large that they were spaced far apart on the ground, yet still touching at the tops, forming a solid barrier to the sun. Even at the top, the tree trunks were so thick that he could have built a handful of houses inside just one tree.

He heard gasps from his friends as they stepped through the final branches and came to a stop next to him.

Crowdal spoke from just behind him, "Gods, I've never seen anything like this before."

Nik whispered, "It is like another world under these branches."

Sid turned and saw all of his friends looking around in wonder. "Come on, let's keep moving. We still have a long way to reach the ground." He picked his way slowly along the trail, careful now not to trip in the diminished light. He couldn't tell how long it took since he couldn't measure time against the movement of the sun, but it seemed to take forever to finally reach the floor of the forest. As he stepped from the rocky cliff trail to the needle-covered forest floor, he sighed with relief, so glad to be on the ground again. It was darker now and he craned his neck upward. The trees rose straight up to narrow points, looking impossibly tall from this level.

Sid climbed between two of the tree roots, each at least twice his own height, until he got to the actual tree trunk. The bark was so deeply furrowed that he stuck his arm all the way in one and was still not able to touch the actual base of the tree. He was curious how large the base of the tree actually was, so he made his way around it, climbing over the roots, counting the steps, and got to 347 before he returned to where his friends were standing. He created a quick calculation, taking in the size and area of the tree, and shook his head in amazement when he realized that he could have fit eight of the houses in which he grew up inside the base of the tree.

Writhgarth planted his feet wide apart. "I never let myself feel small next to people, but here, well, I have to say I feel pretty insignificant."

Crowdal smiled down at Writhgarth. "My friend, I normally feel like a giant next to everyone I meet, but here I feel like nothing more than an ant."

Nik chuckled. "Serves you right, Trith."

Crowdal laughed and said something in return, but Sid no longer heard what his friend was saying. His vision grew dim and he felt himself fall to the ground. Then everything went dark and silent.

In the void of nothingness, he saw a pinpoint of light. It grew, and as it expanded, he felt heat fill him. It wasn't painful. It actually brought him a sense of comfort. Then a voice... no, it was many voices, spoke to him. They all used different words, but they said the same thing, the mixture of sounds perfectly clear, calling him to them, beckoning him to join them, insisting he follow their voices. He wanted to go with them, but forced himself to pull back, unsure if he should follow them. They grew insistent but he pushed them away until they finally seemed to understand, for their voices became soft, and he thought he heard one voice say, "*It is all right. Follow our voices with your physical body, but come to us all the same.*"

Then all of a sudden he was able to feel a soft bed of long Miq needles under his back, followed by the concerned voices of Crowdal and Agnes echoing next to him.

"I think he is coming to. Sid, can you hear me?"

Sid opened his eyes and saw Agnes leaning over him, her beautiful face still making his heart beat quickly every time he saw her.

"I'm all right." He pushed himself to a sitting position, and felt Crowdal helping him. "Thanks, Crowdal." He shook his head and blinked his eyes a few times, and within a few moments he felt his mind clear up. But he still faintly heard the voices calling to him, more of a whisper now, but still insistent.

Agnes handed him her water skin. "Here, drink this."

Sid took it and drank deeply. The water from the mountain lake where they had stopped after the swarm of flies had attacked them was cool and fresh, easily the best water he had ever tasted. He put the stopper back into the top of the water skin and handed it back to her. "Thank you."

She nodded and sat back as she tied it to her belt.

Crowdal still looked concerned. "What happened, Sid? Are you all right?"

"I'm fine." He got to his feet. When Crowdal put out his hand to steady him, Sid pushed it away. "Honestly, Crowdal, I'm all right." He settled his pack more comfortably, then turned toward the northwest where the voices emanated from, as if they floated on the air itself. "I know where to go. Come on." He started walking, but Crowdal put his hand out to stop him.

"Wait. Let's take a short break. We are exhausted and need rest and food."

Sid started to protest but Crowdal shook his head. "Sid, we won't be any good getting to where we are going if we are exhausted and weak from hunger."

Sid wanted nothing more than to hurry toward the voices, but then his stomach rumbled and he realized he was hungry. "You are right. Let's take a break." He shrugged his pack from his shoulders and dropped it to the ground, then stretched his back and heard it pop in different areas.

Richard and Nik pulled some bread, meat, and cheese from their packs and set it all on a small piece of cloth they used to keep it wrapped up. The smells of food made his stomach rumble again and Sid plopped to the ground with a sound of protestation, then smiled at Agnes.

She raised her eyebrows. "What's so funny?"

Still smiling, Sid stretched his arms behind his head. "It's nothing. I just realized I was making noises as I sat down and was reminded of Mrs. Wessmank. She never just sat down; she made a production of it, groaning and sighing as she situated herself." He shook his head and laughed softly.

Agnes was about to touch his shoulder, then thought better of it and dropped her arm to her side. "I really wish I could have known her."

"Me, too. She would have liked you. You two are a lot alike."

Agnes scowled at him. "I don't make noises when I sit down." Then she smiled when Sid was about to apologize. "Relax, I'm just teasing." She took out her knife and cut two narrow slices from the bread. She added some pieces of meat and cheese onto one slice, then added the other slice on top of it and took a bite from it.

Nik watched her and sidled closer to her. "Hey, what did you just do there?"

She chewed and then swallowed. "What do you mean?"

The mercenary motioned down to the food in her hand. "I've never seen that done before, but... I like it. It seems convenient. Where did you learn to do that?"

Agnes looked down at the bread, meat, and cheese in her hands. "I don't know. I guess I've always eaten this way."

Nik took his own knife and cut two pieces of bread, although his slices were a little more raggedly cut and uneven. He added meat and cheese and pushed the two slices together like she had done. He raised it to his mouth and took a huge bite. He chewed for some time, then spoke around the mouthful of food. "Mmm... this is amazing. You get all of the flavors together in each bite."

Writhgarth shook his head. "It looks ridiculous, if you ask me." He tore a hunk roughly from the bread and held it up. "This is how you should eat bread."

Nik swallowed his food and shrugged. "Hey, suit yourself. I'm going to get rich selling these in the city."

Writhgarth muttered, "mercenaries," under his breath.

Crowdal laughed outright, as did Agnes. Sid enjoyed these lighter moments so much but then felt a sadness fill him as he thought of Melinda, wondering how she was doing. He hoped she was safe. He really missed her.

He casually looked at the people sitting around him. They really felt like family to him. Even the mercenaries. They were more family to him than his father had ever been.

He popped the last piece of meat into his mouth and leaned back on his hands, full and satisfied for the first time in a long time.

A loud and deep burp erupted from Nik, lasting longer than Sid thought possible. Everyone stared at the man, who shrugged his shoulders. "What? Like you've never burped before!"

Writhgarth glanced at Agnes. "I have, but not in front of a lady."

Agnes took a deep breath and let out a burp that was easily the equal of Nik's, daintily wiping her mouth when she was finished.

Nik let out a guffaw and slapped Writhgarth on the shoulder.

They all laughed and Sid lay down on the ground with his arms folded behind his head, staring up at the towering trees around him. He found his eyes closing. The chatter from his friends faded away as sleep took hold of him. He floated in the darkness, but even there, he heard the faint voices calling to him, echoing from a great distance. He found himself wanting, no, needing to go to them. They promised him answers to the Black Numbers. But all too soon, he felt a nudge on his shoulder.

"Sid, wake up."

He opened his eyes and rubbed at them as he sat up. "What's wrong?"

Crowdal knelt by him on one knee, but still towered over him. "We should get moving."

Sid stifled a yawn. "How long was I asleep?"

Crowdal shrugged. "I'm not sure, I can't see the position of the sun. But I would guess it is early afternoon."

He noticed his friend looked worried. "What's wrong, Crowdal?"

Crowdal glanced around, then back at Sid. "Richard just returned. While you slept, he backtracked up the cliff face until he reached the canopy level. Looking through the branches, he saw a group of forty to fifty men making their way down the cliff trail."

Sit stood in a hurry. "You should have woken me sooner." He lifted his pack and slung it over his back. The rest of the group were all ready to leave as he tightened the straps.

The voices were still in his head, calling to him from the northwest. He motioned in that direction. "Come on, let's go." He set out at a quick pace.

The ground was covered in Miq needles that were as long as Sid's arms, brown and thick, and soft as an expensive rug. No brush or other types of trees grew in the area, making the ground easy to walk on. The giant Miq trees were spaced widely apart, but their extensive root systems made it difficult to walk in a straight line, and the group found themselves constantly having to walk around them for some distance before they were able to move northeast again.

There were no shadows, as the sun didn't reach down to the ground, causing the light to be diffused and soft.

They walked in silence, and not even Nik, the man who seemed to talk incessantly, said a word.

As Sid walked, the voices seemed to gain strength, almost like they were growing in volume and density. He started to make out gender in the voices, some echoing deeply, others high and singsong, but all beautiful and melodic. Sid didn't hear any birds, see any squirrels, and not even insects bothered him. The odd silence of the forest was in stark contrast to the voices calling out to him.

The Miq trees grew in a staggered pattern, forming what looked like a wall in front of them; and as they continued, the trees grew thicker together, closing in on them.

Sid heard Richard curse behind him as the man tripped on a smaller tree root. Suddenly Crowdal hissed for them all to stop and be quiet. Sid turned questioningly to his friend. "What is it?"

Crowdal faced back the way they had come. And then he cursed.

Writhgarth nodded. "I hear it too."

Sid was about to ask what they heard, when the soft but distinct clatter of steel armor echoed toward them.

Crowdal turned back around and whispered, "Come on, they are gaining on us."

The voices in Sid's head grew in strength, pulling him onward, also insisting that he hurry. Sid faced his friends. "Listen, I know you have all chosen to follow me, and for that I am eternally grateful. But I honestly can't tell you that you will all be safe if you stay with me. I won't fault you if you want to scatter. The men who are following are after me only. If you go now, they probably won't follow you."

Tulman stepped forward. "I am with you on this, Aleph Null."

Nik and Richard looked at each other then stepped forward. "Us, too."

"I don't have any coin to pay you, and you could very well get killed."

Tulman shrugged. "I've risked my life over and over for coin. I am proud to risk it for you now."

Nik spoke up, "Well, coin would be nice, though."

Richard elbowed him in the ribs.

The talkative mercenary rubbed his side. "Sheesh, I was only kidding."

Writhgarth and Agnes both stood waiting, obviously not going anywhere.

Crowdal turned to Sid. "Well, it looks like you are stuck with us all. Plus, to be honest, I don't want to miss all the fun."

Writhgarth looked up at Crowdal and muttered, "Trith," under his breath before turning to Sid. "Come on, we are wasting time."

Sid stood there, amazed again at how lucky he was to have such friends. It sickened him to think they might be hurt or killed in the coming confrontation, but then the voices in his head called anxiously for him to move.

He shook his head. "I don't know why I deserve to have friends such as you, but thank you." He turned and walked away without another word.

His friends followed him silently, except for Nik, who smacked Richard's shoulder. "You didn't have to elbow me so hard."

Richard rolled his eyes, but a small smile creased his lips.

Sid picked up the pace. He could sense the evil following behind him and wanted to get to the clearing he had seen in his visions. He didn't know why he needed to be there, or what would happen once he go there. He recalled that the strongest part of his vision was of Agnes standing over him holding his Rissen blade, and behind her stood a shadowy figure, the one whose power he had felt numerous times now from a distance.

He turned to make his way around a massive Miq tree, at least twice the size of any of the others. It blocked their way forward like a solid wall. He looked up but couldn't even see the top of it. He followed the curve of the tree, and after four hundred steps he rounded the side of it and saw light ahead. He continued on, almost running now, until he stumbled into a large clearing. It was filled with sunlight, almost blinding after the constant semi-darkness of the forest.

In the exact center of the clearing rose a stone obelisk, black and smooth, standing at least three times his own height and narrowing at the top. The voices he heard in his head seemed to be coming from the stone structure.

Sid walked toward it as if in a dream, the voices softer now, beckoning him forward. He heard his named called and turned around.

Agnes stood right behind him, her eyes wide and frightened. "Sid, I don't think you should go near that thing. Every sense in my body is telling me not to go closer."

Crowdal nodded, standing behind her. "Sid, I think she is right. I don't get a good feeling from this."

The Haissan, Writhgarth, Nik, Richard, and Tulman stood right behind Crowdal, and except for the Haissan, they all looked uncomfortable.

Sid turned his head to look at the obelisk over his shoulder. He felt a sense of peace, a promise of power, of joy and happiness emanating from it. He faced his friends again. "It's all right, but you don't have to come any closer. I... don't know what this is, but it is linked to my power of numbers, to the manuscript, and the Black Numbers inside of me."

"I don't sense that at all, Sid." Agnes looked past him, eying the stone with distrust. "I feel that it is dangerous, that it wants... you."

Sid heard the voices from the stone, but above them all, one voice rose, a female voice, ethereal and seductive.

"Sidoro, come to us."

Chapter 59

Sid turned and walked toward the obelisk and the voices grew more insistent with each step. His numbers bounced around in his head, energized almost to the point where they seemed to be vibrating. The power coursed through him, and mathematical equations greater and more complex than he had ever created himself floated everywhere in his head. He had no idea what most of them meant. Even for his amazing mathematical abilities, they were too complicated for him to figure out. But he did understand them on an organic level, something he had never sensed before. They felt alive, and with a start, he realized that the voices in his head all emanated from these individual equations.

One incredibly long and beautifully-constructed equation floated toward him and hovered directly by his face, twisting slightly as it floated. The ethereal female voice filled his head, and with each word, the equation pulsed, but not with light. It pulsed because parts of it utterly lacked light, and were so black as to be three-dimensionally dark, juxtaposing with the white variables.

The voice, so soft and feminine, whispered to him, "*I let certain parts of myself have light so that you can see me, but my true nature is Nothingness in numbers.*"

Sid didn't understand.

"*I know you don't. Yet. But you will. Come to us... to me, place your hands on the stone obelisk and let us inside of you.*"

Sid found himself walking forward, the obelisk not far away now.

He distantly heard an anguished cry from Agnes, and then a sexual energy exploded inside of him and he felt her hands grasping his arm, pulling him back. The pleasure infused him, but it wasn't enough to overpower the voices of the equations, which grew louder and more insistent.

Sid pulled his arm from her grasp and continued on, but the voices in his head changed, crying out and fading away, one at a time, until just the ethereal female voice urgently warned him to turn around.

The numbers grew sluggish in his head and he felt a numbness creeping upon him.

Then the woman's voice and the amazing equation that hovered so beautifully in front of him pulled away, faster and faster, until it hit the obelisk and disappeared with a pop of energy. He cried out, angry and anxious for her to come back; but she was gone.

Sid felt Agnes grab his arm again, and the pleasure from her touch exploded inside of him. He gasped and turned to her.

She stepped back, releasing his arm, her own breathing labored. "Sid, help us!" She turned and pointed.

Sid looked up and stumbled back in shock. He and his friends were surrounded by huge men wearing blackened armor. Sid turned his head left and right, and noticed that the clearing itself was completely surrounded by Haissen, evenly spaced, just like from his vision.

Directly in front of him, two of the huge men moved aside, and four people stepped through and faced him.

One was the Masteen, the giant man radiating that strange power that dulled Sid's control of numbers, although with Agnes by his side, the effect was lessened considerably. The Masteen stood tall, his black armor absorbing whatever light existed in the clearing. He removed his Kraagiquazz helmet, exposing his scarred and hideous face.

Behind him stood a man with no nose, who constantly patted the oozing discharge leaking from the hole with a piece of crusty cloth. The Masteen laughed, deeply and softly, but it wasn't a laugh of pleasure, it was a sound that promised pain and suffering.

Sid tore his eyes from the Masteen and focused on the two people who looked so small and insignificant next to the giant. They both wore hoods. The one on the left radiated a power of numbers of such darkness and evil that Sid stepped back without even thinking. He knew, instinctively, that this was the Black Robe of the Oblate.

The figure stepped forward, and slowly raised its hands to the hood and pushed it back.

Sid gasped loudly and he became light-headed, almost losing his balance. When his vision cleared, he just stood there, his mouth hanging open at the impossible sight in front of him.

"Now, now, Sid, is that any way to greet your best friend?"

Sid stared at Tris, his mind reeling.

It couldn't be!

Tris couldn't be the Black Robe!

"Ah... that look on your face makes all these years of hiding my true identity from you worth the frustration I felt at not being able to rip your heart out." He laughed, his voice dripping contempt. "You were always so slow, so stupid, yet coddled by everyone because you *might* be the Aleph Null."

His eyes hardened. "You are pathetic... cousin!"

Sid finally shut his mouth at that last word.

Cousin.

He knew it was true, he felt it inside and anger filled him, it bubbled up and broke through his shock. His hands trembled with barely suppressed rage. Tris was responsible for Mrs. Wessmank's death, for everything that had happened to him and his friends. He thought back to the times he had given Tris his absolute friendship, trusting his friend over everyone.

He felt the numbing effect of the Masteen, but he could see it as just an equation, an organic equation that was somehow part of the man's biological make up. Sid dismantled the equation with a simple thought.

The Masteen gasped and his face paled. He took a step back, and then fell to one knee, shaking his head.

Tris turned toward man, looking annoyed by the interruption. "What is wrong, Masteen?"

The Masteen shook his head one more time, then slowly stood up. "I don't know, something... I just don't know. It was as if something was taken from me, but I don't know what."

Tris turned back and Sid felt a nudge against his mind. He blocked it without having to try, and Tris' eyes widened briefly, before a glint crept into them. "So, you have neutralized the Masteen. Bravo, cousin."

Sid pushed back against him, sending an equation of fire, the one he had used to burn up the Haissen in the underground cavern, at Tris. But his childhood friend just shook his head in pity as he dismantled it before it struck him.

"Oh, Sid, you make me sad."

Sid shook with barely-controlled anger. It built up inside him, and Tris seemed to sense the powers building, for he shoved the other hooded figure forward so hard it stumbled to the ground, and as it did, its hood fell back revealing a woman with long, black hair tinged with grey.

Sid felt his power instantly dissipate as he stared at the woman kneeling in front of him. She was beautiful, with large eyes filled with sadness. He felt his own legs buckle and he fell to his knees. She was older, but she was the same woman from the portrait that he carried with him.

It couldn't be!

His voice cracked. "Mother?"

The woman pushed herself back to her feet and stood uncertainly, her eyes filled with love and sadness as she stepped forward. "Yes, Sidoro, it is me." Tears fell down her cheeks, dripping from her chin.

Before Sid could say or do anything, he felt Tris hurl an equation at him. He was so confused by the sight of his mother that he literally couldn't even think of his own numbers, or mount any kind of defense.

Through his own tears, Sid heard a primal scream burst forth from his mother, and then a crackle of energy as Tris' equation clashed with another equation and exploded into nothingness. His sight blurry, Sid watched in horror as Tris stepped forward and punched his mother in the face so hard that she flew to the side and landed on the ground like a sack of potatoes, unconscious.

Agnes rushed over to her side, and Tris spun and kicked her across the face, knocking her unconscious to the ground, too.

Anger surged from inside Sid's mind, released from the deepest area within him that he had blocked since that day in Rugger's hut, an anger so chaotic that it filled him with power he had never before dared to even touch. He stood in one fluid motion, his eyes clear and narrowed.

Tris saw the look on his face and screamed at him. "If you so much as create the simplest of equations, I will have the Masteen's death squad kill your friends."

Ignoring him, Sid stepped forward and created an equation for air and the natural magnetism of the ground, mixing the two with a snick of sound, and flung it at the death squad. As it struck them, it created a bond to their steel armor, instantly magnetizing it. Each man was pulled to the man next to him, crashing together until they were one big clump of men struggling inside their armor but unable to move. Then Sid reversed the polarity of the magnetism in a single burst and each man flew in a different direction as they were violently forced apart, landing up to twenty paces away with a crash of steel.

Sid yelled to Crowdal, "Get everyone out of here, now!"

Chapter 60

Crowdal was about to get his friends moving toward the treeline, but before he could move, the Black Robe muttered something that he couldn't hear and the Masteen smiled murderously, then turned and pulled out his sword, facing Crowdal, his voice rumbling deeply, "I am going to enjoy this."

Crowdal pulled his own sword out and faced the man, all thought of getting his friends to safety disappearing when the Masteen let out a roar and ran at him, his great, black sword held high.

The two giants, one a man, the other a Trith, met each other with such force that their swords crashed together like a crack of thunder across the clearing and flew from both of their grasps.

The Masteen immediately swung a massive, steel-covered fist into Crowdal's chin, and Crowdal flew backward to the ground, his eyesight briefly going dim from the blow. He shook his head and scrambled to his feet as the Masteen bent down and picked up his own sword, chuckling from a few paces away.

"Now, that must have hurt."

Rubbing his jaw, Crowdal eyed his sword as it lay on the ground to his left.

The Masteen saw his glance and stepped in front of the sword, blocking Crowdal from getting to it. "Come and get your sword. It is right here, waiting for you."

Crowdal edged around to his right, and the Masteen turned to follow him, holding his sword up and away from his body. Crowdal knew there was no way he was going to get his sword, so he abandoned the effort and leapt at the Masteen with a scream.

The giant man hadn't expected this and it took him a moment to react and swing his sword in an arc at Crowdal. It was just enough of a delay to reduce the power of the blow as it hit Crowdal in the side.

It was the angle Crowdal had hoped for, and his Trith skin, which was so tough that no sword would penetrate it from that angle, caused the Masteen's sword to bounce away.

The giant man's eyes went wide and Crowdal didn't hesitate. He immediately spun around and kicked the Masteen in the steel plate that covered his chest, sending the man stumbling backward, landing on his back.

Crowdal ran for his sword and picked it up, and as he turned, the Masteen was getting to his feet, struggling out of his armor plate, which was dented so far in that he couldn't fully breathe.

With a clang, the Masteen dropped the breast plate to the ground, then walked over and picked up his sword.

Crowdal approached the evil man, his sword held in the Gaiken position, 45 degrees upward. "Enough playing around. Let's finish what we started back in that forest."

The Masteen grinned, his scarred face stretching like the rictus of a corpse. He rumbled, his voice so deep that it could be felt more than heard, "Yes, Trith. Let's end this."

Crowdal glanced over the Masteen's shoulder and saw that even Sid and the Black Robe were watching the battle.

The Masteen stopped ten paces from Crowdal and set his left foot facing away and his right foot inward, his hips turned slightly.

Crowdal raised his eyebrow, recognizing the beginning of the Shimtune attack. He had never faced a man in battle who had used the method, and was surprised that the Masteen knew it. As far as he was aware, only a handful of men had ever mastered it. It was a complicated maneuver and very difficult to defend against when executed by a master.

Crowdal lowered his sword, letting it hang loosely by his side, then let his muscles relax. The only defense that he knew to the Shimtune attack was to not actively defend against it. He had to leave himself completely open until the last moment because the angle of the Shimtune attack changed fluidly before the final strike landed.

The Masteen started forward, shuffling and shifting his feet, leaned to his left, then right, constantly moving his sword in different angles and positions relative to his body. For such a huge man, he moved lightly on his feet. It was a hypnotic series of moves that were difficult to follow, so Crowdal didn't even try. He just concentrated on the space immediately around his own body, for the Masteen's sword had to connect somewhere, and the space around his body was limited.

Crowdal heard the whistle of the blade and saw it cutting through the air to his right. Instead of bringing his sword up to block it, he closed his eyes and listened, for he knew that his eyes could deceive him at the last moment. Sure enough, the pitch of the whistle changed and Crowdal actually felt the shift in air pressure to his left as the Masteen made the final move.

Crowdal loosely spun his hand, letting his sword rotate in his palm to quickly change its position without having to move his own arms, and at the last moment, he gripped the sword hilt hard, flicked it to the left, and tensed his muscles.

Their swords slammed together, the impact almost shattering his arm.

He opened his eyes and saw the Masteen standing right in front of him, glaring at him, their swords crossed.

Crowdal grinned, then spun, his sword cutting through the air at incredible speed. The Masteen blocked the strike, but the impact of steel on steel was at the wrong angle for him and his sword shattered.

The Masteen struck out with his hilt, and Crowdal was so close that he could not block the strike while holding his own sword. Pain shot through his head as the hilt struck his forehead, and he stumbled back, temporarily stunned.

The Masteen dropped his broken sword and charged forward, smashing into Crowdal like a bull, knocking him to the ground and landing on top of him. His sword landed somewhere behind him as his breath whooshed out of him from the impact.

The Masteen was at least twice as heavy as Crowdal and used the weight to his advantage, pinning Crowdal's arms to the ground with his knees.

Crowdal glared up at the Masteen, struggling with all his might to free his arms, but it was of no use.

The Masteen grinned, then smashed a steel-covered fist down to his face, and there was nothing he could do to avoid the blow. He felt bone crack in his cheek and his vision swam. Then another blow hit him on the other cheek, shattering it as well.

The Masteen raised both of his fists high into the air, preparing to smash them straight down onto Crowdal's face with all of his weight and strength, a blow Crowdal knew he wouldn't survive. So he arched his back, using all of his strength to lift the incredible weight of the Masteen off the ground as much as he could.

The Masteen's grin widened, knowing there was nothing Crowdal could do to get him off. But instead of trying to continue lifting the Masteen, Crowdal instead dropped quickly back down and used the momentum to lift both of his legs up and lock them in a cross-legged grip around the Masteen's neck.

Crowdal tightened his legs together and pulled the Masteen backward as hard as he could.

The Masteen's body bent back, his neck locked between Crowdal's legs. The man hammered at Crowdal's thighs, then grasped at his legs and tried to pry them apart. But Crowdal had them fully locked and continued pulling the Masteen backward. In desperation, the Masteen started punching Crowdal in the ribs, each fist crashing down mightily.

Crowdal grunted, feeling his ribs cracking with each blow. The pain was intense, but he kept pulling backward.

The Masteen's knees eventually lifted from the ground enough for Crowdal to get his arms free, but instead of blocking the Masteen's punches, he wrapped his arms around the man's bent knees and pushed down with all of his might while simultaneously pulling the Masteen back in the opposite direction with his legs.

The Masteen gurgled and his face turned purple as he brought his hands up again to try and pry Crowdal's legs from him, but it was too late, for with a loud, sickening crack, the man's neck snapped back, followed almost immediately by his spine. The Masteen's body slammed backward, his upper torso bent at a 90-degree negative angle to his lower body.

The great Masteen Vorn Maghuur, the man who had battled thousands of warriors from dozens of different lands and destroyed them all as easily as children, twitched once, released his bowels, and went limp with a small whimper.

Crowdal wrinkled his nose at the stench, quickly released his leg lock, and twisted his body, pushing the Masteen from him. Pain flared in his broken ribs as he sat up and looked at the dead man lying next to him.

The Masteen's normally hooded and black eyes were now wide open, like he had been surprised by his own death.

Crowdal touched his own cheeks and winced in pain, and as Writhgarth and the three mercenaries ran up to him, he grinned, then winced again. "Now that was… fun."

Writhgarth merely stared at him, then shook his head. "You are a strange one, Trith."

Chapter 61

Sid had watched Crowdal and the Masteen battle, unable to turn away from the amazing scene.

Even Tris watched the fight, and their own battle seemed to be temporarily forgotten. But as Crowdal snapped the Masteen's back, Tris grimaced and turned back to Sid.

"Well, the Masteen has disappointed me for the last time, it seems. Pity. Now, where were we? Oh yes, that's right. I was about to rip the power of Black Numbers from your mind."

Sid, relieved that Crowdal was all right, turned his concentration back to his childhood friend. He glanced at his mother lying crumpled on the ground. He wanted nothing more than to rush to her aid, for he couldn't believe she was alive. It seemed impossible. He had so many questions for her, and he could only hope against hope that she was not dead now. Rage built inside of him again as he thought of Tris punching his mother in the face.

He faced his friend and pulled out his Rissen blade. "I'm going to split you open like a pig, Tris."

His ex-friend smiled condescendingly. "Oh, Sid, here I was hoping that we could go fishing down by the creek like we always did as kids. Oh wait, that's right, I hated every moment I spent with you. Your weakness made my skin crawl, you spineless fuck. So yes, please, try and kill me now. I've waited for this moment for a long time."

Sid felt Tris gather the same equation again. He concentrated on the formula and saw that it was a beautiful piece of mathematics filled with a power beyond anything he had ever tried himself. He briefly studied it and understood the basics, that it was some kind of array, similar to the one he had instinctively created back in the underground cavern to imprison the Korpor. But this one was so complicated, filled with a combination of formulas beyond anything he had studied, that he couldn't fully understand what it would do.

He sensed that Tris was about to throw it, so he reached for the Black Numbers inside of him. He felt them respond, and while he couldn't fully control them yet, or even understand what he could do with them, the basic building blocks were available to him now and he used them, feeling the pleasurable antitheses of his regular numbers, the void where they couldn't go.

He quickly created an anti-equation of non-numbers and flung them at Tris at the precise moment that his old friend launched his mathematical array. They collided, the array a thing of beauty and terrible power. But the Black Numbers seemed to absorb the power of the array, dissecting the individual variables into their base components, devouring them one at a time.

Then, to Sid's shock, each of the Black Numbers that consumed a variable of Tris' array also winked out of existence because they cancelled each other out.

The array then began stabilizing and Sid realized in horror that Tris was rebuilding it on the fly, repairing the equations as they were devoured by the Black Numbers. Such mastery of mathematics was beautiful in a purely logical way and Sid found himself studying how Tris manipulated the math, memorizing every technique as it was applied. He was so consumed with studying the mathematics, that he failed to realize that Tris had fully rebuilt the array.

With a flash of power, Sid felt the array slam into him, knocking him to the ground, his Rissen blade flying out of his hand. His breath whooshed out of his lungs at the impact and he struggled to breathe. Everything went silent around him, for not even sound could penetrate the array.

Tris laughed although Sid couldn't hear him. His old friend stepped up to where Sid lay on the ground and spread his hands out.

Tris's voice filled his head. *"I have to admit, you surprised me with the Black Numbers, I didn't think you really had any control of them yet. I am impressed. But, unfortunately for you, and as always, you are weak. Even as kids, you and your self-serving anger and childish attempts at learning mathematics were sad. Your father was only an average mathematician, so you really aren't at fault."*

As Tris arrogantly looked down upon him, Sid sat up and examined the array that surrounded him. His mind spun as he studied it. Thousands of numbers and variables, equations and formulas, shifted and spun together, interconnecting and then breaking apart randomly, not staying together long enough for him to reach out and disable any single equation. It was like trying to catch a single snowflake, then studying the exact crystalline structure and rearranging it to make a new snowflake, all before it changed from a solid to a liquid in the blink of an eye. He slammed his hand at the array in frustration, then glared at Tris, who leered down at him.

"Unlike the little array you used to trap the Korpor, this one doesn't require a physical component. You don't have the tools, intelligence, or ability to solve this one. The funny thing is, the solution to deactivate the array is really rather simple. I created it in just a matter of moments."

His childhood friend smiled. *"Now, it is time to rip the secrets of Black Numbers from your mind. This part might hurt a little bit."*

His mocking chuckle filled Sid's head. *"Actually, it will kill you. I hope you don't mind."*

Chapter 62

Agnes felt the hard ground under her head and opened her eyes. Pain washed over her and she moaned, pressing her hand to her forehead. As her vision cleared, she saw the older woman lying unconscious next to her. She struggled to a sitting position and her Haissan reached down to help her. She grimaced, thankful for its help. She gasped softly when she saw Sid encased in a mathematical array, Tris sneering down at him. She heard Tris mockingly tell Sid that he had the solution to the array.

Agnes' eyes widened when she realized she was hearing Tris' words in her head and remembered that she still had the equation embedded in her mind that allowed her to speak with Tris telepathically. He must have implanted the same equation in Sid's mind and when he activated it, hers must have been also activated.

She wondered if she could activate her side of the communication equation to enter his mind and steal the solution to the array. It would be tricky and have to be quick, as he would shut her out as soon as he realized what she was attempting. She would have to forget about using stealth; it would have to be an all-out attack. Get in and out as quickly as she could.

Tris continued speaking telepathically to Sid, obviously enjoying his moment, which gave Agnes a little time. She quickly created an equation that would adhere to any array-solution equation upon contact, but struggled with it, the last few variables not seeming correct.

Agnes felt Tris gathering his own equation as he prepared to strip Sid's mind of the Black Numbers. She had run out of time! Her head ached and she felt blood thudding through her heart. She suppressed the panic that threatened to overwhelm her, and then she had it! The last variable slipped into place and she knew the equation was right. Before she could even think of what she was doing, or of the danger, she hurled it at Tris with all of her might. The equation slammed into him, knocking him to his knees. He put his hands to his head and screamed, and before he could do anything, she ripped the equation back out of his mind. She climbed to her feet, a bit unsteadily, and began stumbling over to Sid.

She heard Tris cursing and felt his anger as he gathered his power of numbers, so she threw the equation at Sid in desperation, but it bounced off the array. She gritted her teeth and ran toward Sid, diving the final distance, but the array physically repelled her, dropping her hard to the ground and hurting her shoulder. She realized that the connection that she and Sid had must be making the array repel her as much as it held Sid inside.

Agnes beat her fist against the array in frustration and fear. Sid's eyes grew wide inside, as if he had just thought of something. He pointed to her left and she turned her head and saw a beautiful knife, the blade sharp and gleaming, lying on the ground. Sid mouthed something but his voice couldn't penetrate the powerful field, so he gestured down at the knife and made a cutting motion in front of him.

Agnes knew Tris was about to throw an equation at her, so she looked back at her Haissan with wide, fear-filled eyes. The creature immediately leapt at the Black Robe, its sword whistling in a downward strike.

Tris turned and hurled the equation at the Haissan instead, hitting the creature in mid-air and throwing it sideways violently. It landed in a heap of robes, unmoving.

Agnes took advantage of the brief distraction and reached over and picked up the knife from the ground. It was heavy, much heavier than a normal bladed weapon. She scrambled to her feet and stood over Sid holding the knife.

Tris turned back, standing not far behind her. She didn't hesitate, slashing out at the array and feeling the subtle resistance of the blade cutting through the powerful field of numbers, almost like it was cutting flesh. The air around her crackled and pain shot through her hand and arm, making it numb. She cried out but finished the stroke, and where the knife cut, she could see an opening in the array. But even as she completed the cut, the opening started to mend back together.

Using all her strength, she flung the equation through the last sliver of the opening. It compressed as it hit the narrow cut, then oozed through and Sid cried out as the equation slammed into him.

Tris roared and threw an equation at her. Pain filled every nerve in her body, burning so intensely that she couldn't even scream as she was lifted from her feet and thrown across the clearing.

She landed hard, tumbled across the ground, and then all went dark.

Chapter 63

As Sid sat inside of the mathematical array, unable to break the equations that held him, he had initially watched in confusion when Agnes had bounced away from him. But then a curious thing had happened. His Rissen blade had vibrated on the ground outside of the array, and even from inside the energy field, he could sense it reacting to the array, almost as if they were connected.

He thought again of his vision, of being in this clearing and having Agnes standing over him with his Rissen blade. Suddenly, he understood the vision's meaning, so he quickly motioned toward the knife. She had looked confused so he motioned toward the field of power around him, as if he were cutting it. He then saw realization fill her eyes and she had picked up the knife and sliced into the array. He had felt the power of the Rissen blade cutting the equations, slicing the variables away like fat from a piece of meat. The equation was powerful though, and self-repairing, and he watched in horror as the missing variables reappeared almost as quickly as they were cut away.

But Agnes had been quick and didn't hesitate. Before the opening in the array could close, she had hurled an equation at him, and it struck him hard.

He shook his head and looked up through his long hair, crying out when he saw Agnes fly through the air as Tris' equation hit her full in the chest. He didn't have time to help her, as he only had moments before Tris turned his attention to him. The array pulsed, the constantly changing equations a blur that he couldn't concentrate on. But the solution that Agnes had given him was in his mind, and he studied it in wonder. It was so complex that he knew he didn't have time to solve it. He didn't have to. All he had to do was implement its central equation, and after that, the rest of the solution would activate one variable at a time and attach to one of the array's variables, neutralizing it.

Sid closed his eyes and saw the single variable hanging slightly outside of the equation. It appeared to be the key, and he guessed that all he had to do was move it down into place and it would activate the equation.

He nudged it and felt disappointed when nothing seemed to happen at first. He wondered if he was wrong about it. But then he saw the equation drift over to the array and stick to it. The variables of the equation that Agnes had sent him began to replicate and peel away, immediately attaching to a variable of the array, and when they connected the variables grew fuzzy and then winked out with a slight popping sound.

The process sped up until he grew dizzy watching all of the

variables rising, connecting, then disappearing. Sid could see Tris narrow his eyes in concentration, repairing the array as quickly as he could, but he couldn't keep up with the self-replicating variables. The structure of the array grew weak, too fragmented to hold in all of its own variables. It stretched thinner and thinner until, with a cry of anger from Tris, the array exploded outward, knocking Tris to the ground, his robe tearing into hundreds of smoking shreds.

Sid cast his mind out and the array was gone, leaving in its place a charred smell that reminded him of burning flesh. The sound of steel striking steel assaulted him, incredibly loud after the complete silence inside of the array.

He twisted his head and saw his friends battling the remaining members of the Masteen's death squad. Crowdal was cut in a dozen places, his hair flying around as he spun and slashed like a madman. Five of the Masteen's men were lying dead around Crowdal. Sid counted and saw only eight of the Masteen's death squad remaining.

He turned in a quick circle and saw that the two Murder of Haissen still stood at the perimeter of the clearing, perfectly spaced and at ease, ignoring the men killing each other. Sid was surprised they were not helping the Black Robe, but he had to put it out of his mind because he heard Tris getting to his feet. He turned back to his childhood friend and felt some satisfaction as Tris cursed and patted at the smoldering bits of his robe.

Tris put out the final smoking piece and looked up at Sid. His eyes burned with hatred, almost black because his pupils were so large. He closed his eyes briefly, and when he opened them, they burned with intensity. "I've always hated your ugly face, Sid, especially that ridiculously tortured look you always have in your eyes."

Tris rolled his eyes, mocking him. "You have no idea how many times I wanted to smash your face to a bloody, pulpy, unrecognizable mess." He sighed. "I used to dream of doing that, but I didn't because of my duty to the Oblate. Well now I don't have to hold back any longer." He spread his hand out, indicating the clearing. "As you can see, you don't have any more friends to help you. They are all quite busy at the moment."

Tris then tilted his head toward Agnes, who lay unconscious halfway across the clearing. "Oh, she flew quite a ways didn't she? It is a shame to damage such a beautiful body like that, but... oh well, that is life." He turned back to Sid. "And, as you can see, my Haissen are here to clean up the mess. So, where were we, Sid?" He wrinkled his forehead in mock thought, then snapped his fingers. "Oh, yes, I was going to rip the Black Numbers from your mind. Unfortunately, without the array, this is going to be even more painful for you." He grinned, his boyish features in sharp contrast to the dark anger in his eyes.

Sid faced his old friend, his own anger growing with each heartbeat. He would kill the bastard or die trying. He heard Nik cry out in pain and glanced across the clearing. One of the members of the death squad had broken Nik's sword, the blow so strong that Nik's arm just hung from his side, useless. The man grinned inside of his helmet and lifted his sword to strike Nik in the head. With barely a thought, Sid sent a single number at the man with such force that it blew through his helmet without slowing down. The man swayed on his feet for a few moments, then the sword fell from his hands and clattered to the ground before he toppled sideways. Nik merely stared in disbelief at the bloody brains seeping out of the helmet.

Sid angrily sent more numbers at the remaining members of the death squad, killing them instantly in a bloody mess, leaving his friends standing around with suddenly no one to fight. Sid was saddened to see that Richard was down, as was Writhgarth. He didn't know if they were alive or dead.

Tris drew in an angry breath. "If you want to play that game, I can do the same thing to your friends."

Sid felt Tris gather his energy and knew, without a doubt, that Tris could just as easily kill his friends in the exact same manner, so he slapped his friend across the face. It wasn't a hard blow, but it was loud and hard enough to turn Tris' face to the side. It had the effect he wanted, for Tris instantly whipped his face back and glared at Sid, his eyes black and piercing in his anger.

Tris reached up and touched his now red cheek.

Sid smiled mockingly. "Tris, you pathetic prick, if you want my Black Numbers, then just come and get them... if you think you can."

Tris grew so angry that he roared and hurled the equation for fire at Sid with such violence that it would have incinerated a half-dozen of the monster Miq trees, but Sid was at peace and had the powers of Black Numbers simmering inside of him. He merely held his hand up and absorbed the frightening equation, turning it inert with a thought.

"Really, Tris? Now that is just embarrassing."

Sid was about to create a complex equation that would combine the matter-eating equation that Agnes had invented, but with his Black Numbers instead, increasing the power by a factor of a thousand. But before he could create it, he heard his friends scream in agony. He turned and saw them all fall to their knees, hands to their heads.

Tris grinned, his eyes glinting. "Ah, there is my pet."

Sid felt a thrill of sexual power fill him and he turned to look behind him. The Haissen had faded into the trees, nowhere to be seen. Then, from around one of the wide Miq trees, the Korpor stepped, thick muscles flexing beneath its glowing white fur, and smiled its hideous smile.

Its seductive voice filled his head. "*Hello, Aleph Null. It has been some time since we last met. You still smell... sweet.*" It glided forward until it stood next to Tris.

Sid felt his stomach turn as he gazed into the huge, blue eyes of the Korpor, so close after all these weeks. The creature still smelled of freshly baked bread and feces. It absently clicked its long claws together, the sound filling the clearing, even overpowering the screams from his friends.

Tris smiled condescendingly. "You remember your old friend, don't you, Sid?" He snapped his fingers again, the gesture annoying to Sid. "Oh yeah, that's right, you also knew the Korpor's son, didn't you. Yes, he raped you when you were eight, didn't he? How was that for you? Did you enjoy it?"

Sid's blood ran cold as the memories of his time in Rugger's hut flooded through him. His knees trembled in shame and anger. He clenched his teeth tightly together. "I am going to enjoy killing you, Tris."

"You keep saying that, Sid, but somehow I just don't believe you have it in you." Tris motioned with his head. "He is all yours, my pet."

The Korpor grinned, its face repulsive, and then it leapt at Sid, moving so quickly that he didn't even have time to react. The Korpor slammed into him, and Sid flew backward, landing hard. The creature straddled him, and despite himself, Sid grew an erection.

The Korpor ground its pelvis against his hard penis and Sid struggled to push it away, despite the pleasure filling him.

Then he felt Tris crash into his mind with such force that he cried out at the pain. The attack was so quick and absolute, combined with the Korpor's lulling effect, that Sid couldn't control his own numbers.

He felt Tris move through his thoughts with dark and malignant mental fingers, ripping and tearing as he searched. Molten stabs of pain pushed Sid to the brink of unconsciousness, and it just seemed to be so much easier to let himself fall into that pain-free place inside of the Korpor's mind. It was over, Tris had won. Sid had given it his all, and it hadn't been enough. He always knew that he wasn't strong enough, that he wasn't worthy of his friends' devotion to him, of their lives given freely.

The image of Mrs. Wessmank's face floated inside his mind, of her frizzy red hair and wrinkled face with its two birth marks above her eyes, giving her the look of having four eyes. He felt love fill him, then he began to shake at the thought of her dying for him, all for nothing.

Sid dug deeply and reached for the rage that had been a part of him since his rape. It was there, waiting for him like always, and he let it fill him. He wasn't going to die without a fight. He owed Mrs. Wessmank and his friends at least that much.

Sid let the pain flow through him, accepting it fully and reveling in it, and as he did this, he reached out and grasped Tris' mental fingers, bending them back. He heard, with satisfaction, Tris scream in pain, and the darkness moving through his mind trembled slightly, the pain lessening enough for him to grapple with Tris, pulling him into a tight grip within his mind. He felt the slick oily blackness of his childhood friend's essence, and wanted nothing more than to push it as far away as he could. But instead, he held onto it as tightly as he could, the vile thoughts making him want to throw up.

Sid felt Tris squirming inside of his mind, oozing between his grasp, impossible to contain, and where Tris touched him, new pain flared as the dark thoughts quested for the mathematical source of his Black Numbers. Sid wanted to reach for the power of Black Numbers, but he was afraid that would make it too easy for Tris to rip them away, so instead, Sid pushed them into the deepest recesses of his thoughts, burying them inside layer upon layer of his mind.

Tris dug into him relentlessly, violently peeling each layer away, and Sid began to tire. He sensed the Korpor pressing upon his thoughts too, and distantly felt the creature pulling his trousers down and caressing his member with its claws. Fear surged through him at the memory of the *Ringing*, of the creature cutting his penis with its claws. He briefly lost his grasp on Tris and felt the icy fingers squirm deeper into his mind. He couldn't battle both the Korpor and Tris, and felt his strength waning.

The Korpor's voice caressed his thoughts. *"That's it, let go. It is inevitable."*

Sid struggled weakly, feeling his grip slipping, his mind opening wider, and with each mental slip, he felt Tris worm his way deeper, questing for the hidden Black Numbers. Sid knew that the numbers were only a few layers down now and Tris would strip the final layer away soon. He cried out in frustration, but it came out as a whimper.

He heard Tris chuckle.

"You always were so pathetic, Sid. Almost there. I can sense the numbers now. Your attempts to hide them are in vain."

Sid found a new strength from somewhere and sunk the Black Numbers even deeper into his psyche, covering them with Agnes' equation of Nothingness, hoping that it would hide them completely.

Tris chuckled again. "Really, Sid? You've tried that equation on me twice now. Yes, the first time it worked briefly, but now it is like a beacon to me, telling me right where you are hiding the Black Numbers." He ferociously dug deeper, flinging Sid's thoughts aside like manure, and with as little concern.

Sid cried out so loudly that he felt his throat tear, arching his back and head at an angle that threatened to throw the Korpor free. But the creature held on, holding Sid down.

And then, the final layer was torn away, and the Black Numbers pulsed in the deepest cavity inside Sid's mind. Tris moaned, and mentally caressed them. "There they are." He scooped them into a ball and pulled them from Sid, backtracking through layer upon layer of Sid's mind.

Sid felt the Black Numbers being ripped from his mind, and there was nothing he could do to stop Tris from taking them. He also sensed that his mind would collapse when the Black Numbers were finally pulled free, and he would die.

He had failed.

Chapter 64

Lorielle sensed the darkness start to fade away, the world around her coming back into focus from the depths where she had been. She didn't want to leave the warmth and comfort of the darkness, but gradually she felt the hard ground pressing against her cheek. She tried to pull back, to return to the comfortable numbness, but pain crept into her, filling her, and she whimpered, squirming away from it. But no matter what she tried to do, she just hurt worse and worse with each passing moment. Just when she felt she couldn't take any more of the pain, she heard the sound of an anguished cry rise up not far away. She gasped and opened her eyes.

From where she lay on her side, she couldn't seem to make sense of anything, the world was tilted and dizzying. She grunted and rolled clumsily onto her back, then pushed herself to a sitting position and shook her head to try and clear it. The pain remained, centered mostly in her chest, but the world stopped spinning and she felt a little better. She heard another cry of pain and quickly took in the scene around her with a cry of anguish.

Sidoro was on his back, the Korpor straddling him, caressing her son's penis with its sharp claws. Sidoro cried out again, thrashed violently, then went still with a soft moan. She watched Tris walk forward, his eyes feverishly bright and focused on Sidoro, a gruesome grin splitting his face. She could feel the power of Tris' mind and knew he was about to rip the Black Numbers from her son.

She pushed herself to her feet, saw the Rissen blade lying on the ground, and her eyes widened. She lunged forward and scooped it up in trembling hands, then stumbled up behind Tris, her balance still off. Tris was fully focused on Sidoro and didn't turn until the last moment. She felt him put up an equation to block her strike, but the Rissen blade cut through it as easily as parchment. She thrust down with all her might, the Rissen blade flashing in the sunlight as it descended.

Tris turned his body away, but he wasn't quick enough, and the blade entered his right shoulder. Lorielle felt the flesh part with almost no resistance as the blade plunged to the hilt.

Tris' eyes widened in pain and shock. He pushed her away with his left hand, and because she was still off balance, she stumbled, then fell to her back, her breath rushing out of her lungs.

Tris stepped back, his face white from agony. His eyes filled with hatred as he pulled the blade slowly from his shoulder, the blood rushing out in thick spurts. He gasped, and put his left hand over the wound to try and stop the bleeding, while still holding the knife in his right hand. The blood pulsed between his fingers and he swayed briefly before gritting his teeth and straightening his back.

Lorielle feared she had not hurt Tris badly enough. Sidoro was pinned to the ground by the Korpor, and she still felt disorientated, too weak to go against Tris mathematically.

Tris turned to her and narrowed his eyes. "Cousin, I am going to burn you from the inside out just like that thief we encountered on the mountain pass." He closed his eyes and she cried out in pain as heat flared inside of her stomach. It felt like a flame was literally inside of her, and she doubled over, unable to stop from screaming. But just as quickly as it had started, the heat disappeared and she heard a gasp next to her.

She opened her eyes and saw the tip of a sword sticking out of Tris' stomach. Her cousin looked down at it in confusion. The blade slid back out of his body and he stumbled forward, letting the Rissen blade he was still holding tip, and then fall from his hands to the ground. He slowly turned around to face the man who had impaled him with the sword.

The Vringe who traveled with her son stood calmly, leaning on his bloody sword with his arms crossed, one eyebrow arched. She was surprised he wasn't doubled over in pain from the Korpor. The only thing she could think was that the Korpor was fully concentrating on Sidoro and was no longer affecting anyone else in the clearing.

The Vringe spoke in a deep, gravelly voice, "That was for Sid, you piece of garbage." He nodded behind him, where the Trith stood. "The next one will come from Crowdal, and that sword of his is quite a bit longer and thicker than mine." He spit to his left, then said, "He is all yours, big man."

The Trith stepped forward and pulled his sword from its sheath with an echoing ring of steel. His eyes burned with deadly intent as he swung the sword in a hissing arc toward Tris' head. But before it could connect, the young man screamed in anger and frustration and stumbled sideways, disappearing with a slight pop of air.

The Korpor leapt to its feet and stared at the empty space where Tris had stood. Both the Trith and the Vringe screamed in pain and doubled over.

The Korpor tilted its head toward Lorielle and blinked its left eye, followed by its right eye. Then it cocked its head as if listening to something. Its eyes grew slightly wider before it turned and ran across the clearing and disappeared into the trees.

Its voice drifted back to her, *"Until next time, Lorielle. By the way, something is approaching."*

She looked around, confused. *"What? What is coming?"*

The Korpor's thoughts were fading. *"Something... ancient."*

Then its voice faded completely.

Chapter 65

Sid felt death descending upon him, only moments away. The pain had faded and he finally gave in, letting it come. But as he felt himself fading into the void, he was pulled violently back. His Black Numbers snapped into his mind so hard that he cried out at the intrusion. He had been ready for the final journey, but now he could hear again, feel the ground beneath him. And he could feel pain.

He opened his eyes. The sun was so bright that he had to squint and blink rapidly a few times until he got used to it. He felt a cool touch on his forehead and the face of the older woman filled his vision. She looked down at him with such concern that he merely gazed blankly at her, not understanding why she was there. But as she caressed his forehead, he suddenly remembered.

It was his mother!

She was alive, and she was touching him.

She was real.

She smiled kindly down at him, her long, graying hair touching his face. She leaned down and kissed his cheek tenderly. "Sidoro, how I longed for this moment all of these years, and now I am here with you." She cried the last words, tears falling from her eyes.

Sid tried to speak but his voice was raw after so much screaming. He tried again, but it only came out as a whisper. "Mother, is it really you?"

"Yes, my son. It really is me."

He struggled to a sitting position, his muscles aching and protesting with each movement.

His mother leaned back to give him some space. She lowered her hand from his face and grasped his hands in both of hers.

Sid felt her cool touch and blinked back tears. "I thought you were dead, mother."

She sobbed, then shook her head. "I was held prisoner for the past ten years."

"Why? Who did that to you?"

Lorielle frowned. "It was your father. He betrayed us both."

Sid felt like he had been punched in the gut. He had known that his father had been in league with the Oblate, but he had never suspected that he would do such a thing to his wife.

Lorielle must have seen something in his face, for she nodded sadly. "Your father is not evil, Sidoro, he just believed in the Oblate above all else. Don't hate him."

Sid couldn't believe that she would defend the man who had destroyed both of their lives. He pulled his hands angrily from hers. "I will kill him if it is the last thing I do."

"Sidoro, please, just let it go. Let him go. He cannot hurt us anymore." She took his hands in hers again. "We are together again, that is all that matters."

Sid felt the pain and anguish of the past ten years rush over him, of missing his mother, of forgetting all but the general idea of her. That is why he valued the drawing of her so much. He had feared he would forget her completely. His lips quivered and he fought back the emotions that threatened to overwhelm him.

His mother, seeing his anguish, leaned forward with a cry and wrapped her arms tightly around him, pushing her face tightly against his neck.

He let his arms hang loosely at his sides, afraid of letting his pain go. But as she sobbed and he felt the tears fall from her eyes and trickle down his neck, it was the final break, and the emotions that he had held in check for so many years finally let loose and he sobbed harshly.

She gripped him tighter and he hung limply in her grasp for a few moments longer until with a loud anguished cry of pain, he wrapped his arms tightly around her. The tears ran so thickly that he couldn't see, and time seemed to stand still. He had dreamed of being hugged by his mother so many times, especially after he had been raped by Rugger, and every time he had cried himself to sleep as a boy. But now she was here, alive, and he clung to her to ensure she couldn't disappear again.

Finally, he felt himself unable to cry anymore, and with a soft hiccup, he pushed himself away from her. She smiled through her own tears, and gently wiped at his wet cheek. He turned away, embarrassed. "Mother, stop that, I'm a grown man now."

She smiled and shook her head. "Sidoro, you will always be my little boy."

Suddenly her face darkened as if a thought struck her. "Sidoro, we must get away from here!"

He looked at her confused. "Why? Tris and the Korpor are gone."

"Before the Korpor left, it told me that something bad was coming."

He looked strangely at her. "Why would you believe anything it had say?"

Lorielle shrugged. "I don't know why, but I do."

Sid studied her for a moment, then stood up, helping her to her feet. "Then we should get out of here." He turned and saw his friends standing off to the side, looking happy to see him.

Crowdal was cut all over, and his face was bruised and broken, but he grinned down at Sid. "Glad to see you are all right, Sid."

Sid nodded as he studied Crowdal, Writhgarth, Tulman, Nik, and finally let his eyes rest on Agnes, who was holding her side. "Is everyone all right?"

Crowdal grinned. "As you can see, we had our own bit of fun." He gestured down at his tunic. "Unfortunately, my favorite tunic is beyond repair."

Writhgarth had a bandage around his head that was soaked red from a fresh wound, but he glanced up at Crowdal and shook his head, muttering, "Trith," under his breath.

Nik grinned at him, his right arm in a makeshift sling. "I'll be fine, if anyone cares. Just a bit of a sore arm is all."

Tulman stood resolutely, looking like nothing could harm him, and even if he were injured, he seemed to be the type of man who would never admit to it.

Agnes merely nodded that she was all right, although her face was bruised and swollen. Her Haissan stood behind her as if nothing had happened.

Sid glanced around but didn't see Richard.

"Where is Richard?"

Nik's grin faded away and he scowled. "Three of those death squad assholes attacked him at once. Richard gutted one, cut the leg out from another before splitting his chest open, but the third stabbed him in the back, bloody coward!" He spit angrily, wiping a string of it from his chin. "But I killed the bastard, at least."

His eyes were moist as he said the last bit, and Sid stepped forward and put his hand on Nik's shoulder. "I'm sorry, Nik. Richard was a good man and someone whom I'll miss greatly."

Nik nodded. "Me, too."

Sid stepped back, but as he did, a wave of dizziness hit him. He stumbled and lost his balance, and thankfully Crowdal was able to reach out and steady him. "What's wrong, Sid?"

"I don't know, I feel... strange." He rubbed his eyes to clear them, but it didn't help. It was then that he heard the whispers, the voices from the obelisk. They grew stronger, all jumbling together.

Then the female voice broke through, loud and clear in his head. *"You must come to us. You must hurry!"*

Sid looked and saw hundreds of complex and pulsing equations floating around him, bumping into him, urging him toward the obelisk. He fought against them, and spoke out loud, "No, it is over with."

"Come to us now. Hurry. It is not over with. You must come now." The urgency in her voice made him tremble with trepidation and fear.

Lorielle stepped closer to him. "Sidoro, what is the matter? Who are you speaking to?"

Sid motioned with his head toward the obelisk. "They want me to come to them."

She looked at the obelisk, then back at him, confused. "Who do you mean?"

"The equations of the obelisk." He paused, then shouted, "No, I don't want to, leave me alone!"

Lorielle gripped Sid's hands tightly. "Sidoro, you must fight them!"

He looked at her with wild eyes. "I don't know how to! I don't know who they are! What do I do?"

She pulled him close. "They are the Absolute Convergence, they are the essence of Black Numbers. Sidoro, they will destroy you as they take back the Black Numbers inside of you and force you to merge with them."

He grimaced in pain. "They are all around me, mother. I can't stop them all!" He felt the equations touching him everywhere, trying to burrow into him. He pushed against them, a dozen here, a dozen there, concentrating on every equation at once.

Then he heard the main female voice, only it was stronger and more insistent, *"Come to us, do not fight us. You will be one of us. You must let us in. You must converge!"*

"No!"

Her voice grew stronger, filling his head completely. *"You cannot let the Unnamed One have the numbers. It comes!"*

He pushed against her. *"Who? Who comes?"*

She didn't answer him. Instead, she pulsed in time with his breathing, wrapping herself around his head. She was a beautiful equation, made up entirely of Black Numbers, the absence of math, completely lacking in a standard mathematical structure, yet complexly built. He stared at her in wonder and felt a sense of peace. She filled him then, entering his ears and curling around the Black Numbers inside of him, merging with them.

Power filled him, power greater than any he had ever felt. He could do and become anything he wanted, he didn't need his body anymore. The Black Numbers beckoned him, pulled at him, expanding such that the physical world seemed small and worthless in its physicality.

He drifted into the nothingness of the Black Numbers and felt the woman join with him, her energy the purest thing he had ever felt.

"I am (E). You are (E) now."

Sid opened himself and felt her as himself.

It was wonderful.

The world faded away.

Chapter 66

Lorielle felt Sidoro go limp and she gently lowered him to the ground.

"Sidoro!"

She screamed his name twice more, but he didn't react in any way. She heard the Trith ask her what was wrong, so she looked up at him, her eyes suddenly hard. "He is merging with the Absolute Convergence."

The Trith simply nodded acceptance. "I don't know that that means, but I can tell it is bad. What can we do?"

She grimaced, then stood and walked over to where the Rissen blade lay on the ground. She bent down and picked it up, turning the glistening blade in her hands. Tris' blood still clung to the steel and dripped slowly from the tip in thick droplets. She wiped it on her shirt to remove the blood, then turned and walked back to Sid and sat down cross-legged, then gently lifted his head and scooted in until she could put his head in her lap. She caressed his hair briefly before looking up at the Trith.

"Sidoro will die in a matter of moments. You must do what I say without question." She held the Rissen blade out to the Trith. "Take this and when I give the word, I want you to plunge it through my back so it pierces my heart and the tip exits my chest."

The Trith took a step back. "What? I can't do that. Are you crazy?"

Lorielle shook her head violently. "Don't ask questions, we don't have any more time. The only thing that can give Sidoro the power to refute the Absolute Convergence is my oxygenated blood, released from a killing blow and combined with my entire power set of numbers, both pushed into him at the same time."

She spoke harshly, "On the count of three, you *will* plunge that blade into my heart!" She hardened her tone even more to let the Trith know she meant every word. "I willingly give the gift of Blood Numbers to my son, so don't you dare hesitate, Trith!"

The Trith set his jaw and narrowed his eyes, then nodded affirmatively. He spun the blade in his hands and set it against her back, just behind her heart. "I am ready."

Lorielle closed her eyes and gathered her numbers, whispering to him at the same time. "On my count of three!"

She didn't just pull a few numbers together to create an equation, she opened her mind completely and assembled the very essence of her mathematical ability, the very knowledge and structure of math intertwined inside of her mind. She pulled all of it into a tight ball of roiling numbers and symbols, of equations and formulas, of every mathematical theorem she had ever learned.

She coiled them all together tightly, binding the incredible energies, and when she was ready, she took a deep breath and counted out loud, her voice steady and calm, "1... 2... 3!"

She felt the Rissen blade slam through her back, just to the left of her spinal cord. Pain exploded into her as the blade punctured her heart and the tip exited through her chest. Her heart continued to beat a few more times, forcing the blood to flow along the blade of the knife and pool at the tip. She gasped, feeling her vision already beginning to fade. She trembled as she leaned forward until the tip of the knife rested against the center of her son's forehead, just above the point between his eyes. Then, taking one final shaking breath, she pushed herself down hard until the tip of the blade pierced his skin, then penetrated the bone of his skull. As it did, the blood ran down the blade and seeped into the hole in his head.

Her vision almost gone, she released the entirety of her numbers in one fierce thrust, forcing them down the edge of the blade, through her blood, and into Sidoro.

As the numbers left her, she whispered with the barest hint of a breath. "Goodbye, my son."

Her heart beat one last time, then stopped.

Chapter 67

The voices filled Sid completely, soft and insistent, loud yet lulling, coaxing him to join with them absolutely. The woman called (E) was now a part of him and he felt blissfully happy. He no longer remembered his own name. He no longer cared as he floated toward the obelisk, surrounded by the equations, all converging to one point.

Then he felt pain enter him.

He screamed in agony and anger at the intrusion. He had been beyond pain, now he felt it again. He fought against it, pushing it away. He wanted nothing more than to destroy whatever was trying to enter him.

And then an overwhelming feeling of power and pure love filled him, warm and calming as it radiated out from a single point. He felt his body again, though from a distance.

He heard the voices rise in anger and the equations vibrated with increased intensity, trying to push and pull him toward the obelisk. He fought against them and felt strength and peace fill him unlike anything he had ever felt before.

His mother whispered his name.

He had a name.

Sidoro.

He remembered now. The power of numbers pulsed inside of him, releasing energy that he soaked in. It filled him, and as it did, he felt his mother as her love filled him with a sense of purpose. He had to get back to his body. His mother's voice called to him, so he followed it, and as he did, he heard the voice of (E) shriek at him. He floated back to his body and could see it lying on the ground, with his mother crouched over him. But something was wrong, there was the hilt of a knife sticking from her back, and blood pooled down her shirt.

His mother's voice whispered up to him, *"Do not be saddened, Sidoro. I did what I did willingly. Now listen to me. Before you again join with your physical world, you must do one more thing."*

He couldn't get any words to form, as much as he wanted to cry out to her, to accuse her of doing something terrible. All he could do was listen.

Her voice began to fall away, growing weaker. *"Sidoro, reach out and take the full power of Black Numbers from the obelisk before the Absolute Convergence enters it and close it off from you forever. Do not be afraid, for they can no longer harm you."*

Her voice faded to the merest whisper. *"I love you, Sidoro..."*

Then she was silent.

Sid cast out his senses but could find no trace of her.

His mother was gone forever.

A rage grew in him, the rage he had always had and relished. This time he let it loose and hurled his mind at the obelisk as the last of the equations were entering it. Sid hit and passed into the stone without slowing down. He found himself floating in a limitless expanse of space filled with millions of equations, and at the exact center there was a black void. It pulsed with Nothingness, sucking in all light. He angrily descended into it, and as he did he felt that which he had always feared enter him, fill him in every way, only now he used his anger to force it to his will.

And the Black Numbers were his completely!

He was the Black Numbers.

The Nothingness became solid, the solidness easily manipulated with just a thought. They didn't destroy his regular numbers, they fully complemented them, forming a new type of power.

The power of Blood Numbers.

Sid felt complete control of everything around him, and the equations of the Absolute Convergence cried in fear and pulled as far from him as they could. Ignoring them, Sid left the obelisk and floated back to his prostrate form, looking down at his mother's body with sorrow.

He blinked his eyes and opened them. His mother's body was lying on top of him, and as he shifted, the tip of the Rissen blade settled even deeper into his skull. Sid reached up and pushed her gently away, feeling the blade tip slide out of his head without pain.

"Crowdal, could you please pull my mother from me?"

Crowdal, who had been kneeling next to him, lifted his head and opened his eyes wide. "Oh gods, Sid, I thought you were dead, too!" Crowdal carefully lifted Lorielle's body from him and laid her on her side, setting her head gently down the final distance. He then turned to Sid. "Are you all right?"

Sid nodded and sat up. He rubbed at his head and his hand came away bloody. "Do you have a piece of cloth?"

Agnes hurried to her pack and returned with a clean white bandage, and handed it to him, her eyes sad. "I'm sorry for your loss, Sid."

Sid took the cloth and thanked her. He pressed it to his forehead and held his hand out to Crowdal, who pulled him to his feet.

Crowdal put a hand gently on Sid's shoulder. "Are you really all right?"

Sid nodded absently, then turned and knelt by his mother's body. He reached out a trembling hand and caressed her face. Her eyes were closed and the skin on her face hung loosely, as if, with the loss of her life-force, her body had sunken in upon itself. He leaned forward and kissed her forehead. "Thank you, mother."

After a few more moments, Sid stood shakily up and turned to Crowdal. "Where is your pack?"

Crowdal raised his eyebrows quizzically, then pointed toward the treeline. "It's over there. Why?"

"Could you get it, please?"

"Sure." Crowdal jogged over and picked it up, returning in just a few moments.

Sid opened the waterproof pocket inside and removed the Black Numbers manuscript. He held it to his chest, closing his eyes. He no longer felt it as a source of power. The Black Numbers that him overshadowed the book, making it feel insignificant.

He turned and gave it back to Crowdal. "I don't need this anymore, but I think it is important to keep it safe. Can you do that for me?"

Crowdal took the manuscript and nodded. "With my life." He put it back into his pack.

Sid heard a rustling of cloth and saw the two Murder of Haissen gliding toward him. He heard his friends pull their swords from their sheaths, but he put his hands up. "There is no need for that."

As the lead Haissan approached, Agnes' Haissan stepped forward to meet it. They whispered together for a few moments, then they both approached Sid, and to his surprise, they each knelt down on one knee. As they did, the remaining twenty-five Haissen also knelt down.

The lead Haissan raised its voice, the hiss quite pronounced, "We pledge ourselves to you, Aleph Null, now and forever."

Sid lifted his hand. "Please, do not kneel before me."

The two leaders of the Haissen pushed their hoods back, showing their alien faces. They hissed in unison, "We kneel before you willingly, Aleph Null."

Embarrassed, Sid didn't know how to respond.

The Haissan to his right spoke quietly and with reverence, "We would like to tell you our story, then make the greatest of requests. Will you allow us to proceed?"

Sid nodded, curious. He had no idea what they would ask of him, and he worried they thought too much of his abilities. His friends moved closer, curious what was going on.

The Haissan spoke quietly but quickly, recounting a brief history of the Haissen, of how they had lived far across the sea, but their race had almost completely died out from a strange sickness. Then, a few millennia ago, their leader had a vision of a human who would one day have the mathematical ability to cure their deadly malady. So they had all come to this land to create the Oblate, and ultimately the Aleph Null, to make the vision come true. It finished up the story, stating that the Haissen in this clearing were the only ones that remained in all of the land. It hissed, "Will you do us the honor of altering or destroying the sickness that lives inside of us?"

Sid reeled from the information and request. The history of the Haissen was his history. He existed because of them. Everything that had happened was because of them. Sid knew he should be angry at them, but the fact that they did what they did simply to survive as a race was honorable, not done out of maliciousness.

Sid wiped a few strands of hair from his face and looked directly into the Haissan's eyes and saw neither hope nor anxiety. The creature merely stared blankly at him, waiting for his answer.

He reached out with his mind and studied the mathematical makeup of their bodies. They were perfectly-built creatures in every way. Their blood flowed quicker through their bodies despite their hearts beating at one-third the rate of humans. He calculated the Haissen nerve impulses and he couldn't believe the results. They were so fast as to be almost incalculable. Lastly, he studied the rate of cellular decay and had to redo the equations three times to ensure they were correct.

Sid studied his own cellular decay and compared it to the Haissen and was astounded. While human cells decayed and regenerated constantly, the Haissen cells decayed and regenerated every forty-three days. Combining this with their slow heartbeats and fast nerve responses, they were almost perfect beings who had reflexes that were too quick to register, and who would likely live for thousands of years.

They were almost perfect, but it was the almost that made Sid sit back with a sigh. While studying them, he had seen one strange aberration in their cellular makeup. When he figured it into an equation, the results always returned a negative. He cast out the equation to every Haissan in the clearing and the results all came back the same.

Sid changed the cellular equation to remove the malignant variable. He realized that in doing so, the surrounding variables became unstable because they were dependent on the aberrant variable. Sid modified the surrounding structure of the equation, changing the linear factorization, and the equation pulsed as he added a final polynomial. He studied it and knew it was correct. Without hesitating, he replicated the equation and sent it into all of the Haissen at once.

He heard them all hiss and fall to the ground as one. Sid raised a shaking hand to move the hair from his face, worried that he had made a critical error, but then, as quickly as they had fallen, the two leaders of the Haissen who had approached him opened their eyes and jumped to their feet in one fluid motion, then knelt before him once more.

The other Haissen around the clearing also leapt back to their feet, then turned and knelt before Sid, holding the position. The two lead Haissen removed their swords from their scabbards and held them out to Sid, holding the blades across their hands. "Thank you, Aleph Null. We can feel the sickness is absent from our bodies. Our swords are forever yours."

Sid put up his hands, his face reddening. "Thank you, I am glad I could help you." His own words sounded trite, considering he had just fulfilled an ancient prophecy and saved an entire race. But he honestly didn't know how to react.

The Haissen stood and bowed, full of dignity and self-assurance, then returned their swords to their scabbards and said nothing more.

Sid turned back to his friends and found them all staring at him in wonder. He felt his face flush. "What?"

Crowdal shook his head in amazement. "You just saved an entire race, and earned forever fealty of the Haissen, and you ask 'what'?"

Sid felt his face grow warmer, embarrassed. But before he could say anything, he felt the ground vibrate. He looked down, not sure he had even felt it. But then it vibrated again, then again. He looked up at his friends and saw that Agnes' face had turned white and blotchy.

"What is wrong, Agnes?"

She lifted a shaking hand to push her hair behind her ear, and when she spoke, her voice trembled and broke on the last syllable, "It is coming."

Sid took both of her shoulders in his hands. "Agnes, what is coming?"

She looked fearfully around. "It. I don't know what it is. I ran across it before I met you..." Her voice trailed off.

Her Haissan stepped forward and hissed, "It is the 'Unnamed One.' We had hoped that it would not find you. It has."

Sid turned to the Haissan. "What is this 'Unnamed One'?"

The Haissan spoke calmly, without emotion, "We do not know, exactly. We've run across a few references to it, but that is all. But those references all say one thing. It is ancient and may have been created by the first wielder of Black Numbers."

Sid looked at the Haissan in confusion. "The first wielder? I thought you created the Black Numbers."

The Haissan shook its head minutely. "No, we had documents from millennia ago that referenced Black Numbers. It is what gave us the idea to bring them back into existence." It stared at Sid. "Which we did."

Sid's mind raced with thoughts. 'Black Numbers existed in the past? He wasn't the first to wield them?' Then the ground vibrated even harder and he put those thoughts aside as he glanced into the forest again. "Whatever it is, can we fight it, or should we try to outrun it?"

The Haissan shook its head. "No, on both accounts."

Nik spoke up from the back of the group. "Oh great, just great!" He threw his sword to the ground and sat down, holding his bad arm close to his chest.

Tulman kicked him in the leg. "Get up, soldier. We will not die without a fight."

Nik yelped and stood up reluctantly, picking up his sword with a grumble

Tulman looked like he was going to kick him again, so Nik quickly stepped back.

The ground was shaking in regular intervals now, and then a horrible scream echoed toward them. It started low and rose in volume, going on for a long time. Agnes put her hands to her ears as tears streamed down her cheeks.

Nik lifted his good arm and covered one ear awkwardly while holding his sword, cursing.

Sid grabbed Crowdal's arm. "Listen, get everyone behind me, I don't want any of you in that thing's way when it comes."

Crowdal looked gravely down at him. "You can't fight it alone. Maybe between the Haissen and us, we can wound it enough for you to take it out."

Sid shrugged. "Maybe. But I don't know if that will help anything. You could be killed."

They could all clearly hear the thunderous footsteps now as the thing approached, still hidden somewhere behind the massive Miq trees. Abruptly, the footsteps stopped and silence descended on the clearing. They all stood closely together, staring into the treeline.

The moments stretched out for so long that Nik finally yelled out. "Either come or don't come, but make a decision, you motherless goat!"

Everyone, including the Haissen, turned to look at Nik.

He shrugged. "What? I'm tired of waiting."

Another scream erupted, though shorter this time, and the thudding of the steps began again, increasing in tempo. Whatever it was, it was running toward them now.

Sid turned back toward the treeline and yelled at Crowdal, "Get everyone behind me, now!"

Crowdal pushed everyone behind Sid, except for the Haissen. They fanned out on either side of Sid, swords out and held in the Gaiken position, held up at a slight angle.

Sid motioned at them. "Get behind me, there is no need for you to die."

The lead Haissan who stood closest to Sid, merely shook its head. "We will attack first."

Sid could see the Haissan's eyes shining intensely, and it was the first time he had ever seen a Haissan show anything remotely approaching emotion. It was looking forward to this fight. Sid shrugged, knowing he couldn't make them do anything.

The thudding grew in intensity, growing closer and louder, until, from around one of the giant Miq trees, a colossal creature thundered into the clearing and slid to a stop.

Sid tilted his head up, his mouth hanging open at the awesome sight before him.

The creature stood on two legs and was at least three times taller than Crowdal. It had gray skin filled with open sores that leaked a thick, yellowish pus, the sickening smell washing over him even from so far away. Sid put his hand to his nose and looked up at the thing's face, but he couldn't make out any definable features. Its skin looked like melting wax, sagging and drooping unevenly. It had two strangely-spaced eyes, one slightly higher on its face than the other. It sniffed wetly at the air.

The creature raised its head to the sky and screamed again so loudly that Sid thought his ear drums would pop. The creature stuck out a long blackened tongue as it screamed, spittle flying thickly out. The creature finally lowered its head and stopped screaming. It turned its head back and forth to take in the entire area, then it stopped and focused on Sid, its eyes narrowing as it stared at him from the edge of the clearing.

Sid heard Nik and Writhgarth cursing behind him, not in fear, but in anger. He ignored them and created a powerful equation that mimicked fire and hurled it at the creature. But as the equation neared the beast, Sid gaped in astonishment as it veered away at the last moment and struck one of the Miq trees. The tree trunk burst into flames, and without thinking, Sid dismantled the equation and the fire quickly went out. Sid send some numbers toward the creature and they moved around it. He trembled slightly, realizing the creature was immune to any mathematical attacks.

The creature seemed to watch the equations that Sid had thrown, even though they should have been invisible to it. Then it screamed and charged, the ground shaking as it ran.

Twenty of the Haissen sprinted forward while the remaining stayed to guard Sid. The Haissen spread out and leapt at the creature, their swords blurring as they attacked. They cut the creature's legs, back, arms, all as one, like flies on a dead animal. One Haissan jumped onto the shoulders of another Haissan and leaped into the air at the creature, sword raised for a deadly downward strike, but the Unnamed One simply swatted the Haissan sideways with a massive three-fingered hand. The Haissan flew halfway across the clearing and tumbled to the ground end-over-end before coming to a rest, crumpled in an unnatural position.

The creature screamed at the sky when another Haissan leapt upon its back and began hacking at its skull so hard and fast that it looked like it was chopping at a fallen tree, but it did little damage. The Unnamed One reached back, grabbed the Haissan by the head, and crushed it like a strawberry.

The whole time, the other Haissen relentlessly moved in to attack, slicing and stabbing at the creature, sometimes drawing blood, other times having their blades bounce off the creature's thick skin.

Sid watched in horror as the Unnamed One smashed a fist down on two Haissen, crushing them both into a pulpy bloody mess. Then the creature bent down and bit a Haissan in half before raising its head and gulping down the body in two bites.

Sid was sickened at so much death and knew that the Haissen would not halt their attacks until they were all dead. So he created an equation that would push them away from the creature and imprison them, like he did to the Korpor in the cavern. He replicated the equation thirteen times, for that was all the Haissen left alive, and threw it at them all at once.

All thirteen Haissen were thrown far away from the creature and found themselves stuck in the mathematical array. They struggled at first but quickly gave up when they realized they couldn't get out.

The Unnamed One screamed again and charged Sid, its black tongue flicking out of its mouth violently as it ran.

Sid angrily castigated himself for using his normal numbers with his first attack on the Unnamed One. He brought forth the Blood Numbers again, and they pulsed with both darkness and light, physicality and nothingness. They were alive inside of him.

The Unnamed One was almost upon him, just three strides away. But in the space of those three strides, perhaps no more than one-and-a-half heartbeats, Sid created an array equation made from Blood Numbers, proofed it, double-checked it, then activated and threw it at the creature.

The Unnamed One froze, its hands stretched out, almost touching Sid. The creature's eyes moved, following Sid as he stepped out of its way. The Unnamed One vibrated with rage. Its mouth slowly opened and its black tongue slipped out, its fingers beginning to twitch.

Sid didn't now for how long the Blood Number array would hold the creature. He studied the Unnamed One's structure in the space of a heartbeat and saw that the creature somehow seemed to repulse even his Blood Numbers, and now he knew why. The creature was not made from the same matter that everything else around him was made of. Its molecular structure was different, unable to be broken down. He couldn't destroy it.

He only had moments before the creature would break free from the mathematical array. He had to find a way to permanently imprison it. He ran through hundreds of calculations and formulas in the space of a few more heartbeats, but they all failed at some point.

He saw the creature's arms begin to move, the muscles flexing as it strained against the array. Sid felt failure settle in, he just didn't have enough time. He glanced back at his friends, who watched him from a distance, their faces filled with panic and fear.

Something nagged at him.

He turned in a fast circle, moving his eyes back and forth, searching the clearing. And then he saw it and felt a thrill of hope.

The obelisk!

He sent his thoughts into the space inside of the obelisk, seeing now that the interior existed on a different plane than the outside world, an emptiness that stretched forever. He turned back to the Unnamed One and replicated its strange molecular structure and matched the frequency emanating from the obelisk. He concentrated so hard that sweat beaded on his forehead and his body shook with the effort because the energy waves of the two wanted to push against each other. With pure force of will, Sid bent them together and added an equation that bridged the two, bonding them. He left a single variable free, which would activate the equations.

The creature screamed at the sky, spittle flying as it finally broke free from the array. It turned on him, mouth gaping wide, sharp teeth glistening in the sun, and as Sid hurriedly activated the bridge equation, the creature lunged at him.

A flash of light and energy blew out across the clearing, throwing the creature toward the obelisk. As it flew backward, the Unnamed One screamed, and as it did, Sid felt it rip into his mind and grasp at it with a blackened, vice-like mental grip.

Sid felt his mind jerk viciously toward the obelisk as the creature screamed. Pain filled him, pain worse than anything he could have imagined and his vision faded. In the back of his mind he felt his body strike the ground, but he couldn't move. The molecules within his mind felt like they were stretching out, splitting and tearing away at the place where his power of numbers originated. Sid couldn't concentrate, the pain obliterating any sense of control that he had of his Blood Numbers, his Black Numbers; all of his numbers clenched tightly in the psychic grasp of the Unnamed One as it hurtled toward the obelisk.

The creature slammed into the stone structure and its body melted into it, and as the creature disappeared into the obelisk, it screamed once more and yanked mightily at Sid's mind one final time, and Sid felt something snap inside of him.

The creature's scream faded until silence filled the clearing.

Sid lay on his side, gasping for air, the pain gone so suddenly that he felt a sense of emptiness within him where it had been. He reached up with a trembling hand and rubbed his eyes and then heard his friends moaning. After a few moments, his vision began to clear and he sat up, putting a hand down to the ground to steady himself.

He looked around the clearing and felt a surge of relief when he saw that the Unnamed One was gone. Where it had stood, the ground was now charred, the grass still smoldering. He quickly turned toward the obelisk and saw that the side was blackened, but intact.

His friends were all struggling to sit up, rubbing their heads in confusion. The array he had created to hold the Haissen back from attacking the Unnamed One had broken, and they fanned out, searching the area for any further danger, their swords reflecting the sun in brilliant flashes as they moved. They must have realized the danger was gone, for they all spun their swords and smoothly slid them into their scabbards.

Sid slumped his shoulders, then let himself fall to his back again, closing his eyes. He felt so weary that he didn't know if he would ever stand again. As he always did, he reached for his numbers to calm himself, but as he felt for them, he realized they were not there. In a panic, he searched within his mind, but the area from where his numbers normally sprang was now empty.

His numbers were gone!

He cried out, refusing to give up his search for the numbers. They had to be there somewhere. But as he searched, he realized with certainty that they were indeed gone. He thought of the snap he had felt as the Unnamed One had fallen through the stone of the obelisk and he knew that the creature had somehow ripped his power of numbers from his mind, taking them with it into the unknown abyss that existed inside the obelisk.

Sid screamed and slammed his fists against the ground in fear and frustration. He felt around within his mind one final time in desperation, and it was then that he noticed a thread of light, faint and so thin that he could just barely see it, stretching from himself toward the obelisk, disappearing inside. He followed it, knowing somehow that his numbers were connected to it, but as his consciousness made contact with the obelisk, it bounced away, unable to follow the thread of light into the structure.

Sid slammed his consciousness forward, willing himself to penetrate the obelisk, but the harder he hit it, the further back he bounced. He mentally looked around, not willing to give up, and it was then that he saw that the thread of light stretched away to the Black Numbers manuscript inside of Crowdal's pack. The light pulsed stronger around the pack.

Hope filled him, even though it was faint. Maybe there was a chance for him to find a way to get his power of numbers back. Just knowing this was enough for him right now and he took a ragged breath. He was too tired to concentrate on the Black Numbers manuscript right now.

He heard footsteps approaching and slowly opened his eyes to see his friends gathering around him. Agnes and Crowdal knelt down by him.

Crowdal spoke quietly, "Sid, you did it! That creature is gone."

Agnes was about to put her hand on his leg but stopped at the last moment.

Sid smiled tiredly. "Don't worry, what happened to us before won't happen again." He reached out and took her hand.

She flinched at first, expecting the sexual jolt, but when nothing happened, she squeezed his hand.

Agnes must have seen the look in his eyes, for she leaned down and kissed him softly on the lips. "Thank you, Sid. We owe you our lives."

While the feel of her lips didn't send him into orgasmic bliss, he felt a surge of emotion fill him, a sense of peace, a feeling deeper and more meaningful than the sexual connection they had shared earlier. He had never felt love for a woman before, other than for his mother and Mrs. Wessmank, but this was a much different feeling. As he looked into her eyes, he found that he didn't want to be apart from her.

Sid felt the emptiness within where his numbers had been and a sense of loss filled him again. He looked away, suddenly feeling as if he didn't deserve her gratitude.

She put a finger under his chin and lifted it. "Sid, what's the matter?"

Sid didn't know how to tell her that his power of numbers was gone.

Looking embarrassed, Crowdal stood and motioned to Writhgarth, Nik, and Tulman. "Come on, let's gather the friends we lost today and give them a proper goodbye." They set out and seven of the Haissen joined them. They carried Richard to the center of the clearing, and the Haissen carried their fallen brethren, two of whom were nothing more than a pulpy mess wrapped in their robes.

When they were alone, Agnes stroked his cheek. "Please, tell me what is wrong."

Sid stared into her eyes and knew he had to tell her the truth. She deserved it. He struggled to a sitting position again, then leaned toward her and whispered, "It's my numbers. They are gone."

She looked questioningly at him. "What do you mean, gone?"

Sid pointed at the obelisk, his hand shaking. "When I imprisoned the creature in the obelisk, it somehow latched onto my numbers and dragged them into the structure with it."

Agnes' eyes opened wide. "Oh, Sid, I'm sorry. What are you going to do now?"

"I don't know for sure. I think the answer is in the Black Numbers manuscript."

She looked involuntarily to Crowdal's pack, then back at him. "Then let's get them back! I will help you in any way that I can."

He smiled slightly. "Thank you, Agnes. One thing... please don't tell the rest of the group yet. I want to see if I can get this sorted first. No need to worry them."

Agnes touched his face again, softly. "Of course. I won't say a word."

He closed his eyes and wanted nothing more than to keep them closed, to drift into a deep sleep, but there was one more thing that he had to do. He stood up, swaying slightly in exhaustion, then stumbled over to where his mother lay on the ground and knelt down. She still had the hilt of the Rissen blade lodged in her back.

He gently rolled her to her stomach. Blood caked her back, thickest where it had pooled around the handle of the Rissen blade. He grasped the handle and pulled it slowly from her spine until it was free from her body. He put it back into its sheath, the sound somehow comforting to him, and then rolled his mother's body to her back again.

He studied her face one last time. Even though in death her skin had seemed to sink into her face, she still looked similar to the drawing that he carried of her, although the sadness was now gone from her face, as if she were finally at peace.

Tears fell down his face and he sobbed softly. She had miraculously come back into his life when he thought she had been dead, and then was taken from him again just as quickly. It wasn't fair. He took her hand and held it tightly to his face. It was still warm and he closed his eyes, not wanting to let her go.

Agnes knelt down and rested her head against his shoulder and he appreciated the simple gesture.

He slowly put his mother's hand down onto her stomach, then lifted her other hand and did the same. He touched his mother's cheek one last time, letting his fingers linger on her soft skin.

Crowdal walked over to him and spoke quietly, "She looked a lot like you, Sid."

Sid glanced up at his friend, then behind him to see that all of the dead had been piled together on top of a carefully stacked pile of thick Miq branches, ready to burn. The Haissen stood around the bodies, one of them holding a burning torch.

Agnes stood up to give him some space, and he looked back down to his mother, unable to respond to his friend.

He reached his arms under her body and tried to lift her, but she slipped from his grasp and fell back to the ground.

Crowdal bent down with him, saying in a soft voice, "Let me do that for you, Sid."

Sid pushed his friend gently away. "No, I am going to do it. I have to do it." He rolled her body slightly until he could get his arms fully underneath her, then grunted as he lifted her up. His mother's head fell back, hanging as he stumbled toward the pile of bodies. By the time he reached it, he was gasping for air, his knees shaking so hard that he worried he wouldn't be able to lift his mother onto the top of the pile of bodies. But with one last grunt of effort, he lifted her high and set her down on top of Richard and the dead Haissen. He stepped back a safe distance and fell to his knees.

Everyone gathered around him, their heads bowed in silence for their lost friends.

When Sid got his breathing back under control, he struggled back to his feet and spoke quietly, "We thank the brave souls who gave their lives today. Richard was a good man and we will miss him. These Haissen did not hesitate to give their lives in battle, and we are forever in their debt. And to my mother. She gave her life so that I might live."

Tears fell down his cheeks. "Thank you."

It was quiet in the clearing for a few moments, then Nik cleared his throat a few times before speaking. "Richard, I am a little pissed at you for going and getting yourself killed like you did, but at least you took two of those giant bastards with you." He paused for a long moment, swallowing twice before he could continue, his voice thick with emotion, "I will miss hunting with you, my friend."

When Nik didn't say anything more, Sid turned to a Haissan and held out his hand. The Haissan handed him the smoking torch, and Sid stepped forward and pressed it against one of the branches on the bottom. It flared quickly and soon the pyre was burning hotly.

After a few moments of silence, Crowdal motioned to the dead Masteen and his death squad. "Not to ruin the moment, but what about them?"

Tulman spit to his side. "I say let 'em rot."

Sid nodded. "I agree. Let the animals eat them." He turned and made his way back to where most of their packs sat on the ground a good ways from the fire, and almost fell as he sat down in exhaustion.

Everyone sat down also, except for the Haissen, who stood casually around the clearing, on guard.

Agnes joined him, and he took both of her hands in his, enjoying the feel of her warm skin against his.

She leaned against his shoulder.

Sid noticed that Agnes' Haissan still stood behind her, and didn't join the rest of its brethren.

Nik lay on his back with a sigh and closed his eyes. After a few moments, he spoke up at the sky, his eyes still closed, "Hey Agnes, would you mind making us some of those bread-meat-cheese combination things?"

Tulman kicked him in the leg. "Why don't *you* make us some of them, you ass?"

Nik yelped and rubbed his leg.

It was just what was needed to break the solemn atmosphere and Writhgarth and Crowdal laughed, and Sid silently thanked Nik.

Agnes glared at Nik, although her voice betrayed her good nature. "Yes, I think you should make us some food, Nik."

Nik guffawed. "Since when does a man have to do a woman's job?"

Tulman kicked him again. "Be nice to the lady or I'll break your *sore* arm."

Nik jumped to his feet to avoid a third kick and grumbled, "Fine, I'll get it."

Crowdal grinned at Nik and leaned back with his hands supporting his body, his long legs stretched out.

No one spoke, all of them enjoying the silence.

Sid squeezed Agnes' hands and felt her return squeeze. He wanted nothing more than to try and figure out how to get his numbers back, but he felt so drained that he knew if he tried now, he would fail for sure. He closed his eyes, feeling like he could sleep for a fortnight. He leaned his head against Agnes' head, enjoying the feeling of her soft hair against his cheek.

Soon, Nik returned, awkwardly carrying a blanket, a large loaf of bread, and some meat and cheese in his good arm. He dropped it all on the ground, then roughly spread out the blanket and piled the food onto it. He removed his knife and began cutting a rough slice from the bread, but the loaf kept sliding away from him because he couldn't hold it down with his bad arm.

Writhgarth sighed and took the knife from Nik. "You're pathetic. Let me do it." He cut a bunch of ragged slices of bread, all the while muttering, "I can't believe I am doing this to perfectly good bread." He then cut some meat and cheese and slapped them together haphazardly between the bread slices.

Nik reached forward to grab one when Tulman smacked his hand. He pulled it back, shaking it.

The large captain growled, "Let Sid and Agnes have first choice."

Agnes took her hands from Sid's and picked up two of the meals, handing one to Sid.

The rest of them grabbed some food, and Crowdal pulled his bread apart and tossed the hunk of meat back onto the blanket and picked up three extra slices of cheese to replace it. He took a bite and closed his eyes as he chewed. "Gods, these are good."

Nik nodded. "See, I'm going to get rich from these, you just wait and see."

Sid popped the last bite into his mouth and chewed, then drank some water. With the food in his stomach, he felt his eyes closing, so he leaned back and folded his arms behind his head. In moments he was snoring.

The rest of the group followed suit.

One of the Haissen built a fire and set up camp, the rest of them keeping watch. Nothing bothered them for the rest of the day and through the night.

Chapter 68

The morning sun shined down upon the clearing, though the forest of giant Miq trees that surrounded them remained dark and foreboding. Sid opened his eyes and saw that everyone was awake and sitting around a small fire. Crowdal and Writhgarth were smoking pipes and talking softly.

Sid yawned and stretched, then got to his feet, his bones creaking and popping as he stood.

Crowdal turned and chuckled. "You sound about as good as I did when I got up." He put his pipe in his mouth and took a metal cup and filled it with hot water, then added some tea to it, handing the steaming mug to Sid.

"Thanks." Sid cupped his hands around the warm steel mug, enjoying the heat. It had gotten a little cool during the night, and a chill still hung in the air even though the sun was bright and warm. The grass was covered in dew, and the air smelled clean, with a lingering hint of ash and smoke from the funeral pyre.

He motioned to the pipe. "I haven't seen you smoke since we took all of that tobacco from the storage room of Writhgarth's friend."

Writhgarth blew thick smoke into the air, making rings. "Aye, it has been a long time. Being chased like we've been for so long, I didn't feel much like a smoke."

Crowdal nodded but didn't say anything.

Agnes sidled over to him. "How are you feeling?" Her eyes showed that she was asking about more than just his physical injuries.

Sid rotated his shoulders, making sure to hold the mug of tea steady as he did so. He felt his joints crack, but didn't feel any lingering injuries. Without having to check, he felt the emptiness in his mind where his numbers had always been. While he had memorized the Black Numbers manuscript a while ago, he wanted to physically go through the book to see if there were any clues as to how he might get his numbers back. He felt stronger this morning, and rested.

He locked eyes with her and nodded slightly. "I'm much better, thank you." He reached out and touched her cheek, bruised black and blue. "You look bad."

She playfully slapped his hand away. "Gee, thanks."

Sid chuckled. "I didn't mean you looked bad. I just meant you looked sore."

Agnes touched her own cheek and winced. "It hurts, but it will heal. Could have been worse."

Writhgarth nodded. "Aye, we were all lucky, except for poor Richard." He motioned to Crowdal's face. "How is your face, big man?

You took some hard hits from the Masteen."

Crowdal felt his cheek and winced. "I'm fine. While it's difficult being a Trith, at least we heal quickly."

Writhgarth winced as he shifted positions. "Yeah, it must be hard being a Trith. I'm going to feel these bruises for a fortnight."

Crowdal chuckled and blew more smoke into the air.

Writhgarth coughed and spit to his side. "I swear, this travel will be the death of me. I was happy and safe back in Yisk as a Captain of the City Patrol."

Crowdal laughed. "Oh really? I seem to remember finding you hanging in shackles deep inside a dungeon."

Writhgarth rolled his eyes. "I had them right where I wanted them. You came along and ruined everything."

Crowdal's eyes were twinkling, obviously enjoying his friendship with the Vringe. "Oh yeah, you are right. Sorry, my memory isn't that good anymore."

Sid and Agnes laughed, and Writhgarth grumbled, but with a slight smirk creasing his mouth.

Nik walked up and dropped some branches by the fire, looking at them all with a grin on his face. "What'd I miss? What's so funny?"

Crowdal pointed toward Writhgarth. "We were just talking about the old days when we found this guy hanging in shackles inside of a dungeon."

Nik raised his eyebrows. "Oh, I have a story like that. I remember one time in Strandenfel, I was knee-deep in manure, fighting three idiots who..."

Tulman rolled his eyes. "Oh gods, not this story again. I swear, if I hear it one more time I'll slit my own throat."

Nik waved his arm at the group. "Hey, maybe *they* would like to hear it though, did you ever think of that?"

"Whatever." The tall mercenary captain stood and walked away, shaking his head.

Writhgarth got up. "I think I'll skip this one, too." He ambled away in another direction.

Crowdal stood up. "Speaking of manure, I've got some business to attend to." He walked across the clearing and into the darkness of the Miq forest.

Nik yelled out, cupping his mouth with his good hand. "Fine, I won't tell the story! Your loss!" He sulked for a few moments, then muttered to himself as he rooted around in his pack.

Sid smiled. "They're just playing with you, Nik. Don't take it too hard."

The mercenary lifted his head from his pack and winked at Sid. "I know, I like to mess with them too."

Sid chuckled lightly. "Well, you are very good at it." He turned to

Agnes. "I will be back in a while."

She didn't ask him any questions, knowing exactly what he was going to do. "Just let me know if you need my help."

Sid touched her cheek tenderly and walked to Crowdal's pack and removed the Black Numbers manuscript. He held it in his hands, but he didn't feel any power emanating from it now. He made his way across the clearing in the opposite direction that Crowdal had gone, and entered the dark Miq forest. The giant trees towered over him and seemed to swallow him up after the openness of the clearing.

He made his way around trees that were so wide they looked like walls in front of him. The ground was soft from dead Miq needles, and the air seemed thick, the pungent smell comforting to him, reminding him of home. He continued walking until he came across a Miq sapling, no more than the width of his own body, rising up meekly in the shadow of a massive Miq tree.

The sapling was already at least ten times his own height, but it looked insignificant compared to the mature trees around it. Somehow, a shaft of sunlight fell on the sapling, giving it life energy.

Sid sat cross-legged against the sapling and set the Black Numbers manuscript on the ground in front of him. He closed his eyes and still saw the faint line of light connecting him and the manuscript, as well as another thread of light that stretched back toward the clearing, where Sid knew it entered the obelisk. The light pulsed with energy where it entered the manuscript.

He opened his eyes and studied the cover of the manuscript. The blackness sucked in the meager sunlight as if it wanted to obliterate it from existence. He shivered despite the warmth of the sun on his head and shoulders.

He opened the manuscript to the first page and re-read the poem, knowing that it was of no help to him in finding a way to get his numbers back. He paged through the manuscript, already knowing the words that he would find within, even though they were all equations to him now. He didn't have the ability to convert the equations to text like before, but he had already memorized every word in the manuscript and knew exactly what words each equation stood for.

As he paged through it, he began to feel frustrated. There had to be something in here that would help him. He soon came to the final page and closed the manuscript cover in defeat. There was nothing in it that gave any hint on how to regain his power of numbers.

Pinching the bridge of his nose, Sid closed his eyes and felt a headache starting to build. In his mind, he saw the light pulsing as it entered the manuscript, and he reached out without thinking and reopened the manuscript to the first page. The thread of light entered the page through the poem. Sid slowly turned the brittle pages and saw that the line of light continued through each page until he got to the final page where the light pooled, not passing through the back cover of the manuscript itself.

Sid paged backwards, studying the point of light on each page. There had to be a meaning to it all. When he got back to the first page, he felt a jolt of an idea.

With trembling fingers, he touched the point on the page where the thread of light hit it and saw it rested on the letter 'T'. He turned the page and immediately saw that the line crossed through the letter 'R'.

Excitedly, he turned the pages, which were all equations and numbers after the first two pages. Where the point of light entered each equation, he was able to remember the text the equations converted to. He paged through the manuscript, quickly noting the letters the light passed through.

Sid sat back with a gasp, hardly daring to breathe. He put the letters together and read them again.

Trith, Circle, Zranh, Raith, Death.

He felt a sense of excitement and dread, not sure he understood the message and not sure he wanted to. He started to shake, knowing that he would do whatever it took to get his power of numbers back. Tris was still out there somewhere and would use his power of numbers to destroy everything and everyone that Sid held dear.

Sid closed the cover of the manuscript and leaned his head back against the smooth bark of the Miq sapling.

He knew where he had to go first, but he had no idea how to get there. Only Crowdal could help him, and it was the last thing Sid wanted to ask of his friend.

For he had to ask Crowdal to take him to his home, the Trith Nation.

Sid stood up and made his way back to the clearing, dreading what he had to do next.

Chapter 69

Crowdal had returned to the clearing, feeling much lighter and more comfortable. He bent down to his pack and noticed the top flap was open. Curious, he opened it wide and immediately saw that the pocket that held the Black Numbers manuscript was empty. Assuming that Sid had removed it and was just looking it over, he glanced around the clearing and saw everyone except Sid. Panic set in and he was about to yell his friend's name when he saw Sid enter from the opposite side of the clearing, holding the manuscript.

Something was wrong, though. His friend looked sad and anxious. Crowdal had noticed that something had not been right with Sid since the battle with the Unnamed One the previous day, but he had not been sure how to bring it up with Sid. He had assumed at first that it was just exhaustion mixed with sadness, but the hollowness in Sid's eyes was due to something else, something worse.

Sid stopped in front of him and put the manuscript into the pocket of Crowdal's pack.

"Hey Sid, are you all right?"

Sid shook his head, brown hair falling over his eyes, which he unconsciously pushed aside. "I need to talk to you." He pointed to the other side of the clearing. "Can we go somewhere a little more private?"

Curious and a little apprehensive, Crowdal nodded and Sid immediately turned and led him across the grassy area to the edge of the treeline.

Sid sat on the ground and motioned for Crowdal to join him. He picked at scraggly grass for some time before he looked up, and Crowdal saw the pain in his eyes.

"Sid, what's wrong?"

"A lot is wrong, actually. Crowdal… I lost my power of numbers."

The statement was so simple and short that it took Crowdal a few moments for it to sink in. "Lost? What do you mean?"

"Well, I didn't lose them, they were taken from me. When the Unnamed One attacked us, I created a series of mathematical equations to match its physical structure with that of the infinite space inside of the obelisk, and…" he stopped when Crowdal scratched his head.

"Um, could you speak in a language that I will understand?"

Sid nodded, embarrassed. "Sure, sorry. Basically, I sent the Unnamed One to the space inside of the obelisk, where it will never escape from again. But as I did that, it somehow grabbed hold of my power of numbers and ripped them from me before I could stop it."

Crowdal still didn't fully understand Sid. His power was still a mystery because he really didn't understand anything about advanced mathematics in the first place. Just the fact that Sid's power was gone was enough for him, though. "What are you going to do? Is there any way to get it back?"

Sid sat quietly, suddenly unable to meet his gaze. Finally he nodded. "Yes, there may be a way... I think."

Crowdal let out his breath. "Oh, thank the gods. All right then, I am with you in whatever you need to do."

Sid glanced directly into his eyes. "You may not be so anxious once you hear what it is."

Nothing scared Crowdal, especially after what they had just been through. Why Sid was acting so strangely, he didn't know. What could be so bad that he didn't want to say what needed to be done? Sid seemed to sense Crowdal's confusion and slumped his shoulders, as if he didn't want to go on but had to.

"Sid, just say what you need to say. I am your friend and will support you in whatever needs to be done."

Sid spoke quietly, almost in a whisper, "I need you to take me to the Trith Nation... I need you to take me to your home, Crowdal."

It was the last thing that Crowdal had expected to hear. Blood rushed to his face and he clenched his fists involuntarily. He had no wish to ever go back, not even to see his mother and sister. But when he saw the tears falling from Sid's eyes, Crowdal knew just how much Sid understood him. He knew exactly what he was asking of Crowdal. Then Crowdal realized how silly he was being. After all they had been through, going back to the Trith Nation seemed such a minor issue. He would do anything for Sid. He would travel to the edge of the world, face whatever he had to in order to protect him. For Sid was his friend, a true friend, something that Crowdal had not had since he had killed his childhood friend in the circle. Crowdal touched Sid's shoulder. "I will take you there, Sid. But I warn you, it is a long journey, and my reception may not be... well, let's just say, I may not be welcome back home."

Sid nodded. "I can't tell you how much this means to me, Crowdal. Thank you."

"What is it that you need from my people anyway?"

Sid looked uncomfortable again. "I actually do not know. But the manuscript told me that I needed to do five things, but not why or how to do them."

Crowdal raised an eyebrow. "Five? What are the other four?"

Sid picked at the grass a little more violently, a sweetness filling the air as the blades were broken, throwing off their full fragrance. "It is complicated, but the manuscript spelled out the following. 'Trith', 'Circle', 'Zranh', 'Raith', and 'Death'."

Crowdal said the words in his mind again. At the word 'Zranh', his heartbeat quickened. "Melinda!"

Sid nodded. "Yes, I think she is part of all this."

Crowdal hadn't been aware that he had spoken her name out loud. He focused on Sid fully. "Then we are wasting time sitting here. Let's get going!"

Chapter 70

Sid felt a release of tension and stood up. He was glad that Crowdal didn't ask about the final word from the manuscript. It was the word that scared him the most, not because he was afraid of dying, but because he didn't know who would die.

He stood up and held out his hand to Crowdal, who also got to his feet. "Thank you for everything, Crowdal."

The giant who was his best friend took his hand and shook it. "What are you going to do about the rest of our comrades over there?"

Sid looked over and saw Agnes, Writhgarth, Tulman, and Nik sitting around a small fire, talking. The Haissen were fanned out around the clearing, looking ready for violence at any moment. They would follow him everywhere from now on. He turned to Crowdal. "I can't ask them to come with."

"You know they will come with us, though."

Sid frowned. "Yeah, and they could die in the process."

The big man clapped him on the shoulder again, this time a little harder. "Sid, any one of us could die at any time." He moved his eyes upward. "One of these trees could tip over and crush us. Or one of us could trip on a rock and hit our head and die. We can't worry about what might happen."

Sid didn't think those things really compared to putting people in direct danger, but he didn't feel like arguing, so he shrugged and started toward the camp. As he approached, Agnes, Writhgarth, Tulman, and Nik stopped their conversation and turned toward him. The Haissen also made their way over to the campfire as if anticipating that a major decision had been made.

Writhgarth spat. "So what were you ladies up to, acting all secretive?"

Before Sid could speak, Crowdal pushed past him. "Sid won't ask you because he worries for your safety, so I will."

Sid opened his mouth to protest, but Crowdal spoke over him.

"Sid had his power of numbers taken from him."

Writhgarth, Tulman, and Nik all turned to look at Sid in alarm. The Haissen didn't react in any way.

Crowdal continued, "He studied the manuscript and it told him some things that he thinks might help him get his power back. The first part of that is going to my home, the Trith Nation. Any of you feel like coming along?"

Writhgarth nodded immediately and then spat again. "Sounds good to me."

Nik and Tulman quickly agreed also.

The Haissen all nodded slightly, the only acknowledgment they gave.

Sid just stared, amazed to have such friends. They had all suffered painful hardships, lost friends, and had almost died many times, yet they were still willing to travel with him wherever he went. For what seemed like the hundredth time, he didn't feel he deserved such friends. He glanced at Agnes and felt a lump in his throat at the thought of losing her. He stammered, "What are your plans now?"

She put her hand out and he helped her to her feet. She brushed dust from her trousers. "You don't need to ask me that question. I'm going with you, of course."

Sid took her hands in his. "Thank you, Agnes."

She squeezed his hands, then pulled away and started gathering her things.

He turned to the group as a whole. "Thank you all."

Nik pointed at Sid accusatorially, and then turned in a circle, pointing at everyone in turn as he spoke. "I'll put my business plans on hold for a while, but don't any of you even think about stealing my food idea." When his pointing finger came to Tulman, the large man slapped it from his face and growled. Nik yelped and shook his hand and seemed about to say something, but at the look from Tulman, he quickly stepped back. "I... ah, I think I will gather my things now."

Crowdal and Writhgarth laughed outright and also began getting their packs ready for travel. The group was silent as they prepared to leave and Sid looked at the obelisk one last time. The single thread of light still connected him to the stone structure, and for some reason, Sid was sure the connection would not break no matter how far he traveled.

He turned and made his way across the clearing, toward the area where they had first entered it. As he passed by the first giant Miq tree with the charred bark, he ran his hands along the rough wood and saw in wonder that the fire from his equation hadn't damaged the tree at all.

He craned his neck up and almost expected to see his deer stand hanging from the branches. He smiled to himself.

He was a long way from his little woods. One day, though, he would go back home. He felt a tightness in his chest as he thought of his mother, then he felt the familiar anger well up inside as he thought of his father.

The man would pay for all he had done.

Epilogue

T ris stumbled through the opening in space he had created at the last moment to escape the Trith's sword, appearing in his private chamber at the Oblate.

He made his way to his desk and sat down gingerly in the chair. He removed his hand from the blood-drenched hole in his stomach and saw blood seeping thickly out. His shoulder also ran with blood from where the bitch had stabbed him with the Rissen blade.

He grimaced angrily, then with a sharp intake of breath, reached up and pulled the rope that hung from the ceiling. He heard a bell ring in the next room and his chamber door opened almost at once. His servant entered the room and Tris hissed between his teeth, "Get the healers, immediately."

The servant nodded and quickly left.

Tris ground his teeth together in a rage that threatened to overpower him. It was almost unthinkable that events hadn't worked the way he had planned, not to mention that Sid was still alive.

Tris calmed himself down by taking deep breaths. He then closed his eyes and felt the space within his mind where he had planned to store the Black Numbers after ripping them from Sid's brain. Expecting to find the space empty, he took a quick intake of breath instead.

Roiling and tumbling over themselves, the power of Black Numbers reflected dully back at him.

He had done it! The Black Numbers were his!

Tris carefully sealed the space within his mind and sat back with a sigh.

The healers entered his chamber and immediately set to work on his wounds, and not even the intense pain from their ministrations could keep him from smiling.

All had not been a total failure.

He had the Black Numbers. Now he could fully implement the second phase of his plans. The Oblate would no longer be hidden or secret. Everyone in the land would know who he was and tremble at the power of the Oblate. But that was a side-product, really, a step he must take before initiating the third phase of his plans.

Tris also had to take care of Sid, who would die by his hand if it was the last thing he would ever do. He looked forward to their next meeting.

Only this time, he would have a little surprise for his childhood friend.

THE END

Thank you for reading **Blood Numbers: The Aleph Null Chronicles: Book Two**.

If you purchased this book from a website, it would be greatly appreciated if you would leave an honest review.

Look for **Broken Numbers: The Aleph Null Chronicles: Book Three** in 2014.

About the Author

Dean Frank Lappi was born in Virginia, Minnesota in 1968, a place that is part of the well known Iron Range, where most of the iron ore is found in the USA.

In 1996 he graduated with a Master of Arts degree in English and has worked in a number of industries since then as an Information Developer and Web Content Manager.

Dean is very active on Twitter (@DeanLappi), and you can find him on Facebook.